PRAISE FO

MW01094158

"[A] gripping novel
layers of intersectin͜   ͜ ͜ ͜ ͜ ͜ story of
the Mills family and their small-town secrets. Readers will want to see
more from this author."

—*Publishers Weekly*

"Elliot succeeds in creating both a thrilling mystery and a fascinating
character study of the people inhabiting these pages."

—*Bookreporter*

"With her riveting, narrative-driven, deftly crafted storytelling style as
a novelist, Kendra Elliot's *The Last Sister* will prove to be a welcome and
enduringly popular addition to community library Mystery/Suspense/
Thriller collections."

—*Midwest Book Review*

"Suspense on top of suspense. This one will keep you guessing until the
final page and shows Elliot at her very best."

—*The Real Book Spy*

"Every family has skeletons. Kendra Elliot's tale of the Mills family's
dark secrets is first-rate suspense. Dark and gripping, *The Last Sister*
crescendos to knock-out, edge-of-your seat tension."

—Robert Dugoni, bestselling author of *My Sister's Grave*

"*The Last Sister* is exciting and suspenseful! Engaging characters and a
complex plot kept me on the edge of my seat until the very last page."

—T.R. Ragan, bestselling author of the Jessie Cole series

"Thriller Award finalist Elliot's well-paced sequel to *The Last Sister* opens at the home of fifty-two-year-old Reuben Braswell, a devotee of conspiracy theories, who's lying dead in his bathtub . . . The twist ending will catch most readers by surprise . . . [and] fans will look forward to seeing characters from the author's other series take the lead in future installments."

—*Publishers Weekly*

"Elliot skillfully interweaves the various plot threads, and credible, mostly sympathetic characters match the lovingly described locale. Fans of contemporary regional mysteries will be rewarded."

. —*Publishers Weekly*

HER
FIRST
MISTAKE

HER
FIRST
MISTAKE

KENDRA
ELLIOT

 Montlake

Text copyright © 2025 by Oceanfront Press LLC
All rights reserved.

Published by Montlake, Seattle

www.apub.com

Amazon, the Amazon logo, and Montlake are trademarks of Amazon.com, Inc., or its affiliates.

EU product safety contact:
Amazon Media EU S. à r.l.
38, avenue John F. Kennedy, L-1855 Luxembourg
amazonpublishing-gpsr@amazon.com

ISBN-13: 9781662525773 (hardcover)
ISBN-13: 9781662525759 (paperback)
ISBN-13: 9781662525766 (digital)

Cover design by Caroline Teagle Johnson
Cover images: © Single Fin / Stocksy; © Gary J Weathers / Getty

Printed in the United States of America

First edition

For my girls

1

Thirteen years ago

"Did you vote for him?"

"I don't remember." FBI special agent Alice Patmore paused outside the impressive country home, studying the huge porch with its columns and heavy beams. She hadn't voted in the last election and didn't want to start a political discussion. "Does it matter?"

"Not anymore," said Agent Wilson, sounding grimmer than usual.

She often partnered up with him. He was reliable and smart, but his long face—along with his constant pessimism—reminded her of Eeyore. Oscar Wilson could be counted on to point out anything negative within view. What bothered Alice the most about his gloomy outlook was that she felt pressured to bolster him, point out the positive, and be his perky counterbalance.

She was not a perky person.

Oscar lifted the yellow tape so Alice could duck underneath. Two forensics vans and a dozen law enforcement units were parked on the street in front of the striking home. Sacramento County sheriff, California Highway Patrol, and even the nearby city police. A mix of officers from the different responding departments watched Alice and Oscar head up the walkway. Alice swore she could feel their gazes boring through the back of her jacket. She wondered how many of them had trampled the scene inside before being relegated to the street.

The home was in an unincorporated area about twenty miles outside of Sacramento. All the nearby houses were upscale, expensive, and far from each other on small acreage lots. Personally Alice preferred to live closer to people and businesses. Out here she would feel too isolated.

The two agents nodded at the deputy monitoring the log and showed him their ID's. As they signed, Alice scanned the names above. The medical examiner hadn't arrived yet. "Who's in charge?" she asked politely. There was no question that the FBI had to respond to this murder, but she never knew if they'd get a bit of attitude from other law enforcement.

The deputy studied her for a long second. "Detective Rodden. He's inside."

As she and Oscar bootied up and slipped on vinyl gloves, she studied the front door's frame. No damage. The windows facing the street didn't show any damage either.

Who knows what we'll find inside.

Alice knew the name of the victim and little else. She preferred it that way, so she wasn't influenced by someone else's interpretation when she entered a scene. She'd been with the FBI nearly twenty years and had learned early on to assume nothing and always try to see for herself or hear directly from a victim.

"The air-conditioning bills must be ridiculous," Oscar muttered as he looked at the high ceilings and thick crossbeams.

"It's a gorgeous house," Alice stated firmly, quickly scanning the hardwood floor of the formal living room, checking for broken glass.

"It's got to be six thousand square feet and cost a fortune to clean," said Oscar with a deep sigh and a weary shake of his head.

Why do I even try?

She heard voices and followed the sounds to a gigantic kitchen, where two men in plain clothes with sheriff's badges on their lanyards stood on the far side of an island the size of Alice's entire kitchen. They were watching three forensics techs process the kitchen but immediately looked over as Alice and Oscar entered.

Medical paraphernalia littered the floor. Paper packaging for bandages, tubing, gloves, and gauze squares. The island blocked the sight of the victim's body, but Alice could see his lower legs, noting he wore jeans and hiking boots.

The rest of the body came into view as they neared the men, and she saw that several cuts and bruises dotted the victim's hands and arms. She and Oscar held out their ID's as introductions were made. The tallest man was Detective Rodden, the lead on the case, and the other was his lieutenant. Rodden intermittently chomped hard on blue gum as he spoke to the agents.

Studying the body on the floor, Alice was unable to visually confirm that the victim was Assemblyman Derrick Bell, as had been reported. Since he was a member of the California state legislature, the FBI had been notified of his murder.

Bell's face was a bloody, smashed-in mess.

"You positive that's the assemblyman?" asked Oscar. "That could be anyone."

"That's him," Detective Rodden said forcefully. "His wallet was in his pocket, and you can see the small mole beside his right eye. Hair color and its style are correct too."

Alice moved to the other side of the body and spotted the mole. Detective Rodden held out the driver's license; the mole was identical, along with the victim's hair. From the license she noticed the assemblyman had just turned thirty-two, and that Derrick Bell had been a good-looking man.

No evidence of that was left.

She pointed at the cuts on his arms and hands. "These—"

"Defense wounds," said Rodden. "He fought back."

"They're not bloody," Alice stated. "Look at his face. Lots of blood. But these cuts have very little blood in them, if any. They were made when he was already dead."

All the men stared at the body.

"You're right," said Rodden. "Someone beat him up when he was down. They may not have even known he was dead by then." Rodden continued talking with occasional flashes of blue gum, relating a summary of what else they'd found. Alice listened with one ear, knowing Oscar would pay closer attention and make notes. She studied the body's position and then scanned the room. No broken windows. No damaged door or doorframe in the kitchen.

Did the killer simply walk in?

"What is that?" she asked, indicating a figurine on the floor several feet from the body.

"An elephant," said Rodden. "And yes, there's blood on it."

Alice squatted to get a better look at the piece. The cast-iron elephant was a little larger than a coffeepot. It was heavily detailed, and she suspected it had been expensive. She looked around the room, spotting a few more elephants of all sizes and colors.

Someone was a fan.

She pushed at the elephant with her pen, barely able to move it. It was solid and very heavy.

Murder weapon?

Blood speckled the figurine, and its trunk formed a heavy hook. With enough muscle behind the object, it could do a lot of damage. She looked back at the victim's smashed face.

"All the doors were unlocked when the deputies arrived," said Rodden. "Front door was wide open. Didn't find any forced entry."

"Rest of the house?" asked Oscar.

"No signs of a struggle anywhere. The master bed isn't made, and there are clothes in the laundry basket. Other than that, the rest of the home is extremely neat."

Except in the kitchen.

Blood spatter had sprayed across four of the kitchen island's white cabinets. A thick pool of blood with swirling smears was six feet away, where more medical paper packaging clustered. Obvious shoe prints appeared in that blood, and there were more bloody smears on the floor around it. One of the forensic techs was shooting photos of the dark blood pool, a second tech was dusting the cabinets for fingerprints, and the third made notes on a clipboard.

"Blood was still fresh when the ambulance arrived," said Rodden. "I don't think it happened that long before."

"Who called it in?" asked Alice.

"Anonymous 911 call from the house landline." He pointed at a cordless phone on the kitchen wall, its receiver covered in black dust.

"Who still has a landline?" asked Oscar.

"In this more rural area, a number of people," said Rodden. "Cell service can be sketchy. The call was made by a female. Whispering. I listened to it; she sounds terrified."

"His wife?" asked Alice. "House staff? Do they have kids?" She faintly recalled seeing the congressman's wife in media photographs. Together they were an attractive young couple that Bell's political party had high hopes for.

"His wife was attacked too." Rodden pointed at the large bloodstain by the tech with the camera. "She was still breathing when the deputies arrived. No kids."

Alice grimaced. She should have known *that* fact ahead of time. This time her preference for walking into a scene without too much information had backfired.

"Her husband wasn't breathing," Rodden continued. "Deputies tried CPR until the ambulance arrived. He never recovered. As far as staff, according to the neighbors, the Bells use a housekeeping service once a week. We're checking to see when they were last here. The assemblyman has—had political staff that I believe only work at his office downtown. We'll confirm that. We're getting a list of staff names."

"Do you have the 911 recording?" asked Oscar.

Rodden tapped on his phone and held it out.

"911. What is your emergency?"

"They're dead! Oh my God! They've been killed!"

The woman was sobbing, her whispers choked with tears. "You've got to come now!" She whispered the address.

"Ma'am, can you speak up? Who is dead?"

"She doesn't say anything else, but the line stayed open," said Detective Rodden, ending the playback. "When law enforcement arrived, the receiver was lying on the counter, and she had left. Obviously the caller was wrong that both were dead."

"Cameras?" asked Alice. The hair had lifted on the back of her neck. The woman on the recording had sounded genuinely scared to death.

Some people are good actors.

"No cameras here, but we're checking with all the neighbors to see if they have them."

"I'd expect an assemblyman to have better security in his home," Oscar said in a sad voice.

"We've been told the security is tighter at his condo downtown and his office. Supposedly, out here, the crime is low," said Rodden.

"Not low enough," droned Oscar.

"Were the wife's injuries similar to the assemblyman's?" asked Alice, studying the victim's disaster of a face again, wondering how bad the wife looked.

"Not according to the first responders. The deputies said the back of her head was bleeding. Nothing on her face, but she was unconscious and barely breathing. They said it was understandable that the caller thought she was dead. By the time the ambulance arrived, she was stirring."

Surprised, Alice looked again at the pool of blood; it'd made her expect worse injuries.

Head wounds bleed a lot.

"Are the deputies that first responded still here?" asked Alice, wanting to hear their observations directly.

"I sent them back for a full debrief."

"When will the coroner get here?" asked Oscar.

Rodden sighed. "Last estimate was two hours."

Alice exchanged a look with Oscar. Waiting two hours for the coroner would be a waste of their time. They'd learn details at the autopsy and from the pathologist's report.

Right now the best lead was the eyewitness: Assemblyman Bell's wife.

Alice glanced at the wife's bloodstain, realizing that the swirling pattern in it had most likely been made by her hair.

She tipped her head at Oscar. "Let's walk the house and then go talk to the wife."

2

Deschutes County sheriff's detective Noelle Marshall followed the office manager, Melissa, down the hall at the FBI's satellite office in Bend, Oregon. It was a small facility with five special agents and a number of support staff. Noelle knew most of the employees from prior cases and considered Special Agent Mercy Kilpatrick a close friend. She scanned the offices as they passed, keeping an eye out for Mercy, half listening as Melissa chatted nonstop about cross-country skiing.

It was an icy-cold January morning in Bend, and the deep-blue skies made the snow-topped Cascade mountains look crisp and fresh. Her Friday morning was off to a good start. She was having a good hair day, and the man in line ahead of her at the coffee shop had paid for her latte without hitting on her. He'd given her a solemn nod and stridden out the door before the barista had told her what he'd done.

Deciding to pass on the favor, Noelle had glanced back and seen a group of four teenage girls waiting behind her. Her free coffee had suddenly become expensive, but she was in a happy mood. She'd left thirty dollars to cover the girls' drinks and stepped out into the brisk, sunny morning, eager to get to the meeting the FBI had requested, hoping it had new information about her bank robbery case.

The office manager stopped at a door labeled CONFERENCE ROOM 1, still rambling on about skiing. A chatty Melissa was nothing new, but Noelle realized she hadn't made eye contact the entire time. Noelle's latte suddenly felt heavy in her stomach.

Something's up.

Melissa rapped on the door, opened it, and stood back so Noelle could enter. Her gaze briefly met Noelle's and then darted away. Her suspicions raised, Noelle steeled her spine and stepped inside. The sunny conference room contained a long table, and at the far end, two men stood as she entered. Her eyes locked on the video camera set up between them. It pointed at the only unoccupied chair in the room.

They removed the other chairs so I'd have to sit there.

She didn't like being manipulated. Standing at the foot of the table, she studied the two men, each of whom had hung his suit jacket on the back of his chair. White dress shirts and ties. FBI ID's on lanyards around their necks. The man on her left had salt-and-pepper hair. The sun shining through the window behind them kept her from clearly seeing his eyes. The other man had a close beard and—

Hello, latte man.

He was tall with wide shoulders. His lips quirked, and she knew he recognized her too.

"Good morning, Detective," said the first man. "I'm Special Agent Keaton, and this is Special Agent Rhodes. We're out of the Sacramento FBI office. I'll be filming this interview."

"Why?" She felt ambushed.

"For the record," said Keaton.

Noelle let the silence hang for five seconds as she gazed from one man to the other. "No one told me I would be filmed. Something tells me this isn't a meeting about my bank robbery case."

"That's correct," said Keaton. "I'm sorry if you felt misled."

"I *was* misled," Noelle corrected harshly. "Why am I here?"

"We're taking another look at the unsolved murder of Assemblyman Derrick Bell. This is simply a fact-finding interview."

Her lungs stopped, and she fought to keep her composure. "You could have shared that information when you set up this meeting." She looked straight at Special Agent Rhodes, who'd been silent so far.

"Thank you for taking the time to talk with us," said Keaton, not acknowledging her comment. "Please have a seat." He gestured at the solo available chair. "Can I get you some water or coffee?"

Noelle tipped her to-go cup toward Agent Rhodes. "I've been taken care of." She didn't move toward the empty seat.

Another long pause.

Agent Keaton shifted his weight and picked up the pen next to his legal notepad. "It's been thirteen years since the assemblyman's death—"

"I know how long it's been," she snapped. "Is that camera on?"

"It is," said Keaton. "Would you please have a seat?" A hint of pleading touched his tone.

"I have a noon appointment to interview a hit-and-run suspect at the jail," said Noelle. "How long will this take? Or is rehashing an old case more important than yesterday's accident that killed a grandmother?" A faint ringing had started in her ears.

"We're conducting in-depth interviews with everyone involved in the assemblyman's case, looking for new facts and leads," said Keaton. "I recommend you cancel your appointment."

"I don't have any new leads for you about Derrick Bell." She looked at Agent Rhodes. "Does your partner not speak?"

"Please have a seat, Detective," said Rhodes.

His eyes also weren't visible due to the sun. The golden light felt like a spotlight on her face and sent sharp pains through her head.

"Can you tilt the blinds?" she asked, shading her eyes, trying to fight the ache at the back of her skull.

Rhodes immediately reached for the cord.

She paused and then took a seat, fuming at the way she'd been tricked into the interview.

But there's no point in annoying the FBI.

Both men sat, a sense of relief hovering around them.

Now that she could read their expressions, a small sense of control returned.

"Thank you, Detective," said Keaton, his gray gaze meeting hers. "We have several questions about the assemblyman's—your husband's—murder."

3

Special Agent Alice Patmore studied Noelle Bell through the small window in the hospital room door. The assemblyman's wife was alone, her eyes closed, but Alice sensed she wasn't asleep. Bandages were wrapped around her head, and some of her dishwater-blonde hair stuck out, stained pink with blood.

"What did the doc say?" asked Oscar, peering over Alice's shoulder. He smelled like the Big Mac he'd eaten on the way to the hospital. Alice had ordered a chicken salad and after one bite had wished she'd ordered a burger instead.

"Concussion. Cracked skull. Said she's having memory problems," said Alice.

"Convenient."

"Yep."

"Think she could hit herself in the back of the head after killing him?" Oscar's tone said he thought she had done exactly that.

"I guess it's possible. But damn, she'd have to be aggressive about it to crack her own skull."

"If I wanted to hide that I'd murdered my husband, that wouldn't stop me."

Alice said nothing. The assemblyman had been brutalized. She had a hard time imagining a woman doing that amount of damage, but she wasn't letting it cloud her judgment.

She opened the door.

Noelle Bell immediately sat up, her gaze meeting Alice's and then going to Oscar.

"Good evening, Ms. Bell," said Alice. "I'm Special Agent Alice Patmore and this is Special Agent Oscar Wilson. We're very sorry to hear of your husband's death."

As Noelle's dark-blue gaze studied them, Alice noticed red blotching around her eyes from crying.

"You're FBI?" Noelle asked.

"Yes," Alice said simply.

Noelle settled back into her pillows. "Good. I assume you're involved because of his position in the government."

"Correct." Alice pulled a chair closer to the hospital bed and sat as Oscar chose a spot to lean against the wall. They'd agreed Alice should start the interview. From closer up, Alice noticed faint red marks on Noelle's lower and upper arms. Not welts. Not cuts. Thicker marks, as if someone had grabbed her arms.

Those will be black and blue tomorrow.

Clearly there was a struggle.

But with her husband or an attacker?

Alice looked at Noelle's eyes again. They were wet and bloodshot, but Alice revised her opinion on the cause of the red blotching around them. She'd seen it before when someone had been hit hard in the back of the head. The trauma would create bruising around the eyes. She couldn't recall the medical term for it, but tomorrow Noelle Bell would have two black eyes.

The woman's hands were clear, no cuts, no scraped knuckles. Her French manicure was perfect.

Her clothes and shoes had been bagged as evidence. Alice hadn't seen the items yet but had been told there was a lot of blood on them.

Including stains on the front of her dress, where it seemed unlikely she'd be bloody from a blow to the back of her head.

"Your doctor told me you have a cracked skull," began Alice.

Noelle raised a shaky hand to lightly touch the bandage at the back of her head. "That's what they said."

Her words were slow and slightly slurred.

Pain medication side effects or injury symptoms? Both?

Alice silently sighed in frustration. The statements of drugged and injured witnesses couldn't be taken at face value. But they had to start somewhere.

"How did you hurt your head?" Alice asked gently.

The woman frowned. "I'm not sure." Frustration rippled across her face. "I've been trying to recall. It's fuzzy."

"What do you remember?" Open-ended questions were best at the moment.

Noelle studied her and then Oscar. "I remember the ambulance. A woman's face close to mine, telling me I'd be okay and that they were taking me to the hospital."

"What about before the ambulance?"

Noelle grimaced. "I'm not sure. I've been trying to remember ever since the doctor told me—" She froze, pain in her gaze.

If that's acting, she's very good.

"About your husband?" asked Alice.

"Yes," Noelle whispered. Fresh tears started.

"What do you remember?" Alice asked again.

"The ambulance," she said in a frustrated voice.

"What about earlier today? What did you do? Did you go anywhere?" Alice knew she had to take her time questioning this witness.

Noelle frowned. "What day is it?"

"Friday."

"I would have . . ." Noelle blinked several times, her gaze on her hands. "On Fridays, I . . ." She shook her head and winced at the movement. A big breath made her chest rise under the hospital gown. "Do I need surgery?" She looked at Alice, confusion in her gaze.

"The doctor didn't tell me you did," said Alice, wondering about the sudden topic change. The doctor had told her they were watching carefully for any critical swelling of the woman's brain. Inside the skull, there is little room for tissues to swell.

"That's good." She settled back into her pillows and closed her eyes.

"You were about to tell me what you did this morning," said Alice. "Friday morning."

Noelle's eyelids flew open. "That's right. Ummm . . . Fridays I usually meet my sister Eve for lunch."

"Did you see her today?"

"Yes?" Noelle frowned again. "I think so." Her face cleared. "We had lunch downtown. Then I headed to the house. The traffic was horrible getting out of town on a Friday." A small smile touched her lips as she looked at Alice, clearly pleased she had remembered something.

"And when you got to the house?"

Noelle looked around the room as if the answer were hidden there. Her gaze stopped on Oscar, and a hint of fear entered her eyes for a split second.

He's scared her. Because he's a man? Or because he's FBI?

"I don't recall anything besides the heavy traffic," Noelle finally admitted.

"I drove out to your house today," said Alice. "It's a lot of two-lane country roads once you leave the city behind. Traffic doesn't seem bad on those."

"Yes." Noelle nodded and then froze as pain flashed in her eyes from the simple action.

"Beautiful area out there. Quiet."

"It is."

"How long have you been married?" asked Alice, ready to change direction.

"Just over three years." A shadow flickered in her eyes and tears welled again.

"I'm very, very sorry for your loss," said Alice.

"Thank you." Noelle paused. "I was married before. It only lasted for a couple months. I was eighteen."

Alice already knew about the woman's first marriage to Brendon Simon. She'd requested he be tracked down for an interview. "You were young."

"Too young," Noelle agreed.

"Did you and Derrick purchase the country house? It's stunning." Alice had done a quick dive into the Bell family history and knew the answer but wanted to evaluate Noelle's ability to focus.

"No. That house has been in his family for many years, although we updated it recently. He bought the condo downtown a year before we met."

Her husband, Derrick Bell, came from a wealthy family. Alice had learned his parents lived in an even larger home a few miles from the house where Derrick had been murdered. His older brother was single and lived on the other side of Sacramento, and he had a married sister who lived in town. The parents owned other large homes. One in Seattle and another in Park City, Utah.

Alice's mother would have described Noelle as having grown up on "the wrong side of the tracks."

Noelle Bell, née Marshall, had married very well the second time.

For Derrick Bell, a man from a wealthy family who was making a career in politics, Noelle seemed like an odd choice.

Sometimes there is no control over who you love.

"What do you do for work, Noelle?" asked Alice.

"I volunteer," she said. "I'm on a number of nonprofit boards." She looked away. "I can throw a good fundraiser. Most of these groups need all the help they can get."

Alice had learned Noelle had a psychology degree and wondered why she'd chosen to spend her time volunteering instead of pursuing something in that field or getting a graduate degree. The woman had seemed slightly embarrassed to admit she didn't work.

"What kind of groups do you work with?"

"I like working with animal rescue groups, but lately I've been focused on literacy for children."

"Both important," said Alice, hoping the woman would have more to say.

"Yes." Noelle didn't volunteer additional information.

"Were you aware of any threats against your husband?" Alice tossed a heavy question.

Noelle seemed to focus on her hospital blanket as she put her hand to her forehead.

Those perfect nails.

"I don't know," she said slowly. "I'd been told about a few angry letters Derrick received when he was first elected. It was very stressful. I think he told his staff not to tell me about any more. He didn't want me to worry."

"Understandable," said Alice. "Did Derrick have concerns about your safety?"

"I've never felt unsafe, and besides, he doesn't like hiring security. Says it looks bad. Like he doesn't trust anyone."

"What about security for your home?"

Noelle looked away. "I don't know. We must have talked about it. Right now I don't remember what was said." She looked across the room at Oscar, no fear in her gaze this time. "How long have you been with the FBI?"

Alice let the random change of topic go by as Oscar answered. Noelle seemed to do better answering general questions. Every time Alice returned to specifics about what had happened, she appeared to struggle with an answer and then asked or said something outside the scope of Alice's question. As if her brain were avoiding pain, pushing her to a safe topic.

Alice wanted to ask if Derrick had had life insurance and a will, but it was much too soon for that. She searched for a topic that would encourage Noelle to talk.

"I was told you met your husband in a bar."

"I did." Noelle hesitated, then slowly shared the story.

4

Five years before Derrick Bell's murder

"He says you know what he drinks."

Noelle sighed. "That doesn't mean I'm the only one who can pour it for him. He likes Stoli on the rocks. If he complains, tell him I'm busy."

The other bartender rolled her eyes and grabbed the bottle of Stolichnaya. "Men."

"Women do the same thing to Patrick." The male bartender was openly gay but flirted with everyone. His tips were usually 30 percent more than Noelle's.

And her tips were nothing to sniff at.

Using the mirrored wall behind the bottles, she sneaked a glance at Mr. Stoli.

He met her gaze, a half smile on his lips.

Shit.

He'd been at the bar her last five work nights, and she wondered if he'd also come in on her nights off. He'd been polite every time. Never demanded her attention or attempted to engage her in pointless small talk. He used her name—obvious on her elegant name tag—but had never offered his, and she'd never asked. Tonight was the first time he'd requested she wait on him.

He was attractive in an understated way and had something that made women—including herself—take a second glance. He reminded her of the wingman in a romance movie. The one you knew was a good guy but wasn't drop-dead gorgeous like the lead actor. But when you listened closer and watched his actions, you knew he was the real hero of the story. Dependable. Solid. Trustworthy.

Several of the bar patrons appeared to know Mr. Stoli, stopping to talk, offering a few bro-slaps on the back or a brisk handshake. They listened as he spoke, their eyes stating they respected what he had to say. Since the bar was two blocks from the capitol building, she assumed he had a role in the California state legislature. The bar was always packed with bureaucrats.

Since she'd started working there three years earlier, she'd learned that bureaucrats were fast and loose with their business credit cards. Quick to slap them down when gathered with a group; it was a subtle competition over who was the most benevolent that evening. They were generous with tips, and the drinks cost double—or more—than at other bars. It all added up to money in her pocket.

Money was a good thing.

Noelle had lived without money; living with it was preferable. She'd cut her bartending teeth at a chain restaurant outside of Sacramento, deftly deflecting hints from out-of-state salesmen and married men pretending to be on a hall pass. She hadn't smiled or giggled when they grabbed her ass; she'd simply stared them down, her gaze saying, "Don't be a dick." They'd get flustered and stop but often stated their displeasure with a low tip. She added a fake wedding ring, but it made no difference in their attention.

She learned to read people in a flash. Which ones were dangerous or depressed. Which ones just needed an ear for a minute. She was studying psychology and was fascinated to learn what made people tick. She always wanted to discover the why behind everyone's actions.

Adding up her change and single bills every night while her lips were numb from hours of smiles and laughing at lame jokes while paying her way through college had encouraged her to search for a job with better income. A friend had told her about an opening at an upscale bar and strongly suggested Noelle present her most polished self for an interview.

Ready to escape the chain restaurant, Noelle had lightened her blonde hair and carefully coaxed it into an elegant twist. She'd always been told she was stately and stylish, so she focused on enhancing those assets. She was taller than most women and drew eyes when she entered a room, the glances always admiring.

She went to the Chanel counter the morning of the job interview, got a makeover, and then pretended not to care as she parted with hard-earned tips to buy the lipstick. The cost would have filled her car's gas tank, getting her back and forth to work and college for two weeks.

The saleswoman who'd skillfully done Noelle's eyes had deserved more than the commission from just the lipstick, disappointment flashing in her eyes at the small sale after more than a half hour of her time. Noelle understood. She'd felt the same after hustling for rowdy groups of drinkers only to get a subpar tip. Noelle promised herself she'd return to buy the foundation and mascara if she was hired.

Perfect hair and makeup on board. Eye drops to erase the previous night's late shift. A snug black skirt and crisp white blouse borrowed from her sister paired with her own spiked pumps. She got the job.

And I nailed the interview.

Noelle had never lacked in confidence. She'd always lifted her chin and put her best foot forward. It'd shown as the bar manager quizzed her on drinks and customer management, and then he'd hired her on the spot.

She went back to Chanel and bought the mascara and foundation and added an eye shadow palette; the total cost made her stomach churn.

Fake it till you make it was a favorite saying of her grandfather's, and it'd always worked for Noelle. She was a quick study and willingly put in the hours needed to get a leg up on the competition. She believed in hard work. Consistency. Daily efforts.

Chipping away with her eye on the prize.

Mr. Stoli is not my prize.

She lowered her gaze and returned to her other customers after holding his stare for a moment. Long enough to let him know she didn't intimidate easily and that their eye contact meant nothing. But now she couldn't completely avoid him because that would be too obvious.

Obvious about what?

That he'd captured her attention.

Dammit.

She didn't date where she worked. The policy had served her well. The bar environment was rarely where stable long-term relationships were born.

She knew; she was living proof. Her first marriage had lasted two months. She'd been eighteen with a fake ID and seeking an adventure in a small-town bar. He'd been twenty-three with a chip on his shoulder and the most beautiful blue eyes and black lashes. She'd thought he was an adult; he'd thought she idolized him.

Which I did.

Until I didn't.

After her bank account had been emptied and her credit cards maxed out, she'd hung her head as she crawled back to her grandfather's house. He'd listened—unlike she had when he told her not to marry the man. And then welcomed her back home with loving arms.

"Everyone makes mistakes," he'd said. "You're lucky to get this one out of the way early in life."

He kindly didn't point out that he'd never made that mistake. His long marriage to her grandmother had been storybook-worthy. A match built on respect and love. In the six years since Noelle's disaster of a marriage, she'd only briefly dated two men. She was determined to be financially independent before entering a serious relationship.

Noelle glanced again at Mr. Stoli. His attention was focused on his conversation with two men in dark suits and red power ties.

A small sting of disappointment touched her, and she shook her head, annoyed that she wanted to meet his gaze again.

No more mistakes.

The lucrative bartending job was important to her. She'd erased her credit card debt and made a hefty dent in her student loans.

To make herself stand out at the bar, she'd researched techniques to add flair to the simple act of pouring ingredients together, making the customer feel there was value in the experience as well as in the alcohol. Management had paid for her to become a certified sommelier, and she was currently a level two. Wine fascinated her, and she enjoyed sharing her knowledge with customers. She often considered continuing on to become an advanced and then master sommelier. Maybe someday. Maybe a job at a winery in Italy or France in the future.

Right now she was content.

Working at the posh bar suited her. Interacting with the patrons stimulated her mind and enhanced her people skills. She studied each customer, watching their expressions, listening to their tone, and then would guess what their next words or actions would be, putting her fascination with psychology to work.

She threw all her concentration into her new position. She became the person they depended on when someone called in sick. She willingly took extra hours and was the peacemaker between grumpy employees. After six months, she was offered a management position, which she reluctantly turned down because it would mean fewer tips.

She was in a good spot. The customers paid much more for drinks, wore better clothing, and smelled much nicer than at her first job. There were other subtle differences in the patrons at the high-end bar. Men no longer grabbed her ass. Instead, they grabbed her arm or hand to get her attention. The leers were more muted, but the message the same.

The tips were worth it.

A sharp rap on the wood bar made her spin around with an automatic smile on her lips. Every bar seat was taken, but she knew immediately which patron had tapped his glass, the clink of his ice sphere indicating the bourbon she'd poured minutes before was gone. She reached for the bottle of Maker's Mark as she asked him, "How is your teenager adjusting to her new school?" With her gaze, she included his wife in the question. The couple were regulars, and the first time they'd met, she'd immediately noticed the wife didn't appreciate her husband chitchatting with Noelle. The woman had set a hand on her husband's arm and straightened her spine, her expression reserved. Since then, whenever the husband pulled Noelle into conversation, Noelle always directed her answers to his wife, leaning slightly toward her as if they were sharing a confidence, or she would change the topic to discuss something the wife enjoyed. Like shoes. She shared Noelle's passion for Italian heels and red wines.

Neither of which Noelle could spend money on.

Noelle listened as the woman described her daughter's struggle with math, and her husband silently watched Noelle pour his drink, his slouch and sudden lack of eye contact indicating he had conceded the conversation to the women. Noelle added an additional pour of bourbon to his drink with a wink at his wife, making him happy while simultaneously having a silent, companionable exchange with the woman.

Make everyone happy; that was her goal.

She glanced down the bar, checking everyone's drink level and scanning for eye contact.

Mr. Stoli's gaze slammed into hers.

She lifted a brow. *Need another drink?*

He gave a minuscule shake of his head. *No.*

Then he stood, held her gaze for a long second as he pushed in his stool, and turned away.

Disappointment flooded her.

What did I expect?

She straightened her back, remembering her priorities: work hard, get ahead, *then* have fun.

Noelle turned as a patron called her name, and she put Mr. Stoli out of her mind.

He'll be back.

5

Thirteen years ago
The day after Derrick Bell's murder

The morning after the assemblyman's murder, Special Agent Alice Patmore slipped on booties, a gown, a mask, and gloves before she entered the large autopsy suite at the county coroner's office. She paused just inside the door. A half dozen stainless steel tables were in use, a technician and a forensic pathologist examining a corpse at each one. She blinked in the bright fluorescent lighting, hating that the lights reminded her of a grocery store.

The smell in the large room was unique. Putrid scents mixed with industrial-strength cleaners. Even the most expensive ventilation system couldn't fully eliminate it. It slipped around the edges of her mask, and she knew she'd smell it for the rest of the day.

But she didn't mind visiting the Sacramento County Coroner's Office. The science of what pathologists did fascinated her. From the outside, the coroner's building looked as if it belonged on a college campus, a large, stately but reserved building that an outsider might think housed professors' offices and multiple lecture halls. To her, the outside coordinated nicely with what was happening inside: important learning and seeking answers to questions.

But studying with bodies instead of college textbooks.

Alice had been told Derrick Bell was on table four. She scanned the room and recognized his examining forensic pathologist by his unusual height and poor posture.

Shit. I should have asked who was doing his autopsy.

Not that it would have changed anything.

She squared her shoulders and started toward the table. Out of the corner of her eye, she noted the body on table two was very small. She refused to take a closer look.

"Dr. Carvey," she said as she approached. She'd found him to be efficient and thorough, but his sense of humor had twisted her stomach a number of times. The pathologist glanced up and met her gaze through his thick glasses and protective face shield. Lines suddenly formed at the corners of his eyes, indicating he was smiling behind his mask.

"Agent Patmore. Nice to see you again. Sorry it isn't at a different table."

Alice kept her face neutral, pretending to not catch his meaning. The doctor had asked her to dinner a few times, but she'd always turned him down. Under all the gear, he was a good-looking man. She knew he was in his early fifties like her, and that he'd been divorced for more than a decade. Alice didn't mind dating; she'd been single for six years. But she couldn't get past the image of the pathologist with his hands in a body cavity.

Or the weird coincidence that his last name was tied closely to his profession.

"Good to see you, Bryce." She moved her gaze to the body. "How's it going?"

"Coming along, coming along," said Dr. Carvey as he handed an unidentifiable organ to his assistant. The man set it on a scale and made a notation. Alice noticed the tech wore earbuds and lightly bounced his head to a beat only he could hear.

Derrick Bell's rib cage had been cut through and laid open along with the tissues covering his torso. Alice moved closer to study his face under the bright lights, spotting the small mole by his eye that had helped identify him the day before. All the blood had been washed away, clearly exposing the damage to his face. His nose was too short, bashed into his head. His right cheekbone had collapsed, creating a lopsided look. One eyebrow ridge had sunk too deep.

His wife's face hadn't been touched.

Alice ran her gaze down his arms. Cuts. Contusions. One of his fingers was at an odd angle. Clearly broken.

I didn't notice that yesterday.

With his torso open, she couldn't tell if it had suffered injuries, but hints of purple low along his sides indicated that lividity had settled in his posterior tissues. He'd died on his back, the position she'd seen him in yesterday. He had marks on his thighs and knees, but his feet and lower legs looked fine. For a dead guy's.

"He had a high level of meth in his system," said Dr. Carvey. "And some antianxiety medications. Normal levels."

"He was high on meth," stated Alice, recalling that yesterday, Noelle's doctor had said nothing unusual had been present in her blood.

The assemblyman was a meth user?

"Yep."

She gestured at Derrick's hands and arms. "Quite a few cuts," she said.

"Lacerations," corrected Dr. Carvey. "Cuts have clean edges created by something sharp. Lacerations are irregular and ragged from the skin bursting over a bony structure from impact. There was virtually no blood in them, indicating they were postmortem."

"Any idea what was used?" Alice purposefully didn't bring up the iron elephant that had been on the floor by the body. She wanted the doctor's opinion.

The pathologist pointed at several lacerations that dotted the body's nose and crushed cheekbone. "I'm not sure what he was hit in the face with, but I have a good idea for some of the other injuries." He moved to Derrick's thighs and ran his gloved finger along one of many arc-shaped lesions. "The same marks were on his ribs." He met her gaze. "What's that look like to you?"

Alice stared at the marks for a long moment. Then it came to her. "The head of a crowbar."

Satisfaction filled his eyes. "I thought so too."

"A crowbar would definitely break a finger," said Alice, looking at his hand again.

"Agreed. And both his temporal and parietal bones have fractures from impact with a blunt object. A crowbar fits the shapes left in his soft tissues."

"No crowbar was left near the scene," she said. "I'll ask the wife if they owned one." She made a mental note to ask Detective Rodden to have his team check for a crowbar. The home sat on several acres, and a thorough search of the grounds was to be done that day. If the Bells didn't own a crowbar, it'd indicate the attacker had come prepared to do damage.

"These bruises are a different shape." The doctor pointed at an oblong lesion on Derrick's hip. "There were several more on his stomach."

"Toe of a shoe." Alice had seen them before on a domestic abuse victim.

"Possibly," said the doctor, but his tone said he agreed with her. *Someone kicked him when he was down.*

She sighed. "But you're positive his facial injuries were caused by something else?"

"Yes."

Alice took off her gloves and opened her phone to the photo of the iron elephant that hadn't been far from Derrick's body. "Would this do it?" She enlarged the item and showed the doctor.

He glanced from the photo to Derrick's face several times. "I can't say it wouldn't. Is that made of metal?"

"Yes, and it's super heavy."

"Can you get it to me?"

"I'll try. It'll have to be processed at forensics first." She shot a text to Oscar with the request and then put her phone away. "Have you ever had someone purposefully hit the back of their head hard enough to cause a fracture?" She struggled to get her gloves back on because her hands had started to sweat.

The doctor's focus was back on Derrick's open torso. He glanced at her and raised one eyebrow. "Usually my subjects can't tell me they hit themselves on purpose."

"You know what I mean."

He stepped away from Derrick and picked up something that made Alice think of Thor's hammer—but thinner—off his table of instruments. The table didn't hold a set of delicate-looking surgical instruments. The items looked like they'd been found on a garage workbench. Forensic pathologists didn't worry about injuring their subjects.

He handed the hammer to Alice, who reluctantly accepted the shiny item. Its head was heavy. She looked at the doctor, uncertain.

"Hit your head," he told her.

"No, thank you." She hefted the tool, trying to imagine what would drive a person to injure themselves. She'd read the radiologist's report on Noelle's skull X-rays and CT scans. Among all the medical jargon, she'd learned that a single blow with a blunt object had caused Noelle's fracture and bleeding.

No lighter practice blows. One solid impact.

She eyed the crowbar marks on Derrick, wondering if the same tool had been used on Noelle.

Alice positioned the heavy hammer as if to hit the back of her head. The angle was awkward. A crowbar would make the back of her head a little more accessible, but Alice doubted she would hit hard enough on the first blow. Or second.

If Noelle hit her head hard enough to knock herself out, how did the crowbar vanish?

Maybe she wasn't unconscious.

"Difficult, isn't it?" Dr. Carvey said, watching her with the hammer. "Both physically and mentally."

"But not impossible."

"Correct."

Damn.

Nothing ruled out Noelle as a suspect. Yet.

"What killed him?" she asked, knowing full well it was too early to get a definite answer from the pathologist. She laid the hammer next to the long-handled branch cutters on the table, grateful she'd been too late to observe the doctor using them to cut through Derrick's ribs. The sound of snapping ribs during an autopsy was one she hadn't forgotten.

"I'm not done."

"I know." She indicated the damage to Derrick's face. "On its own, would that have been sufficient to kill?"

The doctor paused for a long moment. "I'll confirm when I open the skull."

Sounds like a yes to me.

"Have you seen any other injury that would have killed him?"

He met her gaze. "I have a lot to do."

"Understood." She took a step back and watched silently for the rest of the autopsy. Only looking away when the doctor peeled Derrick's scalp forward, covering the victim's face to access the skull. She let her mind wander, considering other suspects as she tuned out the sound of the Stryker saw on bone.

Derrick's family. Noelle's family. Employees. Disgruntled constituents.

She and Oscar had a lot of people to talk to.

6

Noelle checked the time. An hour had passed since she'd sat down with the two Sacramento agents. The half inch of latte left in her cup was cold, and her annoyance at being tricked into the interview had risen and fallen several times. She focused on reading the agents. Keaton was the older and more senior agent. He occasionally spoke over her replies but was mostly polite. He frequently shifted in his chair, and his gaze was mostly focused on his laptop when he spoke.

She wondered what was on the screen.

Agent Rhodes let Keaton do most of the talking, and his gaze spent more time locked on her than on his keyboard. He listened intently. It seemed as if he knew what she was going to say before she said it. Which was possible. She'd been interviewed numerous times in the past about Derrick's murder, and her answers were always the same. She wondered if Rhodes had done the bulk of the prep work for this interview.

"Have you spoken with Alice Patmore?" Noelle abruptly asked during a pause in Keaton's questions. She knew the FBI special agent, who'd originally investigated Derrick's murder, had retired a number of years ago.

Keaton looked up from his computer. "Yes." His gaze went back to his screen.

Okay.

Not a topic for discussion.

She made eye contact with Rhodes. His shoulder lifted three millimeters in a subtle shrug.

No help there.

"Detective Marshall, I see some of your family has moved to the Bend area over the years," said Keaton.

"Yes."

There was a pause as Keaton waited for her to expand. She didn't. If he could give one-word answers, so could she. She instantly regretted her pettiness.

"My youngest sister moved at the same time I did seven years ago," Noelle added. "My other sister and her husband moved here a few months after we did."

"And your grandfather?" asked Keaton.

She felt Rhodes's gaze sharpen on her.

Noelle swallowed hard. "He passed a year before I moved." She was proud her voice didn't crack. The loss of her grandfather was part of what had driven her out of the Sacramento area. It was too painful to drive past places he'd taken her and her sisters over the years.

I still miss him.

7

Five years before Derrick Bell's murder

Noelle parked on the street. Light shone from the kitchen window, indicating her grandfather had waited up for her. Again. The cheery light made her feel both loved and a little guilty. She wished he'd go to bed; she wasn't a wild eighteen-year-old anymore, but he insisted on being up even if it meant waiting until 1:00 a.m. after her shift. Like tonight.

"Don't sleep much anyway," he'd told her a dozen times. "Don't need it when you reach my age."

Her grandfather had raised Noelle and her two younger sisters since she was thirteen. Their mother had passed from breast cancer when her youngest sister, Lucia, was only two, and their father currently was serving twenty to thirty in prison. Not that his absence mattered; he'd rarely been around before he was convicted of second-degree murder.

Their grandfather and his sister, Daisy, were the only parents little Lucia had known. Unless you counted Noelle. She'd mothered Lucia, giving her advice on clothes and friends as she grew up, the current girly things that Great-Aunt Daisy wasn't in touch with. Their unusual family had done well raising Lucia and Eve. Both women were smart and sweet and caring.

Noelle strode up the driveway, automatically glancing at the empty spot where her sister used to park her car. Eve had moved out six months ago, and Noelle still wasn't accustomed to her absence. The nineteen-year-old now lived with four other girls in a cramped apartment. But she was happy, and that was what mattered.

As Noelle went to slide her key into the door's lock, it abruptly opened. She grinned at her grandfather. He wore baggy pajama pants, slippers, and a bathrobe that belonged to Aunt Daisy. He grinned back, his eyes nearly disappearing in his happy squint.

Noelle never tired of the sight. The two of them had something special.

"Hey, Poppa."

"How was slinging drinks tonight? Did ya see the governor?"

"Not tonight."

He wasn't a fan of the current governor, but he'd been impressed last month when Noelle told him the governor had tipped her twenty dollars on a glass of wine. Cheap wine. She'd tried to steer the man toward one of her favorite Argentine reds, but he'd insisted on a US brand. Important people had sat at Noelle's bar and enjoyed her drinks, even a few celebrities. She treated everyone the same. If she took an order, she gave her best service.

"Are Lucia and Aunt Daisy asleep?" she asked as she quietly closed the door behind her.

"Lucia is. Daisy's been wandering around complaining about the carpet."

As usual.

Her great-aunt hated the dark brown of the carpet. Noelle did too, but she kept it to herself. Money was tight, and she didn't want her grandfather dipping into his retirement account to change perfectly good carpet. He'd been a police officer for two decades in San Francisco, but now he drove a school bus for the local school district and loved it. Always wore goofy hats and learned all the kids' names. But Noelle couldn't help wondering if he worked because he feared running out of money. He brushed her off every time she tried to bring it up. "I've got scads of money," he'd say. And he always refused any money she offered for the mortgage.

Instead, she contributed by purchasing all the groceries and paying any utility bill she could swipe before he saw it.

He was healthy as a horse. Tall and strong. A former college athlete who still lifted weights in the garage and walked a couple of miles every day. He rarely slowed down. He had a close group of friends who liked to bowl and fish, and he spent every weekend working in the yard.

When his daughter—their mother—had died, he'd moved the three girls into his home, where he lived with his sister, Daisy. It'd been ten years. Ten very happy and loud years. Their poppa was extremely outgoing and energetic compared to their quiet mother.

Looking back, Noelle wondered if her mother had been sick for longer than they knew. Or possibly she'd been depressed. Their father had never helped, but Noelle remembered the adoration in her mother's eyes when she looked at his picture. His murder conviction hadn't taken away the adoration; it'd simply made her sad. Perhaps her cancer had fed on that sadness.

Noelle's grandfather had *not* liked his daughter's choice of spouse from day one. He kept it to himself while she was alive but had privately told Noelle—once she was an adult—that he'd known her father was trouble the first time he met him. He'd dealt with enough criminals to see the problems with their father.

It added to Noelle's shame that she'd made a poor decision with her own marriage. She was twenty-four now and figured she'd most likely marry again at some point. She was determined not to make the same mistake twice.

But no good prospects had crossed her path.

I'm not looking anyway.

Right?

8

Five years before Derrick Bell's murder

The elevator's doors opened, and Noelle realized it had stopped inside the penthouse foyer.

"Holy shit." Savannah grabbed Noelle's arm as she gawked at the huge chandelier and fresh floral arrangements.

Agreed.

Sounds of a dozen conversations and light music reached them. A waiter with a tray of appetizers darted across the foyer without a glance for the women.

Which was an uncommon occurrence. Both tall and attractive, Savannah and Noelle captured attention wherever they went as a pair. Tonight was no exception. Savannah had already said three times how good they looked together. The brunette and the blonde. One in red and the other in black. Heels. Makeup. Blowouts.

Noelle and Savannah moved down the marble-lined hall, and the music grew louder. Savannah gave her a light punch on her bicep. "Glad I made you come?"

"Definitely. Sounds like it will be a good party."

"If you feel uncomfortable, just grab a tray and take drink orders. You'll feel more at home," Savannah said with a big grin.

Noelle snorted.

Savannah was her closest friend and a dining room manager where Noelle worked. Rex Duggan, the restaurant owner, had invited his management staff to a party at his home on top of one of Sacramento's luxury hotels, and Savannah had begged Noelle to be her plus-one.

She hadn't needed to beg; Noelle was immediately on board. Rex Duggan was a colorful celebrity in the restaurant world. A former chef, he owned four restaurants in Sacramento and another in San Francisco. That one had been crowned with two Michelin stars.

Noelle had spoken with Rex a number of times over the years at the bar. He'd said one of the reasons he always remembered her was that she was six inches taller than he—and that was without heels. He always had a joke to tell and offered a friendly hand to shake. He was impossible not to like. Everyone got his personal attention during his impromptu visits, but Noelle knew he was simultaneously watching the food, patrons, and staff, all while evaluating cleanliness.

"Let's find a drink and a bite to eat," said Savannah, sniffing the air as a hint of sesame oil and ginger reached them. "I want to see what a food star like Rex serves at a party."

A moment later they paused at the entry to a huge room with floor-to-ceiling windows that gave a 270-degree view of the city's night skyline. The space was packed with people in small groups talking, laughing, and drinking. Noelle spotted a few other employees and several regulars from her bar. Most of whom she knew were heavy hitters in the political world. It was a crush; everyone was dressed to impress. Her little black dress with the low back had been the right choice. Jewelry sparkled on the attendees, an echo of the night lights of the city outside.

The city's elite were present.

A waiter stopped and offered a tray of drinks. Noelle recognized Rex's signature gin and tonic. The women each took one, thanked the waiter, and then clinked their glasses. "Here's to an awesome evening," said Noelle. Excitement was building in her chest. She'd needed a night out where she wasn't catering to everyone's whims.

"Isn't that San Francisco's mayor?" Savannah said loudly in Noelle's ear. Noelle followed her gaze. "Yep." She'd waited on the man a few times. He liked small-batch tequilas. "Let's mingle." Savannah nodded and made a beeline for a group of women Noelle didn't recognize, so she scanned the room and decided to head outdoors. Several of the floor-to-ceiling windows were actually sliding doors that opened an entire wall to the huge terrace. She stepped outside. The dry night air was pleasantly warm from the day's summer heat.

Rex—or his designer—had created a half dozen seating areas with small tables and large overstuffed chairs. Tall umbrellas dotted the space but were tightly closed, ready to provide tomorrow's necessary shade against the season's intense sun. There was a wide roof, but it covered only half of the terrace. She spotted misters and heaters—the outdoor patio was usable in all weather. Neither were needed in tonight's comfortable evening temperature. Noelle leaned against the rail, looking out over the city, the beauty nearly painful.

What would it be like to live up here?

She'd never leave the terrace. Someone would have to bring her food and set up an outdoor shower. Noelle sighed and turned to search out someone to chat with. Her restaurant's assistant general manager caught her eye and gave a jerk of his head to indicate she should join his group. She had taken two steps in his direction when she heard her name and spotted Rex Duggan headed her way.

She'd found Rex genuinely likable. He was outgoing and chatty and had a tendency to name-drop, but he didn't do it in a bragging way. He actually knew and spent time with the people he mentioned; they were part of his broad circle of acquaintances. Other people whispered that he was a snob; Noelle hadn't found that at all. He was a people person and never said an unkind word about anyone. His looks reminded her of Danny DeVito's a bit, but he wasn't *that* short. And his eyeglasses frames were always bright red or blue.

"Damn, you look amazing, Noelle," he said as he squeezed her hand, looking up at her. "Like a silent movie star. Elegant and polished."

"Your home is beautiful," she told him. "The view makes me want to cry."

His eyes lit up. "That's exactly what it does to me." Still holding her hand, he glanced around with a frown. "I want to introduce you to someone. Don't see him, though. You're still single, right?"

Not another fix-up.

She swore every employee at the restaurant had tried. "I am, but—"

"Either you are or you're not."

"I am." She grimaced.

"Stay right here. I'll be back." Rex vanished into the crowd.

She watched him leave, torn between wanting to do as he asked and wanting to blend into the crowd. She guiltily chose the crowd.

He's the host. He'll be waylaid by twenty other people.

She spent the next hour socializing and snacking. Everyone wanted to talk about the latest education bill and the big-name movie star who'd been caught with the wife of the president of a South American country. Others talked books—one of her favorite topics—or critiqued the Broadway musical that'd been in town for two weeks. She smiled and nodded. Books she'd spend money on; Broadway musicals were out of her budget.

A perk of bartending near the capitol building was that she was up to date on every bit of political news and could intelligently discuss most current events. She rarely voiced her opinion, a habit she'd developed to protect her tips, but she was skilled at asking questions and digging deeper into the issues. After one woman relentlessly poked and prodded for her opinion of the recent minimum wage bill—Noelle knew she was just looking for an argument—Noelle excused herself and slipped back out to the terrace, needing a moment of silence. The crowd had thinned a bit, but there was no indication of the party winding down soon.

She asked a server for a glass of Perrier and retreated to the far end of the patio, where it narrowed to a point, creating a snug area between the railing and the penthouse wall. A light, pleasant buzz from the alcohol filled her limbs. She sipped her water and wondered what Savannah was doing. The last Noelle had seen her, Savannah had been trying on the shoes of a local TV anchor, both women deep in conversation about the spiked heels. The red soles of the anchor's shoes had tempted Noelle to join in, but shoe swapping felt too much like a middle school activity.

Red soles. Someday.

"Jessica loves to start an argument."

Noelle turned to the male speaker, instantly in agreement about the woman who'd pressured her about the minimum wage bill.

Mr. Stoli.

"You saw that?" Noelle asked, meeting his brown gaze, realizing she had to look up an inch or two to do so. A rare occurrence.

"And heard it. I was talking to someone behind you. You were the third person I'd heard her try to argue with." His amused smile touched his eyes. "You deflected best."

"Thank you. Lots of practice."

"She was very put out when you walked away."

"I'm not here for her entertainment." Her gaze wandered over his face. He had something compelling that she couldn't pinpoint and that drew her to him. Right now, he was the best thing she'd seen all night. And that included the red soles.

His smile was slightly crooked, an endearing sight. He had a five-o'clock shadow and didn't wear a tie—which she'd never seen him without. Instead, his crisp white shirt made a nice contrast with the dark-gray suit. He wore suits well, clearly comfortable in them, almost as if he'd been born to wear them. She'd never seen him in anything else, but she suspected he'd be just as cool and confident in shorts and a T-shirt.

His glass held a clear, carbonated liquid over ice.

"Not vodka," she stated, gesturing at his glass.

"Perrier."

"Same." She held his gaze and smiled, as if they were sharing a big secret. The moment stretched, and her soft buzz went to her head, a sensation of lightness and wonder. An unspoken attraction filled the space between them. Noelle wasn't surprised and realized that instinct had made her keep her distance at work because deep down she'd known this would happen.

"You know Rex?" she asked.

"Family friend. My dad did some work for him."

She'd later learn that the "work" had been the construction and design of two of Rex's restaurants and the hotel under the penthouse where they were currently standing.

"Do you like pie?" he asked, his gaze searching hers.

"Who doesn't?"

"I know where to get the best."

"Rick's," she said at the same time as he. Her attraction grew, warmth spreading through her chest and arms.

Same drink. Same pie place. What else?

"Do you want to leave?" he asked, his words so quiet she had to lean closer. She smelled a subtle aftershave that made her crave . . . something.

She had always been the responsible one. Looking out for her younger sisters. Keeping an eye on her great-aunt. Working long hours. Getting perfect grades.

Suddenly she wanted to fly in the warm, soft breeze of the night. Step into the unknown and enjoy the heady rush.

With him.

"Yes." She glanced over his shoulder and spotted Savannah, back in her own shoes. "Let me tell my friend."

He nodded and stepped back. She'd been so caught up in the moment, she hadn't noticed his position had essentially pinned her in the corner of the terrace. She strode to Savannah.

"Is that the vodka guy?" Savannah squeaked as Noelle approached, staring past her.

"Shhh. Yes. We're going out for a bite to eat."

"Uh-huh," Savannah said, twisting her lips. "He looks very hungry. You do too." She innocently blinked several times. "I take it you don't need a ride home."

"I don't think so. If I do, I'll call a cab."

Savannah gave her a quick kiss on the cheek, gin heavy on her breath. "Enjoy."

He was two yards away as she turned from Savannah, his gaze instantly locking with hers. He smiled, and she was smitten again. He held out a hand and she set hers in it, his grip smooth and secure. Without a word, he led her away, weaving among the groups of socializers. Two men tried to stop him to talk, but he shook his head and kept moving. Their eyes went to Noelle, and she saw understanding dawn.

She didn't care.

As they waited in the foyer for the elevator, he held her gaze.

Neither spoke.

The door slid open and he led her inside. As the door closed, he faced her and pressed her against the wall and kissed her.

Adrenaline and something primal shot through her veins as she returned the kiss, sinking her nails into his hair and drawing them along his scalp. He gasped deep in his throat and deepened the kiss. The elevator dropped quickly, but Noelle knew that wasn't what created the butterflies in her stomach. Just before the door slid open in the building's lobby, he pulled back and she felt the loss keenly.

His eyes reflected that feeling. And a promise of more.

9

Five years before Derrick Bell's murder

They were silent on the drive to Rick's. He continued to hold her hand, and they exchanged frequent glances and grins. The silence was comfortable, not stifling. She relaxed into the vehicle's leather seat as his thumb rubbed the back of her hand.

What am I doing here?

She didn't care. They had connected on a heady level in that crowded penthouse, and she didn't want to break that connection. The newness and potential still floating between them.

Inside Rick's, he sat across from her in a vinyl booth. The lights were too bright, but they didn't overpower her attraction. They showed her more of him. The tiny scar that crossed a smile line. The small mole near an eye.

His gaze roamed over her in the same way, letting her know he liked what he saw. He set his arm on the table and opened his hand, a silent request. She placed hers in it, slightly embarrassed to realize she'd missed the touch of his skin in the minutes since they'd left his car.

We just met.

"I don't know your name," she blurted.

One brow rose. "No?"

"No. You always paid in cash. No card."

"I know yours."

"I wore a name tag. Not fair." She frowned as something occurred to her. "Did Rex tell you he wanted to introduce us?"

"No."

"Oh." She wondered whom Rex had had in mind and then decided that she didn't care.

"I asked him to introduce us." He smiled, and her gaze locked on that small scar. "He failed, so I had to make it happen myself."

Small shivers went up her spine. She was flattered.

"What kind of pie do you want?" he asked, even though they hadn't looked at the menus the waitress had set on the table.

"Coconut." She didn't need a menu.

"That was my first choice. So peach for me."

"That was my second choice," she said wryly. "I'll share if you will."

"Of course."

The waitress reappeared and then sped off after he gave their orders. Noelle paused, not used to someone ordering for her.

I did tell him what I wanted.

Clearly he operated in a different world than hers. His car, his clothes, his watch. He'd probably been taught it was a courtesy to order for his date. A little old-fashioned in her eyes, but no doubt he meant it as a sign of respect. He'd opened the diner door for her, and she hadn't let it bother her.

She set the thoughts aside. "You said Rex was a family friend. You grew up around here?"

Their conversation took off. She learned they'd attended rival high schools, and although he was three years her senior, they'd attended some of the same memorable football games. They liked some of the same fiction authors, but his taste extended to military memoirs while she read every book on psychology. He loved tennis; she loved running and yoga.

Neither of them had seen the northern lights and both had it on their bucket list. His travel background was extensive; she'd never left the country. A bachelorette party weekend in Mexico didn't count.

He had an older sister and an older brother. His grandparents had all passed, and both parents were still living. She told him that her mother had died when she was thirteen and that she lived with her grandfather and great-aunt. And she told him about her felon of a father.

She never told anyone that.

There was a small lull in the conversation as the waitress returned with their pie and two cups of coffee. Each eyed the other's plate, causing another round of grins. He'd requested his peach pie slightly warmed and with a scoop of vanilla ice cream—just the way Noelle would have ordered it. She plunged her fork into her creamy coconut goodness and took a big bite.

Heaven.

He paused with a forkful of peach halfway to his mouth, his admiring gaze locked on her. "You look like you've tasted the best thing in the world."

"Maybe I have." She took another bite.

They ate in silence for a few minutes, offering each other bites. Noelle laid down her fork and sipped her coffee, studying him over the rim. "Now tell me your name."

"And destroy the mystery?"

"There will be other things to discover."

His gaze heated. "Derrick."

"Derrick what?"

"Bell."

"Nice to meet you, Derrick Bell." His name was slightly familiar—she'd probably heard it in the bar at some point. The one topic they hadn't touched on was their jobs. Again, he knew all about hers while she knew nothing of his. "In my head I called you Mr. Stoli."

"I would have answered to that." One side of his mouth curled up. "I would have answered to anything."

That smile.

"Do you have a wife or girlfriend, Mr. Stoli?"

"No. You?"

45

"No." *Tell him.* "I do have an ex-husband from a two-month marriage when I was eighteen." She held her breath.

"Kids?" he asked, moving on in the conversation.

"No, thank goodness. I wasn't that insane."

"Mistakes happen."

"Yes." Relief flowed over her that he didn't seem to care. The announcement that she had an ex-husband had ended a few dates in the past. "What do you do, Mr. Stoli?"

"I'm a VP at my father's construction company, but I don't want to do it much longer."

"What do you *want* to do?"

"I love politics." He eagerly plunged into the topic.

Noelle listened, attracted by his enthusiasm.

This date won't end soon.

10

"Was Assemblyman Bell a frequent drinker?" asked Agent Keaton. "Could he hold his liquor?"

Noelle stared at him. "Seriously? That's your question for me? You want to know about Derrick's drinking habits." She leaned forward, her arms crossed on the table, and looked Keaton in the eye. "Derrick never got drunk. He was always in control of himself."

"What about drugs? You're aware that he had a lot of meth in his system at the time of his death," said Keaton.

"I was told that. As far as I knew, Derrick didn't use drugs. Legal or illegal."

"What do you think of the meth?"

"I don't know." The question had haunted her for years. Years after his death, she'd recalled that in his always-immaculate car, she'd once seen white powder on her seat. At the time, she'd assumed it was from a powdered doughnut because he'd been very stressed and eating erratically.

He'd been murdered six months later.

Could that have been meth?

Powdered doughnut makes more sense.

Maybe.

"I have no answer for where he got meth or why he'd used it. He'd told me he hated the feeling of being out of control, so he never drank too much and didn't do drugs. He drank lightly for the social aspect." She paused, remembering all the nights he'd sat in her bar watching her. "Derrick's only interest in alcohol was how to use it on others to get what he wanted. He loved to mingle and talk. He had big plans for his future and wanted to meet other people who could help him get there."

"Did that include you, Detective?" asked Agent Rhodes. "Being someone who could help him?"

Noelle swallowed. "No. I wasn't a stepping stone for him."

"Are you sure?" asked Keaton. "You nicely fit the visual image of a political wife."

"You're asking me if the man I married only picked me because he thought I could help him get elected to office?" She laughed. "I was poor. Divorced. I tended bar. Doesn't sound like there are any political benefits at all." She let her face go blank. "We fell in love. That was it. No ulterior motives on anyone's part. I loved my husband, and he loved me. It was perfect."

Keaton leaned back in his chair. "Did his family view your relationship that way?"

"I don't understand what his family's opinion of me has to do with Derrick's murder."

"We're just trying to see the bigger picture," said Keaton.

Noelle waited a long second. "His mother didn't like me. No one was good enough for her son."

That still stings.

11

Noelle fussed with her necklace again and slid on two silver bracelets.

Too much?

She took off the necklace and nodded in satisfaction at her reflection in the mirror. The simple blue sundress was extremely flattering and highlighted her tan, but she wore a small white shrug in case it was cold in the restaurant.

She was meeting Derrick's family.

It'd been three and a half weeks since the evening they'd had pie, and she'd seen him almost every day—and some nights. When they hadn't seen each other, they had spent time on the phone. Long conversations about everything and nothing.

Two nights ago, during dinner at home, her aunt Daisy had loudly whispered to her grandfather that "Noelle is clearly in love." Her grandfather had met Noelle's stricken gaze—she was thankful Derrick wasn't present—and disagreed. "She's just enjoying the giddy rush," he said.

That giddy rush had lasted for twenty-five days. And Noelle didn't see an end to the ride.

Derrick had found tickets to the sold-out Broadway show that people had raved about at the party the night they met and introduced her to the musical theater experience. They'd gone for a long weekend in Wine Country, where they'd indulged in too many glasses of red wine, and he'd boozily bought memberships at four different wineries, making her laugh and guaranteeing constant wine deliveries for him.

They would talk for hours over wine and good food. She told him about her mother's struggle with breast cancer and her father's trial. Things she'd never shared with anyone. She learned about his reading disability that wasn't diagnosed until he was twelve. "I'd learned how to fake it. I fooled everyone until my seventh grade English teacher. He pulled me aside and I denied everything. But I couldn't fake my way through his impromptu reading test." Derrick had given a sad smile. "He knew because he'd experienced the same thing."

Her heart was getting involved, his moments of vulnerability sucking her in.

Derrick somehow got them into restaurants with weeklong waiting lists where the food and service were impeccable. When she asked how he did it, he shrugged. "My father built a lot of this town. People know our name."

She learned his brother and sister worked for the family construction company and also had "vice president" titles after their names. Derrick's brother, Jason, traveled a lot, making connections for the business. Derrick said his sister didn't do much except carry a title and collect a check, but he smiled, his affection for her obvious.

His world of wealth was foreign to Noelle, and she listened in fasciation to his stories of international travel when he and his siblings were young and of new cars on sixteenth birthdays. She'd had to work and scrimp to pay for *everything* and was slightly jealous. Derrick worked hard too but had received priceless opportunities because of his father's success. She noticed he was generous, a heavy tipper with valets, waitstaff, and the baristas at his favorite espresso shop. Trying to pass it on, he said when she commented.

Once she started looking, Noelle spotted the Bell name on several Sacramento construction signs. Three of the five huge cranes that currently marred the city skyline were part of Bell projects. Derrick's apartment was in a building the company had completed five years ago. His place wasn't as grandiose as Rex Duggan's, but it had lovely views and a kitchen that'd stunned Noelle the first time she'd visited. The furniture was simple with clean lines and looked barely used. The decor was scarce, but he had several collections he kept in glass cabinets. Baseball cards, antique guns, cigar boxes, signed footballs, and models of elephants. Some of the larger elephants were artfully scattered around the living room, sitting on end tables and shelves.

"Why elephants?" she asked, eyeing one that was nearly two feet tall.

"When I was thirteen, my parents took us to Africa. We visited an elephant orphanage, and I've been obsessed with them ever since." He nodded at a framed photo in which thirteen-year-old Derrick had his arm wrapped around a baby elephant, pure joy on his face.

Derrick didn't cook; the professional appliances went unused except for the microwave and fridge. He preferred eating in restaurants or bringing in takeout. To his delight, Noelle changed that; she loved to cook and try to duplicate dishes from her restaurant. He'd sit at the kitchen island and watch, a glass of wine in his hand. She'd have him wash and chop vegetables or stir things on the stove, but even in the huge kitchen, he always managed to get in her way and ask forgiveness with a kiss on her forehead or a hug from behind.

She suspected he got in the way on purpose. He loved to run his hands over her body, and she relished the attention, leaning her head against him, closing her eyes and simply enjoying the scent of his skin.

Sometimes their food burned.

Her friends elbowed her at work when he showed up, giving her a wink and him an ogle. She'd meet his eyes and suddenly the bar was silent in her ears; her infatuation—and his—was growing. He stopped sitting at the bar during her shifts. They'd agreed she needed to focus, and he was definitely a distraction. Rex Duggan came in one night and gleefully took credit for their relationship even though he hadn't done a thing.

It was a relationship. They'd had *the* discussion and agreed they didn't want to see other people. She only had eyes for him.

And thank goodness she'd picked a different type of man this time. Fate was smiling on her.

"You look great." Derrick appeared in the mirror, standing behind her, a look of admiration on his face. "That dress is amazing. New?"

"No. Old," said Noelle. "You don't recognize it because I added the belt and shrug." She'd worn the dress on their wine trip.

He put his hands on her upper arms and studied the two of them in the mirror. "Damn, we make a good-looking couple. Jackie-and-JFK-worthy."

Noelle smiled. That night in the pie shop, Derrick had shared his five-year plan, which included an assemblyman run for his district in three years. He was very social and worked hard to be positively involved with politics, which explained the respect from others she'd seen in her bar. "Putting my best face forward," he'd told her, creating his own maxim.

Derrick had the face. It was one of those faces that photographed extremely well. The camera picked up everything she'd first noticed when she sat across from him over pie.

Strength. Kindness. And dreamy deep-brown eyes.

Derrick had the name and the intelligence. He was well versed on issues, knew how to listen, and was a master of small talk. She noticed women loved him and men respected him. She had no doubt he'd be a successful politician. One night in bed, he admitted he dreamed of the White House. "Everyone in politics does."

Noelle easily saw his vision.

"I thought you were wearing the necklace," Derrick said with a small frown, studying their reflections.

"It was too much with my other jewelry. And it doesn't work well with this neckline."

"Let me see." He picked up the delicate necklace from where she'd set it on the counter and fastened it around her neck. He'd bought it in Napa after she'd admired it in a window. "I like it," he said. "How about smaller earrings?"

She realized he wanted her to wear it in front of his family. "I'll do that." She swapped out the hoops for studs. The aquamarine pendant sat too high on her chest for the neckline of the dress, but she knew it pleased him.

Curiosity filled her as she wondered about his family. Again. She'd looked them up online. There were plenty of business articles that referenced his father and Bell Construction, and she'd learned his mother served on several charity boards, and Noelle had spotted her in many photos at various fundraisers. Derrick's slightly lopsided smile had clearly come from her. Little had been written about his sister, Lora, or his brother, Jason. Their professional photos were on the construction company's website, along with some candid photos of them in hard hats at groundbreakings. Jason's name mainly turned up in old articles about high school sports. He'd been a football standout in his day.

A half hour later, Derrick handed his keys to the fresh-faced valet at the country club and helped Noelle out of the car.

"I'll take good care of it, Mr. Bell."

Derrick clapped him on the back. "I know you will, Colton."

The young man beamed.

Derrick took Noelle's hand and led her inside the club, occasionally exchanging greetings with other members. The restaurant hostess directed them to a table outside, where his family was already seated. Noelle checked the time. She and Derrick were ten minutes early.

Prompt family.

Then she noticed their drinks were half-empty. It appeared there'd been a family meeting before they arrived.

Derrick's father, Stan, immediately got to his feet and took both Noelle's hands. "So lovely to finally meet you, my dear."

This is what Derrick will look like in thirty years.

He was tall and had the same brown eyes but with permanent smile lines at the corners. The name of the country club was embroidered on his white polo shirt. She liked him immediately.

Next to him his wife stood and held out her hand. Noelle shook it. "So nice to meet you," she told Catherine. Derrick's mother wore a sleeveless teal patterned dress with bright-pink accents. Large rings glittered on several fingers, and multiple delicate gold chains hung around her neck. Her French manicure matched her toes. Every inch of her seemed polished. She was very petite, and her defined upper arms alluded to time in the gym.

Catherine's gaze wasn't as warm as her husband's.

I'll win her over.

Jason was next. He was smaller than the other two men but had a forceful presence. His grip was tight on her hand as they shook. "Derrick won't shut up about you," he told her.

"Glad to hear it," she said with a grin.

Derrick gave him a gentle shove on one shoulder. "Would you rather I talked about the Kings?"

"Basketball season's over," said Jason. He met Noelle's gaze. "He knows nothing about sports. Or sportsball, as he calls it." He looked back to his brother. "If you're gonna be in politics, you need to sound informed when you bring up sports."

Derrick stiffened. "At least I can intelligently discuss other topics."

The "unlike you" wasn't stated, but Noelle saw it in his gaze.

"Boys." Their mother sat down without another word. The men exchanged one last glare and then looked away.

Looks like a common family rivalry.

Noelle immediately turned to Lora. Derrick's sister was petite like their mother, but she was the only blonde in the family. They shook hands, and Lora conspiratorially leaned in and whispered, "Ignore them." Louder she said, "Noelle, I love your necklace. It perfectly matches the color of your dress."

Noelle touched the pendant. "It's from Derrick."

He put his arm around her shoulders and beamed.

"Good job for once," said Jason, taking his seat.

Again Noelle noticed how Derrick tensed at his brother's words. He pulled his arm from her shoulders and took a piece of bread from the basket on the table, buttering it aggressively, as if he'd like to smear it on Jason's face.

Noelle watched. The anger was a side of Derrick she'd never seen.

"Stop," ordered Lora, giving Jason a deadly side-eye and then turning to Noelle. "I'm sorry my husband, Stewart, couldn't be here. He wanted to meet you, but he had to work."

Noelle knew her husband was a plastic surgeon.

"I saw pictures of your twins," Noelle said to Lora, trying to sound as upbeat as the young mother. "Adorable. They're almost three?"

"Yes." Her eyes softened and she smiled fondly. "They're terrors, but they're my terrors." She looked deliberately from one brother to the other. "Hopefully my boys will get along better than these two."

The table went silent, and Noelle didn't know what to say.

Thankfully, a waiter approached to take drink orders. The women had glasses of iced tea in front of them, so Noelle ordered the same, and Derrick requested a vodka tonic.

Ninety minutes later, Noelle and Derrick waited for the valet to return his car.

"You were perfect," he whispered in her ear. "I can tell they were impressed."

"They weren't impressed when I told them I tend bar." She'd seen the flash of disappointment in his mother's eyes. "I assumed you'd already told them."

"That's just temporary," he said. "You've got the presence of a queen and the intelligence of a rocket scientist. You're perfect."

She snorted. "More like model rockets." Some of her best memories of her father were of working with him on model rockets and then launching them in deserted areas. "But lately I've considered getting a master's in psychology. Maybe even going for a doctorate."

"Hmmm. Lotta school and studying." Derrick said nothing else as his car pulled up and the valet bounded out, darting around to open the door for Noelle. Derrick handed him a twenty and slid into the driver's seat. He pulled her close for a long kiss and then held her gaze. "I'm pretty sure I'm falling in love with you, Noelle Marshall."

She blinked as her lungs seized. "Me too," she whispered.

He sat back with a satisfied smile and put the car in drive.

Noelle sank into the soft seat, her mind spinning.

I didn't realize I was until he said it.

Damn, it feels good.

She watched him out of the corner of her eye, recalling something he'd said earlier. *That's just temporary.* She'd assumed he meant his family's attitude toward her job, but now she wondered if he meant tending bar was temporary. She shifted in her seat. Tending bar was fun and lucrative. She chose to be there.

I'm sure he meant their attitude.

12

"Split up the interviews between us?" Oscar asked.

"No," said Alice, stopping outside the door of the interview room. "I want both our eyes and ears in each one. Let's start with the parents and then talk to the siblings next."

"They'll be waiting awhile."

"Not my problem," said Alice. Her job wasn't to coddle. She wanted to find Derrick Bell's killer, and while she felt horrible for what his family was going through, acting fast was the best way to find a lead. She was frustrated that she couldn't eliminate Derrick's wife as a suspect. Yes, Noelle being involved was unlikely, considering the woman had suffered a debilitating head injury, but it wasn't out of the question. Without a lead, the next people to cross off her list were Derrick's family members.

"Okay," said Oscar. "His brother, Jason, is in the room next door, and sister Lora is across the hall." He opened the parents' interview room door.

Alice adjusted her expression into one of sympathy and stepped inside. Both parents had red, wet eyes. Neither looked as if they'd slept. Catherine Bell held a ragged tissue in one hand, and Alice spotted several more in the garbage near her chair. Stan Bell heavily leaned his arms on the table; he looked defeated. Both looked up as the agents entered, a glimmer of hope in their eyes.

"I'm so sorry for your loss," Alice said as she set her notepad on the table and took a seat. Oscar echoed her words and sat beside her, facing the Bells.

"Thank you," said Catherine. Her husband nodded.

It was a delicate dance Alice and Oscar were about to perform. They had to glean as much useful information as possible while staying sympathetic and not pushing the parents to a point where they shut down.

Alice had found the best way to avoid that was to address it immediately. "I know this is a horrible time, but it's vital that we quickly collect as much information as possible so we can find your son's killer."

Catherine winced at the word *killer*.

"We understand," said Stan. His voice was flat. "We will do whatever you need." Catherine swallowed heavily and nodded, her gaze on the tissue she'd started to shred.

"Some of our questions might feel intrusive. Or pointless," Alice warned. "Please answer as honestly as possible."

"We won't lie," snapped Catherine. "Our son is dead. We want justice." She'd gone rigid in her chair, her chin rising.

"Good," said Oscar. "So do we. Just remember we all have the same goal."

Stan looked bewildered. "Just what are you going to ask? I can't imagine why we'd hesitate to answer anything."

Alice took that challenge. "Was your son involved in anything illegal? Drugs, theft, tax evasion, or possibly having an affair?"

Stan went speechless while Catherine blinked several times.

"Jesus Christ." Stan finally spoke, fury growing in his gaze. "Derrick was an upstanding member of—"

"Do you see our point now?" asked Oscar, holding up one hand. "Tuck away your emotions for a moment. We wouldn't be doing our job if we didn't delve into these things."

"You're acting as if Derrick caused someone to murder him," Catherine spit out. "He was the victim here. You're blaming the victim instead of focusing on who did this."

Alice silently sighed. "We're not victim blaming. We're crossing things off a list that we use with every murder."

"Starting with his family members," said Catherine. "I know you're supposed to clear immediate family first. Have you talked to Noelle? She was there."

Alice's gaze sharpened at the way she said Noelle's name. Something simmered there. "We've spoken to Derrick's wife. You know she was left unconscious with a serious head wound, correct?"

"We know," said Stan. Catherine said nothing.

"Have you visited her in the hospital?" Alice wanted to hear more of the mother's tone as she spoke about Noelle.

Stan shifted in his seat. "We were told she's not thinking clearly and we probably should give her some time before we saw her."

Alice didn't disagree with the description of Noelle's mindset, but she suspected no one had told them to wait.

They used her confusion as an excuse to not go.

Why?

"She'd benefit from family support," said Oscar, clearly thinking the same thing.

"I'm sure her family has seen her," said Catherine.

They don't consider Noelle part of their family.

"How long was she married to Derrick?" asked Alice, knowing the answer.

Catherine looked at Stan. "Two years?"

"Three," said Stan.

Stan wins the prize.

"They loved each other very much," Stan added hastily. "Everyone saw it."

Catherine said nothing.

Alice had no problem being blunt. "Ms. Bell, your posture, silence, and facial expressions tell me you don't care for Noelle."

The mother's mouth opened the slightest bit, her eyes widening.

I bet people never speak to you like that.

Alice knew her words were harsh, but something about Catherine's attitude had rubbed her the wrong way.

"I don't want to speak badly about her," Catherine finally said.

"This is a murder investigation," said Alice. "I want to hear all the bad."

"It doesn't have anything to do with your investigation."

"Why don't you let us decide that?" said Oscar.

Stan looked from his wife to the investigators and back again, confusion in his eyes.

"She just has different values than us," Catherine said with a shrug. "It's not relevant."

Alice had a moment of sympathy for Noelle. No doubt Catherine Bell was impossible to please as a mother-in-law.

"Shouldn't you be focusing on people who might be angry at Derrick?" asked Stan.

"Did Derrick tell you about some?" asked Alice.

"Well . . . no. Just the usual. I mean, he gets hate mail, of course. Everyone in politics does, and he mentions it sometimes, but nothing specific. I don't think nasty emails automatically mean violence, though."

"What about business dealings?" asked Oscar. "I know he left your company after being elected, but were there some issues with his old coworkers or clients?"

"No." Stan was adamant.

Alice watched Catherine's face. It was blank.

Too blank.

"How about bad encounters with people at the gym? Maybe a road rage incident or argument with a neighbor? Did Derrick ever mention something like that?" asked Oscar.

"No," said Stan.

"Catherine, I feel like there's something you want to add," said Alice. "Maybe you weren't done talking about Noelle. Could something be linked to your daughter-in-law that led to this?"

"Not that I know of."

"How about I phrase it as 'Is there something you wonder about?'"

Catherine paused.

Here we go.

"Well, one of my friends saw her eating lunch with her ex-husband about a month ago."

Alice waited, letting the silence hang, hoping Catherine would want to fill it.

She did.

"Can you imagine if the media had seen that?" Catherine asked, looking from Alice to Stan and back. "They would have hinted at the worst, creating all sorts of problems for Derrick."

"Are you implying that Noelle was having an affair with her ex-husband?" asked Alice. "Did you ask her about it?" She didn't think the Sacramento media would care about a lunch. And the personal life of an assemblyman wasn't *that* big a deal.

"Well, no." Catherine wouldn't make eye contact. "But it could have been bad optics and blown up in the press. I didn't ask her about it because it's none of my business."

"Did you tell your son?" asked Oscar.

Catherine paused. "I did and he brushed it off. Said he was aware they were still friendly."

"For being none of your business, it appears to still bother you." Alice mentally moved Noelle's ex-husband further up her interview list.

"I'm just a mother being protective of her son." Sorrow flashed in her eyes and tears welled. Her husband grasped her hand.

"Was Noelle and Derrick's marriage okay?" asked Alice.

"Of course," said Stan. "It was solid, and they were very happy."

Catherine said nothing.

Interview with Derrick's brother, Jason

"Was Noelle and Derrick's marriage okay?" asked Alice.

Jason shrugged. "They were good at putting on a happy front, but I know Derrick was pissed that she continued to communicate with her ex-husband. He told me that since Noelle wasn't going to cut off all contact, he was going to talk to the guy." Jason shook his head. "I had my doubts about her from day one."

"Did Derrick speak to her ex?"

"Dunno."

"Have you visited Noelle?" asked Alice.

"Mom said she couldn't have visitors yet."

Interview with Derrick's sister, Lora

"Was Noelle and Derrick's marriage okay?" asked Alice.

Lora looked at her hands. She'd been rubbing her fingers the entire interview. "I don't think Noelle had an accurate understanding of Derrick when they married. I love him, but he's *very* self-centered. I think he hid that from her at first, but I know she started to see it."

Either she saw a different side of her brother than the rest of the family or she's more willing to speak up.

"Do you know anything about Noelle's first husband?"

Lora looked to one side, thinking. "I think his name was Brandon. No, it was Brendon." She grimaced. "Derrick recently said he was going to run a background check on him."

"Why?" asked Alice.

"That's what I asked him." She lifted one shoulder. "All he could say was that he didn't like the guy. It didn't make sense to me. Why care about her ex-husband? That'd been over for a long time."

"Have you visited Noelle?" asked Alice.

"Mom said she couldn't have visitors yet."

The same thing her brother said.

Alice pushed the button on the vending machine and then grabbed the Diet Coke. "I'm exhausted," she told Oscar, who was sipping his bottled water. "We've talked to too many Bells today. And all of them are cagey. I feel like we're not getting the whole story."

"Who do you think told the truth about the marriage?"

Alice had already pondered the question. "I'd say they all told the truth. I suspect they only saw what they wanted to see between Noelle and Derrick. Or what Derrick allowed them to see."

"Noelle seemed pretty broken up in the hospital."

Alice eyed him. "Still think she was acting?"

Oscar took a drink as he considered her question. "I don't know what to think. Trying to keep an open mind about her so that I don't miss anything. But my opinion on the family today was that the mother and brother aren't Noelle fans. The father saw everything through rose-colored glasses, and Lora . . . well, she was the only one who acknowledged that Derrick wasn't perfect."

"Agreed," said Alice. "I felt as if the others wanted to shine the best light possible on Derrick Bell."

"Understandable. But not helpful if it keeps us from leads."

"I found it odd that not one of them has tried to visit Noelle. I don't buy the bullshit story that they were advised to let her heal a bit more. Her doctor didn't say that to us. I think the mom made that up and told the others—including her husband. I think Lora would have gone if Mom hadn't gotten to her first."

Oscar solemnly nodded.

"The only lead from today is Noelle's ex, Brendon Simon. And we would have got around to him eventually." She unscrewed the soda's cap and took a long drink. She wiped her mouth and met Oscar's gaze. "I don't care that it's late. I want to talk to the ex tonight."

"You're reading my mind."

13

Noelle was tired of the interview. Their questions were tedious, with too much focus on minutiae.

"I'm very sorry about your grandfather," said Agent Rhodes. "I could tell from Agent Patmore's interviews with him that the two of you were very close."

"He was the father figure in my life," said Noelle, the pain of his death rising up again.

"You've had a lot of loss," said Agent Keaton. "Your husband, your mother, your grandfather, and I assume you'd count your father as lost to you."

"I do," said Noelle. "Is there a question in there?" She couldn't keep the annoyance out of her tone.

"Just stating the obvious, I guess." He tapped on his laptop. "Did your grandfather get along with your husband?" asked Keaton.

"Yes. Derrick got along with everybody." She knew she hadn't quite answered his question.

Keaton looked at her, clearly waiting for her to answer correctly.

"My grandfather was a person that did everything for himself and others. Derrick came from a privileged world. It was hard for him to understand why Derrick couldn't build a deck, change his car's oil, or repair the washing machine. They got along, but my grandfather always felt Derrick wasn't good enough for me." She shrugged. "Like a lot of fathers, I guess."

"Would you say your grandfather was overprotective of you and your sisters?" asked Rhodes.

"I'd say he was exactly the right amount of protective. For a cop."

14

Five years before Derrick Bell's murder

Lucia blew out thirteen candles and everyone cheered. Always the ham, Lucia stretched her hands toward the ceiling and whooped. "I'm finally a teenager!"

"Lord help us all," said her grandfather with a wink and a bear hug for the birthday girl.

The love on their faces touched Noelle's heart. Maybe Lucia didn't have her mother anymore, but she didn't lack for love and guidance. Her sister grinned as Aunt Daisy carefully handed her a giant knife to cut the cake. The girl lifted it above her head and made screeching sounds as she pretended to stab the cake.

"The shower scene from *Psycho*?" Derrick whispered in Noelle's ear.

"Yep. She's a horror movie fan. Especially the old ones." Noelle had her suspicions about how Lucia had picked up the obsession because it definitely hadn't come from Noelle's or their sister Eve's influence. But Aunt Daisy had a sparkle in her eye as she watched Lucia wave the knife. Their great-aunt often stayed up late, the sounds of a TV coming from her room, and Noelle wondered if Lucia sneaked in to watch movies with her.

Lucia swung the knife at the cake again, but this time abruptly slowed and gently cut a piece, delicately setting it on a plate and offering it to Daisy, who added a scoop of triple-chocolate ice cream.

"That's a lot of chocolate," murmured Derrick.

Noelle grinned. The chocolate cake had chocolate frosting, chocolate chips, and a fudge drizzle. Together with the ice cream and chocolate milk to drink, it was a bit much, but not for Lucia. In her opinion there was never enough chocolate.

Slices of cake were passed around, and Noelle and Derrick both requested the vanilla ice cream. They stepped away from the kitchen island and went to sit by Eve and her new boyfriend, Adam, in the dining room.

Noelle had been briefly speechless when Eve first introduced him.

"I know," Eve had said with an adoring look at Adam. "We've already heard all the jokes about our names."

"It will never end," Noelle had told her. "Everyone you meet will be compelled to say something."

Both of them had shrugged. "If that's the worst thing we deal with, I'll take it," said Adam.

He was friendly and polite and was currently being grilled by their grandfather at the dining room table. Noelle felt for him. Every male they'd brought home over the years had faced the same third degree.

"My roommate introduced us," Eve was saying to her grandfather. "She's known him since high school."

Her grandfather's thick white brows came together, and he eyed the boyfriend. "How long ago was high school?"

"Four years," Adam said. He wilted a bit at their grandfather's glaring silence. Eve was only nineteen.

"Don't you want a girlfriend who can go out to have a drink with you?" their grandfather asked Adam.

"I'm not a big drinker," said Adam, and he swallowed hard but kept eye contact. "It doesn't matter at all. We have a lot in common. We play tennis and both like to hike. It's nice to find someone as outdoorsy as me." Eve nodded emphatically.

Noelle stayed silent as Eve shot her a glance from under her lashes. Eve had hated camping when they were younger and still complained about bugs and heat whenever they were outside.

Eve must really like the guy.

"Usually at this point I start cleaning my guns in front of you," said her grandfather, still eyeing Adam. "You know I was a cop, right? These girls are my life. Just as their mother was."

"Poppa! Stop it. Not on my birthday." Lucia came up behind him and set a hand on his shoulder. She had the chocolate ice cream container in her other. "Anyone need more ice cream?" Everyone passed, and she took it back to the kitchen.

"Gun cleaning didn't scare off my daughter's husband," their grandfather continued in a quieter voice. "I wish it had. Pegged him for a loser right away. I recognized the type."

"If you'd scared him away, then we wouldn't be here," Eve pointed out.

Daisy appeared, hands on her hips. "Lucia says you're trying to scare Adam," she said to her brother. "Knock it off." To Adam she said, "Ignore him. He can't help it. The girls bring out the protector in him."

"That's a good thing," said Adam, smiling at Eve as he squeezed her hand. "They're lucky."

Noelle gave him points for not breaking. "Eve says you're taking a full college load *and* working full-time," she said, trying to change the subject and make him look good in front of her grandfather.

"I'll finish my marketing degree in December," said Adam. "I work at a car rental place. It's not demanding."

"He's a manager," Eve added proudly.

"Impressive," said Derrick, nodding at Adam. "Marketing *and* management. Knowing how to market a product or company is an important skill. You'll have a lot of opportunities in the future."

There was a loud knock at the door. It swung open, and Savannah stepped inside the home. "Where's the birthday girl?" she shouted. She had a balloon bouquet and a present bag with red tissue sticking out the top.

"Savannah!" Lucia ran to hug Noelle's gorgeous best friend.

The woman had bonded with Lucia the first time they met, and it always warmed Noelle's heart to see them together. Savannah was like the fourth sister in their family. Aunt Daisy and their grandfather also adored her and had encouraged her not to bother with knocking when she came to the house. Just walk right in.

Lucia took the balloons and tied them to her chair. Savannah set the bag in front of her with a flourish. "Enjoy!" The girl yanked out the tissue.

"Ohhh!" Lucia dug into the bag and pulled out two Harry Potter books. She looked in the bag and pulled out more. "It's the whole set! Thank you! I haven't read the last one yet. I think I'll start at the beginning and read them all again first."

"I think more will be published after that," said Savannah. She gave Noelle a loving but awkward strangling hug as she passed her chair and took the empty seat next to Derrick. "Is there any cake left, or am I too late?"

"I'll get you some." Lucia darted back into the kitchen. "Vanilla or chocolate ice cream?" she hollered from the other room.

"Chocolate, of course," said Savannah.

"That's why she loves you," Noelle whispered.

"Oh, she loves me for much more than that." Savannah poked Derrick's bicep. "How's it going, vodka man? You two planning a wedding yet? It's been two months."

"Not yet," Derrick told her with a grin.

"Wedding?" asked Aunt Daisy, looking up sharply from her cake.

"No wedding, Daisy," said Noelle. "Savannah's teasing."

"You better lock him down before someone else does, Noelle," said Savannah, batting her heavy fake lashes at Derrick. "He's a steal."

"You're getting married?" Lucia shrieked from the kitchen. She appeared in the doorway holding a serving spoon dripping with chocolate ice cream, a brown smear of it near her mouth.

"No!" said Noelle. Lucia had a tendency to believe everything she heard. She also fell in love with every date Noelle and Eve brought home. She'd been moony-eyed over Derrick since day one, and she'd been sneaking glances at Adam all evening.

Lucia had had a growth spurt over the past year that had left her with long arms and legs she hadn't quite mastered. At times she reminded Noelle of a newborn foal. Her blonde hair was thin and straight and refused to hold a curl no matter how long she clamped it with a curling iron. Her eyes were the same dark blue as her sisters' but seemed much larger in her delicate face.

Noelle would destroy anyone who hurt her baby sister. She felt the same about Eve, but Eve had more common sense and could fend for herself. Lucia was the innocent baby bird that needed to stay in the nest longer.

No matter how much gore she liked to watch on TV.

"Lucia's too trusting," their grandfather had once told Noelle. "Just like your mother."

Noelle had inwardly winced at his criticism of her mother, but she agreed with his blunt assessment.

"I'm glad you've got a cynical eye for this world," he'd said next, nodding in approval, and Noelle had smarted at the description.

"I just pay attention, Poppa," Noelle had countered. His decades on the police force had lessened his trust in people and made him frequently suspicious. Noelle didn't want to be like that. She knew he wasn't completely sold on Derrick.

"He's got soft hands," her grandfather had muttered after their first meeting.

"Because he doesn't have to dig up rocks or swing a hammer," Noelle had stated. "Nothing wrong with that. Simply a different upbringing than yours—and mine." Then she'd looked at her hands with the blunt-cut nails and tiny scars. The nails she kept short; it was simply easier for her job. The scars had happened because she always sliced limes too quickly and with a wet-handled knife.

Sitting next to Derrick at Lucia's party, Noelle fought the urge to look at her hands and instead focused on him. He was grinning at Lucia as her shoulders dramatically slumped at Noelle's quick denial of a wedding. Just past Derrick, Savannah caught her eye, tipped her head toward Derrick, and fanned herself, indicating how hot Derrick was.

In total agreement, Noelle fought back a grin.

"*Maybe* a wedding one day," Derrick told Lucia. He picked up his glass of chocolate milk and held it out in a toast. Everyone else quickly raised their glass. "But right now, this day is about you. Happy thirteenth birthday, Lucia."

Noelle echoed the toast along with everyone else and then met Derrick's gaze as she sipped her milk. Anticipation vibrated along her nerves.

Maybe.

15

Thirteen years ago
Two days after Derrick Bell's murder

Last night Alice and Oscar had been unable to contact Noelle's ex-husband, Brendon Simon, after hearing Catherine Bell complain about his relationship with Noelle.

They'd found a local address for Brendon, but no one had answered when they knocked on his door and rang his video doorbell at 9:00 p.m. The house appeared to be lived in, although Alice and Oscar hadn't been able to see a vehicle through the windows of the garage door. Alice debated leaving a note asking him to contact her but decided she preferred the element of surprise. They'd be back.

Records showed that Brendon was a radiology tech at a small hospital outside of town, but a pop-in visit to radiology that morning had revealed that he'd not worked there in three months. The receptionist didn't know if he had a job somewhere else.

"Noelle probably knows," said Oscar. "If she was really in contact with him the way the Bells believe her to be."

"Part of me thinks that idea takes up more space than it should in Catherine Bell's brain. She's highly protective of her son and clearly feels the need to blame Noelle for *something*." Alice checked her phone as Oscar drove.

"As most mothers are," said Oscar.

"Since the mother didn't ask, I wonder if anyone asked Noelle about her luncheon with her ex. Or even knew about it—assuming it actually happened. Catherine did hear it from a friend."

"Sounds like Derrick was aware of their friendship."

Is that all it was between Noelle and her ex? A friendship?

"Let's talk to Noelle again," said Alice. "Maybe she can help us find Brendon this afternoon."

A half hour later, Alice and Oscar walked into her hospital room and discovered Noelle already had visitors. A tall white-haired man with crazy eyebrows stood up and glared as they entered the room.

That's got to be her grandfather.

Behind him a young woman leaned forward in her chair, peering around the man to see the two agents. She had the same deep-blue eyes as Noelle, and her straight, blonde hair was slicked back into a ponytail. She was thin and delicate looking, and she grasped one of Noelle's hands as the woman lay in bed.

One of the sisters.

Alice showed her identification to the grandfather. He scowled and took reading glasses out of his shirt pocket to examine it.

"They're okay, Poppa," Noelle said. "They're the FBI agents I told you about."

"Then why haven't they found who killed your husband?" He met Alice's gaze, and she felt as if she were looking into the eyes of a very protective Doberman.

Tact was needed.

"Nice to meet you, Mr. Swanson," Alice said, ignoring his comment. "How are you feeling today, Noelle?" The bruising around the woman's eyes had bloomed into full color. It looked as if she had been punched in the face several times instead of receiving a single blow to the back of the head.

"Better. They said I can go home this afternoon."

"You're coming home with us," her grandfather said firmly.

"That's not necessary," Noelle stated.

The sister gripping her hand frowned and shook her head at Noelle.

"Agents Patmore and Wilson." Alice looked at the young woman as she gestured to herself and Oscar. No one had bothered to introduce her.

"This is my sister Lucia," said Noelle.

The youngest. She looks fourteen, not eighteen.

"How is the security at your home, Mr. Swanson?" asked Oscar in his usual pessimistic tone.

The bushy eyebrows came together. "Security? Do two handguns and three rifles count?"

"Not really," said Alice. She looked at Noelle, whose mouth had opened slightly at Oscar's question. "Until your husband's killer is caught, you should be very careful."

Lucia had paled. "You mean they might come after her? Do you think they meant to kill her too? And now will want to finish the job?"

"Exactly," said Oscar at the same time that Alice said, "We don't know what they want."

Noelle's sister went even whiter, and she added her other hand to the grip on Noelle's. "You shouldn't leave the hospital," she told Noelle urgently.

The grandfather straightened. "No one's getting near my granddaughter. *Any* of my granddaughters."

"I'll be fine, Poppa," stated Noelle.

"How do you know that?" asked Alice.

Noelle blinked. She didn't appear to have an answer.

"We'd like to talk to you for a few minutes alone, Mr. Swanson," Alice said. "Would you step into the hall with us?"

Oscar opened the door.

The grandfather looked as if he wanted to argue but wisely said nothing. "I'll be right outside," he told his granddaughters, and then followed the agents.

The hall was deserted, the nurses' station out of listening range. Alice smiled at the grandfather. She had to look up to meet his eyes. He was taller than she'd realized, and he stood firmly with his arms crossed. *He must have been very intimidating when he was younger.*

She corrected that thought; William Swanson was still intimidating. A good watchdog for his granddaughters.

"What are your leads on the person who nearly killed Noelle?" he asked.

Alice tilted her head a degree. "You mean the person who *did* kill her husband and assaulted Noelle."

"They left her for dead. Lucia had a good point that they might want to finish the job. So what are you doing to protect her?"

His concern is valid.

"We can ask for a local patrol to regularly pass by your home," said Oscar.

"*That's it?*" Thunder raged in his eyes. "Looks like the responsibility for her safety falls on me."

"Mr. Swanson," said Alice. "Do you know of anyone who would want to hurt her and her husband?"

"No."

He said nothing else into the silence that followed, his gaze hard and accusing.

"Has Noelle mentioned any trouble that her husband was having? Anger from constituents?" Oscar added after the long moment. "Or possibly anyone who would have targeted her?"

"No." Her grandfather paused. "She'd mentioned Derrick received some hate mail, but that seems par for the course in politics. Wimps hiding behind their keyboards." His scowl deepened. "Noelle has no enemies. Everyone loves her. Clearly this was about her husband." He met Alice's gaze. "You never answered my question about your leads."

"And we won't. The leads are our business," said Alice. "If we need clarification about something, we'll ask you."

He studied her a long moment. "You've got shit for leads. I can tell." He turned away, running a hand through his hair. "Dammit! How hard can it be to figure out who beat the hell out of the assemblyman in his own home?"

Alice fumed at his implication. "Can you tell me where you were Friday morning, Mr. Swanson?"

His eyes narrowed on her. "That's the most investigative thing you've said, Agent Patmore. I was home with my sister, Daisy."

"All day?" asked Oscar.

"Until I heard that there'd been an attack at Noelle's home, and she was in the hospital. Then I got Daisy and Lucia in the car and picked up Eve at her apartment and came here that evening. Noelle said the two of you had questioned her and just left."

"What did Noelle tell you about the attack?" asked Alice.

"She said she didn't remember what happened. She recalls the ambulance. Nothing about even being in the house that day."

"She'd had lunch with her sister earlier."

"Eve. Yes, she did. Eve said her account of their lunch was accurate."

"Noelle seems sharper today," said Alice.

"Definitely," agreed her grandfather. "But she's told me nothing that she hadn't already said Friday night. Still has memory loss. Her doctor told me it might return or it might not." He frowned in frustration.

"We'd like to talk to her alone again. Could you take her sister to get some coffee or something?" asked Alice.

Her grandfather hesitated, indecision on his face. "Yeah, I'll get her." He headed to the hospital room door. With his hand on the handle, he turned back to the two agents. "Noelle had nothing to do with this," he said firmly. "This is all on her husband."

He's so positive about his statement.

"What did you think of Derrick Bell?" asked Oscar.

William Swanson hesitated. "He was okay. She could have done better. Of course, no one is good enough for my girls."

77

"She could have done better than a wealthy politician?" Alice prodded.

"Wealth has nothing to do with it. Character is the key." He gave a short, affirming nod.

"Derrick Bell lacked in character?" Alice wasn't ready to let the conversation end. "Why do you say that?"

William looked down the hall. "No one's good enough for my girls," he repeated. He looked back at the agents. "Every father will say that. And people today don't have the same values that we did fifty years ago."

Another mention of values. First from Derrick's mother about Noelle and now he's saying it about Derrick.

Alice took a step closer and lowered her voice. "Your opinion of their marriage?"

He pressed his lips together but finally said, "My opinion doesn't matter. I only saw it from an outsider's point of view. Noelle never said a word against her husband."

But she should have?

"What did your outsider's point of view notice?"

He let go of the door handle and turned fully toward Alice and Oscar. "I saw my independent girl slowly change into a quiet one over the last few years. Her smiles were still there, but the wattage had dimmed down, you know?"

"She was unhappy?" asked Alice.

"I asked her that several times. She brushed me off, stating she and Derrick were adjusting to being a couple and that compromises had to be made on both sides." William glared. "Don't know what Derrick compromised on. Noelle's the one who gave up her job and had to learn to fit into a different world."

"Different world?" Alice suspected she knew what he meant, but she wanted to hear him say it.

He thought for a moment. "I've never had a lot of money and always figured the only difference between me and rich people was that they just spent more. But it's more than that. It's like they're in competition with each other. You have to look and act a certain way or you're ignored. Sort of reminds me of when Lucia was in middle school and trying to fit in with the popular kids. Noelle changed to fit in Derrick's world. I'm not sure I can forgive him for that."

"Noelle is an adult capable of making her own decisions," Alice pointed out.

"Yeah. Which is why I've never said my opinion out loud until this second." He looked from one to the other. "Say anything to her about this, and I'll deny every word." He turned away and opened the door.

Alice looked at Oscar and raised a brow.

He shrugged.

Is her grandfather simply overprotective?

16

After the grandfather coaxed Lucia out of the hospital room with the promise of a blended iced coffee, Alice turned her attention to Noelle. The woman's eyes were more alert and her posture better than the day before yesterday.

"I'm glad to hear you can leave the hospital," said Alice.

"Are they sure your head will be okay?" asked Oscar in a cautious voice. "Brain injuries aren't anything to fool around with."

Alice turned to him, her gaze hard. "I'm sure the *specialists* know what they're doing."

"Whatever you say." Oscar solemnly shook his head.

"No, whatever the doctors say," said Alice, looking back at Noelle, who was closely watching the two of them.

"He's definitely the pessimist of the two of you," Noelle stated. "Do you feel like you have to constantly balance him out?" She looked at Alice in curiosity.

Psychology major.

"It's fine," said Alice, even more annoyed with Oscar for exposing a truth about their working relationship. "I bet you're excited to go home . . . well, go to your grandfather's house. That's what you'll do, right?" she said hurriedly to change the subject.

Noelle eyed her for a long moment, clearly seeing that Alice didn't want to talk about herself and Oscar. "I don't think I can go back to Derrick's house just yet." She swallowed. "Do you know if . . . if it's been . . ." Misery flashed on her face.

Derrick's house? Not "our house"?

"It's the right plan to go to your grandfather's. Your home actually won't be available for a while," said Alice, realizing the woman couldn't bring herself to ask if the murder scene had been cleaned.

It hadn't.

The physical investigation continued. Alice and Oscar had made a quick trip though the home on Friday, and forensics had spent the day in the home yesterday, but Alice wanted to go through again, taking her time. "Now that you've had some time to rest, do you remember anything else that happened on Friday?"

Noelle leaned back against her large pile of pillows. "No. I've been trying. It's hard with the pain in my head."

"They haven't given you something for pain?" asked Oscar.

"They've prescribed good stuff," said Noelle. "But nothing fully takes the pain away. And the meds make it hard to focus, but I don't know if my recall would be any better without them. I guess I could go off them for a while and see what happens."

"Probably not a good idea," said Alice. "You'll be done with the medication soon enough." The words were hard to say; Alice wanted answers *now*. But as the swelling went down, she hoped Noelle's memory would fill in some holes.

Alice mentally reviewed her next questions. It was important not to lead the witness—especially when their memory was faulty. "Do you mind if we record this?" They hadn't recorded their first interview with Noelle, and Alice hoped it wouldn't cause a problem down the line. She and Oscar had made careful notes immediately after leaving, and they were pretty confident they'd covered everything.

Noelle blinked and ran a hand through her hair. "No."

Oscar started recording with his phone.

"Just to review, what do you remember from Friday?" Alice started.

Noelle's answers were identical to those in their first interview. She apologized several times for not recalling more.

"What is your relationship to Brendon Simon?" asked Alice.

The woman's eyes widened. "Brendon? What does he have to do with this?" Her voice rose.

"Your relationship?" Alice prodded.

"He's my ex-husband. We were married for two months when I was eighteen." Noelle pressed her lips together, looking from one agent to the other. "Why? Why are you asking about Brendon?"

"We're just trying to get a view of the big picture," said Oscar.

Her eyes narrowed. "Bullshit. What were you told about Brendon?"

"Do you keep in touch?" asked Alice.

Noelle looked at her for a long moment. "We do. We text occasionally. Meet in person every now and then."

"What did your husband think of that?" asked Oscar.

"He hated it, of course. But if someone is insecure over an innocent friendship, that's their problem, not mine."

"Innocent friendship?" Alice pushed. "You were married. It didn't last. Why?"

Noelle's face was expressionless, but Alice felt her annoyance hover in the air. "It didn't last because we were both young and stupid. We knew nothing about money or relationships. It was doomed from day one. Once we got past blaming each other for being naive, we got along. He's now one of the people I could call in an emergency, and he'd drop whatever he's doing and show up."

"Have you called him about this emergency?" asked Alice, gesturing at Noelle's head.

"He knows."

That's not what I asked.

"He's in a serious relationship," Noelle said pointedly.

That's not what I asked either.

"We'll be getting records of your text messages from your cell provider," said Alice.

Noelle held her gaze for a long moment. Then she picked up her cell phone, tapped it a few times, and handed it to Alice without saying a word.

Alice skimmed the text conversation between Noelle and Brendon. Her ex-husband had texted several times starting late Friday night, begging to know if she was okay, stating he'd heard about the attack on the news. Noelle hadn't answered his texts until Saturday morning, explaining that she'd just gotten her phone. Everything since then read as Alice would expect of an exchange between a concerned friend and a victim. She scrolled up, looking at the messages from before Friday. The last one was from three weeks before, Noelle sending him a happy-birthday text with several emoji. He'd thanked her.

Texts can be deleted.

But her wireless carrier will have records with all the time stamps.

Oscar pulled a piece of paper from his suit pocket and set it on Noelle's lap. She picked it up and scowled as she skimmed the legalese. "You're taking my phone," she stated.

"Ask your grandfather to buy a temporary phone for you."

"All my contacts are on *that* one."

"We'll bring in your laptop, and you can print them from that," said Oscar.

"And then you'll take the laptop." Annoyance filled her tone.

"Correct. It's a murder investigation and—" Alice started.

"And you need to eliminate me as a suspect," Noelle finished. She slumped back in her bed. "I get it. It just creates some inconveniences. I'm not complaining," she added quickly. "I want you to find who did this. I can live without my things. They just become an extension of you—a habit, you know?"

"We know," said Alice, and then changed the topic. "Where does Brendon work?"

Noelle named the hospital they'd stopped at that morning.

Alice shook her head. "We went there. They said he left three months ago."

Surprise crossed Noelle's face. "Then I don't know. Why would he not tell me that?" Hurt flickered in her eyes.

Oscar asked about the address they had for Brendon.

"I assume that's his address," said Noelle. "I've never been to his home, but I know that's the part of town he lives in. We've only met up in restaurants or at Starbucks," she said pointedly.

"His girlfriend doesn't mind your contact?" asked Alice.

"You'd have to ask her. All I know is her name is Isabella and they met at the hospital—the one you said he no longer works at." The hurt flickered again.

"Do you know if Derrick ever spoke with Brendon?" Alice watched her closely. She was forming an opinion that Noelle was sharp and observant. Even under the influence of painkillers. Everything she'd said had felt true to Alice, but sometimes the sharp ones were the expert liars and manipulators.

"They met about a year ago," said Noelle. "We were out to dinner, and Brendon and Isabella walked by as they were being led to a table. Brendon spotted me and stopped. It was brief and awkward for everyone."

"What did Derrick say about that meeting?"

Noelle thought. "He said, '*That's* the guy you married?'" Disdain filled her tone. "He didn't give a reason for saying it like that, and I tried not to let it annoy me. He knew we married too young. His comment was unnecessary."

"Obviously his comment stuck with you," said Alice.

"It did," she agreed. "That's the only time I'm aware of that they met."

"How was Derrick's relationship with his parents?" asked Oscar.

Noelle studied him, and Alice could almost see the gears turning in her head.

"They all loved each other very much, and Derrick was close to both of them. I know he missed working with his father after he was elected."

The answer was evenly paced and devoid of emotion.

Still trying for the best daughter-in-law prize?

"Have you heard from his family?" asked Alice.

She paused. "Lora texted. His parents must be absolutely destroyed with grief. I'm sure I'll hear from them later."

Alice noted she didn't mention Derrick's brother.

"What else can I do to help you?" Noelle asked, including Oscar in her question.

A subtle change of topic.

"Information on life insurance, bank and investment accounts, and Derrick's recent activities would be good," said Alice.

Noelle nodded, her brows moving together as she thought. "His assistant, Jon, will have a daily calendar of Derrick's meetings and such. I'll see what I can figure out about bank accounts." She frowned. "I don't think there is life insurance on him. If there is, I'm unaware of it."

"No life insurance?" Oscar sounded surprised.

Noelle shrugged. "He said he had plenty of money. If he died, I wouldn't be lacking for funds. There was no point in buying insurance to get some more."

"Did he have insurance on you?" asked Alice.

Noelle jerked back slightly, apparently never having considered the question. "Not that I know of. Why would he? He's wealthy."

"You seemed uncertain when you mentioned bank accounts," said Alice, pleased to start addressing money. In her experience, murder motivation usually boiled down to one of two things. Sex or money.

Who would gain financially from Derrick's death?

The woman in front of her seemed the most likely. But Alice would dig into his family.

Noelle took a deep breath. "We had a joint checking account and investment account. The rest of the accounts were solely his. I

85

assume I'm the beneficiary on them." She grimaced. "I shouldn't assume anything," she added.

Alice wondered if the sad look in her eyes was from the loss of her husband or what appeared to be a lack of information from him.

"I'll get you whatever I can find," Noelle stated.

"Who else did he have financial dealings with?" asked Alice. "Shared business ventures? Investments in start-ups?"

Noelle looked to one side. "I don't know," she said softly. "We didn't have many conversations about money. I didn't feel it was my place to ask what he was doing with the money he already had when we married. His father or brother might know." She looked back to Alice and frowned. "I sound like a nineteen fifties housewife. But I'm not, I swear. I put myself through school and paid it off. I *know* how to manage money. With Derrick—" She paused. "He had his spending money, and I had mine."

"So you also had your own accounts completely separate from his?" asked Oscar.

"Yes. And credit cards."

"Why did you quit your bartending job?" Alice tossed the question into the room.

Confusion and reluctance flashed in Noelle's eyes. She lifted her chin. "I no longer needed to work."

Alice sat on the corner of Noelle's hospital bed. "You worked hard," she said softly. "You were respected there, and I suspect you enjoyed the environment."

"I did. But it was just a bartending job." She shrugged and picked at the white hospital blanket. "What was the point of staying? I didn't need to."

A silence stretched.

"He didn't want you to stay on, did he?" Alice's tone was matter-of-fact.

"It wasn't a good look for a politician's wife." Noelle was very earnest. "I wanted to do everything I could to help him succeed. He loved politics, thrived on the challenge, and wanted to do good for his community. It was a small sacrifice—not even a sacrifice—to help him out."

Alice felt as if she'd just heard a frequently rehearsed argument.

I wonder who it originated with? Catherine or Derrick?

Noelle had probably stated it dozens of times.

Alice felt an affinity for the woman and admired how perceptive Noelle was. A valuable quality, in Alice's opinion. But had Noelle allowed her husband's wants and dreams to push hers out of the way? Not that being a bartender was Noelle's dream, but Alice suspected being a smiling political wife wasn't either.

But somehow, she'd slid into the role.

"I saw my independent girl slowly change into a quiet one over the last few years."

Noelle's grandfather's words. Alice wondered what had made Noelle decide to change who she was.

"That was nice of you—to sacrifice that for your husband," Oscar stated. He sounded sincere, but Alice had no doubt that Noelle's claim bothered him as much as it bothered her.

So what if Noelle quit her job?

This isn't getting us any closer to finding a killer.

17

"You two looked like the perfect couple," said Agent Keaton, eyeing what Noelle assumed were photos of her and Derrick on his laptop.

"We were very happy," said Noelle.

Agent Rhodes was watching her with a small frown on his face, and she felt as if he knew every thought in her brain. "You don't seem like someone who'd want the political life in their future," he finally said.

"I'm a detective now. I'm a different person than I was in my twenties," said Noelle. "After Derrick died, I took a hard look at my life and decided to go in a new direction. Before that I was more than happy to have politics as our goal."

"Our goal?" asked Rhodes.

"Our goal," Noelle said firmly.

18

"I'm not sure." Noelle smoothed the front of the long white dress with her hands, the fabric silky under her fingertips.

"It's so lovely on you," said Catherine. "So elegant."

"It's definitely a beautiful dress," Noelle agreed, making eye contact with Eve in the huge mirror. Her sister shrugged and gave a small shake of her head.

She knows it's not the one.

Noelle's engagement ring glittered under the dozens of lights in the bridal salon, catching her eye as it constantly had done for the last two weeks.

She and Derrick had been dating for fourteen months. She'd essentially moved into his downtown condo, leaving enough things in her grandfather's home that her family didn't feel as if she'd abandoned them.

She and Derrick were together nonstop. She loved that he knew what he wanted to do with his life and that his goal was to help people by using legislation to improve the lives of Californians. Their paths and goals were almost parallel lines. She wanted to help people too, but in a more one-on-one, personal way, and had started to look at master's programs in psychology, wanting to move forward into counseling or working as a therapist. Her bachelor's degree had only been the first step.

Noelle had cut back her work hours at the bar, realizing she wanted to spend more of her evenings with Derrick. Going to theaters and restaurants or even simply watching a TV show together at home was their happy time. She'd found a person she wanted to spend all her time with. And the more time she spent with him, the more she felt their lives were smoothly meshing together. Like the teeth of a big zipper.

His proposal had caught her off guard. They'd discussed marriage a bit. Noelle was a little gun-shy from her last experience but believed this relationship was the complete opposite. They were both mature adults who knew what they wanted out of life. She could easily see herself as Noelle Bell. The name was a bit awkward to say, but she liked the way it looked on paper.

The night he proposed, they'd had dinner at "her" restaurant. His suggestion of the location had surprised her a bit. He'd said that since she worked there, it didn't make for a special dining experience—and she agreed. She'd had everything on the menu a dozen times and knew every face. So they frequented other restaurants, only falling back on hers when it was convenient.

But before they left for the restaurant, there'd been an odd moment. He'd come home from work and stopped outside their bathroom, studying her as she put on her makeup.

"I thought you had a hair appointment today," he said.

Noelle looked at herself in the mirror, turning her head to see the casual updo her stylist had created. "I did. Tanya put it up for me. Thanks for asking Lora to share her stylist's name. She's very good."

"You said you were going to tone down the blonde a bit."

Noelle froze. She hadn't said that; he had. Two weeks ago.

I didn't think he was serious.

"This is my hair color." She continued with her mascara, not wanting to meet his gaze.

"It might be a little too platinum."

Noelle's hand stilled, the mascara wand an inch from her lashes.

Would Derrick know to call this a platinum shade?

No. But his mother would.

"I like it." Actually she loved it.

She finally looked at him as she put the wand back in the mascara tube. Disappointment filled his gaze. "Maybe next time," she said automatically.

The moment had left a sour taste in her mouth, and she was quiet on the drive to the restaurant. Derrick was as chatty in the car as usual, sharing his day and even singing along with the music. As they entered the restaurant, she was surprised when Rex Duggan greeted them.

"What are you doing here?" Noelle asked in delight, kissing both his cheeks. His visits to his restaurant had been getting further and further apart. Seeing his happy face had immediately cheered her.

"A surprise pop-in," Rex told her with a wink. "Keeping everyone on their toes." Rex asked the hostess for their table, seated them himself, and then dashed off to get the bottle of wine that Derrick ordered.

The dinner was perfect—as usual. Afterward Noelle relaxed in her chair, the wine pleasantly buzzing in her brain, her stomach content. Her annoyance about the hair color comment had vanished.

All he did was state an opinion.

I told him a week ago his hair needed a trim; it's the same thing.

A cup of coffee was placed in front of her as they lingered after the meal. Derrick sat across the table holding her hand on the white tablecloth, his thumb stroking the backs of her fingers. Her gaze drifted over his face. She'd never been so content and happy. And it was all due to him.

Their waiter set down a piece of coconut pie with two forks.

"We didn't—" started Noelle.

"I ordered it," said Derrick, meeting her eyes.

Noelle looked at the pie and realized it wasn't from the restaurant. Her heart melted as she recognized the pie was from Rick's, the location of their first date. And on the plate next to the pie sat a tiny box.

This is it. He's proposing!

Her gaze met his. His eyes were lit with excitement.

"Is that what I think it is?" she whispered, her heart racing.

"Open it and see."

She tugged her hand out of his, opened the box, and sucked in a breath at the sight of the giant diamond. He stood, took the ring out of the box, and knelt next to the table.

"Will you marry me and make my life perfect, Noelle?" he asked quietly.

She couldn't speak. She nodded rapidly, her eyes filling, the tears blurring his face. She felt rather than saw him slide the ring onto her finger.

The restaurant erupted with applause and shouts. Noelle wiped her eyes and scanned the room. All the employees, people she'd worked with for years, had been watching, knowing what would happen that night. Rex rushed over an ice stand with a bottle of champagne, and Noelle glimpsed the Dom Pérignon label.

"You knew!" she accused Rex.

"Of course I did. I'm the one who put you two together. Seems right that I'm here for this part."

They'd argued that point with Rex several times, saying he'd had good intentions but hadn't played a role in their meeting. It was now a long-running joke.

The room quieted down as the employees returned to work. Noelle took a long, shuddering breath as Derrick took his seat, a huge grin on his face. "Surprised?" he asked.

"Very. I had no idea."

"Good." Satisfaction filled his tone, and he held out his hand. She laid her left hand on his, staring at the unfamiliar jewel on her finger. He ran his thumb across it. "How'd I do?"

"It's perfect." The large diamond kept slipping to the side of her finger, the narrow band a bit loose. "I'll get the band resized this week."

Derrick frowned. "I thought I got the right size."

"I'm sure you did." Her words didn't remove his frown, so she gave him an alluring look from beneath her lashes. "You got such a big diamond, the band can't handle it."

That made him smile.

"The pie is a perfect touch."

Pride filled his face. "I knew it would be." He squeezed her hand. "I want to get married next year in September."

She'd always thought a Christmastime wedding would be lovely. "How about December? That would give us a few extra months to prepare. Sometimes things have to be booked way in—"

"December will be too late."

Noelle blinked. "Too late for what?"

"The election is in November. A September wedding will be a perfect way to catch voter attention." He paused and took out his phone, opening the calendar. "Toward the end of the month. Hopefully the weather will be a bit cooler." He nodded in satisfaction.

Our wedding is part of his political strategy?

"Ummm." She tried to look pleased. "If that's what you want."

"Don't you?" He glanced up, surprise in his gaze.

"Of course I do. It'll be beautiful. Do you know where—"

"I'll make sure the country club is available. The grounds are perfect." He sent a text.

"Wonderful." She'd always thought the old stone church near her grandfather's home would be perfect for a ceremony. It had elegant stained glass windows and soaring ceilings.

"Telling my mother," he said as he texted with a smile. "She'll know what to do."

Noelle took a deep breath.

His dream is politics. If this helps him achieve that, I'm good with it.

◆ ◆ ◆

Derrick's mother tugged at the waist of the wedding dress as Noelle stared at her reflection in the mirror. "This is perfect," Catherine said in satisfaction. "You'll make such a lovely bride."

"I'll try on a few more dresses," Noelle stated.

"What for?" Catherine frowned. "It's beautiful and exactly what we need."

We?

"Because as beautiful as this dress is, it's not speaking to me," said Noelle. "I'll know the right dress when I see it."

"Speaking to you," Catherine repeated. She took a step back and looked over her shoulder to where Lora, both of Noelle's sisters, and her great-aunt Daisy sat watching, glasses of prosecco in hand. Apple juice for Lucia. "What do you think of the dress, Lora?"

Daisy cleared her throat. "Noelle's opinion is the only one that counts. We're just here to keep her company. And have free drinks." Daisy emptied her glass and reached for the open prosecco bottle.

Thank you, Daisy.

Lora didn't say anything as she avoided her mother's gaze.

Noelle lifted the full skirts and carefully stepped off the riser. The saleswoman took hold of the skirts and followed her into the large dressing room. "Which do you want to try next?" she asked Noelle.

"That one." Noelle pointed at one of the dresses she'd chosen earlier.

A smile crossed the woman's face. "I thought so."

The slinky dress had a plunging neckline and back. It'd make Catherine panic, but Noelle needed to assert that this was *her* decision. She didn't think the slinky dress was the right one either, but she wanted to see it on anyway. As the saleswoman helped her out of the first dress, musical notes sounded from Noelle's phone. It was Derrick's ringtone. "Give me just a minute," she said to the saleswoman. The woman nodded as she wrestled the full-skirted dress back onto a hanger.

"Hi, honey," Noelle said into her phone. "You've caught me in the dressing room. I'm still trying on dresses." She watched as the saleswoman unzipped the bag for the slinky dress. The fabric was quite lovely, the light streaming through the dressing room windows giving it a unique sheen.

"How's it going?" asked Derrick, clearly calling from his car.

"Good. Lots of great dresses."

The saleswoman signaled that she'd be right back and stepped out of the dressing room.

"Send me some pictures."

"I can't do that. What if I choose one of them? Then you'll have seen me in it before the wedding. That's very bad luck," she teased, as she touched the next dress's soft fabric.

"I don't believe in bad luck. I'd love to see which one you like best."

"I haven't found the one I like best yet," she said. "I'm sure I will soon."

"You haven't liked any of them?"

"Well, I liked a few of them, but I haven't found one I love yet."

"Are you sure?"

Noelle paused as a thought occurred. "Your mother's been sending you pictures, hasn't she?" She turned away from the dress, fighting the disappointment percolating in her stomach.

How could she do that without asking me?

"She's really having a good time," said Derrick. "Don't tell her that you know she's been doing it."

Noelle stared at herself in the mirror. Disappointment wasn't what she should feel while trying on dresses for the most important day of her life. "Which dress have you liked best?" she asked Derrick, dreading the answer.

"There was one with sheer long sleeves that I thought was great."

The dress she'd just taken off.

Catherine is meddling. She must have told him to call me.

"Yes, that was a good one, but I don't love it."

"You looked amazing in it."

Noelle closed her eyes, tightening her grip on the phone. "I'll keep it in mind."

Why is he taking his mother's side when it's my decision?
His political strategy.

It'd been a few months since Derrick had publicly announced he was running for assemblyman. He'd hired a consultant whose main job was to make certain Derrick looked right and said the right thing everywhere he went. Miranda, the consultant, had suggestions for Noelle too. The first one was the toughest: the consultant had said Noelle should leave her job.

Noelle had known this would happen. There'd been too many subtle—and not-so-subtle—hints from Derrick's mother and himself. Simply put, being a bartender wasn't the best look for the wife of a politician. He'd been polite about suggesting it, but Noelle had seen worry in his eyes that she wouldn't do it.

So she'd quit. She'd called Rex and told him first. He'd understood and claimed to be delighted, saying he could see her and Derrick in the White House one day. There'd been many tears as she personally said goodbye to the people she'd worked with for years. Savannah had taken her out and gotten her drunk. She'd also given Noelle a lecture on not changing too much of herself for Derrick. Noelle had nodded and promised, but knew she'd never get in the way of Derrick's political dreams.

Noelle was happy and even excited. His career was something they were building together. Right now that was the priority. She'd have time for herself once he was elected.

"And if he doesn't get elected?" Savannah had asked.

"Then he'll go back to work for his father. And I'll go back to school."

"He'll want to run again," Savannah had pointed out.

"We'll see." Noelle wasn't so sure. She'd learned Derrick didn't like failure, and he'd see an election loss as a big one. She knew he'd think it would look desperate to run again.

That wasn't the image he wanted to project.

This election was *it*. He'd only try once.

She was committed to making it happen for him. And she bit her tongue when she didn't like Miranda's suggestions.

One night as they strategized, the consultant had held up several photos of Noelle and Derrick together. "What pops out at you in these pictures?" Miranda had asked.

"Noelle's hair," Derrick immediately answered. "It practically glows."

That's how I like it.

She'd looked the consultant in the eye, ready to defend her hair color. But the woman had given her a sad smile. "It's lovely," she'd said. "It's definitely you, but Derrick is right. We need the focus on him. It'll just be temporary. After the election, you can do whatever you want with it."

After the election also means after our wedding pictures.

It broke her heart a bit. Her hair color had been part of her own strategy to get the bartending job downtown. She'd grown to love the color; it gave her confidence.

The only difference between what I did to get that job and what Derrick is doing now is that there are two people involved.

The next week she toned down her hair. At Miranda's request, she'd also bleached her teeth and added several simple navy-blue pieces to her wardrobe. The one thing Noelle did really like was Miranda's insistence that she wear high heels. Expensive high heels. Derrick had been happy to purchase them and the new clothes.

"Women will notice how you dress and what brand shoes you wear," the consultant had told Noelle. "We want to shape you into someone they secretly wish they could be, but not make you someone they resent. We'll tone down the clothes but punch up the shoes and jewelry."

Noelle had nodded, feeling fortunate but also guilty to have someone else pay for her clothes. Derrick pointed out that every purchase was an investment in his future.

His future?

Our future.

19

Three years before Derrick Bell's murder

Their wedding was *the* society event.

It was every little girl's dream of what a wedding should be. Masses of flowers, a perfectly sunny day, a dreamy setting at the country club.

Tons of friends and associates Noelle had never met before.

Noelle had chosen the dress with the sheer sleeves after Miranda the consultant agreed with Derrick and his mother that it fit the image they wanted to present. Miranda had then chosen Noelle's nail polish and earrings and added a small tiara. Apparently, along with creating the optimal presentation of a political candidate, her experience included wedding planning.

Noelle had just smiled and nodded as her input on her wedding was consistently overruled by Derrick's mother and Miranda.

Let them do whatever they want.

The end result is what matters.

As she walked down the aisle on her grandfather's arm, her gaze locked on Derrick's, and he wiped away a tear. She blinked hard, keeping her own tears at bay. Her grandfather patted her arm. "You'll be just fine," he told her.

"I know," she whispered back.

Her sisters, Savannah, and Derrick's sister, Lora, made up her wedding party. A lovely palette of pale peach and pink dresses. Derrick's friends and Eve's boyfriend, Adam, were his attendants. Derrick had hired Adam to work on his campaign and been so impressed by his skills that he'd promised Adam a job when he was elected.

Keeping it in the family.

Eve and Adam would be married next spring.

Tears streamed down Lucia's cheeks as her grandfather helped Noelle up the few steps and kissed her cheek. As she handed her bouquet to Eve, Noelle paused and touched her youngest sister's face. "I'm sooo happeee," Lucia managed to whisper. Behind Lucia, Savannah covered her mouth, her eyes dancing at Lucia's wet declaration. She winked at Noelle and set a comforting hand on Lucia's shoulder. Noelle eyed her line of attendants, thankful that she had such good women in her life. She turned to Derrick, who'd been patiently waiting, and he took both her hands. Her heart jumped at the sight of the love in his eyes.

How did I get so lucky?

Her grandfather took his seat next to Daisy and gave Noelle a firm nod. They'd agreed to skip the "Who gives this woman" line. Noelle was her own woman. She wasn't her grandfather's possession to be handed off to another man. Catherine had wanted the traditional line included, saying it would add a sentimental moment to the ceremony.

Noelle had stood firm. She'd allowed Catherine's influence on her dress, the cake, the decor, and the band. But not this.

Fifteen minutes later they turned to their friends and family, and Derrick bent her over backward for a kiss, raising a cheer from the audience. Noelle melted into the kiss as she gripped his shoulder to keep from falling, hearing dozens of camera shutters click. Derrick righted her and raised her hand into the air with a loud whoop, triggering shouts from his friends and a wave of laughter from Noelle.

We did it!

He gripped her hand. "Grab your skirts," he whispered. She hoisted them with her other hand, and a second later he led her in a dash down the aisle, faces blurring as they ran by. At the back of the room, a row of photographers stood ready, and more shutters clicked as Derrick paused to dramatically kiss her again. Then Miranda opened the doors and pointed down the hall as they ran past. Moments later they were alone in a small room with a tall, wide window that overlooked the lake and greens at the country club. Someone had laid out a charcuterie board and sandwiches with several bottles of water on a small table between two overstuffed easy chairs that faced the window.

"What's this?" Noelle managed to gasp after their sprint.

"Sustenance. I don't know about you, but I couldn't eat this morning," said Derrick, leading her to a chair and then plopping into the other. He grabbed a bottle of water and drank deeply. "We've got a long afternoon and evening ahead of us. Miranda said sometimes it's difficult for the bride and groom to eat during the reception, so she wanted to make sure we had a quiet moment alone to do so."

"Bless her." Noelle reached for a sandwich. The consultant was right. She was suddenly starving and grateful for the peace to catch her breath and prepare for the rest of the day. "What was with all the photographers at the back of the room?"

"Press."

"Eeeesh. I didn't know they'd be indoors."

"They practically demanded it." Derrick layered a cracker with meat, cheese, and apricot jam. "It'll be helpful. Six weeks until the election."

Noelle silently nodded, not wanting to discuss politics on their wedding day.

She couldn't wait for the election to be over. Maybe their lives would have some semblance of normalcy then.

Ever since Derrick had won his party's primary last spring, he'd been on cloud nine and their lives had been upended—even more than before the primary. Business associates had backed him, and people they'd never heard of had contributed huge amounts to his campaign. Noelle had been stunned to learn the amount of money required to run a campaign for a simple assemblyman position. She couldn't imagine what it would take to elect someone to a higher office.

Derrick had been busy for months. He'd come home late to the condo, collapse into bed, and then be gone before Noelle woke in the morning.

Her days had felt empty. There was only so much wedding planning she could do. Especially with Miranda and Catherine taking the lead. They'd wanted to carry much of the weight of planning so Noelle wouldn't feel overwhelmed.

So they'd said.

She missed her job, so Catherine and Lora had connected her with volunteer opportunities and invited her to social events to meet other women in the area.

Clones in the area.

That was how she viewed the women she was introduced to at the social events. She'd learned to recognize high-end designer dresses and shoes. And plastic surgery.

So much plastic surgery. Both good and bad.

There was some invisible level that these women seemed to be striving to attain; their lives were a competition. Who was the thinnest, fittest, and tannest and who had the biggest diamonds. Feeling greatly out of place, Noelle had frequently turned to Savannah and her sisters for companionship, doing normal things like going to movies and barbecuing at home, where they wore flip-flops and no makeup. Nothing that took an hour of prep time to make sure her face and hair were perfect.

After Noelle had passed on a few social invitations so she could attend the four nights of Lucia's school play, Derrick had brought it up.

"You missed the heart disease fundraiser," he casually said one evening as they were getting into bed.

"I made a donation." With Derrick's money. She was still uncomfortable spending money she hadn't earned. Even when it was for charity.

"Mother said they missed you."

Aha.

Catherine was on the fundraiser committee. "I couldn't miss Lucia's performance."

"You'd already seen it last night."

"It's tradition that we all go every night the play runs." Lucia had been in drama for three years. This was the first year she'd had a lead role.

"It's important for you to make the right connections."

Connections.

The word was like fingernails on a chalkboard. She'd heard it too many times from both Catherine and Derrick. Their world seemed to rotate around meeting and schmoozing with people whom they could ask later for favors.

Welcome to politics.

Noelle was growing to hate the constant outings. She liked deep, meaningful friendships, not shallow relationships that pretended to be more than they were. Each time she attended an event and was introduced while on Derrick's arm, people labeled her as candidate Derrick Bell's fiancée.

Not as Noelle. Even though they were consistently in the limelight, she felt as if she were disappearing, becoming a new person who was known simply by association. Not for who she was at heart.

Even here, at their long-awaited wedding, she knew the reception would consist of meeting dozens of people whose names she'd never remember who had attended the wedding to keep themselves on Derrick's radar in case they needed a future favor from an assemblyman. And Derrick kept them close in case he decided in the future to move even further up the political ladder; he'd need their money and their support.

She watched her husband (*husband!*) finally relax in the comfy chair looking over the country club grounds. A look of peace on his face. He'd been carrying a heavy weight for more than a year as they planned the wedding and his campaign.

"Achievement unlocked," she whispered. "On to the next."

He turned to her with a grin, and she reached over to wipe some jam from the corner of his mouth. He lightly caught her thumb with his teeth, his gaze heated, and Noelle felt warmth rush from her head to her toes.

"I know what I want to do next," he whispered, squeezing her hand. "And it has nothing to do with this wedding or politics."

She swallowed hard. Their sex life was an active one. Innovative and passionate. The best she'd ever experienced.

He stood, strode to the door, and flipped the lock. "All during the ceremony, I wondered what you had on under that dress, Mrs. Bell."

She grinned and then showed him there wasn't much.

20

Thirteen years ago
Two days after Derrick Bell's murder

Special Agent Alice Patmore stood at the edge of the kitchen in the Bells' giant house. She and Oscar had returned to the home after speaking with Noelle and her family earlier that day.

"I want to know who called it in," Alice muttered to Oscar as she looked around. They'd listened to the recording of the frantic woman more than a dozen times and sent it to the FBI lab for more testing. Alice knew the lab could identify regional accents and sift out background noise, hopefully giving them a solid lead to pursue.

Neighbors had been questioned and their cameras examined. No one had a road view of the winding street that led to the Bells' home.

"How can the Bells not have cameras?" Alice asked for the hundredth time. She'd learned that the home *used to* have a camera system, but it had been removed more than a year ago in anticipation of a new system. Derrick's father had told her the system had been more than two decades old and hadn't worked in years.

"I think Noelle Bell wasn't supposed to survive this attack," said Oscar. It was a 180-degree turn from his previous theory that had leaned toward Noelle as the attacker.

"Maybe," said Alice. "But why wasn't she brutalized like her husband?"

"Interrupted," said Oscar. "Maybe by our unknown caller. Or maybe they simply couldn't bring themselves to do that to a woman."

"A killer with standards?" asked Alice.

Oscar shrugged. "A lot of killers have weird personal rules. Sticking within them makes them feel in control and that their actions are justified."

Alice had heard the same. She stood in front of where the landline had been removed, leaving an empty socket above the kitchen counter two feet from a pocket door to a walk-in pantry. She stepped inside the pantry and looked up and down at the shelves and cupboards. The amount of food gave the impression that a family of twelve had lived in the big house, not simply the two Bells. On a quartz counter in the pantry were a professional-looking blender, a large toaster oven, and two different espresso machines that looked as if they belonged at Starbucks.

Two espresso machines?

She knew from the forensics report that the cost of the four counter appliances added up to more than she made in two months. Turning, she looked out the pantry door to where the phone had been. "How much do you want to bet the caller hid in here? Maybe even while the attack took place?" Black fingerprint powder covered the pantry's countertop, sliding door, and doorframe. Clearly she wasn't the first to consider the idea.

"Could that indicate it was someone who knew the house? A friend of one of them?"

"Or a relative." She and Oscar had already looked into the locations of Noelle's sisters during the attack. Lucia had been at home with her great-aunt Daisy and her grandfather, and Eve had been at her own house, where she'd gone after meeting Noelle for lunch. Noelle's best friend, Savannah, had been at the restaurant working a day shift, as had been verified by a dozen employees.

The women on Derrick's side of the family had also had their locations verified. Catherine had been at home and Lora at a hospital board meeting.

"Someone just pulled up out front," said Oscar. Alice had deliberately parked their vehicle behind the detached garage, not wanting any snooping neighbors to notice someone was at the Bell home. The man living next door had confronted Detective Rodden because the detective's plain SUV had been parked at the house yesterday. The neighbor wore a gun on his hip.

Everyone who lived on the street was on edge.

Oscar and Alice moved into the formal living room and stood to one side of the window, out of sight of the new arrival.

"It's Lucia," Alice stated, watching her get out of a silver minivan.

There was a stark contrast between the Marshalls' vehicles and the Bells'. All of the Bells drove new, expensive leased cars and SUVs. Land Rovers, Mercedes-Benzes, and Jaguars. All of the Marshalls drove vehicles that were more than fifteen years old. But they were paid off.

GPS histories had been requested for all the new vehicles; the older ones didn't have them. Nor did they use devices from insurance companies that tracked a vehicle's movements. The grandfather was firmly against letting outsiders knowing where his family members went.

Outside, Lucia stopped and stared up at the house for a long moment as Alice and Oscar watched.

"What's she doing?" muttered Oscar.

Alice said nothing, knowing the question was rhetorical.

Lucia took a careful look around the front grounds and then started up the stairs to the home's wraparound front porch.

"She didn't try to hide the vehicle," said Oscar. "I don't think she's trying to be sneaky." He reached over and locked the front door. "Let's see if she has a key."

"She knows we haven't released the house yet," said Alice. "She was at the hospital when we told everyone."

"Doesn't mean she was listening."

Alice agreed. She'd noticed Lucia hadn't paid much attention during their conversations. She didn't know if that was normal or a result of the stress of knowing that her sister had almost died.

Yellow tape blocked access at the top of the stairs. Alice and Oscar had ducked under it, and they watched Lucia do the same. They heard the front door's lock rattle, and then the bolt slid. The door opened, and Lucia strode in like she owned the home. Alice and Oscar stood silently against the living room wall, watching the teen. Lucia didn't even glance their way as she made a beeline for the stairs. Alice and Oscar exchanged a glance.

"Lucia," Alice said quietly.

"Shit!" The teenager whirled around, one hand on the stair rail, her eyes wide. "Jesus Christ." Then she visibly relaxed as she recognized the agents. "You scared me! What are you doing here?"

"What are *you* doing here?" asked Alice. "You didn't notice the yellow tape out front? And we said this morning that the house wasn't available for family yet."

"You did?" Lucia looked confused. "I'm getting Noelle some clothes. She's got nothing."

"Couldn't you get them at the condo downtown?" asked Oscar.

"She doesn't have anything there."

"She doesn't?" asked Alice with a frown.

"No. That's just for Derrick while he's working. She used to stay there but moved everything here after the wedding." The teen gave a one-shouldered shrug. "She told me once he needed his space."

But they're married. An entire home is off-limits?

"I'll be quick," said Lucia, moving up another step.

"We'll come with you," said Alice. "Don't touch anything until we say it's okay." She didn't have a problem with the girl getting some clothes as they watched and examined what she took. She and Oscar followed her up the stairs. Lucia glanced back at them a few times, a nervous half smile on her face. At the top of the stairs, they had turned to walk down the hall toward the primary bedroom when Lucia gasped and froze, staring through a doorway into another room.

Alice caught up with her. Derrick's office had been ransacked. Papers and drawers were scattered everywhere. Broken glass littered the floor from photos that had been on his desk, and a file cabinet had been turned on its side, all its drawers opened, their contents spilling out.

"Did you do that?" squeaked Lucia, giving Alice a look of horror.

"No, law enforcement *did not* do that." Alice took her gun out of her shoulder holster, noting that Oscar did the same. Alice stepped into the room and quickly cleared the closet and the space under the desk.

"Lucia," she said in a low voice. "I need you to stay in this room with the door closed. We need to make certain the rest of the house is empty. *Don't touch anything, and do not open the door until one of us tells you.*"

Lucia's eyes were wide as Alice closed the door with her in the office.

"Downstairs?" asked Oscar in a low voice. He'd reported the break-in and requested backup as Alice cleared the room.

"Let's start up here." Alice tried to think of the rooms they'd gone into downstairs. Besides the living room and kitchen, there was a formal dining room, a guest bedroom, and two bathrooms. They'd not looked in those, and now she was angry with herself.

Why didn't we clear the house first?

It hadn't even crossed her mind.

Oscar headed toward the primary bedroom. From the hall, Alice spotted bedding and pillows on the floor. It had been ransacked like the office. "Shit," muttered Oscar. The two of them quickly cleared that room and moved into the primary bath and closet. Nearly every piece of clothing was on the floor, drawers left open. "Thorough."

What were they looking for?

They cleared two other bedrooms that had attached bathrooms and checked all closets and the laundry room. No other rooms had been tossed. Through the office door, Alice whispered to Lucia that they were going downstairs and would be right back. She barely heard the girl's "Okay."

Downstairs they checked the formal dining room, the bedroom, two bathrooms, and the detached garage. Outside they circled the garage and moved on to take a look around the backyard. The Bells' home backed up to a large treed area that Alice knew went on for acres. No neighboring homes were visible. "I think we're good," she told Oscar. "That mess could have happened yesterday after forensics left. Let's find out what time they closed up the house. And get them back out here to go through the office and primary bedroom."

Sirens sounded in the distance as the sheriff's department headed their way.

Alice and Oscar circled around to the front of the house. "I'll wait outside while you get Lucia," said Oscar. "She probably shouldn't take any clothing for Noelle since the closet was tossed. Send her shopping instead."

Alice agreed. She went back inside and jogged up the stairs. "You can come out, Lucia," she said as she opened the door. She didn't see the teenager. "Lucia?"

"In here," came a muffled voice.

She'd shut herself into the closet.

Alice opened the door and found her in the corner, hunched into as small a ball as possible. "We didn't find anyone," said Alice softly, noticing the girl's hands were shaking. "They're probably long gone. This probably happened last night or early this morning." She held out a hand and helped the girl stand. Lucia's eyes were red and her cheeks damp. "I'm sorry you were scared," said Alice. "But we had to leave you here."

"I know. It's okay." She took a deep breath and gave a weak smile.

This feels like an overreaction.

But a murder did happen here.

Alice frowned as she compared how Lucia had confidently stridden to the stairs with how she was now. She definitely hadn't been scared minutes before.

"We can't let you take any clothes today," said Alice. "Perhaps you could buy some things for Noelle?"

Lucia nodded, her gaze on the floor, as they moved down the stairs.

"Too bad you're not the same size." Noelle was several inches taller than both her sisters.

"I'll figure out something." Lucia stopped in the foyer, looking out the living room windows at the sheriff's vehicles that had just arrived. "Are you going to catch him?" she asked in a soft voice.

Alice's heart cracked at the concern in the girl's tone. "Absolutely."

21

Two years before Derrick Bell's murder

Derrick won his election in a landslide, taking out a two-term incumbent.

The election party went far into the night. Derrick had been called the winner with only 30 percent of the vote counted; his lead had been that overwhelming.

Noelle had danced and celebrated with two hundred of their closest friends for hours.

They'd done it.

And she had mistakenly thought their life would change. It didn't. Derrick's new position swallowed all his time, leaving fewer hours than before for them to be together. Noelle found herself communicating more often with Derrick's assistant, Jon, than with her husband. Jon controlled Derrick's schedule, so texting him got her firm answers; texting Derrick got her more questions. Miranda was hired on as part of Derrick's permanent staff, along with Eve's fiancé, Adam.

Noelle found herself questioning the word *permanent* as a description of staff. An assemblyman's term was two years—definitely not permanent. Six months into Derrick's first term, she started to wish it would be his only one. She couldn't imagine going through another election, although Derrick frequently talked about it.

And election plans were already being made.

She missed her husband. The political and social events for which he required her at his side felt awkward and fake. She suggested weekend trips to Wine Country, the coast, and Las Vegas, hoping to rekindle the excitement of the time they'd dated. He brushed aside her suggestions. "No time."

Instead, he suggested she get pregnant.

Getting her pregnant was something he had time for.

She'd agreed, but after two months of trying, she secretly went back on her birth control, feeling guilty that she didn't have the guts to tell him that she wasn't ready. He frequently spoke of having children, wanting a boy and a girl, describing how they would be the perfect all-American family.

Noelle's understanding of his dream's subtext was that it was her responsibility to deliver that family while he served the people of Northern California. Besides, she didn't have to deal with a job anymore, he'd said. She had lots of empty hours, so now was the perfect time.

Deep down she knew she wasn't ready to be locked into that role. Not yet. She loved Lora's twin boys but saw how much time and energy they took. It was true she had many empty hours during the day, but Noelle was still actively involved in Lucia's life, guiding the girl through her teenage years. Not to mention her grandfather and great-aunt were slowing down. Noelle wanted to be available for them. Keeping an eye on her extended family was enough responsibility for Noelle.

She did the best she could. Noelle kept her chin up and always had a smile ready for Derrick when he did make it home from work before she fell asleep. They'd moved into the giant home outside of town, and Derrick had fully taken over the condo, using it as an informal second office in the city. She felt a bit isolated in the big home. Derrick's parents were just a few miles away, but her side of the family was much farther. Neighbors kept to themselves out in the country. She'd met the people on each side of the home, but other than including a wave now and then, there was no depth to their acquaintance.

Derrick had told her to do whatever she wanted with the house yet pointed out all the things he wanted changed. She liked the old-fashioned, almost historic feel of the home, but he wanted it updated into a modern style that she felt clashed with the home's exterior. She worked with a designer, and the two of them revised the remodeling plans a dozen times. Derrick kept vetoing their suggestions and then would turn his attention to his work. She finally realized he wasn't paying attention to the actual changes in the plans and stopped asking his opinion.

She moved his cabinets of baseball cards, antique guns, and cigar boxes into his office, where they were out of her sight. He'd wanted his collections in his home instead of the condo. He insisted on displaying his elephants and added them to the shelves in the living room and the entryway. She let it go and decided to accept the elephants, patting the head of a large iron one every time she walked by.

The designer found a few elephant prints that Noelle didn't hate, and Derrick was pleased when he spotted them in the formal living room.

The end result was one that suited her and did justice to the home, and he barely noticed—except for the elephant prints—apparently forgetting what he'd insisted on for kitchen style and the home's flooring and ceiling treatments.

A few months before their wedding, he'd surprised her with a new car. He'd led her to the driveway, excitement on his face. Parked in front of the home was a dark-green Jaguar coupe. It even had a big bow on the hood. Noelle had stared at the car, struggling to believe that he'd bought such an expensive gift.

"Now you won't have to drive that ancient heap anymore," he said with glee.

She was instantly offended; she loved her old Explorer. The 4WD could take her anywhere and haul almost anything she bought. It'd been her first major purchase after she started the posh bartending job. It hadn't mattered to her that it had more than a hundred thousand miles on it when she bought it. It'd been reliable, and she'd loved it.

"That's for me?" she'd asked hesitantly, trying to pull together an acceptable reaction to the extravagant purchase.

"Of course! My wife has to look good on the road."

Still stunned, she'd walked up to the car and opened the driver's door. The brown interior didn't appeal to her at all. The green wasn't a color she would have ever chosen, and the car was so low to the ground, she suspected she'd be stuck at home when the weather turned bad.

She liked four-wheel drive; it was reassuring.

"It's a beautiful car," she'd said, turning to him. "You didn't have to do this."

His face lit up, and he pulled her tight. "You deserve it."

Locked in his hug, she'd looked over his shoulder at her dusty black Ford, a small pang of sadness touching her heart. It looked decrepit next to the shiny Jaguar.

It's just a vehicle. Get over it. Your man just bought you an amazing gift.

"I can't believe you did this," she'd said. "How did I end up with someone like you?"

"That's just the beginning," he'd promised.

She stood in the new kitchen and breathed deep, smelling fresh paint from the remodel that had taken up eight months of her life. But she loved the result. She checked the pasta on her new range and decided to give it another minute. She glanced at the time. Derrick should have been home ten minutes ago, as he'd promised. Noelle sighed, unsurprised but still let down.

I'm watching pasta boil.

The equivalent of watching paint dry.

Now that the remodel was finished, she wondered what to do with her time and considered Derrick's pregnancy suggestion again. She shook her head, still staring at the boiling pot. "No," she stated out loud.

I'd be a single mom.

She confirmed her decision to not tell him about the birth control. It'd simply create an argument that she'd like to avoid. And she couldn't handle his disappointment in her. Again.

Last week, she'd booked a dinner reservation for one evening because Derrick had promised he'd be done early with work. During a call on his way home, she mentioned the reservation, hoping he'd be pleased that she'd scheduled some time for them, which had been missing of late. Instead, she'd been met with silence.

"Noelle."

She'd cringed, recognizing his cool tone, the one he used when displeased.

"You *know* what today is. I can't believe you'd think I'd want to celebrate."

Her brain had shot into overdrive, trying to recall what was special about the day. She'd checked his calendar twice with Jon; nothing had been planned. "I'm sorry," she'd told him. "I forgot. Are you sure you don't want to do dinner? It doesn't have to be a celebration, just some quiet time together."

He'd gone silent, the sounds of traffic coming through the call.

"Absolutely not," he'd finally said. "Once again you aren't taking my feelings into consideration at all."

Fuck. What is today?

"I didn't mean to do that," she'd said as she checked the same date in her calendar for the past two years and then the date in her photos, searching for some indication of what he was talking about. She'd found nothing. "It was an accident. I wasn't thinking."

"Obviously. You know how much I loved my grandfather."

His grandfather?

She'd Googled his grandfather and learned he'd died on this date eleven years ago. Faintly she recalled Derrick mentioning it . . . probably on the same date last year. "I know you miss him," she'd said, shaking her head. This wasn't the first time he'd expected her to recall every bit of information he'd ever mentioned to her. In fact, she'd disappointed him at least a half dozen times in the last few months by forgetting things. She'd added his grandfather's death to her calendar so it'd turn up each year, and then she'd looked up when his other grandparents had died so she didn't make the same mistake again.

My memory should be better than this.

She took the pasta from the stove and drained it into the sink, clouds of steam filling the air. Two minutes later she heard his footsteps on the porch. She checked her hair in the reflection of the window over the sink. She still hadn't returned to the platinum shade she loved. When they'd received their wedding photos, he'd gushed about how much better it looked, so she continued with the soft blonde.

Derrick came in, loosening his tie and looking very tired. "Hey, babe," he said as he came up behind her and enveloped her in a big hug. He kissed her neck and looked over her shoulder at the pasta, to which she was carefully adding pecorino cheese and pepper. "That smells incredible."

"Hungry?" she asked.

"Starving."

"Good."

"You take such excellent care of me," he said with another kiss, this time on her ear. "I love you so much it almost hurts."

She turned her head to meet his lips.

"You love me the same, right?" he asked, his tone begging to hear the words back.

"I do," she replied. "It's painful how much I love you." She did love him; she was positive about that. But she didn't like the way he always asked her to say it. There was an insecurity in his constant requests that made her uncomfortable. It wasn't as if she didn't tell him enough; she said it frequently. But he always wanted more.

"Good." He sounded satisfied, but she knew he'd ask again at bedtime.

He's working hard. He needs to know that everything is good at home.

She was determined to support him. If it meant constantly telling him how much she loved him, so be it. She mentally kicked herself for resisting. Nothing was wrong with a spouse wanting to hear they were loved.

He reached down and pressed his hand against her lower belly. She knew the question without him posing it. "Nothing yet," she said, infusing her words with disappointment. "Maybe next month."

"You always say that." He stepped back, and her skin missed his heat.

"I'm not sure what else you expect me to say," she said. "The fact is we won't know if I'm pregnant for another four weeks."

"You could at least sound upset," he said. "I think you don't want a baby." His tone was accusatory. "If you truly wanted it, I think it would happen."

He thinks my thoughts can create a pregnancy?

It wasn't the first time he'd hinted that it was her fault she wasn't pregnant.

It *was* her fault, of course. She'd been on birth control for months. Each month she took all the pills out of their special holder and added them to the small Midol bottle she kept in her purse. The bottle contained Midol tablets, but the tiny birth control pills always sank to the bottom. She'd packed her purse with several feminine hygiene products because she'd learned early in their relationship that their presence kept Derrick from looking for anything in her purse. One time she'd asked him to get a pen out of her purse, and he'd nearly dropped the bag when faced with several tampons. He'd immediately thrust it at her to find the pen.

I need a different hiding spot.

She worried he'd grow suspicious enough to overcome his fear of tampons.

Noelle turned to him and smiled, trying to erase the frown on his face. "I'll book an appointment for some tests and see if there's a physical issue that's keeping me from getting pregnant."

"Good idea." He looked pleased.

She waited, wondering if he'd bring up the possibility of low sperm count and perhaps a test for him.

He didn't. "My mom suggested last week that you should get tested," he told her.

Ire shot through Noelle. "That was kind of her."

"Did you try to get pregnant with your first husband?"

"I was *eighteen*! Hell no. And you know the marriage only lasted a couple months."

"If you were really in love, I think you would have wanted a baby with him."

Noelle searched his face, speechless.

"Just shows that you love me more, right?" His gaze stated he needed the confirmation again.

"Absolutely."

He had a deep jealousy of her first marriage and would use a condescending tone when speaking of Brendon. Noelle *never* mentioned her ex. They exchanged an occasional text; Brendon always remembered her birthday and would wish her a merry Christmas. She knew it would be rude to mention him in front of Derrick.

Derrick didn't think it was rude when *he* brought up her ex.

He pulled her into a deep hug. "We're perfect. I know we'll be together forever."

"Forever," Noelle echoed.

She shoved away the growing questions in her head.

22

"How was your marriage the year before he died?" asked Agent Keaton.

"You mean before he was murdered," said Noelle. She was getting antsy and more annoyed by the minute. "Are you asking how our sex life was?" she asked, wanting to see Keaton squirm.

Agent Rhodes tried to keep a straight face at her comment, but Noelle saw his eyes widen and his lips press together. He seemed more in tune with her than his partner. Rhodes was always watching her reactions, while Keaton stared at his laptop. Clearly Rhodes's role in the meeting was secondary, but when he did speak up, he was tactful and to the point. She suspected it'd take more than a sex question to fluster him.

"I'm asking how well you got along," said Keaton, his face suddenly pink.

"Our marriage was great. We both were very lucky we'd found each other. I loved my husband very much. It couldn't have been better."

Noelle forced a smile.

23

Six months before Derrick Bell's murder

"We need to go!" Derrick stood at the front door, eyeing his watch as Noelle scrambled to find her phone and grab her purse. Twenty minutes ago he'd told her about the fundraiser, but he claimed he'd told her a week ago. She'd been fresh from a sweaty run and pointed out it wasn't on their joint calendar. His reply was that she must have deleted it.

His tone implied she'd done it on purpose.

Noelle had bitten her tongue and rushed to the shower, cursing his assistant. Jon was excellent about sending her event reminders; she didn't know what'd gone wrong this time. There was no time to wash her hair, so she sprayed it with a good-smelling dry shampoo and rubbed it into her scalp, then yanked her hair back into a high ponytail. She threw on a simple dress and high heels, put on some earrings, and grabbed a set of bracelets. She caught her reflection in the mirror.

"Fuck." She'd completely forgotten makeup.

She shoved some in a small makeup bag, intending to apply it in the car, and hoped Derrick didn't expect her to drive. Sometimes he did when he needed to review a speech en route. She found her phone and darted toward the front door, her heels clicking a staccato.

"Is that what you're wearing?" he asked.

She froze and looked down at the expensive dress. "When your mother picked it out, she said it's perfect for this type of event."

He yanked open the front door and strode out before her.

Jerk.

She locked the door and breathed a sigh of relief that he was headed toward the driver's door of his Mercedes. It'd taken a year of marriage to learn that invoking his mother's name when he questioned her decisions made him immediately back off. But one time he'd asked his mother about an artwork decision and learned that Noelle had lied. His fury—and his mother's—made him give her the cold shoulder for three days. After that she always reached out for Catherine's opinion on things she knew Derrick would challenge. In fact it had gotten to the point where she asked Catherine about almost every piece of clothing or decor for the house. It simply made life easier.

Derrick hadn't opened her car door as he usually did, and Noelle knew it was a punishment. After she opened it, she waited as he brushed what looked like powdered sugar off her seat, surprising her. He had a firm rule about no eating or drinking in his car.

What is going on?

She silently slid into the car and flipped down the mirror to apply her eyeliner. He backed out of the driveway too fast, and she grabbed the door for balance.

She said nothing.

"It's just like you to forget something like this," he finally said, ten minutes down the road.

"I'm sorry. At least we'll be there on time."

"It makes me feel like you don't care about what I do."

"You know how important your position is to me."

"Then you need to act like it is."

She focused on applying her lipstick, and her grandfather's words from last week echoed in her head.

Her grandfather had cornered her at a family dinner, a gruff look in his eyes. Derrick had been working late and unable to attend.

"You're too thin," he'd said flatly.

She'd looked past him at Lucia and Eve arguing about whether the steaks on the grill were finished. "I started a new workout class," she lied. "It's really intense but has done amazing things for my muscle tone." She lifted a foot and flexed her calf for him, hoping some definition would appear. "I haven't increased my calorie intake, but maybe I should. I've noticed I've felt hungrier lately."

Actually she'd had no appetite lately.

"Yes, you should eat more," he'd told her. "Maybe ice cream every night." He jerked his head toward her sisters. "Those two look up to you. I've noticed they copy your clothes and hairstyles. Last week I caught Lucia vomiting after dinner. She looked like crap. Pale and sweaty and shaking. She said something hadn't sat right in her stomach, but it made me wonder."

"You only noticed it once? Are you worried about bulimia?" Alarm had shot through Noelle, and she'd taken a critical look at her sister's physique. Lucia *had* looked thin, and there were faint purple crescents under her eyes. But she was bubbly and vivacious as ever. "I'll talk to her. I'll ask Eve if she's noticed anything."

"Eve and Adam come around a lot more than you do," he'd pointed out. This was his way of indirectly stating that he wanted to see her more. "Starting to feel like Adam's taken your spot in this family."

Noelle had forced a smile, but inside she was crying. "He's a qualified substitute. I'm glad Eve married him. I can tell he cares about Lucia and the rest of you." She'd rubbed her grandfather's arm. "I'll do my best to get here at least once a week." Noelle squeezed his bicep. "What's this? You been hitting the gym?" The bulk under her hand had surprised her.

He'd lifted his chin. "Damn right. I read somewhere that people my age lose muscle mass if they don't use it within two days. Got me fired up and using the bench in the garage." He scowled. "You're just trying to distract me. Eat more. Check in with Lucia. I've been watching her like a hawk after every meal, but I've only caught her that one time in the bathroom."

"It's probably nothing, then," Noelle had said. "But I'll find out." Guilt had shot through her. She'd been distracted trying to be the perfect hostess for all the dinner parties Derrick had started to schedule at their home. He expected the right wine, perfect food, and an impressive layout of their dishes and decor. Noelle had suggested a caterer, and he'd just stared at her. "You can't make a dinner for more than the two of us? My mom does it all the time without any help."

Noelle didn't dare point out that his mom used two women who cooked and cleaned the home for those meals. Catherine was really good at hiding it. Noelle only knew because she'd shown up early for one party, intending to help poor overworked Catherine. Instead, she found her in the kitchen with a glass of wine, watching the other women cook.

Catherine had sworn her to secrecy.

Noelle didn't dare break that promise.

In the car with Derrick, she finished her makeup and tucked a few wayward strands of hair into place.

"Seriously, Noelle." Derrick's voice was louder, and his knuckles whitened as he gripped the steering wheel. "Sometimes it seems like you've totally checked out from what's going on in our lives."

"I'm two feet away. I can hear you," she said quietly.

"*Jesus!* Is that all you're taking away from this discussion?" He deliberately raised his voice more. "I can speak however I want! When I'm angry, it's important to let these things out instead of having them build up. And trust me, things *have been building.*"

She flinched, recalling how he'd nearly punched a wall weeks ago but turned at the last moment and hit an overstuffed chair instead. He'd won his second election several months back, but this term had not been going smoothly. He'd been stressed and working long hours and would lose his temper at the drop of a hat.

"Then you need to talk to a therapist," Noelle stated. "A lot of people believe what you just said about letting things out, but actually, expressing anger amplifies aggression and—"

She grabbed the car door handle as he yanked the Mercedes to the curb and hit the brakes. He spun in his seat and faced her. "*Do not quote your base-level psychology psychobabble to me. Four fucking years of college does not make you an expert!*"

His face was red, and drops of sweat beaded on his temples.

Something else is bothering him. I pushed him over the edge.

I need to defuse this.

"You're right. I'm sorry, Derrick." She lowered her gaze and saw his hands were shaking.

This is the angriest I've seen him.

Suddenly the inside of the car felt very small and hot.

"Can you forgive me?" she asked quickly. "I'll put on a happy face and talk you up all evening. It'll be good." Clenching her teeth together, she cautiously slipped her hand into one of his and gave a hesitant squeeze. "We'll feel better when we get there. It should be a fun night."

His breathing slowed a bit, and he sat back in the driver's seat, still holding her hand. "I'm sorry I yelled," he said gruffly. "I didn't mean it. It's just . . . work . . . you know."

"I do know."

Thank God he's calming down.

Derrick had never hit her, but damn, he sure looked like he wanted to sometimes. On the days his temper flared like this, he always tried to make it up to her in bed that night with sex. When they were done, he'd hold her tight and tell her how much he loved her and how sorry he was. Sometimes he even cried as he asked her to forgive him for getting angry and yelling. He blamed job stress and said his job was so important, he had to do it right. Thousands of people depended on him.

Noelle always said she forgave him. But she didn't forget.

She should have known better than to suggest he talk to a therapist. Last time she'd suggested it, he'd walked out of the house, stating he was staying at the condo. He hadn't come back for four days.

He guided the car back into the lane and continued to drive. Noelle took deep breaths and tried to slow her heart rate.

What will happen on the day I can't cool him down?

As they stepped inside the hotel ballroom, Jon instantly whisked Derrick away because "there is someone he *has* to meet."

Interpretation: someone with deep pockets.

Noelle watched them leave, irked she hadn't had a chance to ask Jon why this event wasn't on her schedule. Two political wives approached her, and she made polite chitchat for three minutes, then excused herself, saying she needed to check on Derrick. Instead, she made a beeline for the bar and ordered a gin and tonic. A double. She found a quiet spot to drink, keeping an eye on Derrick as person after person approached him, wanting a minute of his time. His gatekeeper, Jon, spoke to each one before allowing them within Derrick's circle. Derrick rarely drank much; he just nursed a glass of wine all night. He never said anything when Noelle ordered something stronger in public, but she'd seen the displeasure in his eyes.

"He's good at this."

Noelle turned to find Eve's husband, Adam, beside her, a drink in his hand too. He held his toward her, and she clinked her glass against it. "He is," she agreed. "And I hear all the time how much he relies on you to organize his thoughts and get his message out to his constituents. You make his job much easier."

Adam shrugged. "That's the first line in my job description: 'Make Derrick's job easier.'" He eyed her. "It's your first line too."

Noelle gave a half smile and took another sip.

True.

"You look tired," Adam stated.

"Thanks a lot. But don't we all?" said Noelle in good humor. Adam never said things to dig at people, and her drink was already taking effect, erasing the tension of her car ride with Derrick.

"Have you seen a doctor?" asked Adam, studying her. "Maybe you need something to give you a boost. We all need a little help now and then."

"Except for Derrick. I swear this type of event energizes him. Sometimes too much," she added, wondering if anticipating the event had spiked his emotions earlier.

"They do—oh, *shit*. I'll catch you later." Adam strode off, raising a hand as if greeting someone a few yards away.

"Chicken," Noelle muttered. He'd seen Catherine approaching. Noelle wanted to sneak away too, but she'd already made eye contact with Derrick's mother.

"Good evening, Catherine," said Noelle with an automatic smile. "Looks like a good turnout as usual." She knew her mother-in-law was on the planning committee for the event.

Catherine returned the same smile. "Lots of people's hard work is paying off." She took the place beside Noelle that Adam had just vacated to look over the room, a creator surveying her work.

Noelle understood the meaning behind her comment: Noelle hadn't volunteered for the planning committee. She scanned the room for a waiter, ready for another drink.

"I've been wanting to talk to you about something, Noelle."

Where's a waiter when you need one?

"What's that, Catherine?" She kept her tone friendly and open while inside she was screaming. She'd experienced enough of Catherine's talks.

"Derrick seems unusually stressed lately. Do you know what could be causing that?"

"Most likely his job," Noelle said dryly.

"You know what I mean." Exasperation filled her mother-in-law's tone. "What's going on at home? Are you two fighting? I know he was disappointed by your tests."

Noelle drained the last bit of her drink. She'd seen a fertility specialist, whom she'd sworn to secrecy about her birth control use—even though legally he wasn't allowed to share anything—and learned she wasn't the only one of his patients who'd made that request. He'd gone ahead and checked some other things and then told her she shouldn't have a problem getting pregnant in the future. "I was also upset that he couldn't find any issues," she lied. "But Derrick doesn't want to get his sperm count checked. And the ball's in his court." She snorted at her pun.

"I'm sure he's not the issue. Maybe you could try a different doctor." Noelle caught a waiter's eye and raised her hand.

Thank God.

"Alcohol probably doesn't help," said Catherine as Noelle handed off her glass and requested another.

"I don't think my infertility is what's bothering Derrick," said Noelle. "He has a lot going on at work. They're already making plans for his third election. It never ends."

"You don't sound very supportive."

Noelle focused on her breaths. Slow inhale. Slow exhale. "What am I *not* doing to support my husband? I make certain he doesn't have to worry about a thing outside of his job. I do everything I can think of to make his job easier." An echo of Adam's earlier comment about their job descriptions. "But I agree with you that he has seemed on edge more than usual. He loses his temper very quickly." She watched Catherine out of the corner of her eye.

There was no visible reaction.

"That happens sometimes. I'm not surprised." Catherine continued to watch her son across the room, seemingly undisturbed by Noelle's comment. "Here comes Lora." Her face brightened considerably.

"Hi, Mom. Hey, Noelle." Lora gave them each a hug.

Noelle's spine relaxed a fraction. Lora made a good buffer around her mother. The waiter appeared with Noelle's drink.

Things are looking up.

She sipped her drink, half listening to Lora discuss the room's temperature because it seemed the air-conditioning wasn't strong enough. Catherine agreed, a concerned look on her face. They debated how to immediately address the issue without causing a stir.

She says nothing when I mention Derrick's increasing temper but worries about a room temperature that is two degrees too warm.

She watched as Derrick laughed loudly and touched the arm of a man who'd apparently said the funniest thing he had heard in years. The man beamed.

Ka-ching.

The clock caught her eye. Two more hours to go. Most likely three, because there was always another person who wanted "just a moment" of Derrick's time.

She tamped down her resentment of his dedication to his job.

His dedication to helping others was one of the things that had attracted her to him.

I'll never stand in his way.

24

"It's too fucking early," groaned Oscar for the fifth time.

Alice didn't care. After the previous unsuccessful attempts to find Noelle's ex-husband Brendon Simon, she'd suggested they visit his home at 6:00 a.m. "Drink your coffee," she told Oscar. He'd insisted on stopping at the gas station for the gigantic cup of black coffee in his hand. Alice had fueled up at home.

"It's not helping yet," he muttered as he took three big swallows.

She pulled over and parked in front of the home that had been empty on their first visit. Today there was a small truck in the driveway. "Got him."

"Yay," Oscar said flatly. He took another swallow and got out of the car. Alice joined him, and they approached the door together. She knocked as Oscar pushed the button on the doorbell camera. Alice fought to be patient. Glancing around the neighborhood, she noticed a woman in running gear walking two French bulldogs on the other side of the street. She stared back at Alice, a frown on her face.

Alice waved.

The woman looked away and continued her walk.

"Neighbors taking notice," she said quietly.

"That's because sane people don't knock on doors at six a.m.," grumbled Oscar.

The other reason Alice had pushed for this time was that something had jumped out at her in the downloaded bank records they'd received last night. After leaving the forensic team to go through the Bell mansion's tossed office and primary suite, they'd received several subpoenaed bank records and phone records. She'd been exhausted after the long day of interviews and the discovery of the mess at the mansion but had perked up when she learned they'd received Noelle's, Derrick's, and their immediate family members' bank statements.

To Oscar's dismay, she'd immediately dived in.

"Go home and sleep if you want," Alice had told him as she scrolled through Lucia's sole bank account. She'd decided to look first through the least complicated instead of tackling some of the Bell accounts. Each person in the Bell family easily had a dozen accounts, while the Marshalls' were much fewer.

"I'll stay," Oscar had said in his Eeyore voice.

Alice had already finished with six months of Lucia's statements and moved on to Eve's, which were the second least complicated. "Start with Derrick Bell's," she requested.

A minute later Oscar groaned. "You gave me his accounts on purpose. This will take forever."

"I did. Enjoy."

Hours later, the agents had made a list of several interesting things that needed follow-up. And one of those things involved Brendon Simon.

Oscar pressed the doorbell camera button again.

"Can I help you?" A tinny male voice sounded from the doorbell. "You know it's six a.m., right?"

Alice held her ID in front of the camera. "Mr. Simon? We'd like to talk to you about Noelle and Derrick Bell."

There was a long pause. "It's six a.m.," he repeated.

"Well, you weren't here when we stopped by the other night. Excuse us for not making an appointment. This shouldn't take long." She hoped.

"Give me a minute. I'm still in bed."

They waited several minutes.

"What's he doing?" asked Oscar. "Taking a shower?"

The door finally opened a few inches, and Brendon Simon studied the two of them. His hair stuck up on one side, and his T-shirt looked like he'd picked it up off the floor. "Can I see your ID again?" They held out their IDs, which he studied without touching either one. "Is Noelle all right?" he asked, opening the door wide.

"Didn't she text you that she's okay?" asked Alice.

"Yeah, but I know she had a head injury. Is she still in the hospital?"

"Can we come in?" Alice asked.

Brendon paused for a moment but opened the door wider and stepped back.

Alice moved inside. "Thank you." Under the messy hair and wrinkled clothes, it was apparent that Brendon Simon focused on fitness. His muscles rippled as he led the agents to a table in the kitchen nook. A coffee maker rumbled, fresh coffee streaming into the pot.

That's why he took so long to answer the door.

He grabbed a mug out of a cupboard as the agents sat. "Coffee?"

"Please," said Oscar. "Black."

"Same for me," said Alice, who wasn't interested in coffee but had been taught that it was rude to turn down an offered beverage in someone's home. A minute later he set three mugs on the table.

"How is Noelle?" he asked as he sat.

With the early-morning sun streaming in the windows, Alice noticed he had startlingly blue eyes. He ran a hand through his mussed hair, and she abruptly knew one of the reasons Derrick Bell did not like Brendon Simon. The man was attractive.

"Still has some memory issues," said Alice. "Doctors are hopeful that she'll get her short-term memory back but won't make promises."

Brendon nodded thoughtfully and sipped his coffee.

"Do you talk to her much?" asked Alice.

131

The man shrugged. "The occasional text. Mostly just a 'How's it going?' type thing. We've met for coffee to catch up a couple times."

"You two divorced," said Oscar. "But you keep in touch?"

"Weird, right? She's a good person. Was very supportive when I went to rehab after our marriage."

Rehab?

Brendon raised a brow as he looked from Oscar to Alice. "Your expressions tell me you didn't know that. I figured you'd turned my history inside out after her husband was murdered and you learned I still talk to Noelle." He paused and fiddled with his coffee cup. "Gambling. Haven't touched it in years."

"Congratulations. That's not easy," said Alice, truly meaning it. Beating addiction took strength.

"I assume you want to know where I was at some date and time?"

"Thursday evening to Friday morning," said Oscar.

"I was at work most of that time. I work graveyard."

"Where?"

He named a big hospital in town.

"Noelle told us a different hospital."

Brendon frowned. "I could have sworn I told her I switched hospitals. I get more money and better benefits now, but I'll be on graveyard for a while. Maybe she forgot?" He wrinkled his forehead, concern in his eyes. "Think it's from her injury? We've had coffee since I moved, so I must have told her." He paused. "I think."

"Doesn't matter," said Alice, wondering the same about Noelle's memory. "We'll confirm your shift with your employer. Did anyone see you in the hours before or after your shift? I assume you worked eleven to seven?"

"I did . . . let me think." Brendon stared into his coffee cup. "Isabella wasn't here. She only stays over the nights I'm off, or I go to her place."

"Did you go to a restaurant?" asked Alice. "Buy gas? Did a neighbor pop in?"

"Might have gotten gas. Let me check my credit card account." He opened his phone.

"Is the truck in the driveway your only vehicle?" asked Oscar.

Brendon looked up. "Yeah. Why?"

"Mind if I take a look at it?"

"Go ahead."

Oscar stood and held out a hand. "Keys?"

Brendon didn't move, still gripping his phone.

"I promise not to steal it," said Oscar.

A resigned look crossed his face and Brendon stretched to reach a drawer behind him and pulled out a key fob. He handed it to Oscar. "Lock it up." He turned his attention back to his phone.

Alice appreciated Oscar's maneuver, asking for permission to "look" before asking for the keys. She knew he'd check the vehicle for an insurance tracking device and anything odd.

"I got gas that Thursday," said Brendon. "I know I did it on the way to work because it's just a few blocks from the hospital, so that would have been a bit before eleven. After my shift, I went straight home. I usually crash for a few hours right away. I need that sleep. Can't think of anyone I saw after I left the hospital that morning." He met Alice's gaze as he set down his phone.

"Thanks. We can check the gas station's cameras." She looked at her map app. The hospital and Brendon's home were more than forty-five minutes from the Bells' home. Assuming cameras and shift clockings confirmed his presence, he was covered for their current window of time.

But she knew that window was an estimate; Brendon Simon's movements didn't rule him out.

"I didn't kill Derrick Bell," he said quietly. "The only time I met him was during a brief chat in a restaurant. And I remember wishing we hadn't crossed paths."

"We're doing our due diligence. Crossing people off our list. Why do you wish you hadn't met him?" she asked.

"It was just a weird situation. I could tell Noelle was uncomfortable, and it made Isabella feel awkward. You gotta put on a happy face, you know? Pretend like you don't care who an ex is seeing now."

"Are you saying you care?"

He leaned on his forearms, a half smile on his face. "Only in a friendly way. Noelle landed in a good situation, and I'm happy if she's happy. Derrick is a bit slick, but he has to be in his job. Just bugs me. I hate it when people act overly happy and interested in you. It's fake."

Alice knew what he meant.

The front door opened and closed, and Oscar appeared. He handed over the key fob. "It's locked."

"Anything interesting?" asked Brendon with a touch of sarcasm.

"You buy a lot of energy drinks."

Brendon snorted. "Isabella hates that I go through so many of them. And she really hates that I toss the empties behind my seat." He lifted one shoulder in a half shrug.

Alice studied Oscar's expression. He met her gaze but offered no reaction.

Nothing of note.

"We've been reviewing bank statements," began Alice.

"And you want to know why Noelle gave me nine thousand dollars three months ago," Brendon finished.

"That's correct." A few large sums had been transferred out of Noelle's account over the last six months. The one to Brendon was the largest. Alice had checked two years' worth of Brendon's records, but that appeared to be the only transfer he'd received from her.

"Don't you think that if Noelle wanted me to kill her husband, she'd pay in cash?" asked Brendon. "She's not dumb."

"That's where your brain automatically goes? A payment for murder? Why would you think Noelle would do that?" asked Oscar.

"That's not what I meant," said Brendon with a glare. "Don't twist my words. You're here about a murder and you want to know why

Noelle gave me money. Any person would jump to a conclusion that you need to rule out a payment for murder."

The testosterone level in the room rose as Brendon and Oscar had a stare-down.

"So what was the money for?" asked Alice, wanting to get them back on track.

"It paid off my student loans," Brendon said quietly. "I've been scrimping and saving and paying off as much as possible for seven years—even in my gambling days, I made sure I paid extra principal. Nine thousand was the chunk that was left. Somehow it came up in conversation, and Noelle offered to take care of it."

"You just let her?" asked Oscar. "I don't know if my ego would stand for that. She's your ex. Why should she care what's going on with your finances?"

Brendon met Oscar's gaze. "I struggled with that. Still feel a little guilty. But the relief from being out from under that black cloud that's been hanging over my head for years was worth it. Long ago I gave Noelle a bit of money a few times when she was in college. She said this was her way of paying me back." He gave a short laugh. "I may have given her two hundred dollars at the most, so it definitely wasn't an even trade. That happened after our divorce, and I think she was in her second year of college."

"You're the oddest ex-couple I've ever met," said Oscar.

"Everyone tells me that."

Alice had been listening quietly and watching Brendon. His body language was relaxed, he sounded forthcoming, and she wanted to believe him. "Can you think of anyone who would kill her husband?"

Brendon sat back in his chair, shaking his head. "Dunno. Noelle didn't discuss him with me much. She seemed happy. Didn't tell me or even imply that anything bad was going on with her husband. Or her."

Alice thought of what Noelle's grandfather had said. "What sort of changes have you seen in Noelle since she married?"

"You mean besides the expensive shoes, clothes, and nails? And that ridiculous little sports car?"

"Yes."

"She's the same," said Brendon matter-of-factly. "The few times we've met up, it takes me thirty seconds to get past how polished she is now and see the young woman I was in love with. She's the same person under the fake veneer."

"What about how outgoing she is?" asked Alice. "Was she a secure person when you knew her?"

"No changes," said Brendon, thinking hard. "She's always been a confident person. Still is."

Doesn't line up with her grandfather's observations.

"Are you planning to visit her?" asked Alice. "Check in on her?"

"Only if she asks," said Brendon. "We both have our own lives now. But I'll always care a bit, and I think she will too. Out of respect for Isabella, we've cut way back on our communication." His eyes were earnest.

"A good idea," said Alice.

A few minutes later she and Oscar moved down the walkway from Brendon's home. "Truck was clean?" she asked.

"Yes, except for two dozen empty energy drink cans. No insurance tracker."

"We need to verify he was on the job that night. And that he got gas."

"Seems like a good guy," said Oscar. "I'm still a bit shocked he accepted her money."

"Not shocked she offered it?" asked Alice.

Oscar didn't answer until they were inside Alice's vehicle. "Not really. I saw her accounts. That money was nothing compared to what she had. And it looked like she handed out money to family a few times."

Alice nodded. They'd found several large dollar amounts going from Noelle's account to Eve's and Lucia's. But not to her grandfather's.

Alice couldn't see him accepting money from any of his granddaughters. No doubt Noelle had offered.

"I wonder if Derrick's family knew Noelle was giving money to her family," said Alice.

"None of their business," said Oscar.

Alice snorted lightly. "I suspect anything financial didn't go unnoticed."

"Derrick was a grown adult. You think Mommy and Daddy were still holding purse strings?"

"Not sure. Still need to tackle the rest of the Bell accounts."

"Don't remind me," moaned Oscar. "Surely we can get extra hands for that. It's busywork."

"Good idea. I'll ask."

Alice put the car in gear, and soon Brendon's home was in her rearview mirror.

Do I believe her ex?

I want to . . . but I don't know.

25

Three months before Derrick Bell's murder

"What's this?" asked Derrick, looking at his laptop.

Noelle was on the couch with a book. It was a rare weekday evening with Derrick at home. They'd enjoyed some Thai takeout with a glass of red wine, and then Derrick had said he had work to do. But instead of going to his office, he'd set up his laptop at the big table in their great room.

Noelle was pleased. There was something comforting about them doing their own things but still being together in the same room.

"What're you looking at?" she asked, not looking up from her book.

"Your bank account."

Instant discomfort filled her limbs, and she clenched her book.

Is it money lecture night?

Derrick liked to go through her accounts and question anything that caught his eye. She suspected she knew what had caught his eye this month.

"What do you want to know?" she asked. She stayed on the couch, wanting the buffer of square footage and the table between them.

"Four thousand dollars," he stated.

"That went to Lucia."

"Oh. Okay."

Noelle froze, waiting for him to say more. It didn't come.

Is he truly okay with me giving money to Lucia?
Or is this one of his games?

She set down her book and turned to look at him. He looked up from his computer. "What?"

"You're not going to ask what the money was for?"

"She's a good kid, but I'll ask if you want me to. What did she need four thousand dollars for?"

"A car. A reliable car. A neighbor was selling one, and we know he takes care of his vehicles. It seemed like good timing. Although she's not wild about driving a minivan."

"I agree she should have a car. A minivan will keep her ego in check," he said with a laugh, and he grinned. "I don't mean to micromanage," he said, closing the laptop.

She squinted at him. "What did you do with my husband?"

Something is very wrong.

He leaned back in his chair, looking as if he didn't have a care in the world. "I know I've been uptight lately."

Lately? How about for years?

The man speaking to her didn't feel like the one she'd been living with. This one didn't mind her giving money to her family and apologized—sort of—for being uptight. She stood and walked into the kitchen and picked up the wine they'd sampled that night. She looked at the label and then showed it to him. "We need to buy a few cases of this," she said.

He laughed and pulled her onto his lap at the table. "Will do." He nuzzled her neck and she closed her eyes, his lips tickling her skin.

"It's a fantastic wine if it makes you not care when I give money to my family."

He stopped and leaned back so he could see her eyes. "What does that mean?" he asked flatly.

She stiffened. Apparently lighthearted teasing time was over. "Just that we've had disagreements in the past when I've loaned money to my family."

"Loaned? You never expected them to pay the money back."

"Sorry, you're right. *Loaned* was the wrong word. I *gave* them money a few times."

"And I was nice about it each time," he pointed out.

She took a breath. "No, you were nice about it in front of them . . . like when I gave Eve some money. It was a different story when you reviewed my account later that month."

It had happened at least three times. He'd acted generous in front of her family, as if they'd jointly decided to give the money, and then he'd been a complete ass about it in private.

It was always my idea.

Although the money had originally come from him. When Noelle quit her job, he'd started giving her a generous allowance each month and had told her she could do with it what she pleased. But for the last year or so, he'd nitpicked her spending and complained when she shared it.

She wanted to share it. Her allowance was ridiculous, and her family was always low on money. Why wouldn't she help out? Even after she bought the clothes and shoes, had her hair and nails done, made donations and investments, and kept up the home, there was a lot left over.

"Sorry. I thought my comment about the wine was funny," she said, lowering her gaze.

"Sometimes I think we have completely opposite ideas of what's funny, Noelle," he snapped. His lecture tone had taken over, and he lowered his hands, leaving her to balance on his lap.

I pushed too far. I ruined his good mood.

"I'm sorry," she repeated. "Usually I have to explain—"

"I know we're opposites in a lot of ways," Derrick began in a condescending tone that she'd heard too often of late. "That's why we were attracted to one another."

A passive-aggressive insult.

Or is it a backhanded compliment?

"You saw us as opposites when we met?" Noelle said softly, not liking the turn this conversation had taken.

"Of course, didn't you? But I think that was why we clicked."

"Studies show similar people attract each other, not opposites. Homophily."

He pushed her off his lap, and she scrambled to stand. "Can't you just go along with what I was saying, Noelle? We were having a nice moment, and then you spout some psychology crap."

She stared at him. "Go along with what?"

"We're opposites!"

"Why are you so insistent on saying that?"

"Because it's true!" Fury reddened his face, and he stormed out of the room.

What just happened?

She slowly sat back down in his chair and realized he'd created a justification for dating and marrying her. She wondered how many times he'd spouted the opposites-attract theory to his family when they said she wasn't the right person for him.

"He was embarrassed to be attracted to me," she said quietly to the glass elephant on the table. She'd thought he didn't mind that she was a bartender from a poor family, and he came from money. A lot of money. He'd said a hundred times that it didn't matter. But apparently it did.

Is that why we hardly spend any time together?

Is he still embarrassed?

She'd done everything possible to fit in. She turned her head to see her hair in the mirror across the room, still missing her platinum blonde. Catherine had insisted she regularly visit an aesthetician to keep her skin at its best, and Noelle cringed every time she saw the cost. Derrick had requested she have a personal trainer. She wore the clothes his mother suggested. Noelle had shown up at events and joined volunteer organizations. She'd quit her job.

Anger flared.

I've completely changed my life, and I'm still not good enough for him.

She believed he'd looked past her roots and lifestyle in the beginning, but now she wondered if someone's constant little voice in his ear was making progress.

She lowered her head to her hands, wondering if that was why his emotions had been all over the place and why they rarely did anything together.

Or he's seeing someone.

She shut down the niggling thought. Every month Derrick asked if she was pregnant. He wouldn't do that if he wanted to be with someone else.

Unless the pregnancy hints were coming from his mother.

I bet he thinks our marriage will be solidified by a baby.

It was also a good political look and tool. "Look at the darling addition to the assemblyman's family! Such good family values."

Again she was thankful she was taking birth control.

26

Two weeks before Derrick Bell's murder

Savannah was late. Noelle shifted uncomfortably on the metal chair outside the teahouse and tugged down the hem of her summer dress. It had slid up her thighs as she sat, exposing more leg than she was comfortable with.

Good thing Derrick can't see it. Or his mother.

Both of them frequently reminded Noelle to be careful about how she looked and acted in public. It was important to not give his constituents something to complain about. A month ago someone had snapped a picture of her car in a crowded grocery store parking lot where her right rear tire had been over the yellow parking line. Social media had shared the photo, calling her selfish and privileged, and complained that she expected the public to work around whatever she wanted to do.

The photo hadn't shown the other eight cars parked in a row at the same odd angle. She'd either had to park the same way or park across the street.

Derrick had blown up while she explained the situation, snapping at her not to make excuses. Noelle's mother-in-law had called and laid a guilt trip on her because three of her friends had shown her the photo.

No one cared what Noelle had to say.

She had stopped trying to explain. She'd kept her mouth closed and tuned out Derrick's threats about driving lessons and selling her car.

The incident had highlighted an issue that had been simmering in Noelle's brain since she quit her job: she was completely dependent on Derrick.

He could cut off her money at any time. The car was in his name, not hers. Their home was in his parents' name because Derrick had never bothered to transfer the title. Her credit cards and bank accounts were solely hers, but he had access to all of it.

Noelle suspected he could instantly close all of them.

After one evening's argument over her clothes, she'd started transferring money in small sums to a different bank, but it was a slow process. Derrick would notice if she transferred large amounts.

Guilt racked her every time she did it.

If he ever finds out . . .

But she had to do something. It felt like the same predicament she'd been in when her first marriage ended. She'd had no money when the relationship fell apart. Now she had money, but it could evaporate instantly at Derrick's whim. And he frequently threatened to make it happen.

At the outdoor table, she leaned forward to check her parking job for the fifth time.

No one can complain that I'm not between the lines.

She hadn't known parking anxiety was a thing. But now it hit her every time she pulled into a lot. She would adjust her car's position five times to get it perfectly straight and even. Or she'd park at the empty far end of a lot.

Savannah's Bronco sped around a corner and swung into a space. She turned it off with both the passenger-side wheels directly on the line.

Noelle tensed.

The lot is three-quarters empty. It's fine.

Savannah hopped out and strode across the lot, greeted Noelle with a kiss on the cheek, and then flopped into a chair. She took a long drink of the bubble tea Noelle had bought her and sighed. "It's hot today. I hate summer here."

"It's ridiculous," Noelle said to be agreeable. She'd lived in the area all her life. Hot summers were normal. There was no point in complaining. "Can you get out of town to cool off?"

"Thinking about going to the coast for a week. We'll see." Savannah put her elbows on the table and leaned toward Noelle. "What's up with you? How's the handsome husband and his crazy mother?"

Three weeks ago, at a spring auction, Savannah had been present for one of Catherine's catty comments toward Noelle about her sisters. Savannah had confronted her about it, making Catherine uncomfortable enough to walk away. Later that night Derrick had told Noelle to keep Savannah away from his mother. He hadn't been at the auction, but obviously Catherine had complained.

When Noelle started to tell her husband that Catherine had insulted her sisters, he'd thrown up his hand in a stop position, cutting her off. "You misunderstood her. Let it go."

Then he hadn't spoken to her for the rest of the evening.

Clearly he can't let it go.

"Derrick is fine," she told Savannah. "I haven't heard from his mother this week."

"Small mercies."

"I'm sure I will at some point."

Savannah leaned closer, her gaze studying Noelle. "You look like crap."

Noelle pulled back. "Thank you?"

"Seriously. You've got purple bags under your eyes, and your arms look like sticks. Is the monster-in-law starving you?"

Noelle looked at her arms, wishing she hadn't worn a sleeveless dress. "I haven't been working out. My trainer moved, and I haven't found a new one that I like. Probably lost some muscle definition."

They do seem thin.

"Bullshit." Savannah scowled at her. "What's going on?"

Noelle looked away as she stirred her drink with her straw. "Nothing. Just lost a bit of weight, I guess."

I'm stressed out of my head.

Savannah snorted. "You and I don't lose weight by accident the same way we might lose a sock in the laundry. I know we both have to work hard at it." She grimaced. "I blame wine."

"And bubble tea? Maybe croissants."

"Don't change the subject." Savannah's expression grew serious. "Spill it."

There's so much I want to say.

I'm miserable.

"Marriage isn't the easiest thing," Noelle started hesitantly. "Lots of compromise. Even more so when a spouse is in politics."

"Is this about quitting your job? That was a hell of a compromise."

"Not really. I do miss it, though."

"You need something to do."

"I have lots to do. So many organizations want a piece of my time, I have to say no a lot."

"You need something *you like* to do," Savannah rephrased.

Noelle lifted a shoulder. She agreed, but that wasn't what weighed on her.

"Are things okay with Derrick?" Savannah whispered even though they were the only people on the teahouse's patio. "You know . . . sexually?"

Noelle nearly choked on a pearl of tapioca as she laughed. "That part of the marriage is *fine*. Jeez, Savannah."

Her best friend was silent for a long moment, and Noelle felt as if Savannah could clearly see into her brain. "I've seen how his mother treats you. What does he think of that?"

Noelle said nothing.

Savannah scowled. "He does see it—or hear it, I should say, right?"

"It's his mother. He won't say anything to her, and I don't expect him to."

"Maybe you should. I didn't think he was a mama's boy, but if he won't stand up for his spouse, then he definitely has an issue."

Noelle checked her parking space.

"Look at me," Savannah ordered. "It's clear that you have something to say."

"He's been different," Noelle started hesitantly, not wanting to be a whiner to her best friend, but clearly Savannah wouldn't let it go until she said *something*.

"Different how?"

"Well . . . I hardly see him, and when I do, he's so wired and stressed that I can't talk to him—"

"What does he do?"

"He doesn't let me get a word in edgewise. He cuts me off or tells me to shut up—"

"He says that?"

Noelle cringed. "It's happened."

"If any man told me to shut up, they'd never see me again."

"We're married," argued Noelle. "You don't understand how it is. And he works so much. He doesn't need me being a bitch."

"You are the last person who could ever be a bitch. Yes, you're frank and say what's on your mind, but you are *not* a bitch."

Noelle was quiet for a long second. She couldn't remember the last time she'd given Derrick her opinion on anything; she always just rolled with what he said. When she first worked at a bar, she'd learned how to get respect from her customers. Even the difficult ones usually responded when she called them out on bad behavior. Why hadn't she done that with her husband?

He didn't respect her.

He loved her—he said he did.

But the respect was gone.

What happened?

She thought back to the night they'd met. She'd been on such a high as she stared at him over pie, and she knew he had been too. "I don't know what I did to make him be like that," she said slowly.

"Stop it! Do you hear yourself?" Savannah leaned across the table and grabbed her hand. "You're blaming yourself for something he's done. Victim blaming. *You* know better than that. It's psychology 101."

"But—"

"Noelle. Stop. This man has been manipulating you for years. Can't you see it?"

Noelle closed her mouth.

Manipulating?

His little tantrums when he didn't like something she did.

His digs about her clothes and hair.

He always made her feel at fault. It'd started with small things. But the incidents had grown. She recalled how angry he'd been when she made them late for an event she'd had no knowledge of.

That's not normal.

Noelle stared at Savannah, suddenly seeing herself through her eyes.

A woman afraid to park a car. Afraid to pick out her own clothes. Afraid to speak her mind. Afraid to stand up to a man who supposedly loved her more than anything in the world.

But didn't act like it.

Savannah's right.

I'm not me.

"Holy fuck," said Noelle, her brain spinning. "How the fuck did I get *here*? I'm not a stupid idiot. *How did I let this happen?*" She straightened in her seat, feeling as if a blindfold had been yanked away.

Savannah laughed. "There's my Noelle. You have no idea how reassuring it is to hear you drop a couple of F-bombs. I haven't even heard you say *damn* since you met him."

Noelle thought back over the relationship. "It was so good at first. Everything was perfect. Our wedding was perfect," she said. "But little by little it changed. Although I swear the last year, he's been a completely different person. *He's changed.* Job stress, I guess."

"Stop making excuses for him. He's been a dick, and his mom has been a bitch." Savannah squeezed her hand. "You have no idea how long I've wanted to say something."

Noelle's eyes widened. "You've always talked about how hot Derrick is. I had no idea you felt this way."

Savannah shrugged. "You were in love—and he *is* hot. It was one of the nice things I could say about him, and it's my duty as the best friend to be supportive. But it's crossed the line, and I had to say something. He's manipulated you into being someone you're not. You need to look at this relationship as if it was one of your case studies from college. You've been on the inside for so long, you can't see things clearly." Savannah paused. "The fact is, you're in an abusive relationship." She lowered her voice. "Has he ever hit you?"

"No! It's not like that," Noelle said, a few of their loudest arguments coming to mind. "Well, not really."

"Explain," Savannah snapped.

"I mean . . . he's grabbed my arm. Maybe a few times. But he didn't hit me. He was just trying to get me to listen to him . . ." Her voice trailed off.

Savannah studied her. "You hear it now, don't you? The excuse you just made for his behavior."

Noelle's brain couldn't keep up. Savannah was right. "What do I do now?" she muttered to herself.

"What would you tell Eve if she was in your situation?" Savannah asked.

Noelle didn't want to say the words. They'd hovered in her subconscious for months, but she kept pushing them away. "Leave him," she whispered. Savannah blurred as Noelle's eyes filled. "I need to leave him."

"Or you could bury him deep," Savannah said, her eyes dancing.

Noelle choked out a laugh. "Can you bring the shovel?"

"For you to hit him over the head with?"

"That would happen first. Then we'd use it to dig."

"I'll bring two."

Noelle took a deep breath, feeling a lightening in every muscle of her body, almost as if each one were uncurling. She'd tied herself in knots and hadn't known it. "Thank you, Savannah," she whispered.

"What good are friends if they can't tell you when to leave your husband?"

Am I really going to do this?

27

The memorial service was as packed as Alice had expected it to be. The assemblyman had been young and popular. His murder had the community in shock.

Alice and a half dozen agents mixed with the mourners. Alice didn't know what exactly she was watching for, but she'd know it if she saw it. She blended into the crowd as they waited to enter, looking at faces and listening to hushed conversations. The doors finally opened, and the crowd politely swarmed inside. The service was being held in a church's huge auditorium, and as Alice scanned the rows and rows of chairs, she wondered if it was big enough to hold the crowd she'd seen. She walked up and down a few aisles, nodding mournfully at the few people who caught her gaze. The agents planned to spend the bulk of the service at the back of the room, but she'd asked Oscar to sit right behind the Marshall family, wanting eyes and ears close.

Will the killer show up?

Will our suspect wear a suit or a black dress?

The previous few days of the investigation had uncovered a wealth of information. The biggest surprise was that a year ago Derrick Bell had purchased an enormous life insurance policy with Noelle as the sole beneficiary. He'd also made a will that left everything to her: his condo and all his investment and savings accounts. The will had been written around the same time he bought the policy.

Noelle Bell was now a very wealthy woman.

Noelle had been stunned, stating again that she'd had no idea about the life insurance or will. Alice also discovered that Derrick had bought a life insurance policy of the same size on Noelle with himself as the beneficiary.

Noelle had blinked rapidly when she learned about the life insurance policy on her and absently touched the back of her head, no doubt understanding how close she'd come to dying. Alice believed that Noelle hadn't known about it; otherwise her sisters would have been the beneficiaries in addition to her husband.

Noelle would never leave out her family.

Three-quarters of the seats in the church auditorium were taken. Alice noted Oscar was in place, then took her position at a side wall next to other standing mourners. Someone flashed the lights, and people rushed to fill the rest of the chairs. Alice could see the back of Noelle's head and her grandfather beside her. Alice knew her sisters were close but couldn't see them through the crowded rows. Not far away she spotted Derrick's sister, Lora, as she turned to speak to her mother. The two families had sat near each other but kept separate.

There was a growing rift between the Marshalls and the Bells.

Catherine and Stan Bell couldn't believe Derrick had left everything to Noelle.

Noelle hadn't recovered her memory of the attack, and the Bells didn't believe she was trying hard enough to get it back.

Noelle had shown Alice texts from Catherine, begging her to see one of her friends who was a psychiatrist or at least try hypnosis. But it was too soon. The doctors said her injury needed more healing time.

Alice had seen the texts because she'd been living with Noelle for the last four days.

Some people believed Alice was there for Noelle's safety, to protect her from Derrick's killer. Others believed she was there to discover if Noelle had killed her husband.

Both were correct.

At first Noelle had thought to stay with her grandfather, but she'd told Alice she was worried someone would come to the home and attack her, putting Lucia, Daisy, and her grandfather at risk. There wasn't room for Alice to move into that house, so she and Noelle found a short-term rental not far from her grandfather's home.

Roommates.

It wasn't unusual for the FBI to embed an agent in a home when the situation called for it. Alice had shortened her office hours and worked as much as possible from her laptop. Noelle often paced the home and its small backyard, as she had little to keep her occupied. Alice had instructed her not to leave the home unless she could go with her. So Noelle had family come to her at the rental, along with Savannah, who'd even spent a night.

There'd been a lot of wine that evening.

Glaringly absent were any visits from the Bell side of the family. Not one of them had offered to spend time with Noelle, which made Alice furious.

Her husband was murdered.

The Bells acted as if only they deserved to suffer.

Alice saw pain every day on Noelle's face. It wasn't just that her husband had been killed; the media hounded her, popping up whenever she stepped out of the house. Noelle started using a grocery delivery service, only to have a reporter pay off a delivery driver, pose as a driver himself, and actually step into the house. Alice had heard him talking to Noelle and immediately thrown him out when the topic turned to the murder.

Alice's protective mother-bear feelings didn't make sense. Noelle was much taller than she and had no problem standing up for herself.

In fact she seemed to have gained confidence since she'd moved in with Alice. She'd brought in some free weights since she couldn't go to the gym. It'd only been a few days, but already Noelle seemed stronger and held her chin higher. Alice was impressed. Many victims would have pulled inside themselves, barely talked, and stopped moving. Noelle was the opposite; she was constantly on the move.

Alice had brought over her freestanding punching bag and shown Noelle how to use it. She caught on instantly. Her aggression had surprised Alice, and Noelle spent hours working with it. Several old coworkers had referred to Noelle as a physical force. Alice hadn't seen that in her until now. Noelle had also mentioned it after her first day with the bag, commenting on her loss of strength. Now she was determinedly working to get back to her former level.

This must be who she was before the attack.

I allowed the battered victim in a hospital bed to color my first impression.

Every day Noelle peppered Alice with insightful questions about the case. She wanted to hear about forensics, lab tests, and even the autopsy. She was curious about everything, and her thought processes mirrored Alice's when she followed the evidence.

Noelle had been genuinely surprised to discover Derrick had been taking antianxiety medications. "He never said a word. Why would he hide that from me?" But then Noelle had dropped her gaze. "I guess he wasn't the only one."

"Meaning?" Alice then learned that Noelle was on birth control and had been faking that she was trying to get pregnant.

"Don't tell his family," Noelle had requested. "It's bad enough that I lied to him about the pill. They don't need another reason to dislike me."

"Why didn't you tell Derrick?" Alice had asked.

Noelle had looked away. "I didn't want a baby."

Alice had stared at her for a long time, but Noelle didn't offer more information.

There's more to that answer.

Alice barely listened as the mayor of Sacramento and a state senator delivered somber speeches at the memorial, but she paid close attention when Derrick's brother walked up to the podium. Noelle had turned down an opportunity to speak, saying she wouldn't be able to get a word out.

Jason Bell read from notecards as a recording of family videos and photos played on the giant screen behind him. He spoke fondly of his younger brother, sharing some funny stories and sparking laughter in the audience. Jason went on to talk about the people who'd been close to Derrick. Friends, coworkers, family.

He didn't mention Noelle.

What the fuck?

Also missing were any photos of Derrick and Noelle's wedding on the giant screen. Alice only saw Noelle in the background in a few political photos, speaking with other people.

Noelle must feel horrible.

Alice watched Jason return to his seat, where his father patted his shoulder and he got a hug from his mother. She'd known the family disliked Noelle, but not mentioning her at her husband's memorial service was a new kind of low. A subtle murmur went through the crowd. Alice wasn't the only one who'd noticed. She glared daggers at the back of Catherine's head, surprised that the woman, who was so concerned about everything her family did in public, would allow this to happen. No doubt there were reporters in the audience; Noelle's absence from the speech and photos would be noted.

And the press will speculate about the murder investigation. Noelle was avoided because the Bells believe she's involved in Derrick's death.

Catherine and Stan had never asked to see photos of their son's body. The medical examiner had started to give a minimal description, but Catherine had tearfully cut him off, saying she couldn't hear any more. Alice understood that. No one wanted permanent mental images of their battered child.

The medical examiner had confirmed that Derrick died instantly when the iron elephant struck him in the face. The elephant's trunk had left a distinctive mark, and Derrick's tissue and saliva had been found in the elephant's crevices. He reported that all the battering from the crowbar and kicks had occurred after death, and Alice recalled that there'd been little or no blood where the crowbar had broken the skin, indicating the heart had stopped pumping blood. The medical examiner had determined the bruises were all postmortem by analyzing the damaged tissue, where he discovered a lack of both inflammation and a specific leukotriene, a molecule found in bruises that occur before death.

Fingerprints from Noelle, Derrick, and their house cleaner plus other prints that couldn't be identified were found on the elephant. No prints were on the landline. The woman caller must have wiped it down.

They never found a crowbar, and no one knew if Derrick had owned one.

Cellular signals indicated that Noelle had driven home from the city after her lunch with Eve. She might not remember much of the drive, but evidence showed she'd done what she thought she had. More signals and credit card charges showed Noelle had gone to a mall before lunch. Once this evidence was presented to Noelle, she managed to recall that she'd bought shoes and two silver bracelets that morning. And Starbucks.

"I wore the bracelets to lunch," she'd slowly added, clearly thinking hard.

Two silver bracelets had been sent with her clothes to the lab.

It appeared Derrick hadn't left the house that day—or at least his phone and car indicated he hadn't. His staff had confirmed that he'd called early to let them know he was taking the morning off, but he hadn't shared his reason with anyone, even his assistant, Jon. That morning Noelle had left to go shopping and meet Eve under the assumption that Derrick was going to his office. She recalled that he'd been in the shower when she left and that he hadn't told her he wasn't going to work that day.

Law enforcement didn't have a suspect, and that fact grated on Alice. Especially since she was getting pressure from higher up and from the media. Tips had rolled in and were being dissected by her team. More people were sifting through a stack of threatening emails going back an entire year, senders being traced.

Alice was surprised at how many people used their regular email addresses to send hate. For some reason, they felt safe at their keyboards while writing angry and sometimes violent emails.

She scanned the mourners. It was a silent and attentive crowd. Sad faces. Many tissues. Several people holding hands.

I bet some of those emails came from these people.

Alice had met many liars in her job. Their faces rarely gave away the ugly thoughts dancing in their brains.

I don't care about catching liars.

I want to catch his killer.

28

Three weeks since Derrick Bell's murder

Alice made another cup of decaf, hoping to trick her body into believing the coffee had caffeine—but not *too* much since it was nearly 1:00 a.m. She pushed some buttons and listened to the machine grind the beans and then watched it fill her cup. The Italian machine had come from Noelle's giant home to the kitchen of their little shared rental house. Alice had thought the contraption was ridiculous until she tasted her first cup.

Now she couldn't imagine drinking the brew from her Mr. Coffee.

She and Noelle had been roommates for two weeks.

They'd settled into a routine. Noelle liked to cook, and Alice didn't, so Alice grocery shopped from Noelle's list and enjoyed her delicious meals. Noelle expanded Alice's wine palate, and Alice taught her how to fold a fitted sheet and fix a frozen garbage disposal. Noelle was easy to live with, and they enjoyed each other's company, but Alice missed her silent apartment and alone time. She'd lived alone for several years since her divorce, and she loved it.

Alice took her cup of decaf to the kitchen table and sat to continue staring at her laptop screen.

Derrick Bell's murder case had not moved forward. Yes, they'd conducted hundreds of interviews and processed a lot of evidence, but they *still* didn't have a suspect.

Pressure from all directions to solve the case continued to build. No wonder Alice rarely slept.

Tips from the public had started to dry up. But the public's crazy conspiracy theories had grown. The most common theory was that Derrick had been killed because of a legislative bill he'd voted against. Depending on the conspiracy du jour, farmers, high-tech companies, construction workers, or transportation companies were accused of his murder.

Each accusation was a load of bullshit. Or bull-methane if you considered the accusations due to Assemblyman Bell's vote on ways to limit cow methane.

The FBI had scrutinized Derrick Bell's bank accounts and learned he liked to carry cash. He'd removed several thousand dollars every week for years. According to Noelle and his family, this was normal. "He's a generous tipper," Noelle had said.

Thousands of dollars in tips?

"He hands out cash all the time," his sister, Lora, had said. "Homeless people. Senior citizens. Lemonade stands. And he almost always pays in cash at stores." His credit card statements had backed up this claim. There were very few charges from grocery stores, department stores, or gas stations.

"Why?" Alice had asked. No one in his family had a clear answer. It was simply what Derrick had done since high school.

Lora was the only member of the Bell family who had been in touch with Noelle. The rest continued to ice her out as if she'd never been married to Derrick. For some reason, the family had chosen to blame Noelle for Derrick's death—they didn't have proof, and they never said it out loud, but after speaking with each family member, Alice found it apparent in their attitude.

"It's not an easy family to join," Lora's husband, Stewart, had said during his interview with Alice and Oscar. "Believe me, as someone who married into the family, I know. I've felt bad for Noelle since Derrick proposed."

"Did you say something to her?" Alice had asked.

He'd shrugged. "I told her Catherine was tough and to never expect approval from the family."

"Is that what they did to you?" asked Oscar.

"I got a reluctant pass—sort of. My job is the kind that automatically gave me some status, so they respected that. Didn't mean they were friendly, but there was a small level of respect. The absolute minimum." Stewart Greer was a plastic surgeon. Catherine had been one of his patients when she suggested he meet Lora. A few years after their wedding, the Bells helped finance his surgical center, which was the envy of every plastic surgeon north of Los Angeles. "I was stunned when I heard that Derrick was dating a bartender. I assumed he wasn't serious about Noelle, but I changed my mind the first time I saw them together. He was nuts about her and vice versa." Stewart had shrugged. "I knew Catherine—and Jason—would never get past that."

"But Derrick's father, Stan, didn't mind that she was a bartender?" Oscar seemed skeptical.

"Of course he did, but he wasn't one to be an ass about it like some of the others."

"And your opinion of Derrick?" Alice had asked.

"Derrick is—was okay."

"But?" Alice could tell Stewart was holding back.

Stewart had looked from Alice to Oscar and back, clearly mulling over something. "He had a veneer, you know? I never felt like I got to know or see the real man. I think he was intimidated by me—well, by my job and education," Stewart said slowly. "He had this way of delivering a subtle dig at me or what I do and then laughing it off. As if that made what he said okay. Deep down I think he was extremely insecure."

Alice had been surprised. "You're the first person to say that."

Stewart had lifted one shoulder. "I could be wrong." His gaze had told Alice he didn't believe he was wrong.

"You're up late." Noelle entered the kitchen. "Not sure why I even say that. It seems to be the norm for both of us." She set a tiny cup under the coffee machine and selected the espresso option.

Decaffeinated espresso.

"Very true," said Alice, closing the laptop where she'd been reviewing the transcript from Stewart Greer's interview.

"Anything new?" asked Noelle.

"No," said Alice. She hated how often she had to say that.

Noelle took her tiny cup and sat at the table, her shoulders low. "I'm worried I'm going crazy."

"Your psychiatrist and therapist claim you're not crazy," Alice said with a smile. Noelle had regularly met with both professionals since leaving the hospital and often shared some of those conversations with Alice. Living together had eased the women into a solid friendship. Noelle had a high respect for Alice's work—even when Alice had nothing to report—and Alice admired how Noelle had pulled herself together after the tragedy. As the two women grew closer, Alice firmly believed she was maintaining her objectivity. She was always on the lookout for signs that Noelle had been involved in her husband's murder.

But Alice had seen gaps in Noelle's short-term memory. She'd occasionally repeat something she'd already said and forget things Alice had told her. Sometimes she had the day of the week wrong. Once she'd let a pot of water boil over on the stove. Alice had been close enough to hear it and turn it off. Noelle had gotten in the shower, completely forgetting that she'd started to make pasta.

Noelle complained of headaches at the back of her skull. Reading was painful after an hour or two, and the pain kept her from doing things that involved close-up work. The doctors had said these symptoms were typical and they could ease.

Could ease.

Their words hadn't given Noelle a lot of confidence, but she continued to work with the professionals, determined to overcome the memory gaps. An aura of frustration often hovered around Noelle:

Derrick's murderer hadn't been caught, her life might be on hold until this person was found, and her brain wasn't performing like it should.

But those things hadn't affected her intelligence, empathy, or drive.

"You have every right to feel like you're going crazy," said Alice. "You've been cooped up in the house for quite a while."

"Doctor visits are the high points of my days," Noelle said ruefully.

"What will you do when this is all over?" asked Alice, trying to redirect the woman's thoughts. As the beneficiary of Derrick's assets, Noelle would never have to work again. But Alice suspected Noelle wanted to do more than serve on nonprofit boards.

"I don't know." Noelle sipped her espresso. "Maybe I'll go back to school and get a graduate degree so I can do something in psychology." She made a face. "As long as I can remember answers during tests, so I won't flunk out."

Her tone was light, but Alice knew Noelle was sincerely concerned. "You can learn other techniques. Use other parts of your brain to help with how you recall things." They'd both read up on the topic. There was hope.

"I know," said Noelle. "But I'm not feeling a strong desire to go back to school. Or to tend bar," she said with a grin. "Although I miss the constant activity and the interaction with customers."

"Have you thought about law enforcement?" The idea had come to Alice as she'd watched Noelle beat the crap out of her punching bag two days ago. "You like to help people, you're intelligent, you love to solve puzzles and always ask good questions."

Noelle stared at her.

"I'm serious." Alice leaned forward. "I think you'd be damn good at it. You'd put in a few years as an officer and then focus on moving up to detective. Maybe even a command position. Or you could consider the FBI."

Noelle still stared.

Now that Alice had said the words out loud, she discovered she liked the idea more and more for Noelle. "You understand people. I think you're a natural at that, and with your psychology background, it'd be a big help when dealing with the public. You'll have to put up with some shit, but I think this could be really rewarding for you."

"My grandfather was a police officer," Noelle said thoughtfully, but skepticism lurked in her eyes.

"I know. And this would be an amazing challenge for you," Alice continued since Noelle hadn't outright rejected the idea. "You could do a lot of good. I started with the Cedar Rapids Police Department. After five years there, I applied to the FBI. I could have done that first, but those five years taught me a lot of valuable skills that I use every day."

"How did you go from Iowa to Sacramento?" asked Noelle.

"You go where the FBI sends you, but I had a little input."

Noelle made a face. "Not sure I like that part."

"Then work for the Sacramento Police Department. Or any other police department around here. I know you want to be near your family."

Noelle looked thoughtful, her gaze distant. "What about my memory?"

"You have to trust that it's going to get better. If anyone can overcome it, you can."

Her eyes suddenly damp, Noelle extended a hand across the table, and Alice took it. "Thanks, Alice," she whispered. "I needed that bit of hope and direction."

"You bet," said Alice. "And if you decide this is a possibility for you, I'll support you with whatever you need. You'd be incredible at it."

"I'm not sure what my grandfather will think. There weren't a lot of women officers in his time." Noelle didn't look concerned.

"Then show him how it should be."

"Maybe."

29

"After six years with the Sacramento Police Department—one year as a detective—I made a lateral transfer to Deschutes County as a detective," finished Noelle. "I was ready for a change of scenery."

"During those six years, the Bells continued to publicly cast doubts on your memory loss," said Agent Rhodes, not unkindly.

"That fed my goal to change my scenery. Everywhere I went, people questioned me about Derrick. I was sick of it." Noelle appreciated the sympathy on Rhodes's face. "I was damn good at my job at the Sacramento Police Department, but it was time for a fresh start. My sister had talked forever about moving to this area. When I visited, I fell in love with it too."

Bend had four distinct seasons. Green springs, hot summers, cooling autumns, and some snow in the winters. And tons of blue sky every month.

"When did you change your last name back to Marshall?" asked Agent Keaton.

"When I moved to Oregon. I was ready to leave the Bells behind, and that included my name." She looked sharply at both men. "When do you interview Derrick's family?"

"We already did," said Keaton.

"Do they still hate me?"

Both men looked taken aback, but neither spoke up.

Noelle relished the discomfort and the truth on their faces. "I see. Don't worry about it. I get occasional emails from Catherine or Jason that tell me exactly where I stand with them."

"They email you?" Rhodes asked in surprise. He exchanged a look with Keaton that told Noelle the Bells hadn't mentioned that tidbit.

"Yep. And let me know they still believe I'm hiding the identity of Derrick's killer."

"They *say* that?" asked Keaton.

"I can read between the lines." The emails stung. She'd never done anything to that family except try to fit in for the sake of her husband. But they continued to blame her. "Have you talked to his old staff?"

"Yes. And we've also spoken to several of his friends," said Keaton.

Neither his staff nor his friends ever spoke to me again.

Noelle checked the time. "It's almost dinner. Are we about finished?"

As Keaton considered the question, Rhodes glanced at him and then back at Noelle. "Yes, we can be done for today. We'll want to touch base again in a few days."

"You're not going back to Sacramento?" asked Noelle as she stood and stretched her back. She was ready to have the FBI out of her hair.

"We have a team working in Sacramento," said Rhodes. "We have more interviews to do here."

Noelle froze and eyed him for a long moment. "The only people in this area who had a connection to Derrick are my family members."

"Correct."

"Shit." She grimaced. Lucia was now thirty-one, and Noelle was highly protective of her youngest sister. College hadn't worked out for Lucia, and she went from job to job, never able to settle into one. Lucia had little focus, and it seemed as if she'd never become a responsible adult.

Noelle didn't know who or what to blame.

Her overprotective grandfather? Their lives' upheaval after Derrick's murder? The fear about Noelle's injury and long recovery? Simply her impressionable age at the time? Genetics?

Most likely a mix of all.

Their grandfather's death a few years later had struck another blow to all the sisters. The death caused Lucia to fiercely cling to Daisy, terrified that her great-aunt would die any day. Moving to Bend had helped Lucia relax. She'd benefited from the change of scenery too.

Lucia currently worked at the humane society taking care of dogs. Working with the animals gave her some peace, but she often sobbed over the abused and very sick ones.

She had a huge, sensitive heart.

Eve had become a rock for Noelle. Always the levelheaded one, she'd recovered quicker than her sisters from trauma in their lives and often held both their hands. Her love of children had directed her toward teaching, and she had taught grade school for several years. Adam had left politics after Derrick's death. He now worked in marketing for a large Oregon tech company. Lucia lived in a garage apartment at their home outside of Bend. Great-Aunt Daisy had lived with them for a while but moved to a retirement home four years ago, where she'd become the unofficial activities coordinator and relished playing Cupid for her friends. She'd been the driving force behind two of the residents' marriages and was always scheming to create more.

For a woman who'd never married, Daisy had developed a touch for creating romance between senior citizens. Her hearing and eyesight had worsened, but she'd grown sweeter every year. All three sisters visited at least once a week.

"Promise me that you'll be gentle with Lucia," Noelle said to Agent Rhodes. "She's very sensitive. The upheaval in our lives after Derrick's death rattled her for a long time. I don't think she's ever stopped worrying that someone will come after me to finish the job." Her hand started to rise to touch the back of her head, but Noelle immediately forced it back down.

Rhodes met her gaze. "Of course."

"Thank you." She was confident he'd soften Keaton's tough questions for her sister. Rhodes had occasionally reworded Keaton's questions during Noelle's interview. Keaton hadn't appreciated it, but Noelle had.

"How is your great-aunt?" asked Rhodes, sliding his laptop into a messenger bag. "Would she handle an interview well?"

"She'll talk your socks off," said Noelle, pulling on her thick coat. "Keeping her on topic will be the hard part."

"I'll make sure we go in prepared," he said solemnly.

Noelle believed him. "Thank you for buying my coffee this morning."

"What?" Keaton looked up from putting away the camera equipment and raised a brow.

"I was behind Agent Rhodes at Starbucks," said Noelle. "He bought my coffee." She watched Rhodes's face, wondering if he'd wanted that little purchase to be a secret.

"I didn't know who she was," Rhodes said to Keaton. "And I wasn't hitting on you," he rapidly added, looking at Noelle. She swore his cheeks pinked a little. "The person before me had done the same, so I continued it."

"Which left me to buy coffee for a bunch of teenagers or else be the horrible person who ended the streak," said Noelle. "My surprise latte made me happy enough to do so, and I could imagine those kids' delight at their free coffee."

"Huh." Keaton refocused on picking up their equipment.

Unable to hold back her grin, Noelle met Rhodes's gaze, and his eyes narrowed as he realized she'd tried to get him in a little trouble with Keaton.

"I bought you coffee," he said in a low voice as they both moved toward the door. "That's how you repay me?"

"Your flash of concern that Keaton wouldn't approve was worth the thirty dollars I left for those kids."

He opened the door for her, and she went through.

My God. He smells amazing.

She'd already noticed that neither man wore a wedding ring, but that didn't mean anything in law enforcement. Many officers didn't wear one simply to keep the public's attention out of their personal lives.

"Noelle!"

She glanced down the hall and spotted Mercy Kilpatrick, the FBI agent she'd hoped to see when she'd arrived that morning. "Hey, Mercy."

The dark-haired woman caught up with them and immediately held out a hand to Rhodes. "Mercy Kilpatrick."

He shook her hand. "Max Rhodes. Sacramento."

"I know," said Mercy. "Everyone here is curious about the secret meeting you're holding in our office." She studied Noelle with her intense green gaze. "You good?"

"Yes. Ready to go home. Long day."

"Sorry about that," said Rhodes. "We're done for the day too."

"Do you need some restaurant suggestions?" Mercy asked Rhodes.

"Actually I don't," said Rhodes. "My sister lives in Bend. Keaton and I are eating at her home tonight."

"Terrific," said Mercy. She and Noelle said their goodbyes to the agent, and he headed toward the lobby. "Wow." Mercy pushed an elbow into Noelle's side as she watched him leave.

"Stop it," said Noelle. "This is a professional thing."

"He looks like a younger version of that actor." Mercy scowled, thinking hard.

"From *The Walking Dead*?" asked Noelle. The handsome actor had crossed her mind several times during the interview. "The psychotic asshole who beats in people's heads with his barbed wire–wrapped baseball bat?"

"Yes, that's him, but he's had lots of nicer roles."

"True, but that was the one I kept thinking of while I was in there."

"The interview was that bad?" Mercy gave a sympathetic look.

Noelle paused. She'd never discussed Derrick or her past with anyone in Oregon, and that included coworkers, neighbors, and acquaintances.

But Mercy is a very close friend.

"How much do you know about our meeting?" Noelle asked Mercy.

"Absolutely nothing. It's been hush-hush. All we were told was that two agents out of Sacramento needed an interview room. We didn't know they would be talking to you until five minutes before you showed up."

"That's it?" Noelle asked skeptically.

"Yes. Why? Is everything okay?" Concern filled Mercy's face.

Noelle eyed her for a long moment. If she didn't tell her, Mercy would hear through the gossipy law enforcement grapevine. Noelle was surprised it wasn't already circulating.

"Do you have time for a drink?" asked Noelle.

"Absolutely."

30

At a small table in the noisy bar, Noelle spilled the story of her marriage and everything she knew about Derrick's murder. Mercy sat with her mouth half-open as she listened, occasionally interrupting with questions.

"An unsolved murder in the California legislature?" Mercy said when Noelle was done. "No wonder the FBI is taking another look. I'd heard you'd been married twice, but I didn't know if there was any truth to it. You always avoided the topic, and people like to speculate."

"At least that fact is accurate," said Noelle. "If anyone had heard a whisper of the murder, stories would be flying, and they would probably be very wrong. You don't know how nice it's been to live without locals or media recognizing me on the street or during an investigative call."

"And in thirteen years, there hasn't been a single suspect in his murder?" asked Mercy.

"Lots of theories. A killer passing through town. Angry ex-girlfriend. Angry constituents. But there were no camera views or physical evidence pointing at anyone. Since I was still living in town and became the recipient of Derrick's wealth, a lot of focus and speculation circled around me."

"I thought they cleared you right away."

"Sort of. It was more that they couldn't prove I *did* do it."

"They thought you'd crack the back of your own skull?"

"It's possible to do." Noelle shrugged.

Mercy's eyes narrowed. "You said you didn't remember the incident when they questioned you. Has there been any change in your memories in all these years?"

Noelle sighed. "Not really. I don't recall being at the house that day. My memory is still crap and—" She stopped, aware she'd almost revealed a secret.

"And what?"

"It doesn't have anything to do with the case," said Noelle, and took a drink from her beer.

"But it has something to do with you. After having your skull cracked, I bet your head still bothers you, doesn't it?"

Dammit.

Tell her.

"You can't repeat to *anyone* what I'm about to say," said Noelle, holding Mercy's gaze. "Not even Truman," she ordered, referring to the agent's husband.

"Does it break the law? Is it something I'd be compelled to report?"

"No."

"Then you have my word," said Mercy.

Noelle breathed deep, searching for strength, the confession swirling around her and fighting its reveal. "I still struggle with some short-term memory issues. I occasionally have gaps," she admitted. "I've trained myself to make notes about *everything*, and I use a dozen recollection techniques, but some things still slip by."

She studied Mercy's face, waiting for a reaction.

The agent didn't disappoint.

"What sort of things?" Mercy asked with a scowl. "Does this affect your job?" She paused, and a confused expression filled her face. "Wait. How would you know if you forgot something vital on a case? Does Evan know about this?" Evan was a Deschutes County detective who often worked with Noelle.

These are the exact questions I wanted to avoid.

"I think I'd be called into my boss's office pretty often if it affected my work. And no, I haven't told Evan." She met Mercy's gaze. "The lapses are very infrequent."

"I'll rephrase what I just said . . . How do you know that? You can't know that you've forgotten things."

"It doesn't happen that often," Noelle repeated. "Years ago I'd head into the bathroom to take a shower and discover that the shower floor was already wet. Or my sister would show up for a dinner I'd completely forgotten. I've barely experienced things like that in years. I firmly believe my memory is improving," she lied.

She *had* thought it was better, but last week she'd been startled to find a frozen lasagna in one of her cupboards. She could picture herself setting it in the freezer next to her ice cream when she unpacked her groceries. But the soggy mess in her cupboard said otherwise.

The week before, she'd forgotten where she'd parked at Walmart. She'd wandered the huge lot, wondering if her vehicle had been stolen, but knew that with her memory lapses she needed to keep looking. She'd finally found it and sat in the driver's seat for a long time, fighting back tears.

"How on earth did you do your job at first?" asked Mercy.

"Like I said, I was careful and made very thorough notes. I've developed routines to avoid forgetting something."

Mercy stared at her, wonder in her eyes.

Noelle tensed, defensiveness stiffening her spine. "I'm good at my job. Damned good."

"I know. Everyone says so," Mercy said slowly. "I'm just bewildered at how you function."

"I'm not broken. I function just fine," Noelle snapped. "It's like people whose vision sucks so they wear glasses. I have work-arounds too."

"But—"

"*Mercy.* Don't make me regret that I shared this with you."

I already do.

Mercy exhaled and slumped on her stool. "You're right. I'm being unfair. There's never been a whisper of a complaint about your job performance, and Evan has nothing but high praise for you." She looked contrite. "I won't tell anyone."

"Thank you."

"Is your head hurting?"

Noelle yanked her hand away from her hair. She hadn't been aware she was rubbing the back of her head. "It bothers me sometimes. Usually in high-stress situations."

Mercy touched Noelle's arm, sincerity in her gaze. "I'm sorry I did that to you."

"It's okay." She sighed and focused on relaxing tense muscles. "It feels good that someone else knows. It's sort of freeing," she said with a bit of surprise.

"Sometimes friends can help lighten the heavy weight of secrets," said Mercy, looking into her beer.

She has her own deep secrets.

"This is a weird question," Mercy said slowly. "And you don't have to answer, but is this part of the reason you don't date?"

Noelle was stunned at the woman's intuitiveness. "I was married twice," she said lamely.

"And one of those marriages came to a horrific end," said Mercy. "I understand how that would make you avoid relationships, but is the fear of someone discovering your memory issues part of it?"

Noelle was silent for a long moment. "Maybe. But I also carry a lot of baggage," she said wryly. "Who'd want to deal with all that?"

"Everyone at our age will have baggage."

"I'm forty-two," said Noelle. "I've got a few years on you."

"Not that many. All I'm saying is don't let this get in your way. I shut people out for a long time because I worried someone would reject me for . . . doing what I do. I wasn't like everyone else."

Noelle knew Mercy had been raised by preppers. She still stored food, fuel, and medication and maintained alternative power sources at a hidden cabin just in case the world went to shit.

"When Truman found out," Mercy continued, "I discovered it wasn't the embarrassing secret I'd thought it was."

"Truman's pretty special. You got a good one." Noelle was often envious of their deep relationship.

"He is. I'm very lucky." Mercy's lips quirked. "Anyway, you get my point."

"I do," Noelle whispered. Mercy had hit a bull's-eye. Noelle had long feared telling a man about her past. And her present.

Hey, my husband was murdered, and I was there, and I have no memory of who killed him. Did I mention I was a suspect?

And by the way, I might forget some of the things you just told me on this date.

For many years, she had kept men at arm's length to avoid any hurt. But according to Mercy, she could be making a mistake.

"Do you work tomorrow?" she asked Mercy.

"Nope."

"Me neither. Let's get dinner."

Mercy's green eyes lit up. "I'm starving, so absolutely. And you can tell me what it was like being married to someone in politics."

Noelle winced.

"That good, huh?" Mercy's tone was sympathetic.

"Let's just say I have many stories."

Like how I was gaslighted and manipulated.

Noelle remembered that she'd told the FBI agents how good her marriage was. She suspected it was more habit than anything, engrained in her so she and Derrick presented a united front for his constituents in public. She'd never said a word about how he treated her, both to avoid conflict with his family and to ward off personal questions.

Maybe it's time to start telling the truth.

31

Fire crackled in the giant fireplace, and Max Rhodes settled deeper into his sister Keira's giant sectional, his stomach feeling more than stuffed. He and Dave Keaton had been treated to the best dinner Max had eaten since the last time he'd visited his sister. Keaton had headed to a hotel after the meal, but Max was staying in his sister's guest room during their time in Bend.

Her husband, TJ, dropped heavily onto the other end of the sectional, kicked off his shoes, and put his feet up on the coffee table. "I'm glad she only cooks like that when you're in town," said TJ. "Otherwise I'd weigh three times what I do."

"She's always been a good cook," said Max. "Mom and Grandma saw to that."

TJ eyed him. "Missing home?"

"Sacramento is my home now."

"Yeah, but you've got roots here."

"I won't deny that." Max had grown up two hundred miles away, in Medford, Oregon. The southern Oregon town was on the other side of the Cascade mountains, but he'd often crossed over the range to ski or to spend summers in central Oregon with his grandmother, who'd lived twenty minutes from Bend.

He had to admit the area still felt like home.

"You visit your grandmother yet?"

"Maybe tomorrow. Depends when we finish our interviews."

TJ sat up. "Now that Keaton's left, can you tell us what exactly you're investigating in town?"

"Leave him alone, TJ," said Keira as she entered the room, a glass of wine in her hand. "You know better than to ask." She took a seat in an easy chair, stretched out her long legs, and added her feet to the coffee table. Everyone in Max's family was tall. He knew Keira had been teased about it as a kid, but now she embraced her height. One drunken night, with his eyes gleaming in admiration, TJ had told Max that Keira reminded him of an Amazon warrior and then gone into some details of their intimate role-play.

The images were still trapped in Max's mind.

TJ was the closest thing he had to a brother, so he hadn't broken the man's neck.

"No wine for us?" TJ asked his wife.

"Help yourself. It's on the kitchen counter. Max?" She looked at her brother.

"Not tonight," he said as TJ vanished into the kitchen.

"Now," said Keira, abruptly sitting forward with a glint in her eye. "Who are you interviewing and why?"

Max grinned. Keira always made different rules for herself. He'd known she'd corner him and ask, so he'd already decided what he could share.

"We're talking to the family of a murder victim. It happened thirteen years ago near Sacramento but was never solved."

"Ohhh." Keira was a true crime TV show and podcast addict. "Do you think one of the relatives did it?" she asked eagerly, making him laugh.

"You watch too much TV."

"I watch the real stuff. And you'd be amazed at how often it was a family member. Statistics back that up."

"They do," Max agreed.

When the FBI had revisited the case, they'd decided they wanted a closer look at Noelle. No one at the FBI would outright state it, but Max had inferred that Noelle was number one on their suspect list. After meeting her, Max sincerely hoped she wasn't involved in her husband's murder.

Everything indicated that she was a good cop. And an interesting human being. He'd learned from their interview that her values seemed to be in the right places.

"It's always the spouse," continued Keira.

"It's *often* the spouse," corrected Max.

She waved a hand. "You know what I meant."

Before they'd left Sacramento, he and Agent Keaton had interviewed retired FBI special agent Alice Patmore, who'd been part of the original investigation thirteen years ago. Patmore still lived near Sacramento and raised alpacas on a little farm to the west with her boyfriend. As they'd parked at her home, Keaton had stared at the animals, standing in a row at the fence, who'd watched them arrive.

"Those are the oddest-looking things I've ever seen," he'd said.

"Haven't you ever seen an alpaca before?" Max had asked, silently agreeing that the long necks and round furry heads made them look like Dr. Seuss drawings.

"Sure. On TV. Never in person."

Inside the house, after she'd poured them steaming cups of coffee, Patmore had been very blunt with her opinion about Noelle. "She didn't do it," she'd stated.

"But you never proved she didn't do it," Keaton had insisted.

"Are you new to the United States?" Patmore had snapped, glaring at Keaton. "Ever hear of innocent until proven guilty?"

Max had wisely kept his mouth shut.

"I've known this woman for thirteen years," Patmore had continued. "We keep in touch, and I can say with confidence that I know her character. She didn't do it."

"Maybe she didn't mean to do it," Keaton had said. "Shit happens. Accidents happen."

"Are you saying she accidentally beat him thirty-seven times with a crowbar?" Patmore asked politely.

Keaton had no answer for that.

"You helped her into the Sacramento Police Department," said Max.

"Is there a question in there?" asked Patmore, turning her probing gaze on him.

"Why did you help?" added Max.

"Why not? Noelle was struggling to find a direction in her life, and I knew she'd be damned good at the job." She shrugged. "I didn't help her get in; she did that on her own."

"So who do you think murdered Assemblyman Bell?" Max had asked.

"I don't know," Alice said simply, lifting her hands. "The evidence never indicated who could have been there that day besides Noelle."

Her name hung in the air for a long moment.

"She was the only one there," Keaton had finally said.

"No, someone made a phone call, and someone walked away with a crowbar." She scowled at him. "Did you not read anything on this case?"

Max knew he had; Keaton was trying to get a reaction out of Patmore.

"She could have made the phone call and hidden the crowbar," said Keaton.

"After she knocked herself out with it?"

"It's inconclusive that she was unconscious from the blow. Paramedics and police assumed she was." He shrugged. "Maybe she was faking it."

"Do you know how many years I've heard, 'Maybe she was faking it'?" Patmore had glared at him.

"Thirteen?" asked Max, earning his own glare.

"She's a good kid," said Patmore.

"Good kids have been known to kill," said Keaton.

"I'm tired of you throwing out clichés as if they're evidence," Patmore had said in an annoyed tone. "If you want to arrest her so badly, go find some evidence. I've got nothing for you."

"You really like this woman," Max had observed.

"Again. Is that a question?" This time there'd been an amused glimmer in her eye.

"No." Max had wrapped his hands around his coffee mug. "Tell me. After the murder investigation finished—"

"It never finished," stated Patmore. "It'll be finished when there is an arrest."

"Correct. I misspoke. After it had drastically slowed and Noelle was into her career with the Sacramento PD and even after she moved to Oregon, you've made it clear that the two of you stayed in contact."

"Correct. Lunches. Coffee. Just phone calls and texts once she left town."

"During those contacts, how many times did Noelle ask for a progress report on the murder?"

Patmore had paused. "We always talked about the case. Every single time we spoke."

"Maybe I didn't phrase that right," said Max. "Did Noelle specifically call to ask for updates?"

"She knew I'd tell her if something had popped up."

Still not what I asked.

The retired agent had held his gaze; clearly she'd known exactly what he was asking.

When a spouse has been murdered, the other spouse hounds the investigators. They flood the investigation with suggestions, bits of past conversations, receipts, any little thing they hope can help.

Noelle hadn't done that. She'd answered every question that was asked and handed over everything requested. But based on what Max had seen in the call records and read in the interviews, she had never initiated.

"Do you have phone calls on the anniversary of his death?" Max had asked.

"Noelle never wanted that. Which is understandable."

"According to our records, Noelle has never contacted the FBI about this case since you retired."

"I'll take your word for it," said Patmore. "Since I wasn't there."

"Why wouldn't she call for updates? She didn't contact the county sheriff's department either," Max had pressed.

"You'll have to ask her," Patmore had said. "If you want speculation from me, I'll guess that she wanted to leave the tragic event in the past. Everyone reacts differently, you know."

"Her husband was murdered," Keaton had said. "Horribly. I'd badger the police for decades if that's what it took to get results."

The retired agent had simply shrugged and sipped her coffee.

Alice Patmore was shrewd. The record of her time at the FBI was spotless and full of commendations, but she offered little insight into the old case other than stating she didn't believe it had been Noelle.

Then who?

Max stared absently into his sister's toasty fire. "I don't think it's the spouse this time," he told Keira. "We interviewed her all day today."

"What's her name?" asked TJ, walking back into the room with a large wineglass filled to the brim. "Shoulda known Keira would get you to talk." He blew a kiss at his wife.

Max paused. He would trust Keira and TJ with his life. And they knew how important it was to keep anything he said about a case to themselves. "Noelle Marshall."

Keira tipped her head. "Why do I know that name?" she muttered as she pulled out her phone and opened her browser.

"I know you won't talk to anyone about this," Max said forcefully.

"Aha." Keira looked pleased at what she saw on her screen. "TJ, remember that shooting last year? A Deschutes County detective shot a man who'd killed a cop and kidnapped several other people? The detective's name was Noelle Marshall. Is that her, Max?"

"Yes." He'd read all the reports on the case. There were a lot of them.

TJ's brows rose. "You're investigating someone in law enforcement?" he asked Max.

"I'm doing my job," said Max. "Doesn't matter their profession."

"They called this woman a hero. She saved several lives by stopping that man," said Keira, still scrolling. "I don't see anything about her having a murdered husband, though."

"Probably because it's old news." Max decided to keep Noelle's previous last name to himself.

"Hmmm." Keira continued to focus on her phone.

She'll figure out the name and Noelle's history soon enough.

"You look wound up," said TJ, studying Max.

"I am," he admitted. "All-day interviews are stressful."

"You need to go for a motorcycle ride. That'll relax you. You can borrow mine. My gear should fit you."

Tempted, Max glanced through the windows at the dark sky. "Too late tonight."

There was nothing Max loved more than to take a bike on an open road. Bend had dozens of twisty country roads with little traffic that were ideal for a motorcycle ride. "Thanks, TJ. Your offer means a lot."

TJ waved a hand. "It's nothing. I know you'd loan yours to me."

"Maybe." Max kept his face expressionless.

"Bullshit! You know you would." TJ's eyes lit up as he laughed.

Riding was an escape. One that lit a fire inside Max and brought joy to his heart.

"Wanna see it?" asked TJ.

"He saw your new bike on his last visit," said Keira, still studying her screen.

TJ exchanged a look with Max, who grinned, knowing his brother-in-law had the same weird habit. Each of them sometimes sat alone in his garage for a long period and simply looked at his motorcycle.

It was a bit nerdy.

"I'll take another look at it," said Max, getting to his feet. TJ had already stood and was headed to the garage, wine in hand.

Keira muttered something that sounded like "Men."

Max grinned, knowing she loved riding behind her husband. She'd ridden with TJ since before they married.

In the garage, both men were silent a long moment, admiring the big KTM motorcycle.

"Miss your old job?" TJ asked.

"It was pretty awesome to be paid to ride a motorcycle every day." Max had been a motor—a motorcycle officer—for the Medford police before he applied to the FBI.

"The best."

"It really was."

"Weather is clear and cold all week," said TJ. "If you can find time, it's yours for a ride."

"Thanks." Max owned the same KTM motorcycle. Although his was a few years older, the Austrian machine had almost the same amount of addicting power. Weighing more than five hundred pounds, it was a beast that ate up the road. "Maybe I'll finish up early tomorrow."

His thoughts went to Noelle Marshall, wondering when they'd bring her back for another interview. First they needed to speak to the rest of her family.

The door to the house opened. "You two done gawking at that chunk of metal?" Keira asked.

"No," stated TJ, his gaze still on the bike. Neither he nor Max moved.

"I want a game of Uno," said Keira. "I deserve revenge."

"The rules of Uno provide no protection for spouses," TJ deadpanned. "If you're sitting next to me, and I have a Draw Four card, I'm going to play it."

"But three times in a row?" she complained.

TJ shrugged. "I like to win."

Max relaxed as their banter flowed around him. TJ and Kiera both liked to win, and games often grew loud with challenges thrown about and good-natured insults flying. Keira became ferocious with cards in her hands.

It made him feel at home.

"I'll trounce both of you," Max announced loudly over Keira's demand for a rematch. "Let's go."

After a last longing glance at the bike, he followed TJ back into the house.

I forgot how much I miss having family around.

32

"I was expecting your call." Alice Patmore's tone over the phone was matter-of-fact.

Noelle grinned as she sat in her vehicle in the sheriff's department parking lot the next morning, procrastinating about getting her workday started. "I expected that you'd expect it."

"Sounds like we know each other too well."

Leaving Alice was one of Noelle's only regrets about moving away from Sacramento. Alice had started as a hand-holder during the investigation but then became a friend and eventually her mentor as Noelle pursued a career in law enforcement. Several times Alice had suggested that Noelle apply to the FBI. When she stopped mentioning it a few years ago, Noelle thought Alice had finally given up but soon realized she'd passed the agency's age requirement.

Noelle was too old.

Ouch.

Noelle had flown back to Sacramento for Alice's retirement party three years ago, where she'd been surprised to meet Chuck, Alice's new boyfriend, who sold antiques. He was quiet, and adoration for Alice shone in his eyes. Noelle liked him immediately. Alice pulled Noelle aside and apologized for not ever mentioning him to her. "I wanted to know if it was going anywhere before I told people."

"You're living together," Noelle had said dryly. "Sounds like it went somewhere." To Noelle's delight, the comment made Alice blush.

They stayed in touch, but phone calls had mostly become texts, and the texts were often alpaca pictures. Alice had a white one named Noelle who she claimed was very bossy.

Noelle enjoyed updates about her namesake.

"What can you tell me about Agents Rhodes and Keaton?" Noelle asked. "Did you know they were coming here to hold interviews?"

"I did," said Alice. "But they'd asked me not to tell you, and I respected that."

Noelle wasn't pleased but she understood. "They blindsided me. Lured me in under false pretenses."

"I'm sorry about that too, but they have good reputations here in Sacramento. I knew you could handle anything they threw at you."

"I think I did pretty well," Noelle admitted. "I was definitely pissed at first."

"I'm sure you were." Alice chuckled. "When I spoke to them, they pushed and pulled at me, and I gave it right back. I thought they were decent interviewers, although a bit transparent. Seemed smart and determined."

"They plan to interview my family too," said Noelle. "Do they have an angle? Are they looking for something specific?"

"I think they're just digging around to see what they can stir up. I didn't pick up on an angle, and there haven't been any recent local rumors about the case. I don't think anything in particular triggered this deep review."

"It almost feels like harassment after this many years. The only equipment they didn't use during our conversation was a spotlight."

"You okay?"

Noelle took stock of her emotions. She was calm, although a touch worried about her sisters' experiences with the agents. "I had nothing new to tell them. I'm fine."

"Still having dreams?"

"You have to ask?" Noelle and Alice both knew she'd probably have them for the rest of her life. "The dreams had eased up for several months, but last night they decided to pay me a visit. No doubt a result of the interview."

"Elephants still?"

"Always." Noelle snorted. "Always the fucking elephants. They're everywhere in my dreams. Doesn't matter where I am during the dream. Even when I dream, I'm in my car or in a restaurant and there's always one in the background somewhere. It's not fair that I had to live in a house of elephants for years and then they decided to reside in my dreams for more than a decade."

"I think it's understandable that they plague you. They were Derrick's and represented him. I think that your old therapist was right that you need to talk about them as much as possible to purge them."

"I had actually liked the elephant that . . . that . . . was found next to Derrick." Noelle didn't need to state that the killer had bashed in Derrick's face with the iron elephant. She had seen the crime scene photos. Back then Alice had kindly edited out all views of Derrick's face, not wanting to traumatize her, but Noelle's imagination had supplied plenty of images.

After she'd made detective, she'd looked up the case and forced herself to view the unedited photos. Her imagination hadn't been far off.

"One time I knocked over that iron elephant, and Derrick yelled at me because it'd dented the wood floor," said Noelle. "I remember snatching it back up and being relieved that it wasn't damaged. Not because breaking the elephant would have made Derrick furious, but because I sort of liked it."

"That was a dream?"

Noelle's lips quirked at Alice's dry tone. "No, that really happened." For a year the floor dent had reminded her of the incident every time she'd walked past, and even today she could still feel the dread as she saw it fall and then clutched the heavy piece in her hands.

Thanks, Derrick.

"Nothing wrong with your memory."

"I wish." Noelle sighed. "Last night I dreamed that we were late for an event because I couldn't find my shoes. I was in an absolute panic, tearing through the house and digging through closets while Derrick shouted at me in the background."

"Did you find your shoes?"

Noelle chortled. "No. My alarm went off and I woke, relieved that it was over, but I swear I still heard faint echoes of his shouts in the room."

"Was that dream from a real event?"

"No. But it was an amalgamation of a dozen similar incidents."

"You suffered a lot of emotional abuse during your marriage," Alice said gently. "It can take years to fully rid it from your system. But you're one of the strongest people I know."

A huge ache filling her chest, Noelle suddenly missed her mother. She'd been thirteen when her mother died, still a child.

But she still remembered the verbal abuse her mother had suffered from Noelle's often absent father.

Why didn't I learn from that?

"I went from one mistake to another," Noelle murmured into the phone, aware Alice knew she was talking about both her marriages. "How could I not see the truth in Derrick? He only cared about himself. Why did I go along with that? I'm not a stupid person."

"Have you done anything stupid lately?" asked Alice.

Noelle went silent, abruptly remembering when she shot and killed a murderer last year.

Justified. Not stupid.

But that haunts me too.

"You were young," Alice continued. "You followed your heart both times."

"I did."

"Maybe you need to talk to someone again," Alice said gently.

"Someone" meant a therapist. Noelle had seen one for years after Derrick died and then again for several months after last year's shooting, but lately she'd simply powered through.

"Why would I talk to a therapist when I have you?" Noelle joked lamely.

"You've been in Oregon for years," said Alice. "Surely there's someone physically closer than me to talk to by now. And I don't mean a therapist. I mean friends."

Noelle thought back to her conversation with Mercy last night. She hadn't opened up like that to anyone outside of therapy since she'd moved to Oregon.

"Yeah, maybe there is someone," Noelle said gruffly, a lump in her throat. "She's FBI."

"I like her already."

Noelle ended the call after a few minutes, promising to keep Alice updated about the agents in town. Afterward she sat for a long moment in her car, thinking about the life she'd built in Bend.

She had a lovely home. She had a collection of amazing shoes. Her family was close by. Her coworkers were smart and capable and friendly.

Her life didn't suck. But she was a bit of a loner.

Alice and Savannah were her closest female friends. But both lived in a different state.

It wasn't just men that Noelle had kept at arm's length. She'd avoided letting women in too. She'd known Mercy for quite a while but had never suggested doing anything outside of work until yesterday. And their time together had been great.

Another possibility was Rowan Wolff, who had expressed interest in going hiking or out for drinks. The SAR dog handler was engaged to Detective Evan Bolton, whom Noelle liked working with very much. Spending some time with Rowan could be nice.

Maybe it's time I reach out a bit.

Noelle had played it safe for a long time. She'd believed that if she didn't let anyone get close to her, she'd never be hurt. But now she felt a little empty.

It always felt good to talk to Alice, who knew her inside and out. She needed more people in her life like that. But she was rusty at making friends.

Trust was a barrier.

Take some risks.

33

"My grandmother lives here," Max said with surprise as Keaton turned their car into the retirement community parking lot.

They had an appointment to interview Daisy Swanson, Noelle's great-aunt.

"My grandmother will kill me if she finds out I was here and didn't stop in to visit for a bit," Max added. "She's a bit of a tyrant." His grandmother Paulette had strong opinions about family. She insisted on regular visits from Keira and from Max's mother and two other sisters when they were in town.

He suspected Paulette had felt a disturbance in the Force when he'd crossed the city limits of Bend. Somehow she always knew when he was in town. He'd told only Keira he was coming because he didn't know what sort of free time he'd have.

"I'm sure we can find a few minutes for her," said Keaton as he lifted their equipment out of the back seat. "Get our work done first, though."

The retirement community was made up of small houses for independent living, apartments for a low level of care, and rooms in the main building for people who needed frequent medical attention. Max's grandmother lived in one of the small houses. After her husband died, she'd cheerfully moved from her home of forty years into the community. She was very social and wanted to meet new people.

After they checked in at the reception desk, a polite young man with a tattooed neck and a southern accent led Max and Keaton back outside to the clubhouse, a large building with a common area for games or parties and several smaller rooms for other activities. The tattooed man directed them to a room where they found a large table with several chairs. Cheerful sunlight streamed in the large windows, and it had a nice view of the manicured grounds. Max approved. It was much more relaxing for an interview than the conference room at the FBI. "I'll be back in a minute with Daisy," the tattooed man said with a grin. "She's quite the character."

The two had just set up their video camera when Daisy Swanson arrived with a young woman in tow, the young woman's relation to Noelle obvious in her face.

Lucia.

They'd requested an interview with Lucia, and she'd agreed to speak with them at the same location after Daisy's interview.

Lucia carefully scrutinized Keaton and himself, her large eyes hesitant. Max had watched videos of the youngest sister's interviews from thirteen years ago. She'd seemed ethereal back then. Delicate and tall and wispy. Now she was an older version of exactly the same. He knew she had trouble holding down a job and often relied on Noelle for financial support.

Noelle Marshall's financial position had stunned him. If he had that much money, he'd own forty motorcycles and a gigantic garage to keep them in. Two gigantic garages. He didn't care about having a nice house. All he needed was space for his toys and a cot to sleep on in the corner. He'd take world trips, traveling through foreign countries on a motorcycle.

And he wouldn't work.

Well, maybe I would.

Max liked what he did and firmly believed that he helped other people. As good as it sounded, he couldn't live on just motorcycle trips. He needed a purpose, and the FBI provided that.

Max and Keaton introduced themselves to the two women. Lucia said her name quietly and shook their hands. Daisy reminded him of Betty White. She had a similar warm smile, a cloudlike hairstyle, and a softly rounded face. Everyone's grandmother.

"My goodness, aren't you a tall one," Daisy said as she looked up at Max. "I like that." To his stunned surprise, she squeezed his bicep through his sport coat. "Strong too."

"Daisy." Lucia shot the men an embarrassed glance.

"Don't *Daisy* me. He knows I'm being silly." She winked at Max, who scrambled for something acceptable to say.

"It's fine," he forced out. "Have a seat, Ms. Swanson," he said as he pulled out a chair.

"Call me Daisy, please." She sat down and looked over at her grandniece. "You can go away now. I don't need you peering over my shoulder while I talk to these fine men. You can talk with them when I'm done."

"But I should—" began Lucia.

"Shoo. I'm just fine." Daisy smiled brightly at Max. "Now. Where are you from?" she asked.

Max paused, wondering if she'd forgotten why they were there. "We're from the FBI—"

"I *know* that. Where did you *grow up?*" She looked at Keaton, including him in her question. "I'm a California girl myself. Grew up on the coast not far from the redwoods but moved to the Sacramento area in my twenties."

Lucia gave the men a glance of sympathy as she went out the door.

"Oregon is nice," Daisy went on. "I don't mind living here now. I like seeing the snow on the mountains."

"It's beautiful here," agreed Max. "I grew up in Medford. I live in Sacramento now."

"Las Vegas," said Keaton, looking slightly stunned that Daisy was using the interview for her own pleasure.

Max turned to his partner in surprise. "I didn't know that."

"See?" said Daisy, clasping her hands in delight. "We're all learning something new. I heard that—"

"Ms. Swanson," cut in Keaton. "I hate to interrupt, but we're on a schedule, so we really need to get to our questions about Mr. Bell."

"I've already been interviewed about Derrick," said Daisy.

"We know," Max said patiently. "But that was thirteen years ago, so we're touching base with everyone to see if we can find anything new."

"You still don't know who killed that young man?"

"Not yet."

Daisy nodded thoughtfully. "It was a dreadful shock. Poor Noelle. We were very thankful she survived that blow to her head." Her lips pursed. "Such a horrible business. I don't know what her sisters—and us—would have done if we'd lost her."

"Us?" asked Keaton.

"My brother and I," said Daisy. "William. His daughter died when the girls were young. It absolutely crushed him, but we took in those girls, and I swear they saved him from drowning in his pain and loss. It was good to have them around. Little Lucia was only two. I don't think she has memories of her mother."

Max scrolled through some notes on his laptop, trying to recall what had happened to the girls' mother. "Breast cancer, correct?" he asked.

"Yes."

Silence hung in the room as they expected Daisy to continue to talk, but she simply looked at them, apparently done. After all her chatter, her abrupt quietness felt very odd.

Not much to say about that topic.

"How was it, suddenly having three more people in your household?" asked Max, simply to prod her along.

"The girls were so sad those first few years, but William and I did everything we could to make their lives happy. It wasn't easy for William either, he mourned the loss of his daughter for a long time. She'd looked like Eve, you know. It was like having her ghost around every day."

William Swanson had passed not long before Noelle moved to Oregon. Max pulled up photos of the grandfather and saw where the height in the family had come from. It'd bypassed Daisy but had clearly been handed down to the three sisters.

He was a police officer for almost three decades.

Max saw hints of the cop he'd been in the man's posture. He stood as if he was always ready for whatever came his way. "Ms.—I mean Daisy, how well did you know Derrick Bell?"

She considered the question. "That was a long time ago, you know."

"Do you remember how you felt about his marriage to Noelle?"

"Oh! What an event their wedding was." Daisy nodded emphatically. "I couldn't imagine the cost. But Noelle looked absolutely stunning. They were madly in love."

Max felt a subtle pang in his chest. He'd heard the words *madly in love* a million times, but he'd never felt it for himself. There'd been a few women who came close, but it had always fizzled out.

"Until they weren't," added Daisy.

"You think the couple fell out of love?" Max asked.

The woman tipped her head and focused out a window. "I know Noelle did. William and I talked about the change we'd noticed in her. It was like she'd had her spine sucked out of her back."

"How did William feel about that?"

"He was angry at Derrick."

A small chill went up Max's back. He recalled that Agent Patmore had written somewhere that William had stated he'd been unhappy about the change in Noelle since her marriage. But when Patmore had asked Daisy if she knew William's opinion of Derrick, Daisy had brushed the question aside and asked about the agent's earrings.

Max recalled reading the transcript and being amused.

Why didn't I wonder about Daisy's evasion?

Because everyone had said Daisy was scatterbrained. He looked up and met Daisy's gaze. It reflected kindness and interest. He saw no sign of confusion. Her question as they'd sat down together had simply been one of a woman wanting to get to know someone.

Max pulled up the photos of William again.

Tall. Strong. The skills of a cop.

Nearly every person interviewed on Noelle's side of the family had spoken of William's deep love for the three girls.

Did he hate Derrick enough to kill him?

Derrick had been severely beaten. Strong emotions had been present. It wasn't kill and run; it had been a prime example of taking out your anger on someone.

Thirty-seven crowbar blows. Kicks to the abdomen.

Scenarios rapidly played in Max's head as he tried to imagine William beating Derrick. Patmore's investigation stated that William Swanson had been at home during the day of Derrick's death. Lucia and Daisy had confirmed it.

Alibied by family.

It wasn't the strongest alibi, but it was accepted in the absence of evidence to place William at the murder scene.

But why would he hit Noelle in the head?

The only reason he could come up with was to keep Noelle from seeing that he'd been there.

Nothing else made sense.

For the first time, Daisy had stated that William had been angry about the change in Noelle. In Agent Patmore's interview with William, he had said the same, but no one else had. Until now.

Max wondered if Noelle's great-aunt was saying it now because they couldn't prosecute a dead man. Possibly she was trying to redirect the investigation toward a dead end.

Is she protecting someone?

Is it Noelle?

"Who else noticed the difference in Noelle?" asked Keaton.

Daisy waved a hand. "Oh, everyone." She glanced at the door through which Lucia had left. "Don't tell anyone I said that, okay? I'm not sure Noelle realized how being with that man crippled her."

"That's a strong word," said Max.

"Thankfully she snapped out of it," said Daisy with a serious nod. "She got away from him in time to return to her old self. I don't know if that would have been possible if their marriage had continued for a few more years."

Max's brain snared on Daisy's words. "She got away from him . . ." Daisy made it sound as if Noelle had escaped, not as if the marriage had been ended by a murder. Max thought back to Noelle's interview.

I loved my husband.

I loved my husband.

I loved my husband.

Max wondered if she had still loved him at the end.

34

Noelle's department line buzzed as she ate lunch at her work desk in the sheriff's department. She swallowed a bite of Cuban pork and picked up the receiver. "Marshall."

"Detective Marshall, you've got a visitor," said the deputy at the front desk.

"What's the name?" she asked.

"Derrick Bell."

She froze, the name reverberating in her brain.

No.

Who the fuck . . .

Anger swamped her. With shaking fingers she pulled up the lobby camera view on her computer and discovered Derrick's brother, Jason, looking directly at the camera, a cocky half smile on his face.

"What. The. Fuck."

Her heart sped up as she stared, and she fought to keep down her lunch.

She hadn't seen Jason Bell since she'd left Sacramento. The last time she'd seen him, he'd confronted her in a restaurant as she ate dinner with Lucia. He'd stopped at their table and acted super happy to see her, going on and on about how she never visited his family anymore, his loud false tone making other diners turn their heads. Noelle had whispered for him to leave, but instead he'd spoken louder about how much she must miss her murdered husband.

Lucia had started to cry.

"Just tell the police what happened to Derrick," he'd hissed at her, and then he'd shot a glare at Lucia and walked away. Noelle asked for their check, and they left behind their half-eaten meals, no longer hungry.

Lucia's terrified face was burned in Noelle's memory. Noelle had been angrier that Jason had scared her sister than that he'd claimed Noelle knew what had happened.

Both Jason and his mother had consistently told the media that Noelle was hiding something. Moving out of state had been her escape.

"Detective?" asked the officer through the phone.

"Have someone put him in conference room three," she said, struggling to keep her voice steady. Unlike the stark interview rooms, this one felt welcoming with soft seating and a coffeepot. The department used it for victims' families. As much as she'd love to throw Jason in a room with a two-way mirror and a locking door, she would take the high road.

Why is he here?

She closed her eyes, took several calming breaths, and then checked her hair in the mirror on the back of her door. It was perfect. But she heard Derrick's voice stating it was too noticeable.

I haven't thought about that in a long time.

Taking her time, she touched up her lipstick, thankful she'd worn her confidence-inspiring dark-plum pantsuit. She clipped her detective's badge to her belt—a completely unnecessary move since she already wore the required photo ID on her lanyard, but she'd earned the badge and wanted it visible to Jason. She took black high heels out of her desk drawer. They'd been there since last week, when she'd swapped them out for flats to visit the jail. She was currently wearing lower heels, but slipping into this red-soled pair was magic.

Instant élan.

Heels on, she strode down the hall, tamping down her anger at Jason's stupid ploy with Derrick's name. From the corner of her eye, she saw a deputy do a startled double take as she went by, and she concentrated on relaxing her face.

Don't let him see you sweat.

She had no doubt Jason planned to intimidate her. He had never been her friend. The vibe she had always received from him was one of disdain and reluctant tolerance.

Exactly what she planned to deliver today.

She opened the door and strode in. Jason stood beside a chair, hands in his pockets, clearly unwilling to sit and put his eye level below hers.

But her heels placed him there anyway. He'd never been as tall as Derrick.

Jason looked the same but older. A bit of silver at the temples and deeper lines around his eyes. A softness under the chin. The gold band on his left hand surprised her.

That poor woman.

Odd that I didn't get a wedding invitation.

The thought made her smile. "Why are you here?" she asked, lifting her chin to make her eyes even higher.

"The FBI interviewed us last week. They said they were coming here."

"Correct."

"I wanted to be certain you told the truth."

She rolled her eyes at his haughty tone. "You came all the way up here because you believed I'd tell you what I said to the FBI?"

"We're all in this together."

Noelle blinked. Then laughed.

That's a new line.

"What is this truth I'm supposed to tell the FBI?" she asked, impatience in her tone.

"That your ex-husband killed my brother."

Noelle had heard this theory several times over the past decade, and she accepted some of the blame for the speculation. Two years after Derrick died, she'd had a one-night stand with her ex-husband,

Brendon, after meeting him for dinner. Someone had seen them go back to his house and told the Bell family. Noelle blew up when she later discovered the source had been a private detective Jason had hired to follow her.

At the time Brendon had been single, and Noelle had been extremely lonely and not ready to date or meet someone new. Their dinner and conversation had felt comfortable, like slipping into a favorite soft sweatshirt.

She had no regrets other than the intense scrutiny Brendon suffered after the Bells made the story public.

Noelle looked at the ceiling, counting to ten in her head. "Brendon did not kill Derrick. It was thoroughly investigated several times."

"I know you paid him nineteen thousand dollars."

"It was *nine thousand* dollars, and the police were fully aware of the circumstances behind it. You know all these facts, Jason. When will you drop this harassment?"

"When I have justice for my brother."

Noelle bit her cheek at the dramatic martyred look on his face. "You barely got along with Derrick. In fact, I suspect you hated him a lot of the time." She'd witnessed many arguments between the brothers. Her theory was that their issues started during Jason's high school and college football career, when he'd lorded it over his younger brother. But then Derrick became a rising political star, leaving Jason in the dust, his football years irrelevant.

"He was still my brother."

"Early on, your mother told me how much it hurt that the two of you fought so much. Lora saw it, and I saw it too. When you weren't putting Derrick down, you turned your sour attitude on me."

"All you care about is that you got his money. Money that should have stayed in the family. You don't seem to care if his murderer is ever found." Jason's face was red.

"How can you even say that? He was my husband. But I'm not going to give weight to conspiracy theories. Especially the ones that involve me." She ignored his comments about money. As much as they didn't like it, she'd been family, and his crack about the money staying in the family was nothing new. She'd grown used to it.

"You've done *nothing* to help find who did it."

Did he really just say that?

She'd sat through hours and hours of interviews with investigators, answering all their repetitive questions, walked the scene with the FBI and county detectives several times, spent endless sleepless nights trying to recall what had happened, and even tried hypnotism.

Noelle held up a hand. There was no point in continuing to talk. Jason would never think differently until the murder was solved. She was wasting her time.

She went to the door, opened it wide, and stepped back to indicate he should leave. She wanted to kick his ass down the hallway, but she had to walk him to the lobby. No one was allowed behind the locked doors without an escort.

Jason didn't move.

"Leave." Her voice held quiet anger.

He jammed his hands farther into his pockets and looked around the small room as if for something else he could do. Noelle knew his little brain did *not* want to do anything she said.

After five seconds of their silent battle of wills, Noelle stepped into the hall and motioned over a deputy. "Mr. Bell requires an escort out of the building," she told the young woman, the quiet anger still filling her tone and clipping her words.

The deputy's eyes crinkled in understanding. "Got it." She moved into the room. "Come with me, Mr. Bell."

This should be good.

When Jason didn't move, the small deputy rested her hand on her duty belt, several inches from her gun. His eyes followed the movement. "This way, sir," she said.

Jason strode out of the room, avoiding Noelle's gaze. The deputy returned Noelle's grin as she followed.

"Thank you, Deputy."

"All in a day's work, Detective."

Noelle returned to her office and closed the door, leaning heavily against it. For a brief moment insecurity swamped her, a remnant of her time with Derrick and the rest of the Bells. She mentally shoved it away and stood tall.

No one has the right to break me.

She plopped down in her office chair and lifted one foot, rotating it from side to side, admiring the shiny black shoe. "What a waste of my time. And his. Why the fuck would he come all the way up here when he knows his story is bullshit?"

Her shoe didn't answer.

But it calmed her as she imagined grinding the narrow heel into his foot.

You've done nothing *to help find who did it.*

Jason's words echoed in her head, and a small wave of guilt touched her.

"There's no point in telling the police about my stupid dreams," she stated to her foot.

She'd had a lot of dreams.

They mean nothing.

The worst one recurred frequently.

In it she pulled up at the house she shared with Derrick on the day he died.

Lucia's minivan was parked in the driveway.

Daisy lay motionless in a pool of blood just inside the front door.

Her grandfather stood over Daisy, a rifle clenched in his hands.

They're just dreams.

35

"Aren't you hot in that getup?"

Max's grandmother Paulette had already suggested three times that he strip down. The two of them were at the retirement village, eating takeout from Paulette's favorite Indian restaurant.

"I'm fine," Max told her again. He'd borrowed TJ's motorcycle and gear for a ride that afternoon, ending with an early dinner at Paulette's. At her home, he'd removed the heavy armored jacket but not the pants and protective boots. He wore a pair of jeans under the Kevlar motorcycle pants, but it was easier to leave the pants on and not deal with having to take off the boots first.

"You look uncomfortable."

"I'm fine," he repeated, shifting in the bulky gear. Paulette's little house was about ten degrees warmer than any sane person's home, and with the temperature, gear, and spicy food, he was having a moment of regret, but he wasn't about to let her know.

"I appreciate you bringing dinner," Paulette said. "How long are you in town?"

"Tomorrow we're going to review what we've recorded so far, but we have a couple more interviews on Monday. Hopefully we'll be finished by Tuesday."

"This afternoon the entire village was talking about the FBI being here. Daisy Swanson was practically a celebrity." A tiny hint of jealousy filled her tone.

Max fought back a smile. His grandmother loved being the center of attention. "Sorry I didn't tell you I was going to be there." She'd been in the small crowd that had gathered in the clubhouse while Max and Keaton finished their interviews in the adjacent room. He'd stepped out of the room and immediately locked eyes with his grandmother. She'd been surprised to see him and then narrowed her gaze at him.

He was in trouble.

"I was going to call you before I got to town," he'd told her as the curious residents swarmed him and Keaton. "But I didn't know if I'd have any free time," he'd finished lamely. "How about I bring you dinner tonight?"

She'd accepted graciously. Probably because they had an audience.

"Daisy seems like a nice woman," Max said. "I'm sure people had a lot of questions for you once they realized you and I were related."

"Most of them asked, 'Why didn't you know your grandson was here?'"

Max sighed, not surprised she wasn't finished with her little jabs of punishment. "Again. Sorry about that." He deeply loved his grandmother, but she had been always slow to forgive.

"Daisy wouldn't tell me why she was interviewed," Paulette said deliberately, raising an eyebrow at him. Clearly she hoped that his guilt would earn her an answer about his work.

"You know I can't talk about that," Max told her. "But I can say it's got nothing to do with Daisy. We were here to see if she could shine some light on a situation."

"She's got a good heart," Paulette admitted. "I like her, but she keeps trying to match me up with Alan Platt. Claims we'd keep each other company." His grandmother shook her head and glared at the rice on her fork. "I don't need company. I've got loads of friends here. Plenty of people to talk to. And besides, your grandfather was the only man for me. Always will be." Her voice softened as she spoke of her husband, who'd passed three years ago.

"The two of you were legendary," said Max, not exaggerating. His grandparents had been deeply in love until the day death separated them. Their marriage represented his relationship goals.

They'd had a sense of joy that he also saw in TJ and Keira's marriage. Envy surged when he was around them.

I'm almost forty.

He'd come close to marriage ten years ago. But she'd been offered a promotion on the East Coast, and he hadn't wanted to move away. There'd been hard feelings on both sides, and the relationship had quickly crumbled, making him realize that they weren't right for each other after all.

Soon after that he worried that he'd become too comfortable still living in his hometown and working in the Medford Police Department, so he took a leap and applied to the FBI. As he arrived at Quantico for training, he acknowledged the irony in the fact that he was standing on the East Coast. Apparently he had been ready for a big change but not ready for marriage.

"Your grandfather was an amazing man," said Paulette, a wistful look in her eyes. "I was lucky."

"You both were," said Max.

Twenty minutes later he kissed her on the cheek and escaped the overly warm apartment. Outside in the cool air, he glanced at the sky, estimating he had a half hour of light left to ride, and was glad that Paulette liked to eat early. He never rode in the dark unless it was absolutely necessary. Max zipped up the heavy jacket as he admired the bike. He'd taken it for a good run before picking up dinner and was ready to go again.

"Agent Rhodes?"

He'd been about to slip on the helmet but turned to find Noelle Marshall studying him, amusement in her eyes. She wore jeans and a heavy coat with a fuzzy collar. And cowboy boots, he noted in surprise. In her hands was a to-go bag from the same Indian restaurant.

Dinner for Daisy.

"Detective." Max nodded at her. "Visiting Daisy?"

"I am. I assume you saw your grandmother." She tipped her head, taking in the motorcycle. "Did you ride this from Sacramento?" she asked in a teasing tone.

He grinned. "No. But I have before. Well . . . not on this bike, but I've made the ride on my own. This one is my brother-in-law's." He liked the lightness in her voice. He hadn't heard it before.

Because she's not being grilled at the moment.

"Do you ride?" he asked.

Her brows shot up. "No. Never been on one. Were you joking that you've ridden this far before?"

"Not a joke. I could easily do that distance in a day with a break or two. And that would be taking back roads. I avoid riding on the freeway. Freeways are dull."

"Aren't all roads dull?"

"That question confirms that you've never been on a motorcycle."

It took her a second to follow his logic. "You're saying the motorcycle makes a difference?"

He couldn't stop his smile. "Riding is like flying at ground level."

Her forehead wrinkled. "That's a good thing?"

It was impossible to explain; the only way to comprehend the joy was to experience it. "It's completely different than a car ride. On a bike you're part of the environment . . . you're constantly involved. You move and react with what's around you. And the sky is wide open."

"I'm sure it's nice."

Nice?

"You need a ride," he said in all seriousness. "Then you'll understand."

Noelle took a half step back. "No, thank you." She lifted her bag of food. "I've got a date."

"Tonight's not a good time," he said. "But I think you should ride with me before I leave. Just a quick one. My sister's gear would fit you," he said. "She's tall."

She blinked at him.

I think I just crossed a professional line.

"I'd take you just so you'd understand," he added quickly, knowing it sounded lame. "Seriously. Everyone needs to experience it at least once. It'll make you want your own bike."

"I doubt that," she said with a little laugh. "But I appreciate your offer." Her smile was sincere.

Max caught his breath. Detective Marshall with a genuine smile was a stunning sight. During yesterday's interviews he'd thought her dark eyes were brown, but now, in the waning outdoor light, they were actually a dark blue. The same color as her coat.

Back off. She's a witness.

Or is she a suspect?

Either way, Max needed to keep things professional. And getting her on the back of a motorcycle with her arms wrapped around his waist wouldn't be professional.

But it's just a ride. An education.

"I'm heading in before Daisy's food gets cold," said Noelle. "You'll let me know when you need to talk to me again?"

For the briefest second, he thought she meant talk more about that motorcycle ride.

She meant another interview.

Mentally kicking himself, he adjusted the helmet in his hands. "I will. Have a good night." He turned and started to slip it on.

"Agent Rhodes?"

He spun back around, pulling off the helmet. "Yes?"

She'd taken a few steps away, but judging by her frown, she had something else to say.

"Derrick's brother showed up at the sheriff's department to talk to me today." Her words were hesitant, as if she was reluctant to share the information.

Max sifted his memory for a name. "Jason Bell? What did he want? Why is he in town?" The previous week, he and Keaton had interviewed

Jason. The man had been adamant that the FBI needed to look closer at Noelle and her first husband. Max had immediately picked up on his strong dislike for Noelle. Further questions to understand Jason's accusations had revealed little evidence. A banking transaction and his disbelief about Noelle's memory loss were his primary reasons.

The interview with Jason had left a sour taste in Max's mouth.

"He claims he came to tell me to share the truth with the FBI." Frustration filled her tone. "He was an ass. He's *always* been an ass. I had a deputy escort him out of the building."

"Did you tell the FBI the truth?" Max asked as he recalled Daisy's comments about how Noelle had changed during the marriage and Noelle's assertions about her love for her husband.

Noelle's face went blank, and she looked at the ground. "Everything I told you was true," she said softly. "But I may have stretched the truth about how I felt about Derrick near the end."

Max said nothing, recalling how Daisy's interview had made him question just how happy Noelle had been in her marriage.

She swallowed. "I was done with him—done with us. He'd changed from the man I fell in love with. He'd become a manipulative gaslighter and was always angry. I'd told Savannah I'd leave him." She met his gaze. "But I didn't kill him. I was going to walk away, but he died before I could."

I want to believe her.

Daisy was right.

"What about his money?"

Distaste flickered in Noelle's eyes. "I didn't want it. I was perfectly capable of taking care of myself, as I'd done before we met."

"Why didn't you say this during our interview?"

"I've asked myself the same question. This may sound lame, but I spent years trying to present our marriage as picture perfect for the public. He wanted to be in politics more than anything, and I believed that was how to support him. I continued after he died. I didn't dare say a word about how our marriage had crumbled. It made things easier for me . . . and for his family."

"You mean they would have eviscerated you in public if you'd revealed anything negative about Derrick or your marriage."

"Correct. For my peace of mind, I stayed silent."

"They did it in a passive-aggressive way instead. I read the reports. Jason didn't even mention you during his eulogy at Derrick's funeral."

Noelle shrugged. "That's how Jason is. I wanted you to know he's in town."

She's acting nonchalant, but I can tell he's upset her.

"He seems the type that likes to strong-arm people into agreeing with him."

"He is."

"Must have been a great brother-in-law." He paused. "Thank you for telling me the truth."

I hope it's the truth.

Noelle looked away. "I'll let you go." She lifted a hand as she turned toward the building. "See you," she said over her shoulder.

"Good night." Max watched her walk away. She was as elegant in cowboy boots and jeans as she was in spike heels and a suit. A confident woman.

Max wanted to believe her story, but she'd lied about it for a long time.

I've got to stay objective.

36

The next morning, after yoga class, Noelle tossed her mat onto the back seat of her vehicle as Eve and Lucia did the same with their mats in Eve's car.

On Sunday mornings the three of them always met for yoga at a little strip mall and then walked three doors down to a French bakery to have pastries and coffee.

Noelle liked to think the yoga canceled out the treats but suspected, since she usually indulged in the almond croissant, she'd probably need two more yoga sessions—or more—to cancel out the calories. Her sisters joined her, and they set out toward the bakery. Lucia pressed on her stomach. "I hate abdominal day. The next day is always miserable."

"I like the pain," said Eve, and received a glare from her younger sister. "It feels like I accomplished something."

Noelle had covertly watched Lucia during the class. The thin woman always struggled with strength moves, and she'd been unable to do several of the ab exercises.

But she's a lot stronger than she used to be.

Inside the bakery, Noelle ordered the almond croissant and black coffee. She sighed as she sat, feeling a twinge in her obliques and knowing she'd hurt tomorrow.

"How did yesterday's FBI interview go, Lucia?" she asked as she blew on her coffee.

"It was okay. They were nice enough, but I always feel like no one believes what I tell them." Lucia sank a fork into her fruit tart.

"It's the intimidation factor," said Eve, touching her sister's shoulder in sympathy. "Two federal agents staring at you over a table and asking questions. Everyone feels nervous."

"Daisy didn't. She was eager to talk to them."

"Daisy is unique."

"She made me leave the room during her interview," said Lucia with a sigh. "So I have no idea what sort of stories she told them."

"She doesn't lie," said Noelle.

"I meant *stories*," said Lucia. "You know . . . where she goes into great detail about some random event."

Noelle grinned, wondering how the agents had enjoyed her colorful aunt.

Lucia proceeded to cut her tart into several pieces and push them around on her plate.

Eve exchanged a glance with Noelle. Eating was difficult for Lucia when something stressed or distracted her, and she was too thin to miss more than a few meals. Eve and Noelle had kept an eye on her food intake since she was a teenager.

She's thirty-one.

It was hard to step out of the role.

"What's up, Lucia?" Eve asked. "Too much ab work upset your stomach?"

Lucia abruptly laid down her fork; she hated being monitored. "No. Those agents yesterday brought up a lot of old shit."

"Tell me about it," muttered Noelle. Suddenly cranky, she bit into her croissant and was instantly mollified by the buttery, warm, sweet gooeyness. Unlike with Lucia, food brought Noelle comfort.

"I hate that Derrick's death continues to hang over our family's head," said Lucia. "My brain gets tired thinking about it."

"I'm sorry," said Noelle.

"Not your fault," said Lucia. She forked some tart into her mouth, clearly not wanting to but trying to please her sisters. "Seems like we can't move on."

"I moved on," said Noelle. "That sounds horrible, but I can't pause my life because his murderer hasn't been found."

Lucia met her gaze. "Every time I think about it, I worry about you."

Translation: she still feared that someone would come after Noelle.

How do I help her move past that?

Lucia's fear had been an issue for a long time. She no longer cried or had nightmares that Noelle had been killed, but occasionally something would pop up that made her obsess about how to protect her older sister.

Noelle understood. She'd lived in fear for a long time too. Joining the police force had empowered her.

That was not a solution for Lucia.

"Worrying about me won't change anything," Noelle said to Lucia. "Whatever happened with Derrick didn't follow me to Oregon. His murder was an isolated incident. And if there's a killer out there concerned that I'm getting my memory back and might identify him, it's been thirteen years. I don't think it'll ever return." She looked hard into Lucia's gaze. "So lucky for him. Eat," ordered Noelle, pointing at Lucia's tart. "It's a gorgeous day. We survived the ab workout, and we've got Paris-worthy pastries in front of us. I don't want to think about something that happened thirteen years ago."

Lucia gave a weak smile and took another bite.

"When do you talk to the FBI?" Noelle asked Eve.

"Adam and I are both scheduled for tomorrow evening," Eve said reluctantly. "Not looking forward to it."

"It'll go fine," said Noelle. "They're professional and polite."

Inviting me for a motorcycle ride wasn't professional.

For the briefest of seconds, she'd been tempted to hop on the motorcycle yesterday. It'd been a long time since she acted on an impulse, but the thought had vanished as quickly as it'd appeared. Logic prevailed. Agent Rhodes was dressed in safety gear for the ride and Noelle had none. Plus Daisy was waiting.

But the curiosity had lingered. Later that night she'd watched some women riders on YouTube, wondering if Rhodes had been exaggerating about what it was like to ride. The stunning scenery had impressed her. Mountains. Cliffs. Rivers. Beaches. According to the women, Rhodes had told her the truth about the joy.

If Eve's interview was Monday, then it was possible the FBI team would leave on Tuesday. By then they would have spoken to everyone attached to the case.

The motorcycle ride wasn't going to happen.

She had a small pang of regret, feeling as if she'd been tempted by something she'd never get to experience.

The women finished their pastries, and Eve and Noelle chatted for another minute while Lucia used the bathroom. She returned, and the three of them headed out the door. Eve and Lucia were making plans to grocery shop, and Noelle had more work to do on the hit-and-run case that the FBI had interrupted. She had just stepped into the parking lot when a giant blast of air knocked her on her back, instantly smashing the air from her lungs.

A thunderous roar slammed into her head, and she felt as if she'd been punched in the face.

Eve! Lucia!

Noelle clamped her hands over her ears and rolled to her side, attempting to pull oxygen back into her lungs. She forced her eyes open to find her sisters and they instantly watered as they were socked with a dust cloud. A few feet away Eve was pushing up to her knees, her mouth open as she stared across the lot.

Noelle followed her gaze and terror rocked her.

My car!

Flames poured out of her vehicle's broken windows as clouds of black smoke billowed toward the sky.

Noelle shoved up to all fours and spotted Lucia sitting against the bakery's door, her legs splayed in front of her, shock on her face.

Thank God.

"Are you okay?" she shouted at Lucia as she scrambled to help Eve stand. Her sister's arm shook under Noelle's hands. Lucia blinked and nodded. She clumsily crawled to one side as the bakery's glass door shoved against her back from customers trying to get out. The first woman through the door crouched beside Lucia, questioning her, concern on her face.

Noelle helped Eve to Lucia, and they collapsed on the sidewalk by their younger sister.

"Are you hurt?" Noelle ran her hands over Eve's shoulders. Eve couldn't speak and simply shook her head.

We're all okay.

Her ears ringing loudly, Noelle looked back at her burning vehicle.

If we hadn't waited for Lucia to use the bathroom, I'd be dead.

Cars don't randomly explode.

Who did this?

37

Max parked as close as he could to the small strip mall but had to jog two blocks to reach the explosion scene. Fire trucks, vehicles from three different police departments, and spectators crowded the area. The scents of burning fuel and harsh smoke had reached him the second he opened his car door.

He approached an officer maintaining the perimeter and pulled out his identification. "Who's in charge?"

The deputy looked closely at his ID. "Why's the FBI here?"

"Trust me," Max said grimly.

The deputy gave him a long look and then pointed at a group of people near the blown-out windows of a yoga studio. "Lieutenant Ogden." He lifted the yellow tape for Max, who ducked underneath and headed across the parking lot.

The strip mall's parking lot was wet, and there were large areas of standing water. Firefighters were packing up their equipment, and a forensic tech circled the burned vehicle, taking pictures from every angle. The investigation had started. The cars on either side of the SUV had broken windows and scorch marks.

Max spotted Noelle and changed direction. She was sitting on the bumper of an ambulance, holding an ice pack to her head and listening to a man in plain clothes who gripped her hand, speaking emphatically. Max slowed his strides, taking in the situation. Mercy sat beside Noelle, an arm around her shoulders as she listened too.

As Max drew closer, Noelle's gaze shot past the speaker and met his. Noticing her distraction, the man turned, and Max spotted a badge on his lanyard.

County detective.

But he still held Noelle's hand.

Max approached and Mercy stood. Noelle started to stand up, but the other two made her return to the bumper.

"Agent Rhodes," said Mercy, holding out her hand.

She had called and told him what happened. The FBI had been contacted immediately since the explosion was possibly caused by a car bomb, which could indicate domestic terrorism. When Mercy learned it was Noelle Marshall's vehicle that had exploded, she'd notified Max, knowing he was investigating a previous attack on Noelle during her husband's murder.

The attack had taken place thirteen years ago. But the fact that Noelle had been recently interviewed about it and now possibly attacked again was too big a coincidence. Max had immediately headed to the crime scene.

He shook Mercy's hand, and she introduced him to Detective Evan Bolton from the sheriff's office, confirming Max's suspicion that he was a coworker of Noelle's. Bolton narrowed his eyes when Mercy said that Max was from the Sacramento FBI office.

"What does your office have to do with this?" Bolton gestured at the vehicle and looked from Max to Mercy.

"That's what I'm here to find out," said Max.

"What?" asked Noelle. Understanding dawned on her face. "It can't be connected. That's a big stretch."

"Are you all right?" Max asked Noelle. Her eyes were red, and her jacket was filthy.

"How . . . how did you hear about this?" she asked instead of answering his question.

"Mercy called me. Where're you injured?"

She lowered the ice pack. "I hit my head. My ears are still ringing."

Max glanced at the black husk of an SUV. "You were lucky. Where are your sisters?"

"They're at the hospital. Lucia banged up an elbow and hit her head. Eve landed on her knees and was limping."

"You're going there next," said Mercy.

"They took my vitals, I'm fine." Noelle returned the ice pack to her head, wincing as it touched.

"You're not fine," said Detective Bolton. "You need your head examined."

Noelle snorted and then winced at the sudden movement. "Maybe."

"Absolutely," said Mercy. "You might have cracked it again."

Max had thought the same thing.

"Again?" asked Bolton, looking from Mercy to Noelle. "Why do I feel like I'm a step behind everyone?"

They can't be that close if he doesn't know about her old injury.

"Long story," said Noelle. She gestured at Max. "Ask him. He's the one jumping to conclusions."

"Have there been other attempts on your life?" Max asked, not giving Bolton time to question him.

Noelle was quiet for a moment. "Only once," she slowly admitted, meeting his gaze.

He knew she meant at her husband's murder. "This explosion happened right after you'd been questioned about your previous attack. Too big a coincidence for me."

"Anyone could have done it," argued Noelle. "I've angered a lot of people in my job. And that's assuming it wasn't some vehicle issue that caused the explosion."

The three of them stared at Noelle, and she squirmed. "Okay. Stationary vehicles randomly blowing up isn't common."

"Not common at all," added Mercy.

"Who's targeting her?" Bolton asked Max, impatience in his tone.

"That's the question," said Max, eyeing the other man, weighing his concern for Noelle.

"Mercy can catch you up, Evan," said Noelle, pressing a hand against her forehead. "It's too much for me right now."

"The FBI lab should be involved," Max said. "They can get faster results." He studied the front of the strip mall. "We'll take whatever video evidence is found too. We can get heavily detailed stills from video better than anyone else."

Noelle slumped and pain filled her face. "I think—"

"You need to get to the hospital," said Mercy. "I'll tell the EMTs." She headed for the cab of the ambulance.

"I don't want to go to the hospital."

"Too bad," Max and Bolton said at the same time.

Noelle looked past them to the SUV. "I'll need a new work vehicle."

Her mind is drifting. She's concerned about the wrong things.

"She needs someone with her at the hospital," said Max to Detective Bolton, not liking her defeated expression. "And at her home."

"Stop it," said Noelle in exasperation.

"He's right," said Mercy, returning to the conversation with two EMTs in her wake. "If this turns out to be what we think it could be, you shouldn't be alone."

"I'll get a deputy on it," said Bolton.

"Let's get you up," one EMT said to Noelle, taking her arm. "Any nausea yet? Dizziness?"

"Yes and yes," Noelle muttered as he guided her into the back of the vehicle. "My vision is off," she told him in a quiet voice.

Max watched her sit down in the ambulance, the EMT speedily getting her settled and bustling to take her vitals again.

She's more injured than she let on.

The driver slammed the back doors and climbed into the cab. The ambulance drove through the parking lot slowly, occasionally whooping the siren to get people out of the way.

Mercy met Max's gaze. "She told me everything the night before yesterday." She turned to Detective Bolton and accurately relayed Noelle's past in Sacramento.

Bolton was stunned. "I had no idea. She's never said a word."

"Same," said Mercy. "Are we bad friends? Did we not try hard enough to get to know her?"

"My impression is that she's a very private person," said Max. "And the murder of her husband is something she's tried to put behind her. I don't think she ever would have brought it up." Mercy appeared genuinely distressed that she'd let down a friend.

"Could Rowan have known?" Mercy asked Bolton.

He shook his head. "My fiancée," he explained to Max. "How likely is it that this attack is related to your investigation?"

"Don't know, but I have to consider it," said Max. The ambulance turned onto the street and sped away as his gaze followed.

Did our interview stir up something deadly?

Noelle had told him last night that Jason Bell had harassed her. Max had seen in her eyes how much it'd disturbed her.

I need to find him.

38

That evening Noelle kept her eyes focused on the far wall in her hospital room. Forget reading or looking at her phone. Other than closing her eyes, only distance viewing didn't make her head hurt.

Well, hurt more than it already does.

She'd knocked it hard. They'd done every scan possible of her head, and the good news was there wasn't a fracture, but the doctors had insisted she stay overnight because of her past head injury.

Eve's fall had been cushioned by her bag, which had been stuffed with a towel and an extra sweatshirt. Her knees had been patched up, and there were no broken bones, but she would be uncomfortable until the swelling subsided.

Lucia's head scans were clear, and they'd taken several X-rays of her spine after she complained about low back pain. Nothing was broken, but soft-tissue injuries had occurred when she landed on her backside. She'd been the farthest from the blast and the luckiest.

Noelle's sisters had been released but refused to leave the hospital. Instead, they'd camped out in Noelle's room. A deputy had been stationed outside the door while the FBI and Deschutes County sheriff handled the investigation.

"Maybe this blow to my head will correct my memory lapses," Noelle joked as her sisters gasped.

"That's not funny!" said Eve, getting to her feet, wincing, then immediately sitting back down in a chair. "Don't joke about that."

Lucia sniffled. "What if it makes it worse?"

Then I'm out of a job.

Noelle had tried to avoid that particular thought, but her brain had other ideas. It'd brought the job loss to the forefront and waved it around every few minutes. She silently recited state capitals, trying to prove to herself that nothing had changed. She got to West Virginia and panicked, no city coming to mind. "What's the capital of West Virginia?" she blurted.

Eve and Lucia stared at her, and then Lucia burst into sobs.

She thinks I'm nuts.

"Why?" asked Eve.

"Because I can't remember it."

Lucia wiped her face, understanding dawning. "I don't know it either." She looked at Eve. "You're the schoolteacher."

"Charleston," said Eve. "I only know it because my fifth graders covered it last month." She looked at Noelle. "You've always lived on the West Coast. That's a hard one."

"What if I'm losing it?" Noelle whispered, fear strangling her lungs.

Eve sat on the side of her bed and took her hand, sympathy in her eyes. "I don't think the capital of West Virginia is an accurate way to test your memory."

"Then what is?"

"What'd you have for breakfast today?" asked Eve.

"Almond croissant. Coffee." Noelle's stomach churned. She'd lost her breakfast in the ambulance and wouldn't be ordering a croissant for a while. It was past dinnertime, and she still had no interest in food.

"Your short-term is good."

There was a knock at the door. It opened a little and the deputy appeared. "Got an Adam Langton out here."

"That's my husband." Eve's voice shook as she carefully stood.

Adam came in, holding a shopping bag and pizza box in one hand. He hugged and kissed his wife, the concern on his face making Noelle's heart melt. "You okay?" he whispered to Eve, touching her cheek.

She nodded, holding his gaze.

Noelle had thought she'd gotten over her envy of their marriage, but the green jealousy monster reared its head for a quick second, then vanished. She was pleased her sister had found someone kind who watched over her so carefully, to the point that Noelle often forgot how ridiculous their names were together.

Adam turned his attention to Lucia, studying her from head to toe as he set down the pizza. "Your head all right?" he asked, holding out the shopping bag as she nodded. "I brought you and Eve some clean clothes. She said neither of you are going home tonight."

"Thanks." Lucia took the bag and examined the contents.

The same scrutiny he'd used on Lucia focused on Noelle as he came to her bed and squeezed her upper arm. "How are you doing?" he asked softly. "Do the nurses have your pain under control?"

"I'm good. Thanks for bringing some food." The smell had stimulated her appetite a bit but not enough for her to consider a slice.

"The deputy made me open the pizza box, and then he went through the bag of clothes."

"They're being careful."

He grimaced. "I don't like seeing you in a hospital bed again," he said, referring to the time thirteen years ago.

"That makes two of us." Making eye contact was painful, and she directed her gaze over his shoulder. "Sorry. Hurts to focus on things that are close up."

"Not a problem." He gave her arm another squeeze and returned to his wife. Eve had sat down in a chair by Lucia, and she shook her head as he gestured at the pizza. Lucia did the same.

No one has any appetite.

Another knock. "Savannah Price?" asked the deputy as he stuck his head in.

"Savannah!" Lucia rose to her feet as Noelle's best friend swept in, her ebullient aura immediately filling the room.

"My favorite girl!" said Savannah as she enveloped Lucia in a hug. Her gaze met Noelle's over Lucia's shoulder, and she blew a kiss.

I can't believe she came all the way from Sacramento.

Tears burned, and Noelle wiped her eyes.

Savannah quickly greeted Eve and Adam and then perched on the side of Noelle's bed, her serious brown eyes missing nothing. "You need lipstick."

Noelle jerked with laughter and then moaned at the pain in her head. "Don't make me laugh!" Tears ran down her cheeks as Savannah carefully hugged her. "How did you know?" she whispered as the light, familiar scent of Savannah's perfume reached her.

"Alice called me."

"How did Alice find out?" Noelle was confused.

"She said the FBI notified her, and she thought I should know."

Agent Rhodes knows how close I am to Alice. And no doubt she made him promise to keep her in the loop.

"Thank you for coming," said Noelle. "It means a lot."

"What the fuck is going on?" Savannah whispered, concern in her eyes. "The FBI spoke to me recently, but they made it sound like they were just doing due diligence, updating files on Derrick's murder."

"Essentially they were," said Noelle. "They were doing the same thing up here, and then this happened." She closed her eyes, pain spiking through her head, unable to focus. "Eyes hurt."

"Jesus. Are you okay?"

"I will be."

"They think this is related?" Savannah said in a low voice.

"They're considering it. And until they figure it out, they're not taking any chances."

"Is the deputy at the door single? I didn't see a wedding ring."

Noelle's eyes flew open as she snorted and then slapped a hand over her mouth. "Oh my God. I've missed you."

Savannah kissed her on the forehead. "I've missed you too."

"And he looks like he's barely twenty-five," added Noelle.

"Perfect." She swung up her legs and snuggled into the bed next to Noelle. "Move over."

Noelle did and rested her head against Savannah's, comfort flowing through her.

Everything will be okay.

39

Max waited in the elevator alcove on Jason Bell's hotel floor with Mercy, Detective Bolton, and two deputies. It was the most expensive hotel in Bend. Aware of Jason Bell's wealth, their team had found him registered at the first hotel they tried.

The agents had asked the hotel manager to call Bell's room and ask him to come down to the front desk, intending to approach him on his floor once he left his room. A safer situation than having him behind a door, where they couldn't see what he was doing once he knew they were there.

Video from two stores at the strip mall and from a gas station across the street showed that no one had approached Noelle's vehicle while it was parked in front of the yoga studio. On the recordings, Max had watched her pull in and get out of her vehicle as her sister parked a few spaces down. Carrying mats and dressed in leggings and heavy coats against the cold, the three women had entered the studio. An hour later they'd put their mats in their vehicles and walked to eat a few doors down.

Viewing the power of the explosion and its physical effect on the three women had been nauseating. The way Noelle and Lucia had hit their heads made him cringe.

"This could have been horrible," Mercy had said as they viewed the explosion for the fourth time. "All three of those women could have been killed." A preliminary inspection of the destroyed vehicle had confirmed that an explosive device had been attached under the engine. Since no one had been seen placing it at the strip mall, the agents were considering a remote detonator or a timer. The remains of the device would be quickly sent to FBI labs to be searched for answers.

With no current evidence to point at a suspect, Max had made his case for questioning Jason Bell. Mercy and Bolton had agreed.

Max checked the time. They'd been in place by the elevators for ten minutes.

"Maybe he has to get dressed," suggested Mercy. "Or else he told the front desk he'd be down later." They knew he was in the room. A key card had unlocked it two hours ago, and they'd confirmed on the hall's video that he'd been the one who entered. A rapid fast-forward of the video had revealed he'd stayed put. It also showed he'd left his room before the explosion and returned an hour after.

"A door's opening," said one of the deputies. Mercy and Bolton moved to stand as if they were waiting for the elevator, and the deputies stepped out of sight, along with Max, in case Jason recognized him. Mercy briefly glanced down the hall and then touched Bolton's arm, her signal to everyone that she'd confirmed it was Jason approaching.

"You didn't push the button," said Jason before Max could see him. A second later Bell stepped into his view, and the two deputies moved behind him. Jason did a double take at their sudden appearance and then spotted Max standing against the wall. Recognition quickly flashed in Jason's eyes. He glanced back at the deputies, who'd positioned themselves behind him and slightly to his sides. Mercy and Bolton had moved to stand near the deputies, where Jason couldn't see anyone else without turning away from Max.

"What the fuck?" said Jason, disgust on his face as he turned in a circle and stopped to glare at Max. "I assume you arranged this, Rhodes? If you had more questions for me, you could have just asked. You need four other people around so you can talk to me?"

"I do have questions," said Max. "Since we both *happened* to be in town, I thought I'd stop in for a chat."

"This is about Noelle, isn't it? I didn't do anything. Did she say I threatened her? It's a lie." Jason's face started to pinken, and Max wondered about his blood pressure.

"What brought you to Bend, Jason?" asked Max.

"I don't have to tell you that."

"True. But it'd be nice if you did."

"I'm here to make sure you're doing your job correctly."

"Weird," said Max. "I haven't seen you around. Are you saying you've got hidden cameras watching me?"

"You *know* Noelle and her ex are behind my brother's murder. She paid the ex to kill him, so she could get Derrick's money when he died."

"Where's your evidence?"

Jason hadn't mentioned the explosion, and Max wondered if the man was purposefully avoiding it so they'd think he knew nothing about it or if he truly did know nothing.

"You *have* all the evidence. You've had it for years."

"You don't have anything new? Because what we have means nothing."

"Fuck you."

"That's the best you can do?" asked Max, not surprised at the man's reply. "Where were you this morning from eight thirty-seven to ten twelve?" Max used the exact times from the hallway videos of Jason leaving and returning.

Jason's mouth dropped open. "You're tailing me? Why? What the hell! I'm calling—" He stopped, frustration filled his face.

Max waited for him to continue, knowing the man had been about to say he was calling the police, but they were already present. "Maybe you could call your mom or dad."

Jason said nothing.

If looks could kill.

"So where were you during those times?" Max asked. Behind Jason the officers tried to keep straight faces. Mercy didn't; her grin was wide.

"I went out for breakfast. Place down the street. Since you're so into video, theirs will show I was there."

"You walk or drive?"

Bell looked confused. "Walked. It was close."

"Have you caught any news this morning?" asked Max.

"Some stuff. Why?" His look of confusion hadn't eased.

Either he's a great actor or has no idea.

"When are you returning to Sacramento?"

"Tomorrow morning."

"Show me your boarding pass."

Bell frowned but took out his phone and displayed his boarding pass.

"Thanks. We'll let you know if you need to change that flight."

"The fuck you will."

Max sighed. "Have a nice day, Mr. Bell."

Detective Bolton hit the button for the elevator, and Jason turned to face the doors, waiting with the rest of them.

"Unless you're going somewhere else, the front desk doesn't need to see you," Mercy said.

Jason whipped his head her way. "Jesus. That was for you guys?" He snorted. "This hotel is going to get the worst online review they've ever seen. And I'll call the owner."

"I suggest you check for some local news first," said Max. The elevator door slid open and four of them stepped inside. "In your review, be sure to explain the reason the front desk cooperated with law enforcement. I'd go into great detail if I were you. Especially when you explain it to the owner."

The doors slid shut as Jason stared at them in confusion.

"Waste of time?" asked Mercy.

"Nah," said Max. "It was worth it to see some of his expressions. He's used to being in charge and blustering his way through things, not being told what to do."

"I'm not sure he was involved," said Detective Bolton.

"I agree," said Max.

If Jason Bell isn't our suspect, then who blew up Noelle's SUV?

40

The next day, just before lunch, Noelle stood at her home's huge windows and looked out at the inch of snow that had fallen overnight. It was just enough to blanket the ground and firs in white and make a beautiful contrast against the deep-blue sky. The world looked peaceful and calm. But inside her head were warring thoughts and memories.

Last night in the hospital had been rough. She'd struggled to sleep, and it hadn't helped that the nurses frequently came in to check her vitals. Eve and Lucia had stayed in her room. One sister had slept on the built-in bench below the window and another on a small cot that a nurse had supplied. Savannah had eventually gone back to her hotel, and Noelle had missed her presence throughout the night.

Her sisters had slept just fine, not having to deal with a light frequently flashed in their eyes. It felt as if Noelle had just fallen back to sleep when the light would come again. She finally agreed to the sleeping medication the nurses had offered. It wouldn't allow her to sleep through the interruptions, but she'd fall back to sleep quicker.

The drug had worked, but it'd kicked her dreams into high gear. Especially the one where she arrived at her home the day Derrick died. But the medication had changed it up. Her grandfather no longer stood over Daisy, holding a rifle as she lay motionless on the bloody floor in the home. This time he held a crowbar, and it was Eve in a pool of blood below him. And Derrick's vehicle had replaced Lucia's minivan in the driveway.

But it ended the same. Noelle frozen with shock as she stared at her grandfather, unable to speak, the world silent around her.

Over and over the dream had invaded her sleep.

Now she felt like she hadn't slept at all. She was on her second cup of coffee, attempting to attack the aftereffects of the medication and poor sleep. The earlier drive home was a blur. Detective Bolton had been appointed chauffeur for the three women after Noelle was discharged.

After he'd dropped off Lucia and Eve, Bolton tried to arrange for a deputy to sit watch outside her home, but Noelle had refused. She had a top-notch security system and knew the department was tight on manpower. She didn't want a babysitter, and Savannah was coming over soon. Her car out front would tell everyone that Noelle wasn't alone.

"What's the latest on the explosion?" Noelle had asked Bolton on the drive to her home.

He'd given her a look. "Why don't you leave that to us?"

Annoyance had sparked in her fuzzy brain. "Seriously? How would *you* react to that answer if you were in my shoes?"

"Touché." He'd told her that the remains of the device had been rushed to the FBI lab overnight and that a new video from a business down the street had shown a different angle, catching a person smoking several cigarettes while loitering in the alley next to the yoga studio. The person had stayed there from the time Noelle parked until the women had gone to the bakery.

"Man or woman?" she'd asked.

"Couldn't tell. The view was distant."

"Did they approach my SUV?"

"Possibly. The person appears to drop down at one point after you go to the bakery where he—or she—sort of blended into the building's shadow, which extended to include the front of your vehicle. Ten seconds later, they walked away down the alley."

"It could have been someone tying their shoes," Noelle had said in exasperation.

"My thought too. But they approached from the alley, waited over an hour beside the studio, and then left back down the alley. Why?"

"Maybe a vagrant? I know there's a group of tents not far from there."

"I've got a deputy questioning the people staying there. Even if someone didn't see that particular person, they all heard the explosion and probably went to see what'd happened. Maybe they saw something we didn't."

As they sat in her driveway, he'd shown her a few of the videos on his phone.

Now Noelle couldn't get rid of the vision of herself and her sisters being knocked to the ground as her vehicle exploded.

That one will haunt my dreams too.

She sipped her coffee, still concerned about the effects of a second major blow to her head. She didn't need to work to support herself; she had plenty of funds from Derrick. But she needed her job to fuel her soul. It was the reason she got up in the morning. She loved to work for the sheriff's office and knew her life would never be the same without it. If she had to give it up because of this . . .

I'm worrying about something that hasn't happened yet.

Or had it? Today she'd opened her fridge and stared at three take-out containers of Chinese food that she had no memory of ordering or eating. They were all half-empty and held her usual order.

Clearly I forgot.

With shaking hands and churning stomach, she'd thrown them out, uncertain of how old they were. She couldn't check her credit card to see when she'd bought them because she always paid cash at the little mom-and-pop restaurant.

Her doorbell rang, jarring her out of her dismal thoughts. Expecting Savannah, she checked her camera app and saw Daisy's smiling face. The woman faced the peephole, not the doorbell. Noelle had explained the camera on the doorbell several times, but Daisy never seemed to remember.

Will that be me soon?
A text from Adam popped up.

I just dropped off Daisy. All good?

He said that like I knew she was coming.

Yes. All good

Noelle strode to the door, checking her call log to see if there'd been a call from Daisy about coming over. Daisy had a simple cell phone she used for calls. She didn't text.

There had been no calls.

She opened the door and Daisy's happy, loving aura surrounded Noelle even before her great-aunt stepped in. "Hi, Daisy."

Noelle was enveloped in a hug, and she rested her cheek against the top of the woman's head, inhaling the familiar scent of her cold cream, which she'd used for as long as Noelle could remember.

I swear she gets tinier every year.

Daisy stepped back and eyed her critically. "You don't look too banged up."

Noelle led her inside to a cushiony chair with a view of the snow. The oddly patterned chair was a bit small for Noelle to sit in comfortably, but she kept it because it was the perfect size for Daisy. "I'm fine," she told Daisy. "Some bumps and bruises."

"And your head?" Her concerned gaze went deep, touching Noelle's heart and making her sniffle.

"I think it will be okay," Noelle whispered, all her fears roaring to life at the question. "Won't know for a while." She forced a smile. "Can I get you some coffee or tea?"

Daisy patted her hand. "Whatever you're drinking is fine."

Noelle quickly brewed an americano but dumped out half of the espresso before adding hot water. Daisy preferred just a hint of coffee flavor, not the deep black stuff that Noelle drank. She set the cup on the end table by Daisy's chair and slid a chair closer for herself.

"You haven't asked me why I'm here," said Daisy.

"I assumed it was to check on me after what happened yesterday. I appreciate you coming all the way over here." Daisy didn't leave the retirement community on her own.

"I asked Adam for a ride," said Daisy. "And I told him you were expecting me. Sorry I didn't warn you."

Noelle blew out a breath and pressed her hand to her forehead. "I thought I'd forgotten that we'd made arrangements." She was suddenly lightheaded as the fear evaporated.

Concern filled the soft, round face. "Oh dear!" Daisy's eyes crinkled in distress. "I didn't even think about that. I didn't mean to scare you. I know you worry."

Daisy knew her secret fear. They'd commiserated over what Daisy called their "senior moments."

But I'm not a senior yet.

"I'm just glad you're here," Noelle said as a rush of affection for her aunt swamped her.

"I had to check on you," she said. "I knew you would be here alone. At least Lucia lives close to Eve for support." She leaned back in her chair with a smile and sipped her coffee. "Now. Tell me what's up. I felt like you were holding back when you brought me dinner the other night."

Noelle had to think back. The Indian takeout they'd shared seemed a long time ago.

At least I remember that dinner.

She remembered that Max had been in the parking lot with a motorcycle. His helmet and heavy gear had surprised her. Before that she had only been able to picture him in a suit and tie. But after they'd talked for a minute, the gear seemed right on him.

"Noelle."

Noelle blinked. "I'm sorry, what?"

Daisy leaned forward, studying her face. "I know you enjoyed the Indian food, but the memory of dinner isn't what put that smile on your face. What on earth did that?"

"Before I went inside your place that night, I ran into the FBI agent who'd interviewed you earlier that day."

"Paulette's grandson or the other one?"

"The grandson. Agent Rhodes."

"Good-looking man." Daisy nodded approvingly. "Tall too. Paulette talks about him all the time. A little too much, if you ask me. *Talks* isn't the right word; she brags about him. Always says he's working on important cases. Good thing I have you to counter her."

"Me?"

Daisy's face lit up. "You're always catching the bad guys. And you're local too, so most of the other residents know about you. That's much more impressive than a grandson in another state."

"So you're saying you use me to win bragging contests." Amusement filled her.

"Yep!" Her great-aunt looked extremely pleased with herself. "I'm one of the few people who can top Paulette's stories."

"Congratulations," Noelle said with a straight face. "Glad I can be of some help."

"Has he figured out who killed Derrick?"

Noelle's brain struggled to follow Daisy's abrupt topic shift. "No, not yet."

"Hmmm. He seems like a smart one. He will." She contentedly lifted her cup to her lips.

She's up to something.

"Daisy, who do you think killed Derrick?" If Daisy was going to be blunt, then Noelle would be too.

Daisy tipped her head. "My dear girl. Do you realize that's the first time you've asked me that in thirteen years?"

"That can't be right." Noelle emphatically shook her head and winced at the stab of pain. "We've talked about it dozens of times."

"Yes, we have, but you've never asked me what I thought."

Noelle attempted to sift through their years of conversations and abundance of topics.

Is that true?

"Maybe I didn't want to know." The words came out of Noelle's mouth before she thought them through.

Daisy arched her brows. "Why on earth would you not want to know?"

"Because I'm scared of the answer," she said slowly, her nightmares spinning through her head. "I don't know what's real sometimes."

Her aunt leaned forward and set a hand on Noelle's knee, worry in her eyes. "I think you better tell me what you mean by that."

Noelle held her gaze, not knowing how to share the madness that sometimes ran through her head. "I've told everyone I can't remember what happened. But I have dreams, and part of me worries that they're true—or at least partially true. Another part of me believes it's simply my brain running wild."

"Tell me one."

Noelle swallowed hard, seeing this woman she deeply loved dying in a pool of blood. "I frequently dream you died that day in the house. You were there."

Daisy tightened her hand on Noelle's knee. "You can see that I'm just fine, dear. It clearly didn't happen. But go on."

Her aunt didn't break eye contact, and Noelle leaned into that invisible rope of support. "Poppa was there too," she whispered. "But he was okay."

"That's good. Right?"

"No." Noelle's mouth dried up. "He had a rifle. He was standing over you."

"I was shot?"

Noelle closed her eyes for a long second, trying to recall a wound on Daisy. "I don't know. I can't see where you're bleeding."

"Maybe because your brain knows I'm not dead?"

"Maybe." She studied her aunt. "In some dreams Poppa has a crowbar."

"Aha. The missing weapon." She gave Noelle a sad smile. "Your grandfather didn't kill anyone, honey. He didn't have it in him."

How many times have friends and family of other killers said that to me?

"Plus he was home with me at the time Derrick was killed," Daisy pointed out. "You can't put any stock in these dreams."

"Last night I dreamed Eve was in your place, bleeding on the floor."

"You three girls could have been killed yesterday. No doubt fear for your sisters was in your subconscious." Sympathy filled her eyes.

Noelle sat very still, feeling something poking around in her thoughts, trying to come to the surface. She had experienced it dozens of times over the years, but nothing ever emerged.

Do I have the killer's identity locked in my memory?

She wasn't sure. She'd been to three different hypnotists without results.

"I'm just thankful you're all safe after that horrid incident," said Daisy, sitting back in her chair. "Now let's talk about something cheery. Did you know that Adam is planning a surprise trip to Hawaii for Eve?" Her face lit up.

"No! I didn't know that." Actually Adam had told Noelle about the surprise last week, but Daisy looked so pleased to spill the secret, Noelle went with it.

"Yes! He is so excited."

Daisy was in full gossip mode now, so Noelle tried to relax and enjoy her coffee, occasionally interjecting a reaction to Daisy's one-sided conversation.

But Noelle was thinking about her grandfather. He couldn't have been involved in Derrick's death.

Why don't I feel more certain about that?

41

Max met Deputy Hartley a block from the scene of the explosion. Overnight, tips about the incident had rolled in to the FBI and the sheriff's office. Officers were going through them, trying to figure out which carried weight and which ones were from bitter people turning in their significant others.

Max had captured some still images from the video of the person lingering in the alley before the explosion. He still couldn't tell if the person was male or female but hoped there would be something visibly distinctive to the people at the homeless encampment. The video and stills would also be distributed to local news organizations to post on social media and show during their broadcasts. But until then, it was Max and Deputy Hartley hitting the street and knocking on doors. And tents.

Groups of tents and old motor homes had popped up in a few places around the city. Occasionally the local government would order them cleared out, but then they would simply show up in another location. Deputy Hartley told Max this particular encampment behind the strip mall had been slowly growing for six months, and the police had been called to the area several times. As they drew closer, Max studied the debris spread around the camp. The light layer of snow couldn't hide the poverty.

Tires, broken storage bins, children's toys, bikes, cardboard boxes, old coolers, and propane tanks were all visible under the thin snow blanket. One decrepit motor home had cement blocks in place of two of its wheels and bedsheets blocking the view through its windshield. Max decided the people inside were lucky compared to those in the tents covered with tarps held down by random pieces of wood and metal.

A tiny bike lay on its side, its broken training wheels catching his eye. *This isn't a place for a child.*

Hartley approached the closest trailer and banged on the door. "Deschutes County sheriff! I just have a few questions!" Max stood back, watching the windows of the trailer, wondering how it had originally parked there since it had two flat tires and there was no truck in sight to pull it. A towel covering one window shifted slightly. Max couldn't see a face, but he waved, attempting to look as nonthreatening as possible. The trailer shook as someone moved inside.

The door slowly opened and a man in a hoodie appeared. "Yeah?"

"Can you step out, please, sir?" asked Hartley. "We have some pictures to show you."

Max moved forward, removing the printouts from inside his coat. The man reluctantly stepped down two stairs, his hands thrust in the pockets of a jacket he wore over the hoodie. His lip was pierced, his beard straggly, and his eyes exhausted, and the hood hid his hair. He could have been anywhere from thirty-five to fifty-five.

Max held up two photos of the person in the alley. "Do you recognize this person?"

The man peered at it. "There's no face. How'm I to tell?"

"The posture, the stance," said Max. "Body shape." He pulled out his phone and showed the video. "The way they move."

The man studied all the images and video. "No idea. That could be anybody."

"What are people saying about the explosion?" asked Max, trying a different topic.

The man's eyebrows rose to vanish under his hoodie. "This guy did it?"

"Don't know. What have you heard?"

He shrugged. "People just saying a car blew up. I heard it. I was outside and saw the smoke."

"Did you go see what happened?"

"Nah. I heard the sirens and decided it was a good place to avoid. Went back inside." He jerked his head toward the rest of the camp. "That's what most everyone did."

"Most everyone?" asked Hartley.

The man lifted one shoulder. "Some people like to gawk, you know? Can't stay away."

"Who?" asked Max. "Who checked out the scene?"

He pointed at three tents that appeared to be connected under several tarps. "They might've. Not sure. She described the burned-up car."

"Any rumors going around about who might have done it?" asked Max.

Genuine surprise filled his face. "You ain't caught no one?"

"Wouldn't be knocking on your door if we had," said Max.

The man looked past them down the line of trailers and tents. "Haven't heard anything like that. Mostly people talking about the sound and smoke." He met Max's gaze and shrugged; he was finished.

"Thanks for your time," said Hartley, handing him a card. "Call if you hear differently." He followed Max to the group of three tents.

Max paused at the tents, looking for what could be considered an entrance under the layers of tarps.

"Sheriff's department," announced Hartley. He stepped forward and shook one of the tarps. "We'd like a word." He shook it again.

"Hang on," came an annoyed woman's voice from inside.

The men waited. Max spotted an extension cord that ran from one of the tents and through a fence. He took a few steps to follow it and saw it disappeared under the back door of one of the strip mall stores. He wondered if the owner had allowed it or if an employee had taken pity on one of the campers. A green tarp vibrated and was suddenly cast aside as a woman stepped out, giving Max a glimpse inside. Blankets, sleeping bags, a space heater, stuffed garbage bags. A sour smell wafted out.

"What do you want?" she asked, looking from Hartley to Max. Like the man in the trailer, she wore a hoodie, and underneath it a knit cap covered her head, but a dark braid snaked out and hung halfway down her chest. Her lower front teeth were missing.

Max held out the photos. "Can you tell who this is?"

She grabbed one and held it a little farther away, squinting. She peered at the other one in his hand and then eyed the video on his phone. "Could be Silver. He walks like that. Sort of hunched, you know?" She spoke the name with a faint lisp.

"Where can we find Silver?" asked Hartley.

The woman pointed down the sad line of makeshift homes. "The plywood place."

Max stepped back for a better view. Sure enough, someone had built a small unit with plywood and covered it with tarps. "You see the explosion?" he asked the woman.

"No, but I heard it. Everyone heard it."

"Go check it out?" asked Hartley.

"Of course. Saw a crispy vehicle and lots of cops standing around."

"Who are people saying did it?"

She wrinkled her nose. "Thought it just blew up. It happens, you know. Maybe one of those battery cars."

Max silently sighed and handed her a card. "Let me know if you hear any claims about who did it. Reputable claims," he added.

She took the card and stared at it. "FBI? Holy shit. Was it a terrorist? One of those Eastern fellas?" Wide eyes looked up at him.

Max held back the urge to reply "Yes, someone from the East Coast" but instead said, "Not sure what happened yet. Thank you for your time." As they walked toward the plywood structure in search of a person named Silver, he told Hartley, "Maybe we should just give out your cards. Less questions and speculation."

Hartley snorted and then rapped on one of the pieces of plywood. "Sheriff's department! We'd like a word."

Max gazed down the line of tents, which went on for another half a block.

Are we wasting our time?

"Fuck. Watch your step." Hartley kicked at something in the snow. Needles. "Not surprised, though."

Max scanned the ground, spotting a few other syringes sticking out of the snow and three yards away a kid's broken scooter.

What if a child stepped on one?

Angry, he knocked on the plywood. "Sheriff's department! Get out here." He studied some black patches on the warped wood. "Is that mold?" he asked Hartley in a low voice.

"Wouldn't be surprised. Probably a lot more inside. Damp this time of year."

"Hold your horses!" said a man inside. "I'm comin' out." Boards scraped and a low makeshift door slid to one side. A man in a John Deere cap and a bulky jacket scrambled out on his hands. He stood, brushing his hands on the thighs of his dirty jeans, and then glared at the officers. Max estimated he was in his late twenties. A dozen piercings lined his eyebrows. He had two hoops in his nose and several in his lips. His ears were bare.

He has to be Silver.

"I didn't do anything," he snapped.

"Didn't say you did," said Max in a casual tone. "Just looking for some help."

"Right." Distrust filled the man's brown eyes.

"You Silver?" asked Hartley, deliberately studying the piercings.

"Who says that?" he asked, folding his arms across his chest.

"I think we got off on the wrong foot," said Max. He held out the two printouts and decided to take a chance. "This is you, correct?"

Surprise flickered across his face. "Don't know." He straightened, getting rid of his slouch, which was similar to the one in the pictures. "Why?"

"You didn't do anything wrong," said Max. "But you might have been in the right place at the right time. We want to know what you saw when you were there."

"Didn't see nothing."

A backhanded confirmation that it's him in the picture.

"You didn't hear the explosion yesterday?" asked Max.

"'Course I did. Whole city heard it."

Max tapped one of the pictures. "You're standing twenty feet from where it happened thirty minutes later. What were you doing in the alley for over an hour?"

"Not a crime to be walking around."

"I agree. Like I said, we just want to know what you saw while you were there."

Silver tugged at one of the rings in his lips. "Didn't see nothing. I always just hang out there. It's my smoking spot."

Max abruptly understood. "And you get to watch the women in yoga clothing during class and as they go in and out of the building while enjoying your smoke."

Silver grinned, showing a lot of black spots on his teeth near his gums. "Not a crime to watch."

"That's true," agreed Max. He showed Silver the video. "What are you doing when you bend down here?"

Silver instantly took a half step back. "Nothing, man." Fear flickered in his eyes.

Got him.

"Did someone know that you frequently hung out there?" asked Max. "Did they ask you to put it under the vehicle?"

Confusion flashed and the brows narrowed, making their piercings move. "Finders keepers. It's the law, you know."

Finders keepers?

Max glanced at Hartley, who was scowling at Silver. "What did you find there?" Max asked.

"Finders keepers," repeated Silver emphatically. "I didn't steal it. I found it."

"Found what?"

Silver shifted his feet. "The cash, dude. That's what I'm picking up in that." He nodded at Max's phone.

"How much cash?"

"Four twenties. I figured it fell out of a pocket, but since I found it, it was mine."

"Where is it now?"

Silver snorted. "If someone reported it missing, they're too late. Finders keepers. Spent it yesterday. 7-Eleven. Got smokes and peanut butter." He nodded earnestly. "Check the store's video, man. I was in there around eleven yesterday."

He's telling the truth.

"I don't care about the cash, Silver," said Max. "What I want to know is if you saw anything going on that could possibly be related to setting up that explosion. You had a clear view of that vehicle."

"Nah. Nothing fishy was goin' on. Was just gonna watch the women." He leered, impressively waggling his eyebrows and piercings. "Got lucky with the cash. It was a good day, you know?"

"Any rumors going around about who caused the explosion?" asked Max, feeling his lead crumble into dust.

"Nope. Don't care."

Also realizing the lead was gone, Hartley handed Silver his card with the usual request for a call.

Max reluctantly moved down the line.

"Keep knocking?" asked Hartley.

"Yep. Has to be done," said Max as he stopped at a tiny tent.

Silver was there the entire time. If he didn't see anything, the device was put on her vehicle somewhere else and then triggered with a remote.

Who would do that?

42

"Do you have any wine?" asked Savannah as she scanned the interior of Noelle's fridge. "Although maybe some hot chocolate with Kahlúa or peppermint schnapps would go better with the snowy weather."

"I do, but I don't want either," said Noelle. "My head is messed up enough. Help yourself."

"You know I will." Savannah disappeared into the large walk-in pantry, where she knew Noelle kept the alcohol.

Noelle sighed contentedly in the recliner as she closed her eyes. Daisy had left an hour ago after the three of them enjoyed the pizza Savannah had brought for lunch. Savannah was right that it was a hot chocolate day. "I changed my mind," Noelle said. "I'll take hot chocolate. Don't add anything to it."

"That's no fun."

Noelle opened her eyes to see Savannah step out of the pantry, a canister of hot chocolate in one hand and a bottle of schnapps in the other. "I don't need fun," Noelle said. "I need a clear head." She watched her friend make two cups, adding a large serving of schnapps to one and heavy toppings of whipped cream to both. She sprinkled a touch of cinnamon on the nonalcoholic one, brought it to Noelle, and then sank into the sofa with her own in hand.

"Daisy hasn't let up a bit as she's aged," said Savannah. "She can still talk and gossip me under the table."

Kendra Elliot

"That's saying something." Noelle had thought the same as they ate their pizza. "She was so excited to see you."

"It's been a long time. She still sends a Christmas card every year," said Savannah. "I make sure I buy a card just for her. I don't have anyone else who mails me one."

"She takes her card sending very seriously," said Noelle. "She monitors and updates her mailing list every year." She snorted. "It was a very big deal when she crossed Derrick's family off her list. She must have asked me ten times if it was okay—which it was, considering they'd been speculating in the press that I knew who'd killed him and refused to tell anyone."

"Bunch of assholes," Savannah stated. "You've been better off without them. And him."

Noelle sipped her drink. She agreed but didn't want to say it out loud. Savannah was vocal enough about it for the two of them.

"I won't be surprised one bit if a Bell was behind that explosion yesterday," Savannah said darkly. "Especially after what Jason said to you at the station."

"He's all talk."

"A wuss at heart," agreed Savannah. "Always has been. Did I ever tell you he hit on me not long after you moved up here?"

Noelle straightened in her recliner. "No! Why didn't you?"

"Must've forgotten." Savannah shrugged. "I ran into him at a party. He was lit. Since Derrick died he's always acted like I wasn't worth speaking to, but that night he was practically drooling around me, clearly had sex on the brain." She scoffed. "As if. The guy is a slimeball."

"What did you do?"

"I sent him packing. Reminded him how he'd dissed you at Derrick's funeral. That pissed him off." Savannah grinned. "He turned red, the little fuck."

"He's always been jealous of Derrick," said Noelle.

Savannah turned thoughtful eyes on her. "He always put you down too, and I know it was because he was jealous. He wanted you. I was

246

around enough to see how he looked at you when you weren't paying attention. I don't know if it was fueled by his feud with Derrick or that he couldn't find his own quality woman."

"According to him, *quality* didn't describe me at all."

"Lies. When he opened his mouth, a lie would slip out."

Noelle couldn't disagree with her statement. Her phone buzzed with a text. "Agent Rhodes will be here in a minute," she told Savannah.

"And his sidekick?"

"Keaton? Maybe. He didn't say."

"I like that salt-and-pepper-goatee thing Keaton's got going on."

Noelle raised a brow. "I've learned he's married."

"I can still admire." She licked her whipped cream, giving Noelle a side-eye and making her giggle.

"You haven't changed a bit, have you?"

"Why would I? I like men."

An understatement.

Savannah had married for the first time six years ago. An impulsive decision during a weekend in Vegas. The wedding had surprised Noelle, but the divorce six months later hadn't. Savannah enjoyed variety and got bored very easily. "If Keaton is with him, keep it under control."

The doorbell rang and Noelle checked her camera. "It's just Rhodes." Unlike Daisy, he looked directly at the camera, a frown on his face.

"Bummer. I'll get it," Savannah said, quickly getting to her feet.

Noelle set her cup aside and lowered the footrest of the recliner. Savannah was immediately back with Agent Rhodes in her wake.

"Where's the deputy that's supposed to be out front?" His frown was now directed at Noelle.

"I refused one," said Noelle, pushing to her feet. "I've barely been alone, and I've got an excellent security system. I'm not going to waste the department's time."

Rhodes raised a brow at Savannah.

"Don't expect me to take your side," she told him. "Noelle does what she wants. Besides, she's got me as her guard dog." She bared her teeth at the agent.

Noelle smothered a laugh. Savannah was flirting, but Rhodes hadn't picked up on it. He still looked steamed. "I assume you're here with news," said Noelle, trying to shift his attention. She gestured at the big sectional. "Take a seat. What's going on?"

"I'll get you some hot chocolate, Agent Rhodes," said Savannah, heading toward the kitchen.

"No booze," Noelle ordered, knowing her best friend too well.

Rhodes blinked in surprise. "Thank you," he said to Savannah. "And she's right, no alcohol." His gaze went to the mug beside Noelle as he took a seat.

"None in mine either," Noelle said. "Savannah's cup is a different matter."

"It's been a busy but frustrating day so far," said Rhodes. He told her about his morning and his interviews at the homeless encampment.

Noelle thought for a moment. "I've seen a guy several times near the yoga studio with a bunch of face piercings and smoking. Just hanging out."

"Yeah, he likes to watch the class and everyone walking in and out." Rhodes's tone was sour.

Savannah laughed as she handed Rhodes a cup with three inches of whipped cream on top and then sat beside him. "He sounds like a normal man."

Rhodes thanked her for the drink, and he eyed the whipped cream for a long moment. Savannah belatedly handed him a spoon, and relief flashed on his face. "Anyway, it's still looking as if someone placed the exploding device when your SUV was somewhere else. Where could that have happened?"

"At my grandmother's, the Indian restaurant," said Noelle, hoping she wouldn't forget any locations. "I doubt it could have happened at the sheriff's department. Our parking is fenced and has lots of cameras."

She thought for a moment. "I met Mercy downtown. Parked on the street."

Rhodes had set aside his cup and was making a list of locations to check for cameras.

"How far back do you need to know?" she asked.

"I'd say since Thursday. That's when we got to town."

Noelle added a few more locations. "Any more word on Jason?"

Rhodes grinned, and from the corner of her eye, Noelle saw Savannah perk up.

Yeah, when he smiles it's a nice sight.

"He called me last night," said Rhodes. "He figured out that we were at his hotel to ask about the explosion and was severely insulted that we thought he could have a hand in it."

"Jason wouldn't know how to put together that sort of thing," said Noelle. "And he doesn't get his hands dirty."

Rhodes shrugged. "He could have hired someone or spent some time on YouTube to figure it out."

"It would have been stupid for him to threaten me in person if he was planning that," said Noelle.

"Maybe that's what he wants you to think," said Savannah. "Covering his ass. How intensely did he threaten you in person?"

"Not that bad," said Noelle. "You're thinking his visit to the department was a lame ruse to make us consider that he'd never threaten me in person if he'd planted the bomb?" She winced. "Your logic is making my head hurt."

Rhodes's phone rang. He glanced at the screen. "I need to take this." He rose and opened the door to Noelle's deck, starting his conversation outside.

"You're staring," said Savannah.

Noelle whipped her gaze back to her friend. "I want to know what kind of call made him go outside." She gave a half smile. "But he's easy to watch," she admitted.

Savannah downed half her hot chocolate. "Nice to see the blow to your head didn't affect your eyesight."

"It was blurry yesterday," said Noelle, purposefully pretending to misunderstand her meaning. "Seems okay today."

Rhodes came back in, his face carefully blank. Too blank.

"What happened?" Alarm started up Noelle's spine as the agent retook his seat and carefully met her gaze.

"For part of our investigation into Derrick's death, we've been redoing a lot of the forensic work where we can." He pressed his lips together. "Since technology has come a long way in the last thirteen years, one of the things I wanted examined again was the 911 recording."

Noelle nodded. His serious tone was making her stomach spin. Even Savannah was paying close attention.

"To do that, I sent in new voice recordings for comparison." He glanced at Savannah. "I gave them yours, Noelle's, Lucia's, Daisy's, and also Derrick's mother and sister. I sent long samples from my interviews, so they'd have as much as possible to make a comparison." He looked back at Noelle. "I'm sorry, Noelle, but they're positive it was Lucia who made the call. No doubts at all."

Noelle couldn't breathe.

I listened to that call. It can't be Lucia.

"That can't be right," she finally said. "I would have recognized her voice. And she would have told us if she'd made the call. She wouldn't hide that fact." Abruptly the dream image of Lucia's minivan in the driveway popped into her head.

Didn't happen.

"It appears she did hide the fact she made the call," Rhodes said gently. "Why do you think she'd do that? Thirteen years is a long time to keep that sort of secret."

"Her anxiety," murmured Savannah. "She's dealt with stress and nerves since then, right? Always worried about someone coming to hurt her and especially hurt you."

"She'd always been a bit flighty," said Noelle. "Even before that. Her emotions ran deep, and she wore them on her sleeve. Poppa always said she was wired a bit differently than the rest of us."

"If she witnessed something horrible—like Derrick being beaten to death and you being hit—then possibly it affected her in a unique way," said Savannah. "And so she didn't do what you or I would have done."

"She's kept it silent for a reason," said Rhodes. "Possibly—"

"She's kept it silent because she wasn't there!" Anger shot through Noelle. "She didn't see anything!"

Minivan.

"She wasn't there," Noelle repeated weakly, her emotional denial rapidly losing steam as the FBI's evidence overpowered her instinct to protect her sister.

She was there.

"She's a good kid," Noelle added, reluctantly accepting the truth. "Honest to a fault."

"She's thirty-one," said Rhodes. "Definitely not a kid now."

"I know." Noelle leaned back in the recliner, her world starting to spin. "But she's always seemed younger. For some reason she's never viewed the world like an adult."

"Could be from trauma," Savannah said softly.

Noelle held her best friend's gaze for a long moment, seeing sympathy and concern. "Why wouldn't she say anything?" she whispered.

"Possibly because she's protecting someone," said Rhodes. "Or else she lives in fear of someone coming after her for what she witnessed. Or maybe she thinks she would be in trouble with the police since she was there."

Is it possible?

"This can't be right." Noelle couldn't think straight, her mind shooting in dozens of directions as she tried to imagine why Lucia would be there and, if so, why she'd told no one. "She'd tell someone."

"It could be she's not the only one keeping the secret," said Rhodes. "Who would she trust?"

"Me," Noelle said immediately. "She knows she can trust me."

But clearly she didn't tell me.

Unless I forgot.

Noelle pressed her palms against her eyes in confusion and disbelief.

"Lucia trusts everyone," said Savannah. "She always has." She looked at Rhodes. "Your voice comparison is wrong. Have them do it again."

"They did it three times. I was told they're one hundred percent positive."

"Oh my God," muttered Noelle. "What does this mean?"

Savannah knelt next to the recliner and took one of her hands, holding her gaze. "They're wrong. They have to be wrong."

I can't deny the evidence, no matter how much I want to.

Lucia made the call.

"Daisy and your grandfather said they were with Lucia during the time of the murder," said Rhodes. "Either they knew something about the situation, or somehow Lucia snuck out and back in without their noticing." He paused. "During my interview Daisy sort of indicated that your grandfather may have done something to Derrick. She may have known Lucia was gone and had been protecting her. Actually it's possible both your grandfather and Daisy were protecting her. I feel like people have deliberately tried to guide the investigation in wrong directions. Both now and thirteen years ago."

Noelle's phone rang and she checked the screen. "It's Eve." Her finger hovered over the button to answer. She was uncertain she could carry on a normal conversation at the moment.

She answered. "How are you feeling today, Eve?" Her voice was wooden as she tried to sound casual.

"Something's happened to Lucia!" Eve was sobbing.

Noelle rocketed up in her recliner, adrenaline kicking through her nerves. "*What?*"

"I don't know! I went to knock on her door because she wasn't answering my texts and found her purse spilled on the stairs and her door left open!"

Lucia's apartment was over Eve's garage. A narrow set of outdoor stairs went up the far side of the garage. "Her car?"

"Still here."

"Call the police now!" Noelle ordered, making eye contact with Rhodes, who was listening closely.

"I already did, and then I immediately called you."

"I'll be there in ten minutes. Don't touch anything." Noelle ended the call, pushed to her feet, and then repeated Eve's words to Rhodes and Savannah. "I need to go." Slightly dizzy from standing quickly, she stumbled forward. Rhodes shot to her side and grabbed her arm before she could fall.

"You're not going anywhere."

She turned a frenzied gaze on him. "Something's happened to Lucia. She would never leave her door open like that, let alone not pick up her spilled purse!"

"I know," Rhodes said firmly. "But we just had a discussion that it's possible she's hiding something and has been scared into silence for thirteen years. It could be someone is worried her silence won't last any longer."

"Like with you," said Savannah to Noelle. "You almost died yesterday. Someone might think you're also a risk."

Noelle was frantic. "But nothing's changed! I don't remember what happened! Why would they think that now?"

"I don't know," said Rhodes. "But your sister could be in a lot of danger."

"Was the explosion yesterday intended for her?" whispered Noelle.

"They'd have targeted Eve's car, not yours, right?" asked Rhodes.

"Yes. Eve always drives her to yoga." Noelle's brain couldn't keep up.

Rhodes sent a text, then pulled on his coat. "I'll let you know what we find."

Noelle opened her mouth to argue that he couldn't keep her away. Instead, she slammed it shut and nodded. The second he was gone, she raced for her coat and slipped on her boots. "You're driving me to Lucia's," she informed Savannah.

"Way ahead of you, Detective," said Savannah, her coat already on and holding up her keys.

Noelle teared up in gratitude. "Let's go."

Lucia has to be okay.

43

When Max arrived at Eve's home, there were three Deschutes County sheriff's vehicles on the street, and he spotted Detective Bolton speaking with Eve in her front yard. Neighbors were gathering across the street to watch, bundled up in their coats, talking in small groups. Keaton pulled up behind Max's rental car. Max had texted him from Noelle's home when he heard about Lucia.

"I just confirmed that Jason Bell was on his flight this morning," said Keaton as he approached Max.

"I want a visual confirmation that he's definitely out of state," said Max, slamming the door of his vehicle. "The last time Lucia was seen was when Detective Bolton dropped off her and Eve this morning. I know Bell's flight was to leave before that, but I want actual eyes on where he is at the moment."

"Got it." Max watched Keaton open Jason Bell's contact on his phone and hit the FaceTime button.

"What the hell do you want, Keaton?" Jason Bell said as he came into view on-screen.

"Show me where you're at," said Keaton.

"I'm in my fucking house." Bell proceeded to turn in a circle, showing the interior of the home.

Max recognized the kitchen from their previous interview with Bell. Keaton met his gaze and nodded. He'd recognized it too.

"Thanks." Keaton ended the call as a pissed-off Bell started to sputter at him. "I'd say he's effectively eliminated. Who's our next suspect?"

"Lucia could have left of her own accord," said Max.

"And left behind her purse, phone, and car?" asked Keaton. "Who would she go with?"

"Maybe Eve has some ideas," said Max. The two men had started in her direction when they heard another vehicle approach, and Max glanced over to see Savannah parking at the curb, Noelle in her passenger seat. "Dammit."

"She shouldn't be here," said Keaton.

"Do you really think Noelle would stay away? It's her sister." Max had noted how Noelle had silently nodded as he left her home and had figured it wouldn't be the last he'd see of her that day. He watched as Noelle leaped out of the car, ignored him, and sprinted toward Eve and Detective Bolton.

"Shit." Max and Keaton got moving too. Max saw that Savannah stayed with her car, smartly staying out of law enforcement's way and leaning against the fender to watch. She lifted a thermal travel mug at him in a casual toast, and he wondered if it contained the rest of her spiked hot chocolate.

A couple of deputies stepped forward to intercept Noelle as she raced toward the scene but stopped as they recognized the detective. Noelle quickly embraced Eve, and her sister rapidly spoke, waving her hands.

"Please restart your story, Eve," said Keaton as he and Max joined the group.

Detective Bolton nodded at both of them. "I'll take you up to the apartment when she's done."

Eve took a deep breath, her hand clasped in Noelle's. "I texted Lucia before lunch, asking if she wanted to eat with me. She said no and that she was going to take a nap. I ate and then lay down and fell asleep too. But a half hour ago I texted her again. When she didn't answer after another text, I went outside to go up to her apartment. That's when I saw her things on the steps. I went up the rest of the stairs, and her door was open, but she wasn't inside. I ran around the outside of the garage and house to make sure she wasn't here, and that's when I called Detective Bolton. Then I called Noelle."

"As soon as Eve hung up, I requested units to her home," continued Bolton. "We've cleared the house and the apartment. Lucia isn't here, and the only camera is on the home's doorbell."

"I checked it while waiting for you guys," said Eve. "The only thing it shows since we were dropped off is me heading to Eve's apartment and then running to check around the house."

"No cars passed on the street?" asked Noelle.

"The angle doesn't catch the street."

"I've got two uniforms knocking on doors, checking for cameras and asking if anyone saw anything," said Bolton.

"Would she go for a walk?" asked Keaton.

"No," said Eve and Noelle simultaneously.

"Not her thing," added Eve. "She would never leave her things on the stairs and her door open."

"When will forensics be here?" asked Max.

"Any minute," answered Bolton.

"I need to see her apartment," said Noelle.

Bolton led the sisters, Max, and Keaton to the far side of the garage. Max looked up the steep set of stairs. They were painted a light gray and had a rubber tread on each step. Halfway up lay a small purse with a long, thick strap. Scattered on other steps he spotted a cell phone, keys, and a sunglasses case. "Could she have fallen?" he wondered out loud as he studied the pavement around the bottom step, looking for blood. If she'd been startled or pushed while on the stairs, it'd have been easy for her to tumble to the bottom, but he didn't see anything to indicate a fall.

The stairs and driveway didn't have a thin cover of snow like the grass below the trees. The sun had been shining for several hours and had melted most of the snow on the streets and in its direct path. Bolton handed out booties and gloves, and the group of five started up the stairs. Max was about to suggest Eve stay behind since she wasn't law enforcement but realized she'd be the most likely to spot anything out of the ordinary in Lucia's apartment. Max lingered behind the others, taking his own photographs of the stairs and items. "I'll grab her phone after I get some pictures," he told the group.

He stopped at the purse, recognizing it from his interview with Lucia and Daisy two days ago. Lucia had worn it across her body, the distinctive red-checked strap standing out against her white sweater. He stared at the small bag, imagining it being ripped off over her head or tugged from her grasp and thrown down the steps. Or perhaps Lucia had taken it off herself, leaving a distress signal for others.

Max picked up the cell phone and slipped it into a plastic bag. Tapping the locked screen showed three notifications of unopened texts from Eve. Hopefully one of the sisters knew the phone's passcode.

The apartment was very neat inside. No dishes in the sink, her bed made, and a knitted throw perfectly folded on the back of her sofa. There was no head print in the pillow on her bed. "I don't think she took a nap," said Keaton. "Even if she'd done it on the sofa, she'd probably have used the throw."

"But she would have folded it back up," said Noelle. "That's how Lucia is." Eve nodded in agreement.

Max motioned for Bolton to follow him into the bedroom and found a laundry basket of clothes on the floor of the closet. He pointed at the clothing on the top in the basket. "Was she wearing those jeans when you dropped her off this morning?"

"She wore dark-green yoga pants," said Bolton. Max fished through the laundry, not seeing the described pants. "I think she wore a green striped shirt," continued Bolton. "She had on a white jacket that covered most of it." None of the items were in the closet or the laundry basket. Max confirmed the detective's clothing description with Eve.

"We know what she's wearing," he said.

Not that it helps us at the moment.

They searched the apartment for anything unusual, checking cupboards and drawers. A laptop was plugged in on her desk. Bolton opened it, but he needed a password to gain access. Neither Eve nor Noelle had any suggestions.

"How about a passcode for her phone?" Max held up the bag with Lucia's phone.

The women looked at each other. "Maybe her birthday," said Noelle hopefully. "Or maybe Poppa's birthday." Eve looked skeptical. The phone still in the bag, Max tried the numbers, but neither date worked.

"Mom's birth date," said Noelle. When that didn't work, she suggested another date.

The phone opened.

"What happened on that date?" asked Max.

"Our mother's death," whispered Eve, reaching out to take Noelle's hand. "I can't believe that's what she uses for a passcode. Lucia was only two when she died," she told the others. "She doesn't remember our mother."

Max was speechless for a brief moment as he wondered why Lucia kept that sad date active in her daily life. Maybe she had chosen it because she didn't have the memories her sisters did. A way to hang on. "I'm very sorry," he told the women. He turned his attention to the phone, scrolling through Lucia's list of texts, noting texts from all her family members. He clicked on names he didn't recognize and quickly scanned their messages. Not counting Eve's, the last text had been to a friend early that morning, reassuring her that she wasn't badly hurt. Her last phone call had been two days ago.

Nothing waved red flags.

"Try the date on her laptop," said Max.

Keaton typed it in with no results. "Leave it for forensics."

Max looked at the sisters. "Call everyone who she knows. Call her work, call Daisy, call her friends."

"I don't want to worry Daisy. This will really upset her," said Eve as Noelle nodded. "And Lucia isn't out visiting friends!" Eve waved at the open front door. "Her stuff is dumped on the stairs!"

"I understand," said Max. "But maybe a friend has an idea of who would do this. Maybe Lucia told Daisy about someone who was bothering her at work. That sort of thing."

"It has to be related to the explosion yesterday," said Noelle. "These two incidents are so close together, I can't see them not being connected."

"I agree," said Keaton. "But we have to explore all avenues. Keep your mind open."

"I know. You're right." Noelle pressed her fingers against her forehead above one eye.

"You hurting?" asked Eve.

"A bit."

"Take her outside and start making some calls," said Bolton. "What did your husband say?" he asked Eve.

She glanced at her phone screen. "I texted him after I called Noelle. He must be in a meeting. Nothing yet." Eve tapped on her screen and opened the text. "It's not delivered," she muttered. She touched Adam's photo at the top of her screen and clicked on his location map.

Max watched as she waited for her phone to locate him, a sense of dread forming in his gut.

"Not found," Eve muttered. She tried again.

Noelle met Max's gaze, concern growing in her eyes. "Call him," he told Eve.

"Straight to voicemail," she said after a moment. With a stunned expression on her face, she looked at the others. "Did something happen to him too?" she asked in a faltering voice.

"Call his work," ordered Bolton. "Does his job ever take him out of range?"

"No." Eve held the phone to her ear, her hand visibly shaking. "Hi, Lorna, it's Eve. Can I talk to Adam? His cell isn't working." She was silent a moment. "Oh . . . okay. No, he's not here. I'll check with his doctor's office. He probably texted me, but it didn't go through." She ended the call, her face pale. "He went in and then left after an hour or so, saying he was sick." She looked at everyone. "Something's happened to Adam," she whispered.

Bolton pulled out his phone. "I'll get a BOLO on his truck. It's silver, right? Make and model?" he asked Eve. "Do you know the plate?"

"Silver Toyota Tundra. I don't know the plate." Her voice cracked.

"We can find out." Bolton headed to the door, his phone at his ear.

"Did you talk to him today?" Max asked Eve.

"I texted him that Detective Bolton was giving us a ride home from the hospital. That text went through," she said, checking her phone again. "But he didn't reply—which isn't unusual since it wasn't a question. I assumed he was at work when I got home. I didn't think anything of it."

"Everyone outside," said Max. "Start calling whoever you can think of that Lucia or Adam could have been in contact with."

"What is going on?" asked Eve, her voice rising. "Does the same person who made Lucia drop her things have Adam too?"

Her question echoed in Max's head.

Or did Adam make Lucia drop her things?

Max exchanged a look with Keaton, seeing in his gaze that they shared the same thought.

He looked at Noelle, who shook her head, disbelief in her eyes. "It can't be."

Eve looked from one of them to another, confusion wrinkling her forehead. "What—no! You're wrong. All of you are wrong!" She stumbled back two steps.

"How close are Adam and Lucia?" asked Max.

"Very close!" said Eve, anger rising in her tone. "He would *never* do anything to her. He's one of her closest friends! He loves her!"

Max noticed Noelle said nothing, but a speculative look entered her gaze.

"You're wrong!" Eve yelled again. "All of you! Something has happened to Adam! Now fucking find him and Lucia!" She spun away and darted out of the apartment.

"Noelle?" Max asked softly. He didn't like how pale she'd grown.

She swallowed hard, her eyes troubled. "I don't know."

"Impossible?" he asked.

"No."

"Why do you say that? Eve seems certain Adam wouldn't do something to Lucia." Max spoke carefully, seeing Noelle was teetering between logic and loyalty to her family.

"I'm not sure. But I can't say it's impossible."

"Okay." Max touched her arm. "I know you're trying to consider all angles."

She jerked her head in a short nod.

Max looked at Keaton. "Our best bet is finding his truck."

44

Hours later there were still no results on the BOLO for Adam's truck, and Noelle was fading, exhaustion and pain taking over her head. She'd numbly sat in Eve's living room, Savannah holding her hand, waiting for word of Lucia. Eve had called everyone she could think of and then sat at the dining table at the far end of the room, silently crying while shooting the occasional glare at the deputies who were currently searching her home, looking for any clue to where Adam or Lucia could be.

After working with Agent Keaton on a script that wouldn't alarm Daisy, Eve called her and asked if she could join her and Lucia for dinner. Daisy suggested tomorrow because tonight was Hawaiian night at the retirement community center, and she was one of the organizers. She didn't mention that Lucia was already there or that she'd seen or spoken with her that day.

Where is she?

Noelle had tried to talk to her sister, but Eve had shut her down. "I can't believe you'd consider the slightest possibility that Adam would do something to Lucia," she'd hissed. "*Who are you?* Turn off your cop brain for a moment and think of your family. The two of them must be in trouble!"

I can't turn off my cop brain. Especially when my sister is missing.

Guilt swamped her that she couldn't swear Adam wasn't behind Lucia's disappearance. She'd known the man for years. He'd always been kind and helpful to her and Lucia.

But is it possible to be too helpful? To the point of overstepping a personal line?

How many times had he inquired about Noelle's health or brought up Derrick's stress levels? And Lucia's anxiety. He watched everyone so closely. She'd always attributed it to his kindness and his determination to make everyone's life easier. But looking back . . .

There was a niggling suspicion that she couldn't eliminate. "You okay?" Savannah asked Noelle for the tenth time.

"It's way past time for my pain meds." She glanced at the front door, where Rhodes was speaking to a deputy. "I want to go home. Eve doesn't want me here."

"I'll ask again if you can leave." Savannah headed toward the agent.

Noelle closed her eyes. She couldn't hear the conversation, but she picked up on the tone. In any argument, Savannah was the person you wanted on your side. A few seconds later she was back.

"He says I can drive you home, but a deputy has to clear the house before we can go inside, and then I'm to stay with you. Your alarm system is *not* to be turned off, and he wants us to check in with him every hour."

"Deal." Noelle slowly got to her feet. She looked down the room at Eve, but her sister deliberately turned her head.

She'll talk to me when they find them.

Later, at Noelle's home, Noelle and Savannah waited in the rental car as a deputy went through the house. He came out a few minutes later. "All clear, Detective Marshall."

"Thanks, Jeff," said Noelle. The deputy waited, watching until both women were inside and the front door had closed. Noelle activated the alarm.

"I'm ready for more hot chocolate," muttered Savannah, striding to the kitchen and into the pantry. "Food too."

Noelle suddenly realized she was starving. Stress and concern for her sister had kept hunger at bay. It was nearly 7:00 p.m., and the sun had been down for hours. She took her pain medication and then checked her freezer, knowing there was nothing worth eating in the fridge.

"I've got frozen pizza, lasagna, or chicken strips," she announced to Savannah.

"Lasagna."

"It'll take an hour. I'm pretty hungry."

"Eat these while you wait." Savannah reappeared, a box of crackers in one hand and a bottle of red wine in the other. She studied the wine label. "This calls for lasagna."

Crackers appealed to Noelle and to the medication she'd just taken on an empty stomach. "I'll slice some cheese for the crackers and start the lasagna. No wine. I want hot chocolate, please."

Savannah turned on some classic rock music, poured a glass of wine, and made more hot chocolate. The sounds of the Rolling Stones filled the house, and a minute later they sat at the table and started in on the cheese and crackers. "What a fucking day," mumbled Noelle, feeling the last of her energy dissipate even though the music was upbeat. She'd be lucky if she stayed awake until the lasagna was done.

"I can't believe Adam would be involved in Lucia's disappearance," said Savannah. "He was probably just there at the wrong time and got caught up in whatever happened."

That sense of doubt struck her again.

I'm overanalyzing everything I ever heard him say or saw him do.

"It can't be ruled out just because we feel it's so," said Noelle.

"I'm sorry Eve wasn't speaking to you."

"She needed to direct her anger and fear at someone," said Noelle. "And I happened to be that person. It'll pass." The betrayed look in Eve's eyes would haunt Noelle for a long time. She'd been horrified that Noelle wouldn't agree that Adam wasn't responsible.

I should have said I agreed, if only to make her feel better.

But she couldn't have brought herself to say it out loud.

She couldn't eliminate a possibility until she had proof. It was too easy to develop tunnel vision when emotions guided an investigation, and she'd learned the hard way not to allow that to happen. She loved her brother-in-law, but right now, something was very wrong.

"I hope Lucia hasn't been hurt." Noelle pressed her hand against her forehead, willing tears not to start. She'd been stoic throughout the day, trying to hold it together for Eve. But she was about to crumble.

"She's fine. For now."

Noelle whirled to face the voice in the kitchen and gasped as a roar started in her head. Adam stood there with a pistol pressed against Lucia's temple.

Savannah sucked in a breath. "Holy shit."

Several thoughts exploded in Noelle's brain at once.

Lucia's not hurt.

My gut wasn't wrong about Adam.

My closest gun is in a kitchen drawer.

How did they get in?

"You knew the code," Noelle said, her gaze locked on Lucia, rapidly scanning her from head to toe. There was a bright-red welt on her cheek, but Noelle didn't see any other signs of injury. Her sister stood tall, her eyes wide and blinking rapidly, Adam's other hand tightly gripping her upper arm.

She's terrified.

Adam's lips curved. "We both know the code. How many times has one of us watered your plants when you've been out of town?"

Noelle had never bothered to change it; she'd trusted everyone who had the code.

Until now.

I was so wrong about him.

"What do you want, Adam?" she asked, sounding calm despite the rush of adrenaline in her veins. Adam was visibly amped up, constantly shifting his weight as he stood behind Lucia, the gun never leaving her head.

Lucia is his shield.

"Cash and your keys," he replied promptly.

"I'll give you both," stated Noelle. "But Lucia stays here."

I can't let her leave with him.

"Nope. I need her. Money and keys now."

"You fucking chicken," said Savannah with fire in her eyes and anger in her voice. "Using her as a shield. I always knew you were a wuss."

"Shut. Up." Adam pointed at Noelle. "Where's the money?"

"I don't keep much cash on hand," Noelle said. She held out a hand toward Savannah, gesturing for her to cool down. She didn't like the crazy she saw in Adam's eyes. Something had pushed him to the edge.

"Bullshit. Derrick always had a ton of cash around."

"And Derrick's been dead for thirteen years," snapped Noelle. "I'm not Derrick."

"How much do you have?"

Noelle only kept cash on hand to pay her housekeeper, and there was a little more in her purse. "Probably about four hundred."

"Now I know you're lying." He sneered. "You've got more than that here."

Fury rocked her. "You think I'm trying to protect a bit of money when you've got a gun at my sister's head? Do you really believe I feel cash is more important than Lucia's life?" She started to stand. "What cash I have is in the drawer by the microwave."

"Sit down!" He pointed the gun at her. Noelle sat.

"You said you wouldn't hurt her!" Lucia begged.

"The police are keeping an eye on my place," Noelle lied. "They've probably already spotted your truck."

"My truck is at work," he said. "I *borrowed* a coworker's car."

Noelle recalled he'd gone to his office for a short while that morning. He'd probably stolen someone's keys. "The workday's been over for hours. They probably figured out by now that you took it."

He shrugged. "I'll have yours. And when I'm done with that, I'll move on to another."

"Lucia," Noelle said, taking a different tack. "The FBI positively identified you as the caller the day Derrick was killed. They have no doubts." She stared hard into her sister's eyes.

Lucia looked at the floor, her shoulders slumping.

"What did you see that day, Lucia?" she whispered.

"Jesus," said Adam. "Let it go. Where are your keys?" He walked sideways, pulling Lucia with him toward the drawer with the cash.

"In my purse. Lucia, why wouldn't you tell anyone that you made that call? It was just a phone call."

Stall him. Maybe someone has seen the stolen car out front.

"Get the money," he ordered Lucia, keeping his eyes on Noelle and Savannah.

Noelle froze. Her sister knew there was a gun in the back of the drawer with the cash.

He'll shoot her if she pulls a gun.

"Lucia, the money is in the blue envelope," Noelle said. Lucia glanced at her, and Noelle gave a slow shake of her head, not looking away, hoping Lucia would understand she didn't want her to touch the gun.

"Okay," said Lucia. She opened the drawer, grabbed the envelope, and shoved it closed.

Relief swamped Noelle.

That could have quickly gone south.

Adam was twitchy, and Noelle suspected it wouldn't take much to push him too far. The best thing to do was to give him what he wanted and let the police catch up with him.

But how do I make him leave her behind?

"Let Lucia go, and I'll write you a check," said Noelle. "You pick the amount."

Adam laughed. "Seriously? You think I'd try to cash a check?"

"I'll withdraw cash. Lots of cash. You can tell me where to leave it."

He sighed. "How stupid do you think I am, Noelle?" He pointed at her bag on the counter. "That the purse?"

Noelle nodded.

Grinding the gun into her head, he ordered Lucia to find the vehicle remote. Tears ran down her face; her hands shook, and she dropped the bag.

"Christ! Pick it up, klutz."

She did and shakily handed him the remote starter.

He pointed the gun at Noelle and Savannah. "Stand up."

Oh, fuck.

Terror shot through her, and she met Savannah's scared eyes.

"Turn around."

Will he shoot? Who is this man?

The women slowly turned, their backs now to the kitchen. Noelle's legs shook as she felt completely exposed. A big mirror now gave her a view of Adam and Lucia, who was trying to pull out of his grip.

"You promised you'd leave them alone!" Lucia shrieked, pushing at him. "Don't hurt them!" He lifted his hand and hit her temple with the gun's butt.

In the mirror, Noelle met Adam's gaze, the image of him raising his hand to Lucia frozen in her brain.

Recognition slammed into her.

His eyes. In a mirror. Adam raising a crowbar to swing at the back of Noelle's head.

I saw him!

She spun back around, her heart racing. *"You were there! I saw you! You hit me and you killed Derrick!"*

"You have no idea how *wrong* you are," said Adam. "I was there, but I didn't kill him. I'm sorry you remember it that way." He gave Lucia a shake. "I guess I should have believed you when you said she still didn't remember anything. Too bad she does now. Even though she's wrong."

He pointed his gun at Noelle.

He's going to kill me.

"You said you wouldn't hurt her!" Lucia screeched, thrashing in his grip.

"Fine." He changed his aim and fired at Savannah.

The roar of the gun filled the room as Noelle dropped to the floor and Savannah let out a bloodcurdling shriek, tumbling to the ground.

"Savannah!" Lucia screamed. *"You fucking bastard!"*

Her ears ringing with the shot and Lucia's screams, Noelle scrambled over to her friend. Blood flowed from Savannah's side as she flailed on the ground and pressed her hand against her wound, digging her head backward into the floor in pain.

So much blood.

It oozed between Savannah's fingers.

"Better stop that bleeding, Noelle," shouted Adam with laughter in his voice.

Focused on Savannah, Noelle was faintly aware as he dragged Lucia into the garage and slammed the door.

He shot her so I couldn't leave.

Noelle pulled up Savannah's blouse. Blood flowed steadily from a hole a few inches from her belly button. Ignoring Savannah's shrieks, Noelle rolled her to her side and checked her back. It was clear; the bullet was still inside. Noelle ripped her own sweater over her head and pressed it against the bleeding, making her best friend cry.

"Hold this." She tore across the room to the kitchen, yanked her phone from its charger, and grabbed all her kitchen towels. She sprinted back to Savannah and landed on her knees beside her, pressing a towel on top of the already soaked sweater.

Noelle put her phone on speaker and called 911. She identified herself as a sheriff's detective, requested an ambulance, and then told the dispatcher that she needed a BOLO and gave a description of her 4Runner, which Adam had taken.

"Noelle! It hurts!" Savannah moaned. "I'm going to kill him! That bastard!"

"I know, honey, you're going to be okay." Noelle added another towel to the sopping mess under her hands.

Dear God. The blood.

"And you can have the first shot at him. I promise," Noelle lied, terrified at how quickly her towels were turning red. "What's the ETA on the ambulance?" she shouted at her phone.

"En route. Ten minutes," said the dispatcher.

"Notify Detective Bolton at county. The driver of the 4Runner BOLO was already suspected for kidnapping. Now this shooting." She wiped her nose and cheeks with the back of her hand, tears streaming.

It should have been me.

Lucia changed his mind.

"I have Detective Bolton on the other line," said the dispatcher. "He's asking if you know the identity of the shooter."

Noelle swallowed hard to get the name out without tears. "It's Adam Langton." Her throat closed up, and she coughed to clear it. "Adam Langton," she repeated over Savannah's moans. "He is armed and kidnapped Lucia Marshall. He threatened to shoot her too."

She tried not to think of Lucia's tear-filled face and her desperate shouts as Noelle's fingers suddenly warmed again with Savannah's blood. She snatched up a third towel and pressed harder, making Savannah groan.

Why, Adam? Why?

45

Noelle's home was a crime scene.

The ambulance had just left with Savannah, its lights filling Noelle's dark street. Her best friend had fallen unconscious right before the EMTs arrived, and they'd had grim expressions as they worked on her. Savannah was loaded up and taken out the door, leaving Noelle sitting on the dining room floor, where she'd tried to stay out of the EMTs' way.

She'd never seen anyone whisked away so rapidly.

Three deputies had arrived before the ambulance. Jeff, the deputy who'd earlier cleared the home, had pulled Noelle away from Savannah to allow the other deputies to take over the lifesaving attempt. "Are you hit?" he'd asked Noelle, quickly checking her torso and arms, which were covered with blood.

"I'm fine, I'm fine." She'd batted his hands away. "It's not my blood."

"Did I miss him when I went through the house? Where was he?" Jeff's tone had teetered on the edge of despair as he watched the others work on Savannah. "I'm so sorry, Detective."

"No one was inside. You didn't miss anyone," Noelle had said quickly, in a rush to reassure him. "He came in after. He knew the alarm code."

Relief had filled Jeff's face, immediately replaced with concern for Savannah. "I'm so sorry," he repeated.

Now that the ambulance had left, he and the other deputies finished securing the scene and Noelle tried to calm her racing heart. Three times she'd automatically walked toward the sink to wash her bloody hands. "Not yet," she muttered, knowing forensics would want to photograph her, swab the blood on her arms, and take her clothes as evidence.

She could wait.

This could be a murder investigation.

She wouldn't do anything to possibly mess it up. She wanted Adam to pay for what he'd done.

My brother-in-law.

Oh my God. I need to call Eve!

Her cell phone was near the stove, where she'd started to cook. She didn't want to touch it much, but she opened it up and called Eve, leaving the phone in its place on the counter and putting the call on speaker.

"Noelle?" Eve's voice shook, and Noelle could tell she'd been crying.

She knows.

"I'm so sorry, Eve," she managed to get out.

"I don't understand," Eve said through her tears. "The police said Adam has Lucia as a hostage and . . . and *that he shot Savannah?*"

"I'm sorry, Eve," Noelle repeated. "But they're telling you the truth."

Eve started to loudly sob. "Did she die?"

"I don't know yet. She was still alive when the ambulance left," whispered Noelle. "I can't believe this is happening."

What do you say to your sister when her husband tries to kill someone?

"But Lucia's okay?" Eve's voice was high.

"Physically she was okay while she was here," Noelle said slowly, thinking of how she'd recalled seeing Adam with the crowbar.

I can't tell her about that yet.

"He won't return my calls," cried Eve. "I don't understand what he's doing."

"You never had any idea something was going on with him?"

"No! How could he do this?"

Noelle cried too. Adam had fooled them all. "I'm sorry, Eve. There's got to be a reason. Something must have happened to him," she added, knowing her words were lame.

"What?" Eve spoke to someone in the background. "I've got to go, Noelle. They want to talk to me. *What am I going to tell them?*"

"Just tell them the truth. Tell them everything you know, Eve. It will be okay."

"I love you," said Eve through her tears.

"I love you too." She ended the call and closed her eyes in exhaustion.

I don't understand what's happened.

Voices came from outside, and a moment later Evan Bolton stepped through the open front door, bootied and gloved, his eyes wide and worried. "Fuck! Noelle, are you hurt?" He rushed forward, and she held up her hands to stop him.

"I'm fine. Not my blood. Don't touch me." Her voice cracked.

He slammed to a halt, horror and understanding in his eyes. He turned and yelled out the open door. "Get forensics in here *now!*" He looked back at Noelle. "They're out front. We'll get you cleaned up as soon as possible."

"I can wait." She held Bolton's gaze. "I want this done right, Evan. No room for error."

"Of course." He paused and appeared to be searching for the way to ask a question.

"She was conscious when they left," Noelle told him. "But there was so much blood, Evan." Her voice cracked on his name. She turned away, her eyes filling.

"Where is she?" came a male voice from outside.

Noelle looked back toward the door as Agent Rhodes strode in. He was bootied, but his gloves were still in his hands. His gaze slammed into hers, and it flashed the same horror and relief that Bolton's had.

"Oh, thank God," he muttered as he moved toward her with intent in his eyes.

Noelle weakly held out her hands. "Don't." Her voice shook as she was abruptly overcome with the need for human touch. A hug. Anything physical to reassure her that everything would be all right. Although her voice and hands said no, she suspected her eyes begged the opposite.

That was confirmed when Rhodes said, "Fuck that," and wrapped his arms around her. "I know Savannah's going to be okay," he whispered.

Noelle leaned into him, pressing her cheek against his shoulder, and felt something inside her crack and quietly crumble. But Rhodes's arms held the pieces of her together.

"We don't know that," she said, letting the tears stream onto his jacket.

"She will," he said firmly as he held her tighter.

Noelle shuddered, and they silently stood that way for a long moment until she pulled back and met his brown gaze. "Thank you." She took a step back to assess how much blood she'd transferred to his clothing. None. Savannah's blood had already dried.

"Anytime," he said gruffly.

She noticed Bolton standing two yards away, watching them. He nodded to himself, as if confirming something.

"I'll light a fire under forensics," Bolton said, and walked out the door.

"You okay?" asked Rhodes.

"I will be."

"The BOLO went wide. We'll find him."

A forensic tech with a camera entered. "Detective Marshall? I need to get some photos and then take your clothes."

"Yes, you do." She lifted her chin. Right now, this was the best way to help Savannah. Gather the evidence to nail her shooter.

Two hours later she sat on a couch in one of the sheriff's department conference rooms, waiting to speak with detectives and the FBI. At home she'd changed and given her bloody clothing to the evidence tech, but she'd come downtown to use the department locker room to shower as quickly as possible and put on another set of fresh clothes.

Savannah was still alive but in surgery. The doctors were cautiously optimistic.

That wasn't good enough for Noelle.

If she dies . . .

Noelle didn't know what she'd do. The only reason Savannah had been shot was that she had been in town for Noelle.

Now it's my turn to be there for her.

Please give me that chance.

Adam and the 4Runner had not been located. Neither Toyota nor her auto insurer had a way to track the vehicle. Noelle had refused when her insurance provider suggested a device and now regretted that decision.

Adam would have ripped it out anyway.

It was nearly 10:00 p.m., and Noelle suspected they'd hear nothing about Adam overnight. Most likely he'd hole up somewhere and be on the move again tomorrow.

He and Eve seemed so perfect.

It's like I don't know him at all.

She sent up another prayer for Lucia.

Eve's home was still being searched for evidence, so the police had taken her to Daisy's little house, where Daisy had stepped up and given Eve the support she'd needed. They'd offered to take Noelle there too, but she'd declined.

She needed to be where she could keep a finger in the investigation. The assigned detectives might not agree, but she didn't care. Right now, she was their best source of information about Adam and Lucia. She'd made herself as quiet as possible on the couch, watching the expansion of the investigation room's equipment. It'd been organized after Noelle's vehicle blew up, but now Adam was their number one suspect. More computers. Phones. Whiteboards. People went in and out. Even though the hour was late, there was a fervency in the air. Everyone wanted Adam caught. He'd messed with one of their own.

Evan finally came in, with Rhodes right behind him with Agent Keaton. Joining them was Detective Lori Shults, whom Noelle was pleased to have on the investigation. The women had worked together for a few years. She was petite, smart, and tough. Lori nodded solemnly at Noelle and sat beside her. "We'll find the asshole."

"That asshole is my brother-in-law," muttered Noelle, her mind still reeling from the knowledge that someone she'd loved had done this. "But I don't disagree with calling him that."

Evan and Rhodes each rolled a chair away from the conference table and parked it in front of Noelle's place on the couch. "Tell us again what happened," said Rhodes.

Noelle had already gone through it once at her home, but she had known they would want to hear it all again. And again.

Standard procedure.

She'd been thinking through her previous story and realized she'd left out one huge element. "First you need to know that tonight I remembered that Adam was there the day Derrick was murdered," she told them.

Surprise lit up their faces. "Are you certain?" asked Rhodes. "He had an alibi."

"Adam confirmed it when I accused him," said Noelle. "I told you how he made Savannah and me turn away. When we did, I watched him in the mirror and was suddenly hit with the memory of seeing him in a different mirror holding a crowbar."

"Your husband was beaten with a crowbar, correct?" asked Lori.

"Yes." The vision of Adam back then rose in her mind. "And when I accused him of killing Derrick, he denied it. But he admitted he was there. He seemed to think it was funny that I was accusing him," she said slowly. "He said I was completely wrong about that."

"And Lucia?" asked Evan.

"I brought up the 911 call. She didn't deny it. Her whole demeanor sagged when I asked her," said Noelle. "But she didn't admit it either."

"Doesn't matter," said Keaton. "The evidence confirmed it was her."

"It had to be Adam who killed Derrick," said Noelle, thinking hard. "He had the crowbar."

"You said he was behind you in your memory?" asked Lori.

"Yes." Noelle could easily picture it now. "I can see him start to swing the crowbar at me."

But is it real?

"When you saw Adam, can you recall where Derrick was at that moment?" asked Keaton.

Noelle closed her eyes. The memory—was it really a memory?—of Adam was growing clearer each time she thought about it. But she couldn't see Derrick. She shook her head, her eyes still closed.

"Can you say how you felt at that exact moment?" asked Rhodes. "You're obviously feeling shocked to see Adam—what else are you feeling?"

"Confused," murmured Noelle. "Scared."

"Is Derrick already on the floor?"

Noelle opened her eyes. "I want to say yes, but I don't have a reason to say it. It just feels like it—which means nothing."

"Can you recall anything else in the room?" asked Rhodes. "Are you sure the memory is from your Sacramento home?"

"I *know* that mirror. It was a wedding gift," said Noelle. "And besides seeing Adam in the mirror, I recall the flash of an elephant print on the wall. And I can see the iron elephant. The one that was smashed into Derrick's face. It's definitely my house."

"Is Adam holding that too?"

"No. It's on the floor." She frowned. "I don't trust anything I can recall. But Adam confirmed he was there, so at least part of my memories are accurate. The rest may be bullshit."

"Did he say anything about yesterday's explosion?" asked Evan.

"No." Noelle briefly kicked herself for not bringing it up, but she'd had a damn gun pointing at her. Her brain had been focused on other things. "Did Eve have an idea of where he would take Lucia?"

Because I sure don't.

"She didn't. Eve's struggling to think clearly," said Evan. "Like you, she's also had a major shock tonight—on top of the explosion yesterday."

"It's been a fucked-up few days." Noelle saw guilt flash in Rhodes's eyes. "Not your fault, Agent Rhodes. You were doing your job, but somehow you hit a hornet's nest during the interviews."

"I think by now you can call me Max," he said. "We didn't even get to interview Adam. He and Eve were our only interviews left to do, and then we were headed back to Sacramento."

"Did he feel the need to act before the FBI questioned him?" asked Lori.

"Possibly." Max turned a thoughtful gaze on Noelle. "Or maybe he thought this latest investigation would prod your memory and you'd recall he was there."

"He's been within arm's reach for years," said Noelle. "I didn't think anything of him and Eve moving up here after I did. But now I wonder if he did it because he wanted to keep close tabs on me. Maybe he thought he'd hear quickly if I started to remember that day."

"I still don't understand why Lucia didn't admit she made that phone call," said Evan. "That call most likely saved your life, Noelle. Why would she hide that?"

"Don't know." Both Lucia's and Adam's betrayals cut deep. Tears threatened and she fought them down, not knowing if she would ever comprehend the why of what they had done.

Should I forgive?

She couldn't forgive Adam; Savannah might die.

Lucia? Most likely Noelle could forgive her for keeping a secret. Lucia had only been eighteen and—

I know why. "Adam made Lucia keep the secret," she said, looking at Evan. "It has to be the reason, but I don't know how he did it or why. Maybe he threatened her?" She thought about how Lucia acted when Adam was around. "She always kept her distance from him unless she had no choice," said Noelle. "Looking back I can see it. I always chalked it up to her being a bit shy around men."

"You told me she's struggled with anxiety for most of her life," said Max. "Do you think Adam added to that?"

Nausea suddenly made Noelle lightheaded. "Oh my God."

How many years has Lucia feared him?

And we didn't see it.

46

Max glanced at the glowing clock on the nightstand in his sister's house. It was nearly 6:00 a.m., so he gave himself permission to get up. He'd looked at the damned clock a dozen times over the last two hours, determined to get more sleep. But it had never come.

Both he and Keaton had been at the sheriff's station until two in the morning, trying to figure out where Adam had taken Lucia and silently hoping she wasn't dead in a ditch somewhere. Every time someone's phone rang, he'd tensed, worried a body had been found. He'd seen the same thought also appear each time in Noelle's eyes.

Around midnight they'd learned that Savannah was still holding on and the surgery had removed the bullet and part of her small intestine. It was considered successful, but her prognosis was guarded. The doctors were worried about infection.

Noelle had visibly sunk into herself in relief. She swayed gently in her seat and was unsteady when she stood to get more coffee. Bolton asked Detective Shults to take her to Shults's home and stay with her. Noelle's lack of protest gave all of them a clue to how deeply exhausted she was.

She'd been attacked physically and emotionally. Max couldn't imagine the toll it was taking on her. When he'd seen her covered in blood, his heart had skipped a beat, terrified she'd been shot even though he *knew* there was only one victim.

He swung his legs out of bed and pushed to his feet. His room was freezing, and he liked it that way when he slept—but not when it was time to get up.

His cell phone vibrated on the nightstand. It was Bolton.

He's got something.

Max grabbed his shirt and tucked the phone between his neck and shoulder.

"Rhodes." He slipped his arms into the sleeves and looked around for his pants.

"Noelle's 4Runner has been found," said Bolton without a greeting. "Adam parked it off a rural road southeast of here. State trooper spotted it. Said someone tried to hide the 4Runner in the brush, but his headlights caught one of its rear reflectors."

"Anyone there?" Phone still held at his neck, Max pulled on his pants.

"Empty. But it's in a foot of snow. The trooper said there are footprints that head into the brush. He called it in before following them and was told to back off. He's probably lucky he didn't get shot."

"That's assuming Adam was nearby. Maybe he dumped it and got picked up by someone. Faked the prints going into the brush and doubled back. Were there two sets of prints?"

"The trooper thought there were at least two."

"Thought?"

"Said they were erratic."

"Shit. Where are you?"

"Headed to the scene."

"Text me the address."

"Just did. I've got Detective Shults meeting me there, along with three other units."

"Did you tell the detective to inform Noelle?" asked Max, slipping on his boots.

There was a long pause. "No. This isn't Noelle's place," said Bolton.

True.

"She'll disagree."

"Too bad for her. See you in a bit." Bolton ended the call.

Max looked at his screen and opened the address Bolton had sent in his map app. He could be there in thirty minutes. He quickly called Keaton and passed on the information. Two minutes later he was getting into his freezing car in the dark. He started the engine and backed out of his sister's driveway.

Someone should let Noelle know.

He shook his head, knowing she would blow a gasket when she discovered no one had informed her. Her sister was with a very dangerous man.

We've got nothing concrete to tell her.

I'll update her when we do.

Thirty-five minutes later Max parked his rental on the narrow shoulder of the country road. He'd had to drive slowly the last few miles. It appeared the roads had been plowed yesterday, but a thin layer of snow had fallen since then. The area was at a higher elevation than Bend and had received much more snow.

It was still dark, so he left his headlights on as the other six vehicles had done. There were no streetlights on the winding country road, and groups of trees and brush darkened the sides of the road. He spotted the state trooper in his wide-brimmed hat talking to Detectives Bolton and Shults. County deputies were off the road in some brush, their flashlights highlighting their positions as they studied the 4Runner and footprints. Max sat in his vehicle for a long moment, studying the terrain on the satellite map on his phone. The area was consistently covered with brush and trees but occasionally broken up with home and farm buildings. From this location, he saw three possible homes or farms where Adam could have gone to take cover.

Assuming he wasn't picked up.

He got out of the vehicle and approached the Deschutes detectives and the trooper. The trooper looked very young. He was baby-faced but had the carriage of former military, and his eyes were wide with excitement over his find. The state troopers out here covered a lot of territory on their own. Finding the 4Runner was probably the most interesting thing that had happened so far in what had to have been a short career.

"Rhodes," Bolton greeted him, and he made introductions. The trooper was Findley.

"What have the deputies found?" Max asked.

Bolton pointed down the road to where two deputies held flashlights. "There's an odd formation in the snow back there and then footprints leading from it. I think Lucia bailed out of the vehicle, fell, and then ran. Tire tracks show that the 4Runner stopped in the road and the driver got out. He ran toward the first set of prints, turned around, came back, then got in the vehicle and moved it off the road to there." He pointed at the 4Runner in the brush. "He must have realized it would take longer to find Lucia than he first believed, so he parked it and left. Both sets of prints head south."

"Can you tell if he caught up with her?" asked Max.

"I've got two deputies following the prints, and I've requested a K9," said Bolton. "It's slowly getting lighter, but the sun won't be up for another half hour. What I don't like is that there are homes in that direction. I was just about to send Findley and a deputy to knock on those doors, telling them to keep everything locked up. We don't need a hostage situation." His mouth tightened in a grim expression. "More of a hostage situation than we already have with Lucia. It's an impossible location to set up a perimeter. There are a few long, winding driveways and a ton of open space."

"And who knows how long ago they left," added Lori. "The vehicle is cold, but it was twenty-two degrees overnight. Currently thirty-one."

Max was glad he'd put on an extra sweatshirt under his coat. "They'll need to have found shelter. Quickly."

This could turn ugly.

"Keaton will be here soon. Which homes need to be approached?" asked Max.

Bolton pulled out his phone. "I'm sending two deputies here," he said, tapping a building on his satellite view. He enlarged the view and indicated another house. "You two can take this one." Max studied the house, noting the three outbuildings and where the driveway turned off the road they were on. He glanced back as another vehicle stopped and he recognized Keaton.

"I'll be right back," Max said. Bolton's phone rang as Max strode toward Keaton. As the other agent got out of the car, Max updated him on their assignment.

"Rhodes!" The stress in Bolton's voice made him spin around. "Someone just called 911 and said they've got a man with a gun in their home! It's the house I assigned you!"

It just got ugly.

47

Noelle woke in the dark, not sure what had disturbed her sleep. She abruptly sat up straight, realizing she wasn't in her bed.

I'm in Lori's house.

Noelle had gone home with the detective in the early hours, when she could no longer keep her eyes open at the sheriff's department. She swung her legs out of the bed, took a few breaths to get her heart to slow, and then grabbed her phone to check for texts.

There were none.

No news is good news?

She started to search for the hospital phone number to call about Savannah and realized the staff wouldn't share medical information with her. The detective assigned to the case would be the only person outside Savannah's family to get updates. She shot Bolton a text, asking for one.

While waiting for a reply, she got dressed and went downstairs, smelling coffee. The kitchen was empty, but Lori had left a note saying she'd gone to work. It was nearly 7:00 a.m.

Lori never works this early.

Something happened.

She fired off a text to Lori and a second one to Bolton, demanding answers. She quickly scanned local headlines online, looking for any mention of Adam Langton. Nothing. She glared at her unanswered texts.

They're avoiding me.

I'm not assigned to the case.

"Dammit." She called dispatch and identified herself, asking for the locations of Detectives Bolton and Shults. The dispatcher informed Noelle of the discovery of her vehicle and the recent 911 call about an intruder with a gun in the same area. She thanked him, hung up, and raced to grab her bag and coat. Then slammed to a halt.

I don't have a vehicle.

I'm stuck.

Her mind searched for solutions. It was too early to rent a car. She didn't want to take an Uber to a crime scene. Who would loan her a vehicle?

That 911 call has to be about Adam.

Is Lucia okay?

I can't just sit here.

Her gaze fell on the door to Lori's garage. She yanked it open and hit the light switch. Parked inside was a shiny new Ford Bronco. Her heart lifted.

"Hello, gorgeous."

She knew Lori had waited months for the custom vehicle; the detective had talked about it dozens of times, totally infatuated with the SUV. Noelle turned back to the kitchen and started pulling open drawers. She found a remote for the Bronco in the second one.

"Sorry, Lori," she whispered. "I'll take good care of it." She grabbed her things and pressed the garage door opener. She opened the Bronco and slid into the driver's seat as the early-morning light filled the garage. She hit the start button and a pattern of happy musical notes sounded.

They won't be pleased to see me.

But nothing would keep her away.

48

"The caller hung up," Bolton told Max and Keaton with his ear to his phone. "911 heard a man in the background telling the caller to stop talking or he'll shoot someone."

"Shit," said Max.

Bolton ordered the deputies into a perimeter around the house in question and requested a SWAT team and negotiators. The female caller had said she was the homeowner and that her two adult daughters and a son-in-law were also in the house. 911 had asked if the intruder was alone and the woman had said she didn't know.

"We don't know for certain that it's Adam," said Max. "It's very likely, but wouldn't the caller have known if Lucia was with him?"

"If she's with him," Bolton said grimly. "Maybe he didn't catch up with her after she got out of the SUV or maybe . . ."

She's dead.

"SWAT says they're a few minutes out," said Detective Shults.

The home wasn't a great setup for a tactical advantage. It was a two-story, white, traditional-looking farmhouse that sat on a small knoll, which put all law enforcement at a lower level. There were no trees or brush near the home to provide cover. It was exposed from all angles, which meant law enforcement would be exposed too. The closest outbuilding was a small barn about fifty yards from the home. Max knew SWAT would set up snipers there but would have to use their BearCat vehicle to get anyone close to the home.

Their best option was to get Adam—assuming it was he—to leave the house. Or else to free the hostages.

That was the job of the negotiators.

Max had a high level of respect for negotiators. He'd been a SWAT team member in his time at the Medford Police Department. The negotiators were always used first to avoid as much violence as possible. It didn't sound difficult to be on the phone with a subject for hours, but Max knew it was mentally and emotionally exhausting. It took patience and skill. They had to sound genuine and establish a rapport with a subject, not come off as the voice of authority. Their goal was to convince the person to see that violence wasn't the only answer.

It wasn't a simple task when the subject was angry and scared.

"Here they come," said Shults.

Max turned to see the BearCat vehicle and a mobile command unit behind it appear on the long driveway. Bolton had established an incident command area approximately a half mile from the house, out of its sight. Six officers in heavy gear filed out of the armored BearCat.

That's not enough people.

He knew there should be more. But things happened. Officers took vacations or got sick. Some couldn't respond fast enough.

"Shit," said Shults, recognizing the same problem.

SWAT officers were a team. They trained extensively together, and they knew how to adapt when they were shorthanded, but Max wished they had more people today. The team leader approached, and Bolton went to greet him. Max watched the rest of the officers double- and triple-check their equipment. His gaze landed on a specialized rifle, and he quickly scanned the other officers' weapons.

Only one sniper?

Sniper had been Max's primary role. He'd also trained in containment and entry, but sniper had been his specialty. Most of his time had been spent as a forward observer—common for snipers—watching through his scope and passing on descriptions and movements, but he was always prepared to shoot if necessary. Multiple observers were ideal in dangerous situations. Max had only fired his rifle once in his five years on the team.

He hadn't missed.

When snipers miss, hostages and officers can die.

It was a heavy responsibility to shoulder. He'd been glad he had taken the shot, but it'd left him with a mental and emotional burden that would never go away. It was lighter now, but it lingered.

He looked away from the grim faces of the officers getting ready and strode to the small RV that was the command vehicle. He knocked on the door and showed his ID to the older officer who answered. Max was invited in and learned Officer Hillyer was one of the negotiators. He sounded like a kindly grandfather—a good voice for the phone. Inside, two other officers sat in front of computer monitors, each screen showing several different views from the body cams on the SWAT team. At a small desk was the other negotiator, Squires, who looked a bit like Max's sister. She had the victim's phone number from the 911 call and was waiting for the go-ahead to make contact.

"You know the subject is related to a county detective, correct?" asked Max.

"We do. Detective Bolton told us," said Squires. "We contacted her and asked her to come in. Any insight she can give us will be extremely valuable."

It made sense. Noelle knew more about Adam than anyone except his wife.

"Should be here any minute," said Squires. "She was already on her way when I spoke to her."

"Of course she was," Max murmured. He knew Noelle wouldn't be kept away if her sister was in danger. At that moment he heard tires crunch on the snow, and he stepped out of the small RV. A Ford Bronco parked behind the other vehicles, and he recognized Noelle behind the wheel.

"What the hell?" Max turned to find Lori Shults glaring down the driveway. "That's my Bronco! I just got it."

He looked back and noticed the Bronco didn't have license plates yet. He smothered his smile. "I think she did what she could to get here."

"Still."

"Sorry, Lori," said Noelle as she strode up. "I was in a bind, and no one was answering my texts." She looked tightly wound and had dark circles under her eyes. "Morning, Max. I assume the negotiators are in there?" Without waiting for an answer, she opened the RV door and stepped inside.

Max exchanged a look with Lori.

"She's not happy with Bolton and me at the moment," said Lori, with a guilty frown. "We didn't answer her texts this morning as this was coming together."

"I can imagine her stress from being kept out of the loop," said Max, understanding Lori's situation. "It's her sister." He followed Noelle into the RV, where she was introducing herself.

"What's the plan?" she asked the negotiators.

"We need to establish some trust with Adam," said Hillyer. "Would telling him you're here be a good or bad idea?"

"Bad. I'm on his shit list, and he's on mine, but you can't hide my presence from him. He'll assume I've been contacted."

"Any topic we should avoid with him?" asked Squires. "Anything that would set him off?"

"I wouldn't mention the explosion we suspect he set the other day. It might make him defensive. Same with him shooting Savannah last night."

Squires nodded while making a note. "We don't want him to worry about possible charges from those incidents. We plan to help him focus on getting out of his current situation as smoothly as possible."

"By minimizing the consequences for him when this is over," said Max.

"Always," said Hillyer. "Want to make that more appealing than what could happen if he goes down the road to more violence."

"I need to know if my sister's okay," said Noelle. Max caught the subtle desperation in her tone.

"We won't jump into that with him right away," said Squires. "If he's done something to her, he might believe there's no going back."

Noelle looked stricken.

"But we'll figure out something," said Hillyer kindly. "We'll work it in somehow."

"Explain again how he's related to the murder of your husband," said Squires, pausing in taking notes to look at Noelle.

"He admitted he was there thirteen years ago but claims he didn't kill him," said Noelle. "I think he did it, but I'd also avoid that today if you want to keep him calm."

"If he wants to speak to you, are you okay with that?" asked Squires.

Noelle hesitated. "Yes."

"We'll be listening," said Hillyer. "We'll give you prompts if needed. Just remember to keep him calm."

"Thank you."

Max could tell Noelle didn't want to speak to Adam. "What worries you about talking to him?" he asked her.

"That I'd say the wrong thing, and someone dies," she said bluntly.

He understood. Completely. "I was a sniper for SWAT when I was in Medford. I get it. I had a lot of fear about making a wrong decision."

The officers looked at him, respect dawning in their eyes. "It's difficult enough being on the end of the phone," said Hillyer. "I can't imagine being on the end of the rifle."

"If you think of anything else we should know while we're working, write it here." Squires tapped a yellow pad. "Ready?" she asked Hillyer. He nodded.

"Negotiators are ready," said Squires, speaking into her radio. Ten seconds later the door to the RV opened and the SWAT commander stepped inside. The SWAT members did an oral verification of their microphones, each counting off using the code word *Blue* and a number.

Watching one of the monitors, Max focused on Blue-six, the sniper, who'd set up in the barn as he'd expected. The team member had propped up his body cam a few feet away and pointed it at himself, showing that he lay on his belly on the barn's upper level, his eye at his scope. An odd tingling sensation shot through Max. One he hadn't felt in many years. A mix of anticipation, fear, and determination. He exhaled and noticed the sniper doing the same.

He feels it too.

Other body cameras showed the officers waiting outside the BearCat. The last view was from Blue-five, an officer on his belly in the snow at the opposite angle of the property from the sniper. He was solely a spotter, not a sniper.

"All right," said the SWAT commander into his microphone. "I know we're shorthanded today, but we've got eyes on the entire property." He turned to the negotiators. "Call that cell number. Let's see what we've got."

Squires dialed. The phone rang, sounding through the speakers in the RV.

No one answered. Squires called five more times, waiting a few minutes after each call.

Finally someone picked up. "What?"

Squires glanced at Noelle, who rapidly nodded. It was Adam.

"This is the Deschutes County sheriff's office," said Hillyer in a conversational tone. "We're outside and would like to know what's going on in the home."

"Fuck off." Adam hung up.

Squires and Hillyer looked pleased. "He answered the phone and he spoke to us," explained Squires when Noelle gave a sigh of disappointment. "We'll take it. This process can take hours."

"If no one's being hurt, we have time to spare," said the commander. "The longer this goes, the better chance we have at defusing the situation."

Noelle shifted her feet. "I don't have your patience."

"Patience is key for this job," agreed Squires. "We'll call him again in a few minutes."

"Adam's not dumb," said Noelle. "He's very sharp, and you'll need to be honest. He'll catch on quickly if you play games with him."

Max disagreed on Adam's intelligence. The man's behavior proved Noelle wrong.

Noelle leaned against a wall, exhaustion on her face, and Max wondered how much sleep she'd gotten recently. It'd been a rough few days for her, and now, in the crowded RV, the air felt thick and tension was high.

"Maybe we should wait outside until he actually joins a conversation," said Max. "Someone can get us then."

Noelle glanced at him, her dark-blue eyes thankful.

He tipped his head toward the door, and she followed him out.

49

Noelle pulled her coat tighter as she faced Max outside the mobile command unit. She felt as if she were a half step outside of reality, watching what was occurring from a distance, struggling to believe that this was truly happening.

Lucia kidnapped.

Savannah shot.

Her vehicle blown up.

Adam's attempted murder. And now he'd taken more hostages.

What's next?

And what can I do?

"We'll catch him," said Max, his gaze tough but sympathetic. "He'll answer for this—for all of this. These negotiators know what they're doing."

"Adam isn't easy," said Noelle. "He's stubborn. And I think he's past caring about anyone or anything. That makes him dangerous."

"He's got to care about his wife," said Max. "Everyone says they're close, a perfect couple. Those feelings can't vanish overnight."

"You'd think so. But now I don't know. Why would he do this to Lucia?" Noelle paced in a small circle. "Fuck. Eve is beside herself. She says she doesn't recognize who he is. None of us do."

"When did you last talk to Eve?"

"On the way here. She's still at Daisy's."

"And Savannah?"

"I got ahold of a nurse friend of mine at the hospital this morning since no one here would return my texts." She shot a glare at Evan, who was thirty feet away, talking to Shults and a deputy. Evan hadn't approached her yet. No doubt he could tell she was pissed about the lack of communication. "Savannah's stable. Prognosis is good."

"I think Evan and Lori didn't want to worry you when they found the empty 4Runner."

"He kidnapped my sister!"

"Do you know why he did that?"

"No." Noelle rubbed her eyes. "I've asked myself a million times, but I assume it has something to do with Derrick's murder."

Voices suddenly rose in the RV. Noelle spun around, pulled open the door, and bounded up the short flight of steps. The negotiators were now watching the cameras with the rest of the inside crew. "What happened?"

"Blue-six. She's running toward the barn." A voice crackled through the speakers.

Noelle scanned the cameras, seeing only the officers in the BearCat, the sniper, and the other observer. The sniper's mouth moved. "She's twenty feet from the barn."

"Who?" Noelle's heart was in her throat.

Is it Lucia?

"They're not sure who it is," Squires told her. "They saw her crawl out of a basement window and start sprinting toward the barn."

"Blue-four. Get to the barn," ordered the commander. One of the body cam views from the BearCat suddenly jerked and bobbled as the wearer went out the back of the vehicle. The camera view shakily showed the barn rapidly getting closer as he ran.

"Let me see your hands!" Blue-four hollered.

Noelle tensed. Lucia wouldn't be armed, but there was no way for the officer to know that. He had to protect himself. A hand squeezed her shoulder. Max.

"Get them up, up, up!" the officer shouted.

Do what he says!

Noelle couldn't breathe. The situation could go sideways in a split second.

A woman's boots and jeans came into the officer's camera view, and she halted, the wood walls of the barn behind her. "Turn away from me and get on your knees," ordered Blue-four.

"There's someone in the house! He's got a gun!" gasped the woman.

Noelle closed her eyes at the voice. "It's not Lucia," she whispered, disappointment flooding her.

Where is Lucia?

"On your knees!"

The woman dropped to her knees, her long, dark hair contrasting with the back of her white shirt.

"What's your name?"

"Katie. Katie Amidon." She was crying.

"Has to be one of the daughters," said Squires. "The caller said she had two of her daughters with her, along with a son-in-law. We know the owner of the property is Janet Amidon."

"Blue-four, get her over here," ordered the commander.

"I'm going to handcuff you until I can confirm you're not armed, all right?" The officer's voice had gentled.

"Okay," she sobbed.

Even though she'd said a name, her identity had not been confirmed. They knew not to take chances.

Minutes later Katie Amidon had her cuffs removed and was led to one of the county SUVs to be questioned by Evan because the RV was too crowded. Noelle poured a cup of coffee in the RV and stepped outside. She slid into the SUV's back seat with Katie and handed her the cup as Evan took the front passenger seat and turned awkwardly to address the women.

"This is Detective Marshall," said Evan with a tentative glance at Noelle.

He wants forgiveness for avoiding my messages.

"Who else is inside the house?" asked Noelle, letting go of her annoyance with the detective and studying the young woman. She looked about sixteen.

"My mom. My two sisters and my brother-in-law." Katie shuddered and clung to the paper cup of coffee but didn't take a sip.

"On an earlier phone call your mom said she had two daughters in the house," said Evan. "Not three of you."

Katie wiped at a tear. "My bedroom is in the basement. She probably didn't want him to know I was down there, so she only told him about my sisters. When I woke up this morning, I heard a strange voice upstairs. I was halfway up my steps when I realized he was threatening them. I tiptoed back down, and I didn't know what to do at first, but I finally decided I needed to get out, so I got dressed and slipped out the window. I was going to call 911 when I got to the barn, but then that army man yelled at me."

"They're police officers, but I understand how they look like soldiers in their SWAT gear," said Noelle. "Was the man threatening your family all by himself?"

"I only heard one man asking questions," said Katie. "My mom replied, and I could hear both my sisters crying. I could tell everyone was in the family room."

"How old are your sisters?" asked Bolton.

"Twenty-eight and twenty-two. I heard Drew trying to calm Kendall. They're married but live here too." Katie sniffled and struggled to hold herself together.

"How old is Drew?" asked Bolton.

"I think he's thirty-two."

"You have your phone?" Evan asked, and the girl nodded. "Can you send me photos of everyone? The most current ones you have. We'll need a good one of Drew that shows how he looks right now. Does he have a beard or any facial hair?"

Katie frowned but started going through photos on her phone. "No. Why?"

"We need to be able to identify everyone," said Noelle. She didn't tell Katie that the sniper needed to clearly distinguish Drew from Adam in case he needed to shoot. The men were close in age, and Adam didn't have facial hair either. She glanced at Katie's photos and saw that her brother-in-law's hair was the same color and length as Adam's.

I can tell them apart, but the sniper needs to know who is who.

Just in case.

"Is he dangerous?" Katie's voice cracked. "Is he going to hurt them? I know he has a gun."

"We don't know anything yet," Noelle said, keeping her answer vague. "We're trying to find out what he wants. Trust me, everyone wants to get him out of your house."

Katie AirDropped the images to Evan, who immediately sent them to the SWAT commander, who would get them to his team.

"Katie, did you hear any other voices you didn't recognize?" Noelle knew she was essentially repeating a previous question.

"No."

We still don't know if Lucia is with him.

Evan's face turned grim as he met Noelle's gaze. "Katie, I need you to draw me a floor plan of the house," he said. "And then draw where the furniture is in the family room, okay?" He handed her his little notebook and a pen. "We're going to have a lot of questions. Just answer the best you can. We also need the numbers to your sisters' and Drew's phones."

"Okay."

Noelle took back the cup of coffee the girl hadn't sipped. Katie bent over the notebook on her knee and started to draw. She seemed calmer. Having something to do kept her focused, and the maps would be vital to the SWAT team.

"I'm going back inside," said Noelle to Evan.

He nodded. "Thank you, Noelle." His eyes transmitted the same message.

Yes, we're good.

There was a heightened air of tension as Noelle stepped back in the RV, and Max immediately put his finger to his lips as she realized Adam's voice was coming over the speakers.

"I don't need to show you proof that they're okay. You can take my word for it," he said. "Everyone is fine."

"We appreciate that, Adam," said Hillyer. "Right now your situation isn't too bad since no one has been hurt. This is fixable. Can you tell me the names of who's there with you?" Hillyer glanced at Noelle.

He's trying to feel out if Lucia is there.

They heard Adam turn away from the phone and ask for names. Noelle listened hard, hoping to hear Lucia speak.

"Janet," said Adam into the phone. "Drew, Kendall, and Kristine."

They must all be sick with worry that Adam will eventually discover Katie.

Noelle wrote on the yellow pad, *How can we let them know Katie is out of the house and safe?*

Squires nodded slowly, pondering the question.

"How about you let one of the hostages go?" said Hillyer into his headset. "Do you need that many people in there? It'd go a long way in letting us know you don't want to hurt them."

"Who said I didn't want to hurt them?" snapped Adam. "I'll hurt whoever I need to get my ass out of here."

Gasps from the family sounded through the speakers.

Noelle was stunned.

Is this the type of person Adam has been all along? Did he fool us all?

"The safer that family is, the better your situation is," said Hillyer. "Let's not do anything you can't come back from."

"Maybe I already did," mumbled Adam.

Noelle froze, terrified he was about to admit he'd hurt Lucia.

"We'll cross that bridge when we come to it," said Hillyer, purposefully easing past Adam's comment. "Right now let's figure out how to end this. What do you want from us?"

Adam cut the connection.

Hillyer wiped his damp forehead and slumped back in his chair. "Jesus."

"You're doing great," said Squires, patting his shoulder. "Your tone is perfect. You kept him talking a long time and planted the seed that we might give him what he wants. That'll make him want to talk more with us."

"But what can we give him?" asked Noelle. "The only thing he'll want is to walk away with no repercussions at all."

"We'll help him see that's truly not an option," said Squires. "Maybe offer a reduced charge of some sort. Play everything down."

"He'll see through that bullshit," said Noelle, knowing they didn't have to stand behind anything they told Adam.

"You'll be surprised. After a while they want out of the situation so bad, they'll start to believe us." Hillyer took a sip from his water bottle. Both he and Squires had water instead of coffee. "We'll give him a bit of time to think, and then I'll call again."

Noelle scanned the monitors. The SWAT team members in the BearCat were quiet as they waited until they were needed. She'd never been on the site of an active negotiation before. Several years ago, as a patrol officer, she'd had to do her own negotiating when she came across a man about to jump off a bridge. She barely recalled what she'd said to him, but she remembered how terrified she'd felt and how willing she'd been to say whatever he wanted to hear. Anything to get him to safety.

It'd been a delicate dance of give and take.

This was a similar dance but with more lives at stake.

The SWAT commander tapped his phone's screen and enlarged Katie's sketches of the home's layout. "She says it sounded like everyone was sitting on the sofa in the family room when she left. Makes sense. He'd want them in one place where he could watch them. The family room is on the east side of the home, which is why Katie was able to run west to the barn without being seen. Adam would have had to be in one of the bedrooms to have seen her through a window. But it also means my sniper in the barn won't see much unless Adam or the hostages move outside. The spotter on the east side said window blinds are closed on the first-floor windows—which includes the family room. I don't think Adam will move to a different room, because he'd have to take his eyes off someone." He glanced up, meeting several gazes. "The front of the home and the west side are blind spots for Adam if he stays in the family room."

"He won't sit there being blind," said Noelle. "He'll want to know what's going on outside."

"Most likely he's checking the east side and south side windows since they're in the family room," said the commander. "But to look north, in our direction, he'd have to move down a long hallway to the foyer at the front of the house. I can't see him leaving his hostages to do that." He met the negotiators' gazes. "He might be willing to let some hostages go so he has fewer people to watch."

The commander headed toward the RV door. "Sending Katie's sketches of the layout to everyone. Gonna talk over a plan with my team."

"How can we find out about Detective Marshall's sister?" asked Max.

Noelle shot him a look of gratitude. She was worried about all the hostages, but not knowing Lucia's status was eating at her.

"We're still figuring out a way to bring that up," said Squires with deep concentration on her face. "Somehow get him to volunteer the information."

A phone rang, and the negotiators swung back into position.

"Hillyer here," he answered.

"I want to talk to Noelle," announced Adam.

All eyes turned to her as her muscles froze.

What if I say the wrong thing?

50

"You want us to get Detective Marshall for you?" Hillyer asked, phrasing it as if they were doing Adam a favor.

The negotiator's head is much cooler than mine at the moment.

"Sounds like your ears work just fine, Hillyer," scoffed Adam.

Squires's face lit up.

She likes that Adam used his name.

"Okay. Give us a few minutes to get her on the line," said Hillyer.

"I know how Noelle is," said Adam. "She's probably right there, looking over everyone's shoulders. You don't get a few minutes."

"She's outside," said Hillyer. "Hang on." He hit the mute button and turned to Noelle. "You ready?"

"Yes."

No.

"What do I say?" Her fingers had turned to ice.

"It'll come to you. Just remember to keep him calm. Take your time answering his questions, and don't rush. We'll help if we think you need it." He handed her a headset.

She slipped it on, a sense of numbness setting in as the white noise of the computers was suddenly blocked. Hillyer lifted his brows and gave a thumbs-up. Noelle responded in kind. He hit another button and pointed at her.

"Adam, it's Noelle."

"How you doing? How's Savannah?" His tone was teasing.

You asshole.

"Savannah's going to be fine," Noelle forced out. Squires quickly wrote out that Adam was trying to push her buttons, get her off balance, take control of the conversation. Noelle focused on the words.

I need to keep my composure.

She felt as if she'd been thrown in the deep end of the pool.

"I'm glad to hear that," said Adam. "Lucia was very upset with me about it. Which was stupid since she's the one who told me not to shoot you. What did she expect me to do?"

He's using the past tense.

"No doubt it was traumatizing for her to see anyone get shot." Noelle sought Max's gaze. It was calm, and she held on to it like a lifeline. More than anything she wanted to beg Adam to tell her that Lucia was okay. But she knew she shouldn't; she couldn't give him that power.

"She got over it," he said.

What does that mean?

"I'm surprised you asked to talk to me instead of Eve." Noelle held her breath, wondering if the question would make him angry.

"I should've."

Is that sadness I hear?

"We can get her on the phone," said Noelle, looking at Squires, who nodded.

"Not yet." His tone was still odd.

"What do you want, Adam?" asked Noelle.

"I didn't kill Derrick."

That was out of the blue.

"That's what you told me last night." Noelle's mouth was dry. "But you said you were there when he died."

"Yeah. I don't want to talk about it right now."

You brought it up.

"What do you want to talk about?" asked Noelle, earning a nod of approval from Hillyer.

"I want to talk face-to-face, Noelle," he snapped. "None of this over-the-phone shit with twenty people listening in." He was suddenly fired up, his words clipped and angry.

What did I do?

The negotiators shook their heads, signaling that she shouldn't meet with him.

He might kill me if we meet in person.

Noelle felt it deep in her bones.

"I don't think it's time for face-to-face yet, Adam. How about—"

"You want answers, Noelle? You want to know what happened to Lucia? You want to know who killed your dick of a husband, Derrick? Then you'll walk over here in the next few minutes. I'll be watching for you."

"Do you think I'm stupid?" She matched his angry tone. "You'll shoot me the first second you can, and I don't understand why! I haven't done anything to you. *You're* the one who blew up my car and shot my best friend. And now you expect me to trust you?"

Hillyer waved his hands. Noelle ignored him.

Adam has done something to Lucia.

"You're going to have to trust me, Noelle. Otherwise I'll start shooting hostages. You've got five minutes to get your ass headed this way. I won't shoot you, but every five minutes you waste, someone will die."

The connection abruptly ended, and Noelle's mouth fell open as she stared at the stunned faces in the RV.

I fucked up.

Noelle looked as if she'd been hit by a bus, and Max struggled to speak. He grabbed her hands, making her look at him. "That wasn't your fault, Noelle. He manipulated you on purpose. He had every intention of directing the conversation that way, and that's why he asked to talk to you."

Hillyer and Squires spoke at the same time, agreeing with him. But Noelle just stood there, wide-eyed, stunned, and pale. None of their reassurances were reaching her.

"Did I get them all killed?" she whispered.

"The only person responsible for anyone's death is the person who pulls the trigger," said Max.

Noelle nodded, comprehension finally sinking in. "He's going to kill them and insist it's my fault." Anger flooded her face. "That fucking asshole is trying to mess with my head. How much time do I have?" Determination filled her tone.

"You can't go out there," Max said with a sinking feeling that she wasn't listening.

"Agent Rhodes is correct," said Squires. "We don't give in to this sort of demand."

Noelle yanked her hands out of Max's and whirled on the negotiator. "And when he shoots one of those innocent people? He shot Savannah on a whim, and he's *known* her for years. Do you think a bunch of strangers mean anything to him?" She caught her breath and straightened. "I'll go talk to him."

"No!" said Max along with several others.

"I'll wear a vest. Get me a helmet and whatever other gear you want me to wear."

"What does he want with you, Noelle?" asked Max, not liking the stubbornness he saw in her jaw. "You've been his focus for a while. He's nearly killed you twice—I noticed he didn't deny blowing up your vehicle. What makes you think he won't try to kill you today?"

"I don't know why he's fixated on me. How much time is left?"

"You can't walk up there," said Max, knowing he was fighting a losing battle.

"Maybe what you just said is why I'm willing to try, Max. You said, 'He's nearly killed you twice.' But for some reason he *hasn't* killed me.

Maybe deep down he doesn't want to. He could have shot me instead of Savannah—or shot me in addition to Savannah—but he didn't." Her blue gaze held his. "I think something stops him. He might want to—but he doesn't do it." She turned to the two officers at the monitors. "Can you ask someone outside to get me a helmet and vest?"

Hillyer stood up. "I don't like this."

"No one likes it," said Noelle. "Especially me, but I'm going to fucking do it with or without anyone's approval." She put her hand on the door to pull it open.

"Noelle!" Max knew he couldn't stop her.

She turned. "What?"

I can't tell her what to do.

"Be careful."

She gave a solemn nod and studied his face for a long moment. "I always am." And then she went out the door, slamming it behind her.

Max was left with four silent and stunned people in the RV. "What does the negotiator's handbook suggest for this situation?" he asked.

No one answered.

51

Noelle had just strapped on a ballistics vest outside the BearCat when she heard the first gunshot come from the house.

Her hands stilled in shock.

I'm too late.

The commander was at her side, holding a spare helmet with a mic and headphones, which he had been about to hand her. "Report!" he shouted into his mic.

Noelle took the helmet and thrust it on in time to hear two voices say they couldn't see what had happened inside the home.

"Adam is calling," came Squires's voice through Noelle's headphones.

The commander's hard gaze met Noelle's. He signaled to his team in the BearCat, and they all exited the vehicle.

"Adam, what just happened?" Hillyer asked, his voice clear inside her helmet. "We heard a gunshot."

"Noelle is late," said Adam with fury in his tone. "Now she's got five minutes until I shoot another. Oh. And if I see a weapon with her, she's dead on sight."

"He hung up," reported Hillyer.

"I need to go," said Noelle, fighting to keep her voice even. "Call him back. Tell him I'm on my way."

Who did he kill? The brother-in-law? One of Katie's sisters?

"It was quiet in the background of the call," Hillyer pointed out. "And he didn't say he killed anyone. Possibly there is a bluff going on."

"Tell him what I said." Noelle handed her pistol to the commander, who reluctantly accepted it.

"Blue-six. Has there been any movement with the blinds at the front of the house?" asked the commander into his mic.

"Blue-six. Negative. I have a clear view of the front."

"We're going to escort you," the commander told Noelle.

"No," said Noelle. "If he looks out the front windows, it'll be to check on my progress. Since he said no weapons on me, he won't be happy to see your officers, and he'll kill every person inside." She looked down the snowy driveway, the house out of sight. "I'll keep my mic on, so that you'll know what's going on. Wait until I'm in the family room, and I'll try to get him talking in there," she suggested. "Move in then."

The commander considered her for a long second and then pushed her mic up, nearly tucking it under her helmet. "Say something."

"Something."

"We can still hear you. I'm hoping he doesn't realize your helmet has a mic and speakers." He handed her a shield. "Good luck."

Noelle hefted the heavy SWAT shield and started down the driveway.

"Noelle!"

She looked back.

Max had stepped out of the RV, and he held her gaze for a long moment. "Give him hell," he said.

Her lips trembled into a half smile, and then she continued her journey.

I can't look back again.

The home came into sight as Noelle rounded a curve of the driveway. It was as described. White farmhouse. No cover of any sort near it. The scene was quiet and calm. A winter wonderland. It didn't look like a place where an execution had just occurred.

Again she wondered whom Adam had chosen to shoot. Her stomach churned as she wondered fearfully what kind of disaster she would encounter inside.

She studied the barn to the west of the home, unable to see any hint that Blue-six was there with his sniper rifle.

But she did spot two trails coming from the east where the snow had been broken. The trails led to the house. Her heart lifted with hope.

Two people.

Lucia must have made it this far.

But Noelle had no idea what had happened next to her sister. Adam had given no clue as to Lucia's status.

"Blue-six. I have eyes on Marshall," said the sniper through her headphones.

He's got my back.

A small sense of relief touched her. The sniper could watch the front of the house for any movement until she went through the front door. Then she was on her own.

Maybe Adam will show himself before I get there.

Adam had proved beyond a doubt that he was willing to kill. The sniper had been given permission to take a shot to stop the threat that Adam presented to his hostages and the officers. Noelle felt for Blue-six. He would have to make a life-or-death decision in a split second.

The sniper wouldn't shoot to wound. Adam would still be a danger to everyone with a gunshot in his leg or arm. Being knocked down wouldn't take away his ability to fire a gun over and over.

Noelle continued her progress toward the home. One snowy step after another. Her situation felt surreal. The sky was bright blue, and a cheerful sun peeked over the trees far beyond the home.

I might be walking to my death.

Her legs shook, and she strode more forcefully, trying to ignore the ache in her arm from the heavy shield. This was not the time to let her fear dictate. She thought of her grandfather, and she knew he would be proud of her. She'd built her ethics and integrity on his examples.

He would make the same decision I did today.

Ahead she saw a flicker at the blinds. "The blinds moved," she said.

"Blue-six, copy."

She'd known Adam would watch for her. The family was most likely too scared to move since he'd shot one of them, and that would give him confidence. Maybe too much confidence.

She lifted her arms away from her body, her shield arm not even coming close to the height to which she could raise the other arm, and continued to move toward the house. "Adam, I'm not armed!"

She reported, "The blinds moved again."

"Blue-six, copy."

Noelle reached the steps, which led to a traditional farmhouse front porch, and stopped. She paused, scanning the windows. "Adam, do you want to open the door?" she asked loudly.

A second later it was opened by a young woman with a strong resemblance to Katie. Her stance was stiff, her countenance full of terror. Several feet behind her, Noelle saw someone move in the shadows.

He made her open the door while he stays back.

"Are you Kendall or Kristine?" Noelle asked.

"Kendall."

"Katie is safe," Noelle whispered to her, and Kendall's face brightened.

"Get your ass up the stairs!" Adam shouted from far back in the room.

The relief in Kendall's eyes vanished at the shout, and she took a jerky step backward.

Noelle slowly moved up the stairs, her steps heavy. "He's too far inside," she said softly for the SWAT team.

"Blue-six, copy."

"Leave that thing outside," ordered Adam.

Noelle set down the shield on the porch.

"Place your hands on your head and walk in backwards."

She turned and gazed out over the smooth blanket of snow broken by only her footsteps and the two other trails that led to the house. Her hands on her helmet, she inched backward into the home until Kendall could close the door. She turned the lock with a loud clack and faced Noelle. In the dim light, she noticed Kendall's eyes were red and puffy.

"Blue-six. Marshall is in the house. No eyes." The voice was quiet in her headphones, but she worried Adam would hear it.

"On your knees," said Adam.

Noelle knelt, and he used one hand to thoroughly search under her ballistics vest and everywhere else for weapons.

"Get that helmet off."

Noelle's hands shook as she fiddled with the strap under her chin, knowing she was losing her one connection to the outside world.

"Hurry up!"

"Hang on. I can't see the latch under my chin," she stated, hoping the team would cut all sound to her speakers but leave on her audio. The fastener clicked open, and Adam yanked it from her head.

"Get up. Lead her back," he told Kendall.

The young woman passed by Noelle, who turned to follow her, getting her first sight of Adam, who pointed a gun her way. He kept his distance, her helmet in his other hand. "Why are you doing this, Adam?"

"Shut up." He hung back and then followed.

Kendall led her down the hallway to the family room. All the blinds were drawn, and the other three members of the family were on the sofa. All were gagged and their hands tied.

No one is shot.

What about Lucia?

"Where's Lucia?" Her voice cracked.

"I'm right here."

Noelle spun around to see her youngest sister calmly standing in the kitchen with a can of Diet Coke in her hand. No gag. No bound limbs.

She's okay. But . . .

"Lucia," Noelle said, trying to steady her voice. "I don't understand. What's going on?"

Her sister looked at Adam, who said nothing. He tossed Noelle's helmet onto the floor in the kitchen like it was garbage. "Get rid of that," he told Lucia.

"Why is everyone else gagged and sitting on the sofa?" Noelle quickly asked, hoping the mic on the helmet picked up her voice. "Did they talk too much for you?"

"*You* talk too much. Gag her and tie her." He motioned at Kendall.

Lucia eyed the helmet on the floor and then picked it up and stared at it in her hands. Then she smoothly deposited it in the garbage can under the kitchen sink as if she tossed junk in there every day.

Can the team still hear me?

Something caught Noelle's eye. She looked up and realized that Adam had fired a round into the ceiling, leaving a neat hole. The threats had been a bluff; Hillyer had been right.

Adam wanted me inside. Why?

"You didn't shoot anyone," Noelle stated.

"Nope." Adam grinned. "But the day's not over yet."

Kendall approached her with a short length of narrow twine in her shaking hands. "Can you turn around?"

Noelle ignored her. "Last night in my house, you were petrified of Adam," she said to Lucia. "He shot Savannah right in front of you. Why the fuck are you listening to him now?" Her sister didn't answer. She slowly took a sip of her drink as if she didn't have a care in the world.

Her eyes aren't focused.

Yesterday Lucia had been highly agitated and unable to hold still, her eyes full of terror about what Adam might do in Noelle's kitchen. But today . . .

She's drugged.

"I said tie her up!" yelled Adam.

"Please," Kendall begged with tears in her eyes. "Help me do what he says."

"Fuck him," said Noelle. "What did you give Lucia?" she asked Adam as she took several steps toward her sister, studying her intently.

"No closer!" shouted Adam. He lunged forward, his gun leading.

Noelle halted, lifting her hands to show she was done, but never took her gaze from her sister. Lucia gave her a weak smile and blinked several times as she tried to focus.

"I gave her what she wanted," said Adam. "What she's always wanted from me."

Does he mean . . . ?

Noelle examined her sister and let her mind roll through the hundreds of times Lucia had been anxious or deep in depression. The days when she'd talk a million miles a minute and the days when she was silent and couldn't get out of bed. How Adam had always been so concerned about Lucia's emotional and physical state.

Lucia had always lived near Adam.

Noelle suddenly knew.

He's been giving her drugs for years. He wasn't concerned. He was simply watching what the drugs did to her.

"I see you figured it out," said Adam. "And you call yourself a detective."

Noelle recalled how he'd asked in the past if she needed "a boost." And he'd asked more than once.

"You couldn't see what was going on under your own nose," continued Adam. "In your own family. Even in your own house."

There weren't drugs in my house.

Noelle sucked in a breath.

White powder on his car seat.

Derrick's volatility.

Her husband had been up and down the last year of their marriage. Derrick would make love to her, telling her how much she meant to him, and then another day tear her down with his words, call her names, and grab her arm in anger. Over a matter of months, she'd grown deathly scared of him.

Suddenly she saw the truth.

Adam was supplying Derrick with meth.

He was high the day he died.

Noelle looked at Adam, standing next to a sofa full of tied-up strangers. He wore an odd smile as he watched her, and she ached to wipe the smug look off his face.

"It looks like you're thinking hard about something, Noelle," Adam said in a playful tone. "I wonder what that could possibly be."

I'm finally remembering that day.

In her gut, she knew that truth was breaking through.

Suddenly a crash of shattering glass sounded from the front of the Amidons' home, and then something hit the floor behind her. The room abruptly exploded with sound and light and smoke. Noelle dived forward and took Lucia to the floor in the kitchen, covering her with her body.

Flash-bang!

Shouts and stomping boots came from the front of the house, and more glass shattered as the family room slider burst. Muffled screams sounded from the Amidons.

"Gun! Gun! Gun!"

A single shot sounded, and a deafening rush of shots followed it immediately.

Noelle pressed Lucia into the floor. "It's okay. It's okay," she repeated over and over into her sister's hair, knowing what the mass of rapid shots meant.

"He's down!"

"Check him and cuff him!"

"Got him! Clear the house."

Her heart pounding out of her chest, Noelle rolled off Lucia and faced the family room. Adam was crumpled on the floor, part of his skull missing. Blood spatter covered the wall where he'd been standing, and SWAT frantically worked over him, applying medical aid, but Noelle could tell there was no point. Adam was dead.

The Amidons had slid off the couch and to the floor, crying and leaning on each other as SWAT members tried to calm them and cut their bonds.

"Noelle?" Suddenly Max crouched in front of her, wearing a helmet and vest. "Are you hurt?"

"No." She couldn't say more, overcome with a dozen different emotions at the sight of the concern and relief in his eyes.

I'm so glad to see him.

Lucia had sat up and was staring in confusion at the brown puddle spreading from her Diet Coke can.

"It's over," said Max as he touched Noelle's hand. "Adam won't hurt anyone again."

"I know." But she was watching Lucia.

Part of this isn't over.

52

Four days later

Noelle hugged Alice and tears burned in her eyes.

"You didn't have to come," she told the retired FBI agent.

"I couldn't stay away," said Alice, squeezing her tightly. "You'd been through hell, and we finally have some clarity about what happened all those years ago. It's been my white whale, you know. Trying to learn what happened that day in your home when Derrick died. It was the case I could never solve, and it's never left me."

"Come sit down." Noelle led Alice to the little table and chairs by the windows in Eve's home. Noelle had been staying with her sister since Adam's death. Eve needed the support, and Noelle didn't want to go back to her house. Savannah's blood still stained the carpet.

It was good to see Alice. When Noelle was with her, she pushed Noelle to be the best version of herself. She'd always admired Alice's no-nonsense way of speaking and calm attitude. She'd represented the woman Noelle wanted to be when she grew up.

I think I'm nearly there.

Noelle poured two black cups of coffee and joined Alice in the winter sun streaming through the windows. "How's Eve?" asked Alice.

"I think she'll be okay," said Noelle. "It's been a nightmare for her, but she's admitted something was off with Adam for a long time. She ignored it because she loved him, and I believe he truly loved her.

Somehow he kept that separate from the other parts of him that did horrible things."

"Like being a drug dealer," said Alice.

"I believe so," said Noelle, staring into her coffee. "I'm not sure when Adam started supplying Derrick with meth. Looking back, I feel so stupid that I didn't see it. Derrick's slow slide into irrational behavior. I was determined to make that marriage work, you know. I was convinced that I was the problem—Derrick convinced me." She gave Alice a wry smile. "So much gaslighting."

"It started subtle and small," said Alice, kindly. "It was hard for you to see it was happening."

"I *knew*, though," Noelle said as a familiar anger burned in her chest. "Part of me always knew that he'd changed me. And not for the better."

"You got through it," said Alice. "You're one of the strongest women I know."

"A lot of it is thanks to you," said Noelle. "You gave me the guidance I needed. I'm not sure what I'd be doing with my life if you hadn't guided me toward law enforcement."

"I can only take part of the credit for that," said Alice. "Your grandfather was a huge influence."

"True." A wave of emptiness hit her.

I miss him so much.

"Did Lucia agree to talk to me?" Alice asked hopefully.

"No." Noelle grimaced. "Sorry about that. She doesn't feel up to it, but she told me everything she knew about the day Derrick died. That was one of the toughest conversations I've ever had with her. We were both bawling. Lucia feels horribly guilty that she hid the truth for so long, and I feel guilty that she went through it." Noelle slowly shook her head, meeting Alice's curious gaze. "I think she told me the truth. I struggled to accept it, but it lines up with what I've finally remembered."

"You mentioned you were recalling things," said Alice.

Noelle sighed. "Turns out I didn't need to recall certain recent things because they never happened. Lucia told me that Adam made her enter my house and move things from where I kept them or plant things like Chinese food containers in my fridge. He even had her move my vehicle one time. I assume his goal was that I'd never trust my thoughts if I started remembering things about the day Derrick died. I honestly thought I was losing it, Alice. When I'd discover something wasn't where I'd left it, I'd become terrified that my memory was going to shit. I didn't tell anyone because I feared I'd lose my job."

"That's horrible," said Alice. "She'd easily get into your home because she knew the alarm code."

"Yes," said Noelle. "I've also had weird dreams showing things that I doubt ever happened. But I *think* I pieced everything together after talking to Lucia." She pressed her lips together and studied the retired agent. "This is hard for me," she said. "What will you do with the information I'm about to tell you?"

Alice tilted her head, assessing Noelle. "Are you saying charges should be filed?"

Noelle looked away, uncomfortable with the woman's scrutiny. "I don't want that to happen. But on the other hand, it's probably the right thing to do."

"If you *don't* tell me," said Alice in a curious tone, "will charges be filed?"

"No." Guilt hit her as she said the single word.

Alice considered for a long moment. "Maybe it's best you don't say anything."

I need to tell someone.

She was miserable, sick to her stomach over what she'd learned from Lucia.

"Will anyone be harmed if charges aren't filed?" Alice asked quietly. "Is anyone in danger?"

"No."

"Then I'll take it to the grave."

53

Thirteen years ago

Noelle parked her little sports car next to Lucia's minivan, pleasantly surprised to see that her sister had stopped by. She gathered her purse and admired the new bracelets that jangled on her wrist as she closed the car door.

Lucia would love these.

As she went up the stairs to the front door, she decided to give the bracelets to her sister. She paused at the front door, and her shoulders abruptly tightened as she heard Derrick shouting.

What did I do now?

A woman shrieked. *"Stop it!"*

Is that Lucia?

Noelle thrust open the door and strode into the home.

"You almost ruined me with your fucking loose mouth!"

Her strides slowed. *That's Adam.*

She entered the kitchen and froze. Lucia was yanking on Adam's arm, tears streaming down her face as he swung a crowbar at Derrick, who darted out of reach to avoid the crowbar smashing into his face.

Adam fought to keep his balance as Lucia pulled him backward, and Derrick lunged at him, his fists swinging.

"Derrick!" screamed Lucia. *"Don't!"*

Derrick awkwardly landed a fist on Adam's shoulder and then tripped, falling to his hands and knees. Derrick gasped for air as he struggled back to his feet. He paused, swaying as if dizzy.

Is he hurt?

Noelle darted forward and grabbed his upper arm to steady him. "Are you okay?" She turned him toward her. He was covered in sweat, his eyes wide and frantic. He blinked several times as he fought to focus on her face.

"You!" he bellowed at her, his cheeks instantly red with fury. "You did this!" Spittle flew from his mouth, his pupils huge.

Frozen, she stared at him.

What's wrong with him?

"Derrick—"

"Shut up!" His gaze focused on hers with a laser intensity and she stepped back, her heart trying to beat out of her chest.

He's going to hit me.

A split second later his hand shot out to slap her in the face. Noelle stutter-stepped back, avoiding his blow, but lost her balance and hit the ground, which sent pain rocketing up her tailbone and spine. She scrambled backward, her sandals sliding on the wood floor as he came after her again. Her back hit the sofa, and she clambered to her feet, intending to run.

But he grabbed her upper arms and shook her, causing her head to whip forward and back as if she were in a car crash. *"Derrick!"*

What did I do?

She threw her body to one side, breaking his grip and landing on her knees. She clambered across the floor, the understanding that he wanted to physically hurt her ricocheting in her skull. He grabbed her hair and yanked. She flung her arms outward, futilely searching for something—anything—to hold on to. Instead, she fell over and landed on her side. He towered over her. He shouted, but her brain didn't register his words. Only his fury.

She faintly discerned that Lucia and Adam had left the room.

It was only her and Derrick.

He will kill me if I don't get away!

She'd known this day could come.

Noelle grabbed both his lower legs, closed her eyes, and thrust her body forward with her feet, pushing her shoulder into his shins. He landed heavily with a shout and kicked, breaking her hold. She crawled away and pulled herself to her feet, leaning heavily on a sofa arm, panting.

Get out of the house!

She took a step, and he slammed a fist into her shoulder, nearly knocking her into the marble stand holding her favorite elephant. She snatched the elephant, digging her fingertips into its iron grooves, and swung around, using her momentum to slam the elephant into his face.

Derrick fell to one side, dropping to the floor as if every muscle in his body had stopped working, blood flowing from the wounds in his face.

Noelle stood over him, panting, clinging to the elephant.

Oh my God! What did I do?

She flung the elephant aside, and it hit the wood floor with a crash. She backed away from Derrick, her gaze locked on his smashed face. He didn't move, the room suddenly silent. But blood roared in her brain.

He was going to kill me!

Something caught her eye, and she looked across the room at the huge mirror on the wall.

Adam stood behind her. His crowbar raised.

54

"I killed him, Alice. It was me. I'm the person you've been looking for all these years." Noelle shuddered as she stated the words and fought back a wave of nausea. "I know the ME said the blow to the face was the one that killed him."

"That's correct," Alice said softly, her eyes wet.

As she'd told the story, Noelle had grown dizzy with relief. She trusted Alice more than she trusted anyone else. Even Savannah and her sisters. "You heard it was confirmed that Lucia made the 911 call, right?" she asked the agent.

"Yes."

"I'd seen in my dreams that her minivan was in the driveway that day. I thought it was just a dream, but it wasn't. She was there."

Alice held up a hand. "Lucia, Daisy, and your grandfather all alibied each other, said they were all home together."

"I haven't asked Daisy, but I think she suspected Lucia was involved in some way. Both she and my grandfather must have known Lucia wasn't home at that time and alibied her. They weren't about to point a finger at her. Max—Agent Rhodes—believes that people did a lot of intentional misdirection of the investigation during their interviews back then. My family tried to protect each other even though they didn't know the truth."

"How *is* Lucia?" asked Alice.

"She's only been at the inpatient program for a few days," said Noelle. "Adam gave her a few different drugs for a lot of years. It's going to take a long time to learn how to live without them." Noelle paused, thinking of her younger sister. "I don't know what sort of permanent damage those chemicals might have done to her." She met Alice's gaze. "How could I have not seen it, Alice? Neither Eve nor I had any idea. What kind of sisters are we to not know she was suffering all those years? How can I call myself a detective?"

"You went through a lot of trauma when Derrick was murdered," said Alice. "And now we know that Lucia's experience during that was much worse than we realized. I suspect that by the time you were mentally and emotionally back on your feet, she'd established herself in your family's eyes as a deeply affected person. I hate to say it, but I've heard all of you make excuses for how she acts. 'She's different.' 'She's emotional.' 'She has extreme anxiety.'"

"They're not excuses," Noelle said defensively. "They're true."

"*Excuses* was a bad word choice. I'm trying to point out that all of you accepted any odd behavior and chalked it up to . . . her struggles. No one looked deeper."

"We made sure she had good doctors and went to therapy."

"And clearly she lied to all the doctors. She learned how to cover up things."

Noelle thought back. "Her doctors tried her on several different antianxiety medications. Whenever she acted a bit off, she complained of their side effects, and we accepted that explanation. I suspect they were actually from whatever Adam had given her."

"She knew to hide it from you," said Alice. "She was good at it. Good enough to fool a detective for a long time."

◆ ◆ ◆

"Lucia said Adam was angry that day because Derrick had nearly revealed to his office staff that Adam was dealing," said Noelle. "He was also furious because Derrick owed him a lot of money for drugs. Derrick then told Adam he was going to report him for the drug dealing and tell the police that Adam had been supplying a minor—her— and that he'd go to prison. Lucia had run to hide just before Derrick attacked me. She came back into the room as Adam was bent over Derrick. He told her Derrick was dead because I'd hit him in the face with the elephant and then Adam had hit me to stop me. And then Adam went after Derrick's body with the crowbar. Beating him over and over. She said Adam was red with fury as he kicked and hit him. Yelling at Derrick even though he was dead."

"She took the time to call 911."

"She thought I was dead too. She said I was on the ground, and it appeared I wasn't breathing. She called 911 while Adam was still focused on beating Derrick. When he looked at her, she put down the receiver. She said he'd ridden to the house with her, but he drove when they left. She was too upset."

"Adam was supplying Lucia at that time?" Alice asked with disgust. "She was a teenager!"

"Yes. I guess it started a year or two earlier with something like Ritalin and then progressed to other things." Noelle took a deep breath. "Adam threatened her to keep her quiet. When he discovered I hadn't died, he told her it would be revealed that *I* was the one who killed Derrick and that I would go to prison. In some twisted way, Lucia thought her silence was protecting me. I hope life will be easier for her when she returns."

"She has you and Eve," said Alice. "That girl will be just fine." She reached across the table and patted Noelle's hand.

"It's so good to have you here," Noelle admitted. "Everyone is so stunned. Daisy, Eve, Lucia. I feel like I'm having to emotionally prop everyone up. It's exhausting." Her brain still struggled to accept what had happened. "I murdered Derrick," she said in a small voice. It didn't feel real.

Alice shook her head. "Your action was in self-defense."

Noelle clung to Alice's words, wanting to forgive herself. "But I didn't have to hit him *so* hard."

"Stop second-guessing yourself," said Alice. "You were threatened; you reacted. No jury would convict you."

Noelle wasn't confident about that. She'd mentally convicted herself over and over since her memory had returned. She buried her face in her hands as the tears flowed.

Alice came around the table and wrapped her arms around Noelle. Not speaking, simply comforting. It took several minutes for Noelle to pull herself together.

Alice returned to her own chair. "Adam was never on my radar for Derrick's murder. Now, your grandfather, that was a different story." She gave a solemn nod. "I took a hard look at him several times. He was not a Derrick fan. He'd made it clear he did not like the way Derrick treated you."

"I know. I was almost convinced my grandfather had done it," said Noelle. "While he was alive, I was afraid to push the investigation because they—and you—might discover he'd done it. Once he passed, I simply wanted the investigation to be in the past. I think Daisy had the same worry about him. She sort of hinted about it not long ago."

Alice nodded. "You said she also might have suspected Lucia had been involved, so Daisy alibied her. I wonder if Daisy and your grandfather agreed to alibi each other and Lucia or each thought of it on their own."

"Is it wrong that I'm relieved it wasn't my grandfather? That it was me instead?" Noelle struggled to hold her head above the sea of conflicting emotions that threatened to drown her.

"That's not a surprising reaction. You love him. You hate to think that he would purposefully do something like that."

She is right.

"Law enforcement believes Adam hit Derrick with the elephant and the crowbar," said Alice.

"I know," whispered Noelle. "Lucia believes that too. She's convinced Adam lied to her when he said that I'd done it. Should I tell them the truth?"

Alice studied her face for a long time. "That's your decision."

"I don't know," Noelle said. "Lucia is more relaxed now that Adam is gone, and she thinks I'm innocent. It was a lot of stress on her shoulders for years. But what do I do now?" Noelle was adrift.

"You pull yourself together and keep doing good things in this world," Alice said quietly in a determined voice. "You're in the right profession to do that. What happened is in the past. Would you have lived your life differently if you'd known your blow was the one that killed Derrick way back then?"

"I would have struggled with a lot of emotions," Noelle admitted. "I don't know if I would have had the confidence to enter law enforcement. I wouldn't have felt worthy."

"Maybe that's why it didn't come out until now," said Alice. "I'm a big believer in fate. You saved your friends' lives not too long ago. What would have happened to Evan and Rowan if you hadn't been in law enforcement?"

"I don't know."

They'd be dead.

"I know exactly how that incident would have ended." Alice leaned forward in her chair. "Spend some time thinking about it, Noelle, and then figure out how to get past it. Because this world needs you to do what you do best."

She's going to make me cry again.

"I love you, Alice." Noelle grabbed a napkin to stop her nose from running.

"I love you too. You've made me proud."

Noelle put her head in her hands and quietly fell to pieces.

But she knew in her heart that it would pass.

55

One month later

"Are you sure she's ready?" Max asked into his cell phone.

"Yes," said Savannah. "She'll be completely surprised, but I've made sure she's ready."

"Okay. I'll be there in two minutes."

"Can't wait."

Max tucked his phone away and started the motorcycle. He'd only talked to Noelle a few times since Adam had been killed. He'd seen her during her debriefing and then met her for a cup of coffee at the same coffee shop where he'd unknowingly purchased her latte the first day he interviewed her.

I know there is something between us.

That spark. That absolute awareness in my gut.

He suspected she felt it too. But she'd been through hell, and so he'd given her space.

Max had returned to Sacramento the day after they had coffee, and since then they had exchanged a few emails and texts. She'd sounded better as the weeks went by and that horrible day when Adam died melted further into the distance.

So Max contacted Savannah, who'd been staying in Bend with Noelle as she physically healed from her gunshot wound. It hadn't taken long for Savannah to return to her sassy self. And she was fully on board with his surprise for Noelle.

He turned onto Noelle's street, came to a stop at the curb, and swung off the motorcycle. He removed his helmet and balanced it on a mirror. The February day was clear and cold. A perfect day for a ride as long as he bundled up.

"Max! What are you doing here?" Noelle stood in her doorway, and he spotted Savannah at her side with a huge grin. She gave Noelle a little shove in her back and said something, earning an over-the-shoulder scowl from Noelle.

"I promised you a ride." Max watched her walk toward him, a smile widening across her face, and a goofy happiness spread through him.

I missed her.

He had it bad. He'd been attracted to her from day one, and he'd had to squash it the entire time he worked on her murdered husband's case. But now that was over.

"When did you get to town?" Noelle asked as she reached him. She wore jeans the color of her eyes and a white sweater, her blonde hair pulled back in a high ponytail.

She looked perfect.

"I got in this morning."

"You should have let me know you were coming. Are you here for long?"

"I haven't decided." He had decided, but he wasn't ready to share that with her yet.

"That's a nonanswer." She scanned the motorcycle. "Looks like you have a good day for a ride."

"You're coming with me."

She laughed and took a step back. "Sorry, I don't have anything to wear."

"I came prepared." He opened the top box and pulled out a helmet. "See how this fits," he said as he handed it to her. Then he opened a pannier. "I borrowed my sister's riding gear. I told you before that I thought it'd fit you." He pulled out a black-and-gray jacket and pants. "I've got her boots too, but I'll warn you she's got giant feet."

Noelle looked at the helmet in her hands, bewilderment in her eyes. "You're joking."

"I never joke when it comes to motorcycles. Please come with me. I promise you're going to love it."

"Just do it, Noelle!" hollered Savannah from the front door.

Noelle eyed him as if she still didn't believe he was serious.

"Okay," she finally said. "Give me the boots."

Noelle felt as if she were dressed for battle. The gear was heavy, made of Gore-Tex and some other engineered fabrics along with armor at her elbows, shoulders, knees, hips, and back. The boots were a little too roomy in the feet but buckled snugly around her ankles and calves. She awkwardly shoved the helmet on her head.

"How's that feel?" asked Max.

"Like a helmet."

"Anything poking you?" He wiggled it. "Doesn't feel loose."

"I think it's okay." She fumbled with the strap under her chin. "I can't see how to buckle this."

"I got it."

He focused on the strap, and she studied his face, which was so close to hers.

Damn, he's attractive.

She'd been pleased every time she heard from him after he left but had to play it cool. He lived in another state. She wasn't interested in a long-distance romance, but now, with him right in front of her, she was having second thoughts.

He wouldn't be here if he didn't feel the same way.

But neither of them said it out loud.

She'd needed the weeks to absorb what had happened to her family, in both the past and the present. Before the FBI had blindsided her with that interview, she'd believed she'd moved past the questions about Derrick's murder. Now she knew that hadn't been true. She'd simply buried them.

The truth about that day had been tough to accept. But once she did, she'd finally felt like the door had closed on that chapter in her life. The rest of her family was working on closing the door too, putting Adam in their past.

Only Noelle—and Alice—knew that she'd hit Derrick with the elephant.

She looked at Max's brown eyes as he focused on fastening her clasp.

Maybe I'll tell him one day.

Max finished her chin strap and showed her how to raise and lower the visor. Then he handed her a pair of gloves, put on his own helmet, and got on the bike. He released the kickstand and looked at her. "Let's go."

She found a foot peg for her left foot and awkwardly heaved herself up, grabbing at his shoulder as she maneuvered her leg between him and the top box.

"Ready?" he asked.

"Where do I hang on?" She didn't know where to put her hands. It didn't feel right to wrap her arms around him.

"You can hang on to me, or there're handles at the sides of your seat."

She fumbled with the thick gloves to find the handles. Gripping them felt almost as if she were sitting on her hands.

This doesn't feel secure at all.

She tentatively put her arms around him. She couldn't reach all the way around him, but she could sort of grip his jacket at his sides. It still didn't feel secure, and she didn't think it would take much to make her topple off. At least the top box was at her back to keep her from going over the rear of the bike.

"Ready now?"

"I guess we'll find out."

The bike started up with a loud rumble, and she tightened her grip. He smoothly pulled away from the curb, and they were moving.

I didn't ask where we're going.

She had no means of talking to him. She knew some helmets had microphones and speakers, but apparently theirs did not. She sat in silence and concentrated on not falling off.

Twenty minutes later she was in love.

Not with Max but with the ride. He'd described it as flying at ground level, and she completely agreed. She'd relaxed her death grip and sat back a bit, enjoying the scenery and giving her brain a break. No thoughts about work or Lucia or Adam. It was the lightest and most serene she'd felt in a month.

Max had quickly taken them out of town, giving stunning views of the snow-covered Cascade mountains and green forests.

The roads were dry and clear, and he stuck to quiet two-lane country highways with little traffic. After about an hour, he pulled off at a scenic overlook and cut the engine. She didn't move.

"Can you get off?" he asked.

"I think so." It was awkward in her heavy gear, but she managed.

He got off and removed his helmet, so she did the same.

"That was amazing," she told him. "I was smiling the entire time. I don't think I've felt that happy in a long while."

Max's smile was warm, and his eyes were pleased. "That's exactly what I wanted you to experience." He opened the top box and handed her a water. "There's a bench over there. Need to sit down?"

"It feels good to stand for the moment." She followed him to the fence at the edge of the overlook and they both leaned against it, enjoying the sight of the mountains. "Now will you tell me how long you're in town? I could tell you knew when I asked you earlier."

"I did," he admitted. "I was hesitant to tell you."

"It's going to be that short of a visit?" she joked as her heart sank a little because they wouldn't have much time. She was absolutely certain that this was a relationship she wanted to explore.

"A long visit, actually," he said, turning to face her. He had a few silver hairs at his temples and in his short beard that she found charming.

I find a lot charming about him.

He was a good man. She knew it in her heart.

"How long?"

"Permanently."

She stared at him, searching his eyes. "Are you joking?"

"Nope. I spoke with the Bend satellite office. They wanted to add another agent. And that agent is me." He paused. "What do you think of that?"

He looks nervous about my answer.

"I think that's fantastic." More happiness bubbled up inside her. "Between the ride and that news, this has been the best day in a long time."

His face lit up. "There will be more rides."

"Promise?" She knew he meant more than just rides.

"Absolutely."

I can't wait.

ACKNOWLEDGMENTS

I hope you loved learning about Noelle's story as much as I did. She's always been a mystery to me, but I knew something horrible had happened in her past. I've barely touched on Max's background and plan to expand on that in the next book, *No One Knew*. He appears to be a chill guy, doesn't he? But he's got secrets.

I want to thank the wonderful people who helped me put this book together. Anh Schluep, Charlotte Herscher, and Meg Ruley have had my back for many years. My books would not be the same without them, and I'm very thankful to have them on my APub team. I look forward to more books with them.

Thank you to my readers. I've received frequent emails asking when I'd write Noelle's story. I'd planned to fit her book into the Columbia River series but realized this was a character who deserved her own series. I hope you enjoyed this book and the Noelle and Max books to come.

ABOUT THE AUTHOR

Photo © 2016 Rebekah Jule Photography

Kendra Elliot is the *Wall Street Journal* and Amazon Charts bestselling author of the Mercy Kilpatrick novels, the Columbia River novels, the Bone Secrets series, and the Callahan & McLane series. She is a three-time winner of the Daphne du Maurier Award an International Thriller Writers Award finalist, and an RT Award finalist. Kendra was born and raised in the rainy Pacific Northwest but now lives in flip-flops. For more information, visit www.kendraelliot.com.